FOUL PLAY

Fiona McIntosh is an internationally bestselling author of novels for adults and children. She co-founded an award-winning travel magazine with her husband, which they ran for fifteen years while raising their twin sons before she became a full-time author. Fiona roams the world researching and drawing inspiration for her novels, and runs a series of highly respected fiction masterclasses. She calls South Australia home.

BOOKS BY FIONA MCINTOSH

AVAILABLE FROM PENGUIN RANDOM HOUSE

Fields of Gold

The Lavender Keeper

The French Promise

Nightingale

The Tailor's Girl

The Last Dance

The Perfumer's Secret

The Chocolate Tin

The Tea Gardens

The Pearl Thief

The Diamond Hunter

The Champagne War

The Spy's Wife

The Orphans

The Sugar Palace

In the DCI Jack Hawksworth series:

Bye Bye Baby

Beautiful Death

Mirror Man

Dead Tide

FIONA McINTOSH

FOUL PLAY

MICHAEL JOSEPH
an imprint of
PENGUIN BOOKS

MICHAEL JOSEPH

UK | USA | Canada | Ireland | Australia
India | New Zealand | South Africa | China

Michael Joseph is part of the Penguin Random House group of companies
whose addresses can be found at global.penguinrandomhouse.com.

Penguin
Random House
Australia

First published by Michael Joseph, 2024

Cover image by Silas Manhood/Arcangel
Cover design by Louisa Maggio Design © Penguin Random House Australia Pty Ltd
Typeset in Bembo Std by Midland Typesetters, Australia

Printed and bound in Australia by Griffin Press, an accredited
ISO AS/NZS 14001 Environmental Management Systems printer

A catalogue record for this
book is available from the
National Library of Australia

ISBN 978 1 76104 801 2

penguin.com.au

MIX
Paper | Supporting
responsible forestry
FSC® C018684

*We at Penguin Random House Australia acknowledge that Aboriginal and Torres Strait Islander
peoples are the Traditional Custodians and the first storytellers of the lands on which we live and
work. We honour Aboriginal and Torres Strait Islander peoples' continuous connection to Country,
waters, skies and communities. We celebrate Aboriginal and Torres Strait Islander stories, traditions
and living cultures; and we pay our respects to Elders past and present.*

For Nathan Giaccio, whose house really did burn down while I was writing this, and whose cat, Poppy, was nearly lost. Both of you safe and sound now ... and looking forward x

PROLOGUE

LONDON, OCTOBER 2009

Just five minutes ago – less time, even – his life had been perfect. With the slice of a letter opener, it had changed. His world had shifted . . . and now it was different.

It had catapulted from blessed to frightened.

No longer that glowing, star-dusted, exquisitely modelled exist-ence that others envied and he lived. If Luca Bruni had written a script for it, his life would look just as it had before he reached for the expensive Montblanc blade – a gift for the man who had everything – to open the envelope.

He found himself reading the note for the third time, as if by focusing intently on it he could somehow change the contents.

It had come via courier. Ally had signed for it and put it in his hands as she had paused to kiss him, walking by with her satin dressing gown open to reveal the outline of her suddenly blos-soming breasts and her ripe belly carrying his children.

'Hope you didn't greet the courier like that,' he'd joked.

She'd turned back and smacked him playfully. 'Like they'd be interested in a plump has-been.'

She was so far from plump, and a has-been, that he didn't bother correcting her. He knew she was playing down just how good she looked as a mother-to-be, not fishing for a compliment. Contrary to what many might presume, Ally was modest, and a long way from the egotist that all those glamorously posed, tanned and pert celebrity snapshots might suggest.

'What is it?' she asked, not sounding all that interested.

'Dunno. I wasn't expecting anything,' he replied, turning the envelope over. There was nothing to give away the sender.

'I've put a brew on,' she said, fingers trailing away from him but her smile lingering.

They received packages and documents all the time, so this was nothing out of the ordinary. The envelope was A5-sized and regulation post-office stock. It had been delivered by a normal courier service called Donkey Express that was hugely popular, not just for its silly name but its proven superior service on motor-bikes. He knew this by the instantly recognisable rubber-stamped image of a laughing donkey.

'Come on,' Ally said, tapping his chest gently. 'Tea.'

He grabbed for her, grinning. 'Any chance of an early morning—'

She swatted his hand gently. 'Only in your dreams, Bruni. You've got training anyway, haven't you?'

'Always time for a quickie,' he said hopefully.

'Hold that thought, lover boy. I need food. Besides, I've just showered,' she said, pointing to her wet hair. 'If you hurry up, I'll still give you something hot before you go,' she said suggestively and then added, 'Scrambled eggs?' She laughed as she pulled away completely.

'Sure,' he said, vaguely disappointed, but he was now on a promise for tonight. Something to look forward to. 'I'll just open this. It's probably something to sign for Jon.' He started wandering back towards the office.

'Don't be long,' she said over her shoulder as she moved towards the kitchen. 'I'm pouring fresh tea this minute.'

He knew Ally hated it if he let a newly poured cuppa turn cold. He walked into his private sanctum. Ally never came in here; she wasn't curious about his behind-the-scenes stuff of sponsorship and appearances. She'd had enough of that in her own working days as a television actress in a popular soap drama. Now she was enjoying the peace of impending motherhood and the reflected glory of being his wife. She didn't seem to mind being out of her own spotlight; magazines still wanted to feature her in the newest season's clothes to add to their fashion pages. In fact, a top London designer who had just released a pregnancy range had sent her a pile of outfits and was paying her to be seen in them.

Luca only now realised how little Ally missed the attention that had previously followed her every move. It was as though becoming pregnant and looking forward to motherhood had made her grow up overnight – all that celebrity status, everything that used to be part and parcel of her life, no longer offered the same attraction it once had. She didn't interfere in his business either, trusting his decisions implicitly and offering opinions only when asked. She never wavered in her support and, through hail or shine, never failed to be present at a home game for the Huxley Arrows football team. She also got to as many of the away matches as she could so he would always know she was there, cheering for him.

He loved her so much for that. Many of the other players' partners dropped that vigilance once they had a ring on their finger or became busy with family duties. He suspected Ally, however, would still wrap up her newborn twins and bring them to the London games. The fans hadn't missed her commitment, either, and it only made them more popular as a couple. When he scored, he'd look up to where he knew she'd be sitting and touch his heart, as though each goal was for her.

Smiling, he slit open the envelope with his ridiculously expensive letter opener and pulled out a single sheet, a polaroid dropping onto the desk below. He picked it up and stared at it, dumbfounded at its provocative content, while absently unfolding the letter.

'I've poured!' he heard her yell.

'Coming!' he yelled back. But his attention was riveted.

What had begun as bafflement now created deep creases in his forehead as he frowned, beginning to connect the perplexing words with the confusing photograph. A man on a bed, in repose, arms flung carelessly against the pillow, his head in the distance, blurred, turned to one side. The lens was focused lower, where his shirt had been pulled out and unbuttoned to reveal a flat belly, defined with toned muscles to the hips and a small, heart-shaped discolouration just below the man's navel.

It was a masterful image. The angle was just right to show Luca's birthmark; his mother had often joked through childhood that it was her farewell kiss on his body as he'd left hers. Out of focus, awkwardly lying on top of his boxers, which had been pulled only half down, he could see the post-coital flaccidness of an erection he didn't remember. In sharp focus, though, was a hand with nails painted like red talons.

Fuck! his mind screamed. *What is this?*

His frown deepened and triggered an eruption of fury. He controlled it how he'd been taught, feeling its tension leak into his jaw as he clamped hard; his even, well-cared-for teeth, white enough for any toothpaste commercial, fit together neatly to grind that rage. Yes, a memory was returning to him slowly, like an old-time negative gradually revealing an image. How had he not known this, or rather, how had he buried it? Forgotten it? Dismissed it?

He recognised the fingers with their red nails, which held a used condom. It was coming back fast now, a rush of memories he didn't know he possessed; those fingers had been all over him, undoing his clothes, caressing him, teasing him. Was it possible that he'd lost this knowledge? Surely not.

This scene related to an event that was two – no, nearly three – months back, at the launch of a new GT convertible car from Bentley. Handpicked guests, only a few likely buyers or Bentley executives, staying in luxurious rooms. Media and other celebrity guests came for the glamorous launch, adding lustre to the event. It was held in the Thames Valley at what the property's spin doctors liked to call a six-star spa and health resort to differentiate it from an everyday five-star venue. Lark's Hill was a grand old pile that had seen its fair share of aristocratic owners before a fire finished its life as a personal residence. The ruin, which wasn't as bad as many had believed, was bought and renovated over several years by a top hotel group to become a relaxing play space. Its glittering gala opening had been attended by the rich and famous.

Celebrities were regularly snapped by the paparazzi on the gravel drive of the heavenly place of rejuvenation. Some stayed for a week, others for a weekend burst of cleaner living, the in-house nutritionist and chef providing sumptuous but healthy feasts. And now the wealthy, like him, held their weddings and private functions there, too.

Luca and several other London-based footballers had been invited with their wives and partners. He suspected his invitation was initiated because he'd already indicated his interest in the new two-hundred-thousand-pound convertible. Ally, sadly, couldn't come; her morning sickness, which still seemed to last all day and night, had been so bad she'd begged off. He hadn't wanted to go without her but their close mates Harry and Gina were attending the event itself, so he was hardly without company, and he'd agreed to check out the venue so they could go together later.

And they had. About four weeks back she'd taken full advantage of his promise to share an indulgent weekend together at Lark's Hill and pamper her to the hilt before she got too big to enjoy it.

Ally was now just days from delivery of their twins, and huge – she'd stacked twenty kilos onto her former model-thin frame. In the early days, before she showed, she'd worried briefly about the weight gain. 'Fans of the show aren't going to recognise me. And what if I never get back to my body again?'

'You'll never fully get that body back, love,' he remembered her mother saying. 'It will be a new version. But you're young and feeding twins will turn you hollow. Besides, your fans adore you – you're the favourite character in that silly soap. They'll write you back in if you want to return . . . but why would you?' This was the moment his respect had turned into genuine admiration and even affection for Ally's mother. She'd happily counselled her daughter, pointing at him and saying: 'You're going to marry one of the country's most adored sporting heroes and you've got a whole life of good times ahead of you. Look where you live, look what he can give you while you raise your children. Ally, my love, if I were you, I'd make sure I asked nothing more of the universe. Focus on being pregnant and a mother to those two babies, and a good wife to Luca, who worships you.'

Even before the whirlwind romance they were already independently darlings of the media, as they each had an almost uncanny ability to woo the paparazzi and keep them kind.

Both had come from the most ordinary of backgrounds too, and that had a strong appeal for their fans. Her slight northern accent was treasured, while his Italian background gave him credibility as a battler who had made it.

Everyone thought of them as a perfect couple. No fractures – not even a hairline crack, according to friends. They were fast becoming an A-list power couple, and they knew it too. Made a promise to each other they would always protect their bond . . . protect their names.

There was one other promise.

Fidelity.

Ally demanded it. 'We're both really young, so if we're going to do this whole marriage and kids thing, I need to know it's real. I can marry anyone I want. So can you. But if we're choosing each other, I want to trust you and rely on you for the rest of my life.'

'Ally, you can. I'm not like those others.'

'I've known girls going out with footballers,' she said, shaking her head. 'They're treated well for a while and then cast aside like yesterday's rubbish. My hair, my boobs, my TV show might make me seem like a bimbo, but I'm not going to be your plaything for a while. If we're going to commit, take vows, wear each other's rings and raise these children, then it must be for keeps . . . and only for each other. If you make a fool of me with another woman, I'll make your life a misery. I'll leave and take our kids, and then take you to the cleaner's.'

It was a serious threat, delivered in a grave tone. He had nodded and kissed her to seal his promise. 'I will never let you down.'

Now he stared at the photo again.

How would he ever make Ally understand? She had been very clear. No mucking about with other women was number one on her short but emphatic list of intolerances and here she was, about to give birth to these precious children, and she would soon learn he'd failed so soon into their life together; they had only married a few months ago, while Ally could still fit into her dream wedding frock.

He'd broken her golden rule.

Except . . . he hadn't.

That might be him lying there with the family jewels on display and a full condom supposedly condemning him, but he had no memory of being a willing participant. He did not buy that he would forget having sex.

He read the note again.

Want to be a winner . . . or a loser? We all win if you pay £500,000. If you do, I'll destroy all evidence and no one will be any the wiser about your misbehaviour. Don't pay and we all lose, but you especially when I leak it to the press, tell your wife and sell your sperm on the dark web. Let's face it, who wouldn't pay to have your DNA in their child? Involve the police and you lose. Pay too late and you lose. I know that amount is small change for you.

Don't be a loser. Details of how to pay soon. We'll give you a week to organise the money.

Be assured. I keep my promises. Remember, if you involve the police or the club, I'll send Ally the photo anyway. No mistaking that's you, right? And you really don't want Ally looking at that right now.

He hurled the photo and note onto his desk with a visceral fear that had begun deep in his belly the moment he'd opened the envelope. It curled and twisted, squeezing at his insides until he could feel the tingle of panic at his crotch and in his throat.

Yes, that was him in the photo.

But he had not broken faith with Ally. No way.

He didn't understand how any of this was possible, but he would not capitulate without a fight.

He picked up his phone and tapped in the number. When it

was answered, before the usual cheerful pleasantries could begin, he said, 'I need to see you. Right now.'

'Wow, slow down. Is something wrong?'

'Yes.'

'What's going on?'

'Not over the phone. Come here.'

'I promised the family—'

'Jon, I pay you a cold fortune to have my back. So have it. I wouldn't insist if it wasn't urgent. In fact, it's dangerous.'

'Dangerous? What are you talking about?'

'Just get here, as soon as you can. This could blow my life up . . . and yours!' He rang off. He'd never spoken to his agent like that.

1

Jack hadn't wanted to go but Kate had pleaded with him over the phone. 'I haven't had a birthday party since I was a child. Besides, I haven't seen you for months,' she grumbled. 'And don't say you've been busy. I know you've been in a quiet job since Australia.'

'Neither have I,' he countered, ignoring the jab.

'Neither have you what?'

'Had a birthday party since I was a child,' he said, remembering the last one before the car crash that had killed his parents. He banished that memory quickly. 'I don't like parties, Kate, you know that.'

'But this is mine!'

He laughed that hers should be the special one. 'You've never invited me to a birthday gathering before.'

'I've never been this close to forty before.' She groaned.

'You've still got a few years up your sleeve,' he said to soothe her. 'Kate, don't ask me to—'

'But I am. I haven't seen you for months because you've been hiding away in Cold Cases and I've been at Anti-Corruption. Did you even know I'd moved to CIB?'

'Yes,' he answered, knowing full well she was in the Complaints Investigation Bureau 3, the proactive branch of that division, gathering intelligence on suspected or detected serious misconduct.

'You brute. And you didn't ring to congratulate me?'

'I should have, but I'd also heard about the teacher, and I didn't want to put my foot in it.' He didn't say: *And I didn't want you to get the wrong idea while you were vulnerable.* There was a soft silence. The break-up obviously still hurt. 'Sorry, I should've—'

Now she gave a moan of frustration. 'Jack, yes, you're the one person who should, because you're the one person I don't mind talking about it with.'

He didn't ask why. 'I thought he was a keeper.'

'He is, for someone. He should have been for me, but I have a habit, as you may have noticed, of pushing nice people away. He deserved more than I was giving. My workload at the time was crushing.'

'No chance of getting back together?'

'Doubtful. I'm a bit of a mess, as usual, in that regard. I don't know if it's wise either – I couldn't bear to hurt him again. Deep down I think I'd feel grateful if he told me he'd met someone. But in the meantime, this party will be a good distraction, I'm assuring you, though it wasn't my idea. It was Gabriella's. Have you met her?'

'Not that I recall.'

'You wouldn't forget her if you had. I thought you might have come to her thirtieth as my plus one, but you have a marvellous way of wheedling your way out of stuff like that. And yet I know you're not antisocial.' She gave him a pointed moment of silence.

He didn't want to tell her that going anywhere as her plus one was dangerous . . . for both of them, but especially her. 'Kate,' he began.

She sighed loudly. 'Don't take that tone.'

'We're colleagues. We can't . . .' He didn't finish.

'Jack, colleagues can be more than just fellow workers. You know, some are even lovers, but I'm talking about something innocent . . . just a birthday party my friends are throwing for me. And you are one of my best friends, even though I could be forgiven for thinking otherwise. I'm asking you to be a guest – not a partner, not a date, not a plus one. Just be my friend.'

He sighed. 'Okay, okay. Send me the when and where.' He smiled at her soft squeal of pleasure that sounded through the phone.

So now he found himself in a swanky basement bar in Soho that prided itself on serving the best gin cocktails 'in the world' according to those in the know.

'You look amazing.' He had to yell in her ear over the noise of the music and not just her gang of partygoers but the bar's general clientele, who seemed to be in high spirits this Friday night. And it was true, Kate had never looked more attractive than she did this evening, in a black metallic party frock that was all fun, showing off toned arms and tanned, shapely legs. A teardrop black pearl hung on a long gold chain contrasting with her dress, which was the colour of mercury and flowed effortlessly around her trim figure. Her hair, normally tied up neatly for work, now flowed in soft golden waves, only adding to her beauty.

'Thank you,' she said, kissing him a fraction too close to his mouth but just far enough away for him to accept it might be a clumsy hello. 'I'm so glad you came.'

'Happy birthday,' Jack said, holding out a small wrapped gift.

'You really didn't have—'

'I wanted to,' he said, cutting off her protest.

She held up the black pearl around her neck and waved it in front of him. 'This will always be my favourite.'

'From one of my Australian trips. Do you remember what I told you?'

'Yes.' She smiled, leaning in close. 'That the only naturally black pearls are Tahitian. I only wear it on special occasions. You couldn't top it.'

He shrugged. 'You don't have to open that now,' he said, looking around with disguised horror at the already busy dancers and flowing alcohol.

'We're not on duty,' Kate said, reading his mind as she undid the wrapping.

'Are we ever off?'

'Oh, Jack!' she breathed in awe, lifting out black pearl earrings that matched the pendant.

He couldn't help smiling. 'I'm glad you wore that tonight.'

She was already pulling the hoops from her ears. 'I have to put them on right now,' she said, excitedly. 'My gosh, this is too much. There, what do you think?' She glanced around, and a couple of her friends leaned in and made the right noises of approval.

Jack was still holding the hoops she'd flung into his hands. 'They're up to the job of matching how insanely gorgeous you look this evening.' He kept his tone just right for a friend offering a compliment.

'Right answer, Jack!' She laughed and gave him a huge hug, saying, 'I love them, thank you,' and then, without warning, she did kiss him on the mouth, very briefly, before turning away hurriedly to order a drink. She looked over her shoulder. 'What are you having?'

'Er . . .'

'Don't bother, let me choose.'

A few moments later she returned with an intriguing amber-coloured cocktail with a twist of burnt orange in it. Jack had watched the bartender light the spritz from the zest as he peeled off the skin from the fruit.

'You're going to love this, Jack. It's called a—'

Before she could finish speaking, a raven-haired woman eased up to them. Over her skin-tight black dress, cut away in places to reveal smooth olive skin, she wore a scarlet jacket. No one could miss her in any crowd. 'Oh my, Kate, who is this handsome fellow?' she asked in a smoky voice.

'I'm Jack,' he answered for Kate.

'The policeman?'

'Detective Superintendent Jack Hawksworth,' Kate said, pointedly.

Jack cast her a look of soft despair.

'Aha,' the newcomer drawled knowingly. 'I know who you are now.' She gave him a wink.

'Jack, this is one of my school pals from a hundred years ago, Gabriella Ferrari. It was her idea to have this party, and at this venue.'

He could detect disapproval in Kate's tone that perhaps her friend could not, but then she wasn't looking at Kate but at Jack, with a sort of open hunger. 'Ferrari?' It was all he could think of to say under her hot gaze.

Gabriella made a growling sound, like a car engine revving. Jack obliged with a chuckle, although her overt seduction was unnerving. 'I prefer my pet name of Bella among friends,' she said, only a trace of her heritage perceptible in her southern English accent. 'Kate, I had no idea the mysterious Jack you've spoken of was so alarmingly attractive,' she said, leaning in to kiss him slowly on both cheeks. She smelled of alcohol and Chanel No.5 Eau Première, which was all the rage in the department stores, being sprayed on every available female wrist that passed by. 'You should know that Kate makes you sound awfully stuffy and conservative.'

He grinned. 'Regularly guilty of both, actually.'

'Not with a wicked smile like that, you can't be,' she said with authority and took the glass he was yet to sip from. She helped herself to a swig. 'Mmm, scrumptious, just like you,' she said, smiling with that famished look again.

Kate clearly thought it was time to intervene. 'As I was saying, I ordered you a—'

'Hanky panky,' Gabriella finished, shutting down Kate. 'So appropriate, you tease.'

'I've never indulged before,' Jack said, instantly regretting the opening he'd given Kate's friend.

'Never indulged in hanky-panky?' she replied in an arch tone. 'We must fix that.' Then she turned to Kate. 'Don't you love this bar?'

'It's great,' Kate agreed but Jack knew that tight cadence in her voice meant she was telling a fib. 'Listen, I think Annabelle was looking for you.'

'Why?'

Kate gave her an airy look and a slight shrug. 'Not sure. Cake stuff probably, so I'm not meant to know.'

'I'll find her and then I'll come back and find you, Jack Hawksworth.' Gabriella sashayed away, no doubt presuming they were both watching her shapely behind disappear into the crowd.

Jack blinked and Kate turned to stare at him.

'What?' he asked, sounding defensive.

'Beware of Bella. She's a man-eater.'

'Odd that I didn't pick that up,' he said, lifting an eyebrow.

'I mean it, Jack. She'll have you twisted around her finger in a heartbeat.' At his sigh, she continued. 'No, really, it's a badge of honour for her. She's always been like this. Any new guy around and she needs to leave her mark on him. I don't know if it's simply because she can, or perhaps she has a missing chromosome or something.'

Jack gave a tsk. 'That's catty.'

Kate grinned unhappily. 'Look, she's an old friend, and she has a big heart, but she's also scary when she's in the mood she's in tonight. She believes she can have any bloke she chooses.'

'That's because she probably can,' he replied, as though that fact was obvious. Then he added, 'Anyway, I didn't come to meet Bella. I didn't want to be here at all, other than for you and to wish you the happiest of birthdays.' He picked up his drink, rotating the glass away from the lipstick half kiss that Bella had left for him. 'Here's to you. I hope this is a special year for you.'

'Cheers, Jack.'

They clinked glasses. As he sipped, he gave Kate a look of awe. 'Wow. Delicious!'

'It's my new favourite cocktail.'

'Why aren't you drinking one, then?'

'Because champagne is slipping down easier tonight.'

'Right, well, I think you should go off and mingle with your friends. Let them spoil you.'

'What are you going to do?'

'Nurse my hanky panky and—'

'Look for your moment of escape?' she asked.

He grinned. 'Something like that.'

'Don't you dare leave without saying goodbye.'

'I won't.'

Kate didn't want to leave Jack leaning against the bar, where he watched her friends erupt into song and dance, her in the middle, having to do a solo. She could see him on the fringe, laughing at the celebrations, and couldn't help but think he'd never looked more distant or desirable at once. Tonight he was in black, like her, but something about a man in a black suit and an open-necked white shirt did funny things to her. All he needed was the undone black bow tie and he'd look like he'd walked straight off the set of *Mad Men*.

She knew she shouldn't be thinking about Jack like this. He'd made that clear. But what had happened between her and Dan had been desperately sad. For just a moment their relationship had felt so grown-up and real; she had even allowed herself to imagine being his wife, coming home to his smile, their children, nagging each other about who was doing the ballet run or the football pick-up. Just a heartbeat of supreme comfort in their future, and then her career had begun to get in the way. He knew her work was demanding, with far from friendly hours, but for nearly a year she'd kept her time at the office as lean as she dared, so that had probably lulled them both into a false sense of how life might be together.

Was any job really worth losing an important relationship?

He had not been the unreasonable one. If anything, Dan had tried harder than her to find ways around the demands on her time, even getting special permission to arrange a rooftop picnic on a building she was working at when they'd barely seen one another for a month. His attempt at a romantic solution had only made it worse, though, with Kate resenting what she'd viewed as an interruption of her work.

'Childish and embarrassing,' she remembered hurling at him. She winced now at how viciously it must have come across when she'd suggested they were not lovelorn teens who needed to hold hands every moment that they could. So unfair. Dan had simply been trying to keep them connected around her exhausting work hours. He'd never once complained about the meals he'd cooked for her and had to throw away, the countless times he'd gone to bed alone, or the many dinners or meet-ups with friends he'd found himself stood up for. If she was being honest, his complete reasonableness, his affability in all situations and his constant forgiveness had begun to wear away at her and build a mountain of guilt.

In the end it was sweet Dan, once again being generous, who'd suggested she needed space and some time alone to work things out. She'd agreed, not even putting up a fight for him. And now there was Jack, looking highly desirable as he leaned against the bar. Perhaps he was the true source of her angst, the real reason she couldn't settle down: the man that could change everything if only he'd permit it.

He wouldn't, though. They'd had this conversation time and time again. So she would take friendship as a consolation prize, because at least it meant they could remain close.

Kate's gaze narrowed as she watched Bella make a new advance, and she gasped as Bella draped herself over Jack, who, gracious as always, tried to disentangle himself gently instead of rebuffing her straight out.

Kate should rescue him. But she moved too late, hesitating just a fraction too long. Bella had heard a favourite song belting out and by the time Kate got to them her friend was *beep-beeping* and *toot-tooting* seductively to Donna Summers' famous disco track.

'Come on and join the bad girls, Jack,' Bella suggested, tugging on his hand.

He politely declined; no doubt Jack could see that Bella was already well on her way to being drunk.

'Oh, here's the *sad* girl,' Bella said to Kate, playing on the song's lyrics.

'Hey, Bel, I didn't invite Jack to my party so you could hog him.'

'*Oink-oink!*' Bella said in perfect time over the *beep-beeps* in the lyrics and gave a hog snort. 'Green isn't your colour, Kate . . . or is it? I was simply asking him to dance. And I must say, I think it would be rude if he rejected me,' she said, eyeing Jack, daring him to turn her down.

He sighed. 'Right, ladies. I don't want to be the party pooper. One quick turn and then I'll leave you to it.'

Kate was staggered. No, deep down she was feeling venomous, watching Bella lead Jack to the small dance floor suggestively, holding his hand dangerously close to her half-exposed and beautifully pert breast. Once she'd reached the centre of the dance floor and thus the centre of attention, Bella twisted around and began gyrating her body in that 'come to bed' way of hers. It didn't matter that the song had a disco beat – she'd managed to slow her movements to half its pace. Kate wanted to scream.

Meanwhile, Jack surprised her by showing rhythm she'd never thought he possessed. She couldn't tell if he was enjoying himself or not; she couldn't see past her own despair. Kate needed the song to end.

'What's with the long face on your birthday?' It was another schoolmate.

She shook her head. 'Nothing.'

'It's Bella, right?' They were both watching her dance. 'Is he your date?'

'No,' she fired back a bit too smartly. 'Er, I mean, he's a really good friend.'

'Single?'

'Yes.' Kate nodded.

'Then what are you worried about? So's she. Two consenting adults and all that. Come on, we're going to do the cake and shots soon.'

Jack didn't stay for the cake. His phone began to vibrate inside his jacket pocket just as Bella decided to link her long, olive-skinned arms around his neck and curl herself closer than he'd prefer. He pulled out the phone, glanced at the screen and killed the call because, as he expected, Bella had all but passed out in his arms.

He helped her off the dance floor. 'You've had enough for one night.'

'Take me home, handsome Jack,' she slurred and in a split second he decided to do just that, walking her from the club and helping her up the stairs into the cool of the evening.

Some passing merrymakers whistled and cheered. 'You're on tonight, matey,' one encouraged him.

'Take in some big breaths,' Jack urged Bella.

'Did you say you like my big breasts, Jack?' she teased with glazed eyes.

He sighed, looked around and walked her unsteadily to a taxi rank.

The guy behind the wheel looked dubious. 'She going to vomit in my cab, mate?'

Jack wasn't in the habit of flashing his warrant card under anything but formal circumstances, but the situation was becoming urgent. 'Listen, I need to get her home safely. I have to be somewhere.'

'Hop in,' the cabbie said wearily. Jack bundled a mercifully cooperative and very flexible Bella into the back seat, where she collapsed like a fold-up toy. She suddenly looked small and fragile.

'She all right?' the taxi driver asked.

'Too much champagne,' Jack said as a throwaway line.

'Where to then, boss?'

'Oh,' Jack said, crestfallen. 'Good question. Er . . .' He found Bella's handbag on the floor of the car and rummaged around in it, finding only a single credit card, phone, lipstick and other para-phernalia that a woman can't leave the house without. 'Hold on,' he said, with a smile and a finger in the air. He called Kate; as she answered, he could hear the music had gone up a notch and was thumping away in the background.

'Where are you?' she asked flatly.

'I had to go. Can you give me Bella's address, please?'

'Why?'

'Kate, just tell me.'

Something in his tone persuaded her to not hedge any longer. She reeled it off. 'It's an art deco block just south of Clapham Common.' Her own tone was blunt and humourless, and he could tell she was angry with him. 'Have fun, you two,' she snapped. 'She's wearing a bodycon dress, Jack. It takes two to get it off!' The line went dead.

Jack stared at the screen with astonishment, murmuring 'bodycon' to himself in puzzlement before giving the cabbie the address in Balham. 'It's flat four.'

'Well, I'm not carrying her up the stairs, mate. That's your problem.'

'Yes, of course,' he said, feeling stupid for saying it. 'Can you wait while I take her up?'

'How long?'

'I'm just going to get her inside her flat with a bucket nearby and make sure she's safe. Ten minutes tops.'

'It's your money,' the cabbie said, not unfriendly but firm.

They travelled south of Charing Cross for approximately four miles, entering the borough of Wandsworth. At her flats in Balham, a low 1930s deco block, Jack again asked the cabbie to be patient. He took Bella to the main door and saw a panel of bells that included Ferrari and Barclay on one. He rang it and waited with his cargo, who was slumped over, kissing his neck.

'You smell so nice,' she slurred.

'You smell of liquor,' he countered. 'Who is Barclay?'

'Hmm?' she said from his collar. He repeated his question. 'Loulou.'

'Hello?' came a dislocated voice.

'Er, is that, um, Ms Barclay?'

'It is, who is this?'

'Loulou, darling, it's me,' Bella cooed.

'Bella, oh dear, you sound untidy.' She buzzed the door open and Jack hauled his load over the threshold. Above him a woman's voice called down. 'Need help?'

'Please.'

The flatmate arrived in stripy pyjama bottoms and a T-shirt, skipping down the centre carpet barefoot. Her hair was casually clipped up and she had a pencil stuck behind one ear. Jack had to look away from the nicely rounded breasts beneath her T-shirt. 'Hi, I'm Louise . . . Lou,' she said with a smile.

'Loulou.' Bella suddenly stirred, more alert now. 'This is handsome Jack.'

'Hello, Jack.' Lou grinned. 'Um . . .?'

Jack cleared his throat. 'Just bringing her home safely from Kate Carter's party.'

'Ah, the birthday bash. Is it over already?'

'Just warming up, but I had to leave − I have something to attend to. Bella here was looking a little frayed, so I thought it best to get her home.' He looked over his shoulder. 'I've got a cab waiting.'

'I can take her from here.'

'Are you sure?' he asked, looking up the flights of stairs.

'Oh, we've done this a few times.' Lou laughed. 'Leave her with me.'

'She's, um, well, a lot of champagne and no food, to my knowledge, so a bucket is probably in order.'

Lou gave him a salute. 'Got it.'

He paused a moment, meeting her eye. 'Why didn't you come to the party?'

She grinned. 'I'm not part of that set. I know Bella and a couple of the others, but not the birthday girl very well.'

'Well, it's nice to meet you,' Jack said.

'I'll be better dressed next time,' she promised.

He grinned. 'I think you look perfect. Sleep it off, Bella,' he said close to the other woman's ear. She tried to grab him, but he gently shifted his balance to avoid being wrestled into a smooch of any kind. 'Sorry to leave her like this.'

'Go,' Lou said. 'He'll charge you heaps otherwise.'

'Night.' He nodded.

She smiled again and he turned, reaching for the heavy front door.

'Jack?'

He twisted back, raising his brows in query.

'Thanks for doing the right thing by her.'

'You're welcome.'

'Come for coffee, or drinks, or even a meal sometime. We should thank you properly.'

He raised a hand in a friendly wave. 'Sounds nice.'

And then he was gone, ducking back into the cab.

'Where to, sir?'

'Scotland Yard.'

'Might've guessed. Here we go ...' the guy said, swinging the black cab around effortlessly and heading back towards Westminster.

Jack rang his boss on her after-hours number.

'Hawksworth?'

'Ma'am.'

'Tell me you didn't cut me off an hour or so ago.'

'I was in a nightclub and couldn't hear a thing. I thought it best to get to a quieter spot.'

'You were in a nightclub?'

He couldn't tell if she might be smiling. Likely not. 'Er, a night out for a friend's birthday. I didn't have anything to do with choosing the venue. I managed to steal away early, anyway. Just arriving home now,' he lied. 'Has something come up?'

'It has. I realise you're off duty, so forgive me calling you.'

'No problem. Do you want me to come in now?'

'No, it can wait, but I'll see you at the office in the morning. Just before nine, all right? I've got someone else coming in, but I want to talk to you first. I'm sending you some stuff you can look over.'

'Right.' The line went dead. Women were ringing off on him too often tonight. 'Change of plan,' Jack said to the cabbie. 'Can you take me to Kew?'

'Station or street?'

'Head for Burlington Riverside,' Jack said, giving the neighbourhood where he'd bought his townhouse six months prior. 'Do you know that area?'

'Course,' the fellow said, only just hiding his disdain. 'Very nice it is too. Pricey.'

Jack didn't comment.

Just over half an hour later, he was glad to close the door on an altogether unsatisfactory evening, although he felt glad that he'd shown his face at the party and not let Kate down. Still, he had apparently let her down in another way by taking her exceedingly drunk friend home to the safety of her flatmate and pillow. He was reminded of the cheerful disposition of Lou Barclay and how entirely at ease she seemed, confident in herself. He found that deeply attractive and tried not to think of her cute PJs and T-shirt. It had words on it that said: *Don't even think about it.*

That made him smile. He was thinking about it.

The pencil behind her ear. What did that mean?

Distantly he heard the familiar ping of his email and sighed. He'd better get to it. Carol Rowland would expect him to be up to speed by the time he walked in tomorrow morning.

2

Luca Bruni was the one.

The cheer as the Huxley Arrows ran out roared through his body. He could feel the adoration, along with the presence of his childhood coach, speaking while they had stood shivering on the pitch when he was around nine years old.

'Of the one and a half million children playing organised football up and down England at any one time, fewer than two hundred will enjoy a career in the sport. And of that tiny figure, only a handful might go all the way to the Premier League with one of the top clubs. Do you know what that means, boys?'

'No, sir,' they mumbled in chorus.

'It means that only one of you clowns charging around the pitch this afternoon might have a shot at the bigger stage.'

Some of the bigger, lippier lads joshed that it would be one of them. They didn't understand. It might not be any of them; it was just a statistic. Luca was smarter than most gave him credit for, but school didn't interest him. He wanted to use his smart mind to become one of the best footballers in the country.

It wasn't always natural talent, the coach told them often enough. 'It's up here, lads,' he'd say, tapping his temple. 'This is where a lot of the training should go. Training your brain to make smart decisions during a match. You have a dream? Start in here,' the coach said, gently tapping the heads of various boys crowded around him.

And Luca's dream? That was easy; leading his national team to victory in the World Cup was his ultimate aim . . . had been since he was seven and his parents first enrolled him in football training. It hadn't been cheap; even so young he'd known they were making sacrifices for him to capitalise on what his father believed were 'silky skills'.

'And what about his sister, Corey?' Luca knew his English mum only called his dad by his proper name, Corrado, when she was anxious or angry; otherwise, he was Corey.

'Sofia can be anything she wants, Deb, you know that. If there's something she wants to specialise in and we can help her to achieve it, then it's the same deal. But she's tried everything, surely?'

Luca's mother had nodded, then said dryly, 'Yeah, well, she wants to be a hairdresser,' and grinned.

Sofia had become just that but in Australia. Luca hadn't seen that coming. First it was a holiday to meet their Italian family, all of whom – bar his grandfather – had taken the ship to the other side of the world, settling in Adelaide. Luca hadn't expected to love Australia as much as he had and his sister, Sofia – a few years older – had fallen for the hot summers and beach parties. He couldn't even recall how the decision had been made but suddenly their family was packing up life in overcast England and heading 'down under' too.

He recalled it vividly. It had felt enormous when he was nine, leaving his friends, his school, his neighbourhood and especially his local club at Hove. He swore Coach Patton had become misty-eyed saying goodbye, and he remembered him shaking his father's hand, sounding reluctant as he said, 'I have to say it – I reckon you're stealing his future, Mr Bruni.'

'They play football over there,' his father had assured the other man.

'It's religion here, though. Over there it's just another sport. They have their own code full of jumping and catching the ball . . . using their hands!' Coach Patton spat the final word as though it burned his mouth to say it. And then he gave a mirthless chuckle. 'No, I'm wrong. That lot worship at the altar of the crease wearing baggy green hats. It's all cricket for them.'

His father had smiled tightly but Luca knew he was just being polite. 'I promise you, I'll enrol him in a club straight away. I know the boy's got potential, and they'll see it.'

'Potential?' Coach Patton shook his head. 'You have no idea what you're walking away from.'

Did the coach really think Luca's father was going to change all their plans just because Luca was showing some talent with a football?

'Mr Bruni, it's so much more than potential. Look, kids like Luca come along now and then. Remember Georgie Best?'

Luca's father had nodded.

'I know I'm old-school, but his name didn't lie . . . He was the best of his era. Even Pelé called him the greatest footballer he ever saw. These guys like Best, Messi or Ronaldo.' He shook his head helplessly. 'They arrive on the scene and we don't see their equal for years and years. Mark my words, if your lad keeps going on the trajectory he is, he won't need a second name. He'll be known simply as Bruni and the world will be at his feet.'

'Are you saying he can't do that from Australia?'

Coach Patton shrugged, looking suddenly defeated. 'We'll see. He'll be missed,' he said, ruffling Luca's hair and surprising him because the coach had never shown that kind of affection before. 'Come back soon for a visit, eh?'

'I have to do what's right for my family,' his father had said. 'For all of us. This is a great opportunity for the kids to know their family. All of my wife's relatives are gone – we've been a tight foursome here for all their childhood but now there's a chance for them to be part of something larger, and to know something of their Italian heritage.' He grinned. 'Australia does Italy quite well,' he quipped, hoping to lighten the mood, but the coach didn't respond in kind. And so his father had shrugged, a hand finding its way protectively onto Luca's shoulder. 'Besides, these kids will have some great opportunities in Australia that they won't get here.'

'We'll agree to disagree,' Coach Patton said in a tight tone. 'Good luck, Luca. You keep practising that cross with both feet, okay? You're a bit of a magician already, so make sure you follow through on all your promise.'

'I will,' Luca had said, embarrassed and a little sad, but he couldn't tell his coach that he was also excited and really did want to go to Australia.

By eighteen, he had the experience to understand that the coach's statistics were all up the creek but that hadn't mattered – it probably did all boil down to the one kid who got a chance. Coach Patton had made his point.

And Luca had made his; not through words, but with stellar ability and his naturally ambidextrous feet. This skill had been fully honed over the previous decade through Adelaide United's Youth system, and Luca could play one wing as comfortably as the other. That would be enough for any rising soccer talent, but Luca had so much more to offer. In his heart he was a striker . . . every schoolboy player's dream but also well within his reach. His ability to kick the ball hard and powerfully low, with a dead-eye aim, so far from the goal that even the goalkeeper had to shield his eyes and hope to stop the bomb coming at him, was breathtaking, or so the pundits were saying.

'His free kicks close to goal are just sublime,' one had said after Luca's first few opening games for Adelaide United's A-team. 'I would hate to be a defender against this kid, and that's all he is. Still wet behind the ears. Imagine him in five years when he's put on some muscle and fully develops his football brain. He's a new Thierry Henry, in my opinion.'

'Why do you say that?' the other commentator asked, purely for the audience's sake. Luca had already demonstrated why.

'Listen, this kid is fast and powerful. He can score from anywhere, any angle if he sees the opening. He doesn't have a trademark goal, so you can't see it coming. He can bend around a wall of players or on the run. You can't get a feel for when his brain is thinking "strike". He's like a wizard when the ball's at his feet. But add to that, Mike, he's an assist machine. Watch him carefully. He sets up as many opportunities for others as he takes for himself. He's every kind of striker you could want all rolled into one, and off either foot. He's going to be devastating, and I hope the Reds take full advantage of the kid, because he is going to be hunted the moment his contract is up for grabs. And I don't just mean from Australian clubs.'

'All the way, eh?'

'Oh, yeah, no doubt at all. Listen, I'll put down money that the kid has his own chant within a year. He'll score so often they'll be singing his name loud enough to lift the grandstand roof.'

The commentators had liked that and shared a chuckle. So had Luca.

'Don't get cocky listening to this drivel,' his father warned, coming in from the garden.

Luca had shaken his head. 'No chance, Dad. I've seen it happen to others. When they do, they become targets.'

'Well, I note the leaf basket hasn't been cleared in the pool. If you want to swim in a few weeks, you'd better get to it. If that one breaks, it's coming out of your wages, not mine.'

'Corey, don't make threats,' his mother said in a tone that suggested everyone knew they were empty. 'Anyway, son, you'll be targeted in new ways soon.' She kissed his head. 'Here's your gear for school,' she said, handing him a freshly ironed uniform for the week. 'Go hang it up.'

'What do you mean, targeted in new ways?'

'Don't think I don't hear that phone pinging all the time. Boys don't talk like that. That's the ping of a girl on the other end.'

Luca had blushed, and noticing, Sofia joined in the teasing. 'All the teenagers who come to the salon ask for me simply so they can see if I can hook them up with my brother! It's very annoying, Lukey.'

He'd put his head down and passed his Year 12 with higher-than-average scores that qualified him immediately to take an engineering course he'd applied for at Adelaide Uni, but he'd instead signed on for two years with Adelaide United. University would have to wait.

At twenty, he was known by various affectionate nicknames from Golden Sprigs to Mafiaboy to simply Bruni, just as Coach Patton had predicted. He'd grown broad rather than especially tall, but his five foot ten was more than enough height for a footballer. His wide, strong shoulders had put on muscle in the gym over the years, and he moved like a panther, low to the ground. At times he seemed impossible to nudge off the ball because he had such a firm grip on the pitch. But when he made a dash, thigh muscles pumping like well-oiled pistons, even the commentators would yell because he would light up the stadium with his speed.

He had become the consummate footballer, and everyone wanted Luca signed to their team. The bids when his contract

was up were eye-watering. The European teams offered money
that his family could and would never have dreamed of. Perhaps
Coach Patton had, but not the Brunis. Bayern Munich offered
a staggering amount that equated to nearly a million Australian
dollars per month.

'Per month!' his father had exclaimed repeatedly, looking at
Luca's mother. 'You and me and Sofia combined won't earn his
month's salary in our lifetimes.'

Luca had kept his head through all the negotiations and the
outrageous pitches from clubs with their gargantuan promises.
There were loyalty bonuses, sponsorship deals and even something called 'objectives' payments. He'd wisely parted company
with his local agent and signed on with a new group in London,
who were experienced with brokering such enormous sporting
deals. Luca just wanted to play football and privately his heart
was set on playing back in England. When an offer came
through from the recent sensation – the Huxley Arrows –
it wasn't a hard decision. The tipping point had been the
Australian connection through the club's new billionaire owner,
Roger Tallis.

The Tallis family had made its fortune through mining, beginning with Roger's grandfather and gold mining in Kalgoorlie.
Roger's father had then diversified the company interests into
diamonds as well as bauxite and coal. Roger, the only heir, had
added lucrative iron ore to the company's projects. He'd attended
university in England and developed a passion for the World
Game, as it was known. In 2006 he'd taken that passion to a new
level, acquiring his own English football team and replenishing
their 'stock' with some top players and a new coach with a fine
track record in Europe. Now he was about to cut the ribbon on
a new stadium and home base for the Arrows. His latest project,
however, had been to recruit Luca Bruni at any cost.

'They're matching the Bayern Munich deal and then some,' Luca's agent, Jon Mason, had said over a new system they used for face-to-face calls. Skype was apparently old hat. Jon had smiled, moving his gaze to take in the family – Luca had wanted his parents to be present for this conversation. 'They really want your boy.'

'The Arrows.' Luca's father had given a low whistle. 'Bloody hell. Their rise has been spectacular.'

'Yep, they've moved out of Division One and into the Premier League, touted to win the FA Cup this year. Luca would be the cherry on top of an amazing five years for the club with Tallis in charge. You know how much he likes your lad, and he wants an Aussie spearheading his team. Luca, you'll be playing in the World Cup for Oz before you know it.'

His mother couldn't speak, holding back happy sobs.

Mason smiled. 'What do you think, Luca? Tallis is clearly impressed. Apparently the technical gurus at the club reckon you've got the ideal composure and sense of commitment. You're a perfect fit for them. He says he'll build the club's list around you.'

'Yeah, I like their ambition. I want to be part of it. Huxley it is,' Luca had said with conviction.

His agent had nodded. 'Good decision.'

Luca's parents had accompanied him to England to set him up in a flat with a slightly older, more experienced player, also Italian, who was part of the buddy system.

'I promise you, we'll take very good care of your boy,' the Arrows' player-care manager had repeated to Luca's anxious parents.

And they had. Meanwhile, Luca had rewarded them with an astonishing golden goal in his first game. It had been an upward, enviable trajectory from there over subsequent years until it was now almost expected that the likely scorer in any meet would be Luca Bruni. He was dependable, he was modest, he trained hard and he continued to assist goals for his fellow strikers. He was popular with the media, happy to give interviews and his self-effacing style was appreciated. He was liked by his fellow players for being fair and unselfish when he had the ball. And he was generous towards and thus adored by fans; Luca would pause to sign their scarves, their shirts and sometimes their bare skin.

Soon enough, one had snared him properly. Ally Gold had caught his eye at a nightclub and by the time he was twenty-two and about to negotiate one of the biggest football contracts known in the sport, Ally was pregnant with twins and busy setting up the nursery in their vast flat at Kew, though they were planning a move in the near future.

'We've found a huge old pile at Highgate that Luca's going to renovate,' Ally had gushed to her parents, who lived in a tiny house in Barnet, North London.

When they saw it, their eyes had grown wide with disbelief. 'Blimey, luv, you can take a walk around your garden with the babies. You won't need a park!'

She'd giggled. 'I know, Luca's hired a gardener. What do I know about gardening?' She rubbed her huge belly and kissed Luca's cheek.

Luca had smiled, enjoying knowing he made his wife happy and impressed her parents. Although she was as young as Luca, she seemed to be relishing the idea of motherhood and never having to struggle again financially. Luca had thrown some money her brother's way to help out with a business he was setting up, and her parents were all-round thrilled with how Luca had given their two children security. He'd also set Sofia up in her own salon back in Adelaide, which she'd named after him.

'It's leverage,' she'd said, laughing. 'I'll take all the reflected glory I can.'

He'd also been able to pay off his parents' home in Prospect on the outskirts of Adelaide's city and, despite their protests, buy them a holiday home in Victor Harbor.

'You love the beach, Mum. Now you can spend the summer walking along it and enjoying the sea,' he'd said on a visit.

He liked what his money could do – especially for others – and his latest plan was to build a new clubhouse for his old childhood team. Coach Patton was still there barking orders at them and had shed a few tears to see his star student turn up, much to the delight of the squad.

But money wasn't as important to Luca as it appeared to others. It was nice, sure, but he simply loved the thrill of the match, the roar of the crowd, the tension of the Premier League. He couldn't have been happier in his life until the moment he'd opened the letter.

Through his sporting life he'd been tagged, fouled, bullied and pushed around, but he'd expected and been coached to cope with all of that. What he hadn't expected or been coached for was the dilemma he was facing right now. Blackmail.

A stranger was threatening his whole way of life; his career was at stake, and certainly his relationship might not survive. He pressed his fist into his brow now as he tried to make sense of it all.

'I'm told an elite senior officer is being briefed tomorrow,' Jon Mason had assured him in a tense phone call the previous night.

'This is killing me. The Arrows are gearing up for the treble, and my head's all over the place with this. What am I going to do?'

'Luca, I know it's easy for me to say, but you have to dig deep and focus on your work. Let others clear up this mess. The officer's name is Jack Hawksworth and he's a detective superintendent. They're not messing about. He's one of the best.'

3

Jack was seated across from his chief, Carol Rowland, sipping his specifically chosen takeaway coffee while she accepted a ghastly stir-in-the-mug brew from her assistant.

'I can see the revulsion in you, Jack,' she remarked, clearly enjoying his discomfort.

'I thought I was doing a good job of disguising it,' he quipped as the door closed to leave them alone.

She shook her head. 'Your expression gives nothing away, but it's in your eyes, I'm afraid.' She smiled. 'Thanks for coming in on the weekend.'

'What's a weekend?' he replied without any rancour.

'Well, I think it should be respected. You all work long hours. How are you finding your time in Cold Cases?'

'Very good. It has an enjoyable academic quality – studying a case, going back over details, considering what might have been missed, what else we might do. We've already established some leads on eight old cases.'

She nodded, impressed.

'Anyway, to answer what I think you were really asking,' Jack continued, 'the quieter job has been exactly what I need after the Australian mission.'

'You got all the follow-up material I sent on it?'

He nodded. 'Thank you for including me.'

'You cracked that syndicate open, and we owe you a debt of thanks for that.'

'How's Mrs Maddox doing?'

'I don't know. I was simply assured by the South Australian Police that their investigation is satisfied she had no knowledge of her husband's criminal activities. She's been fully exonerated, and is, I suspect, trying to rebuild her life.'

'She has three children. It won't be easy.'

'No,' Rowland said, in a tone that told him she was done with that conversation. He knew she didn't have a family of her own, though he suspected that perhaps she had wanted children. During a recent visit Jack had made to catch up with Martin Sharpe, his former chief had mentioned that Rowland had once been married, adding that when she'd found out about her husband's affair, the relationship had been brought to an abrupt end.

'Rowland's a straight shooter, Jack. Doesn't hate men, don't get me wrong, but it might be a chip on her shoulder.'

Maybe that explained her candid conversation when they'd first met about his personal relationships bleeding into his professional life; even though he'd explained, she didn't show much sympathy.

He knew he should drop the subject; Rowland had already made it clear Jack had far too much crossover from cases into his personal life. No one knew about his romantic few hours with Jem Maddox, but he often wondered how she was getting on. He stayed silent.

'So, Jack, it's because of that particular case that I think you may be able to plug into this one.'

'I don't see how, but I'm all ears.' He'd read the files she'd emailed through the night before.

She glanced at her watch. 'I'm expecting someone to join us in fifteen minutes or so. Let me take that time to tell you about it.'

Rowland briefed him on a letter and polaroid photo that Premier League football superstar Luca Bruni had received.

Jack listened quietly and carefully to all the facts. When she finished speaking, he nodded and began with the obvious. He had to admit to himself that he was intrigued. The footballer was a star, no doubt about it, and it made sense that he'd eventually become a target. But this wasn't the usual sort of thing. 'Nothing amiss with the courier firm?' Jack asked.

'We haven't begun digging deep yet, but it doesn't seem so.'

'And why do you think I might be a good fit for this case?'

'Several reasons. First, you're effectively between jobs; let's be honest, your current one is just tiding you over to get some space from what was a fairly dramatic episode in Australia. Second, that particular case gave you something of an education into human reproductive material that most of us don't have.'

He nodded thoughtfully as she continued.

'Finally, this needs sensitive handling, and I think you have the right touch and, shall we say, mix of experience, seniority and charm to help these people.'

At his frown, she held up a hand. 'Let me explain. The black-mailer, which could be more than one person, has threatened that if Bruni or his family come to the police, the photo will be released to the media. It will become a feeding frenzy – you and I both know how popular this couple is. The wife knows nothing at this stage.'

'He needs to tell her.' Jack was blunt.

'I agree, and that's what you will be advising, possibly even helping with. But at this stage, we must tread very carefully because of the threat about involving the police.'

'Who brought this to us?'

'Bruni. Through a third party.'

'Okay,' Jack said, even more intrigued now. He felt admiration for Bruni's defiance. 'It's just one blackmail item so far. Are you setting up a full op because he's high profile?'

'No. I've learned that this is not an isolated incident, as we'll hear about when our visitor arrives. He's speaking on behalf of a group of sports agents who collectively represent some of Britain's highest-earning athletes.'

'How many others?'

'I have no specifics, but quite a few, I gather. All the same – a compromising photo and a full condom. And each time, they've paid.'

'They've paid because they're frightened not to?' Jack asked.

'Yes. Quite worrying. We've not had any inkling about it either. They've handled it all quietly – in-house, so to speak.' She drew imaginary quotes in the air at the word 'in-house'.

That would have annoyed Kate, Jack thought, but then a lot of things annoyed Kate.

'Presumably a condom without spermicide, if they have any chance of going through with their threats.'

'Is that a question? Because I don't have the answer.'

'No, a thought. It would be the way to protect the sperm. Most carry spermicide.'

'Right, well . . . it's not just footballers, apparently,' Rowland continued. 'It's happening across all the big sports. This seems to be the latest in a line of carefully planned events.'

'Am I to understand that Luca Bruni refutes what seems to have happened in the photo?'

'Vehemently,' she confirmed. 'Claims he was drugged.'

'So that's not his semen in the condom?'

Rowland took a deep breath and sighed it out. 'I'm sure he doesn't want to believe it is.'

'Surely he'd know?'

She shrugged. 'I'm not a man, I can't attest to anything. You're in a much better position to answer that.'

'He would know if he ejaculated, ma'am,' Jack said in a firm tone.

Rowland cleared her throat. 'The fact is – and why we're here talking about it – that Luca Bruni is so determined not to capitulate to their demands that he has risked the blackmailer's threats by bringing us in on it.'

'Well, I admire his resolve.' Jack was being honest.

She gave a small smile. 'Yes. I do too, as it happens. It's a daring move and would have taken courage. The others paid just to shut the blackmailers up.'

'And they did shut up?' Jack asked, surprised.

'Apparently so. Each time, the contents of the condom were shown being destroyed in a follow-up video and the blackmailers were never heard from again.'

Jack gave a low whistle. 'Gentlemen blackmailers?'

Rowland shrugged.

'And the victims trust that?'

'I guess so. There have been no repercussions, I'm told, for those who paid.'

Jack's mind was whirring now. 'So whoever this is must be freezing the sperm . . . that's going to need some tech.'

His boss waited, clearly happy to hear more. Jack obliged, remembering the details he had learned from the Australian case. 'Sperm can live within the female for as long as five days. Outside of the body, it's my understanding that three days is about their best effort, but that's requiring all the right conditions.'

'Which are?'

'Well, no cooler than 21 degrees, no higher than body temperature. And the bigger threat is evaporation. The, uh, material tends to dry out quickly.'

'Go on.'

'I guess they could protect against that by using some special chemical media. It can't be just seminal fluid, as I understand it.' Jack blinked. 'Egg yolk,' he said.

'I beg your pardon?'

'Egg yolk helps.' He'd just remembered that.

'Ugh. Semen on eggs yolks?'

'Not a nice image, I agree. That's a backyard option. If they have access to a lab, then I imagine they'd have a proper sperm-friendly fluid – don't ask me for the technical name, I can't recall it – but the method they use is called the "swim-up procedure".'

His boss looked baffled.

'Take a test tube,' Jack began, 'with that fluid, then in goes the sperm, which is now able to swim up easily in that fluid to find the surface, which I seem to remember takes approximately an hour.'

'You'd need specialist equipment, surely?'

'Yes, if they don't have a proper lab, they'd need to create one of sorts at home, I guess, which would include an incubator to keep the sperm at body temperature. When the sperm makes it to the top of the test tube and settles, it can be collected and put in what's called culture media. Gosh, I know it wasn't all that long ago, but I'm feeling a bit vague on it.'

'No, Jack. Already your knowledge is helpful. Truly.' She frowned. 'So if it was treated like that, how long would the sperm last?'

'If frozen, indefinitely.'

'So if they want to sell it, it would require speedy work.'

'Yes. And then I'm trying to imagine what that all looks like to the buyer. Let's say all of this is in place. The sperm is sold. The recipient has to meet somewhere, collect the sperm and then, forgive my vulgarity, ma'am, but get it inside within, let's say, forty-eight hours.'

'Easier ways to make money,' Rowland said, sounding contemplative.

'So what are we doing—'

He was interrupted by the buzz on Rowland's desk phone.

She held up a finger in apology. 'Yes, Shirley?'

'Mr Shaw is here.'

'Good, bring him in.'

The door opened to a man who smelled of strong cologne and Savile Row. He looked entirely out of place in Rowland's teak veneer office, with its nasty grey carpet, but he smiled politely as though it was perfectly natural to be here. Jack did his best to alleviate the awkward moment by standing to shake the newcomer's hand as his boss got busy with introductions.

'Coffee, Mr Shaw?' Rowland offered.

Her visitor glanced at her half-drunk cup and the takeaway one near Jack.

Jack gave a tiny shake of his head.

'Er, no thanks.' Shaw smiled. 'I've just had one.' Whether it was a lie didn't matter; Jack was glad the newcomer had made the right decision.

'Mr Shaw, Detective Superintendent Hawksworth is weighing up how we should best approach this latest episode of blackmail. I wonder if you'd be kind enough to brief us on the previous incidents to bring us up to speed and answer any questions he may have.'

'Certainly. Er, Detective Super—'

'Jack's fine,' he offered, watching the fellow struggle to remember the long title.

'Jack,' Shaw said gratefully. 'Thanks. And please call me George.'

Jack momentarily wondered whether the man's middle name was Bernard, but tucked his silly thought back where it belonged.

'I think it's important I tell you that I represent a group of agents, normally rivals,' Shaw said with a soft smirk, 'but in this instance we are allies.' He took a slow breath. 'This goes back about three years.' He noted Jack and Rowland's surprise and nodded. 'It began in motor racing. I won't tell you who the victim was, but he paid up within twenty-four hours and was satisfied not to hear from the blackmailer again, other than receiving video proof that the, er, semen had been destroyed.'

'And you trusted that?' Rowland asked.

Jack was glad she'd made that query.

Shaw gave an expansive shrug. 'Short of the material being returned for a DNA test, we can't be sure, no. The guy in question didn't want that. But as I said, nothing more was communicated and the problem disappeared.'

Rowland nodded and gestured for him to continue.

'To be honest, none of this was common knowledge between agents until a rumour began to circulate. I couldn't tell you from where it emanated, only that it began to gain currency as more people fell prey to these blackmailers. As I say, we're quite a small fraternity, even though we're competitors, and we all know one another. Anyway, it happened again, this time in tennis, and soon I caught wind of another incident, so I phoned around. It turns out similar blackmail incidents had occurred in cricket, too – that's my area. A different agency to mine handled that transaction, thank heavens. But it's also happened in motor-bike racing, golf and, of course, football.'

'Why "of course"?' Jack asked, hoping Rowland wouldn't mind his interruption.

'Oh, simply because there are so many highly paid footballers to choose from, and they're often exceptionally young and thus make easier targets.'

Jack nodded.

'In fact, there were three incidents in football – that I know about.' Shaw shook his head. 'Once we began to come clean to each other, those involved admitted that they'd each given similar advice to their clients.'

'To pay?' Carol asked.

Shaw nodded.

'Why?' she pressed. 'Why not go to the police?'

Shaw shrugged. 'Because they could. These people earn enormous sums of money. What was being asked certainly made them angry, but my advice would have been the same – why bother with the hassle of trying to fight back if you have the cash? These incidents came out of left field and we all just wanted it to go away.'

'But then it happened to one of yours?' Jack asked.

Shaw nodded. 'We don't talk about it.'

Rowland frowned. 'How much is generally involved?'

'Collectively? Many millions. I'd rather not get specific; this is a touchy and protected secret, you realise.'

Jack sat back, shocked but silent. He had more questions but he'd let Shaw finish.

'If you're wondering why we're coming to you now, it's because we're tired of wondering who's going to be next. We can't insure against it, and we can't prevent these young, wealthy athletes from letting their hair down every now and then, particularly during season breaks. The bad guys pick their marks perfectly; young, stupidly wealthy guys, often with huge egos and on the cusp of something big.'

'What does "something big" mean, Mr Shaw?' Carol asked. 'I can hazard a guess, but I'd rather hear it from you.'

Shaw puffed out his cheeks and blew out the air. 'Everything from a monster sponsorship deal to a transfer to a Premier League club or a huge international club, maybe a wedding or, I don't know, a TV deal. A pivotal, life-changing event that could be destroyed if news leaked of their night of fun.'

'Why should a young, single adult man feel worried that he was being shown to have had sex with a woman – prostitute or not?' Jack asked. 'It's almost a rite of passage these days, it seems. Is it really worth millions to cover up?'

'Well, you're right, of course. In that situation, it might not be a huge issue, but who needs that kind of media hassle, right when you're about to sign on to something huge? It's so much easier to pay up and make it go away. Not everyone's single though – like Bruni, whose wife is about to give birth to twins. Not to mention the potential embarrassment for their families. Add to that the idea that the world wants our top-tier athletes to be setting good examples. I'm not talking goodie-two-shoes here – that's boring. But no one out there in the real world, who works in a dreary nine-to-five office job or on the factory floor, wants to know that their heroes are fallible, just like them. Yes, we want them to have some vices to keep them normal, but we also want them to be superhuman.'

Shaw paused to scoff. 'Certainly the big-name sponsors want someone, if not squeaky clean, then aspirational for their younger customers. Morals do come into it too, somewhere in the blurry background. Imagine a player is about to marry the woman of their dreams. A photo like this could ruin their whole life. What if they're known in the media as straight but it's a young naked man in the picture instead of a woman? If you're a heterosexual A-grade player, married, engaged or about to start a family, you really don't want a photo to get out that implies you're gay, even if it's nothing to be ashamed of. Let's say you're about to sign a huge deal and then a photo gets out of you in a sleazy pose with a near-naked woman and a couple of lines of cocaine. People trust what they see, and these photos are no joke. Someone's set them up really cunningly. It ruins the mystique and destroys their marketability.' He shrugged. 'And that's what it's really all about. The damage in their personal lives is one thing, but losing a potential sponsor could cost them millions.'

Shaw sighed. Jack and his boss waited, sensing that he had more to say.

'We had formed a loose alliance where we were all prepared to put in money to hire a private investigator. We had to take some action to stop it, because we didn't believe it was going to stop on its own. We planned to secretly hire the best, pay whatever was asked, and hunt down this bastard.'

'It may be a group rather than an individual,' Carol cut in.

Shaw nodded. 'Yes, very true, it could be a team but we would have remained patient until we had them all rounded up and ready to hand over to you. But then Jon Mason contacted me in rather cloak-and-dagger fashion about this threat to Luca Bruni.'

'Cloak and dagger?' Rowland wondered aloud.

'Oh it was like the Secret Seven.' Shaw laughed. 'Go here and wait there ten minutes, then take a taxi to this place and then another taxi to a pub in darkest Putney. Unlike his predecessors, Bruni has flat-out refused to pay and is not interested in using the private detective. He really is not going to do as he's told. He was about to blow it all up in the media – including telling the world that there had been numerous other incidents – but Mason calmed him down by promising that he would bring the police in quietly through a third person.'

'You,' Jack said.

'That's right,' Shaw said. 'We all want the same thing – for this to go away – but Bruni isn't going to let that happen the way we planned. He's adamant he wants to go public, but I have to think about all the other players who have already coughed up and want to keep their names out of the media.'

'Why is he the one standing up to the blackmail?' Jack asked.

'He says it's a scam.'

'Obviously,' Rowland remarked.

'No, I mean he believes it's a bluff. He won't capitulate to their demands because he is sure that he did not participate in the act depicted in the photos. He wants the police involved so whoever this is can be prosecuted properly.'

Jack spoke. 'Did the others participate in the act?' It seemed the obvious question.

'No one's owning up to that, nor have we asked.'

'Why not?'

'Because it seems irrelevant. The photos are more than enough to convince anyone who sees them, no matter what the truth is.'

'Is this happening to women too?'

Shaw shook his head. 'Not yet. Or, I should say, not that I know of. Really, it's only a matter of time. Women are equally vulnerable. In the world of sport there is a lot of opportunity for playing up, though I would suggest the boys see more action.' He gave a shrug. 'Their big egos demand it. The women players I represent are more cautious.'

'What is the "opportunity" you refer to?' Rowland asked.

Shaw looked embarrassed. 'Er, well, all sorts of people, companies, focus huge attention on these athletes. They're wanted at all the events, celebrity gatherings, to wear the latest fashions, drink the latest cocktail, wear the cologne, drive that car, and so on. And the corporations behind these products stump up a lot of money to entertain them, win their favour, putting them up in hotel suites, giving them alcohol, drugs. High-end prostitutes . . . escorts, if you prefer, can often be part of it.'

'I see,' she said, no judgement in her tone.

Shaw gave an awkward chuckle. 'I could tell you things that would curl your hair, Chief Superintendent.'

'You'd be surprised how unshockable I am, Mr Shaw,' Rowland said in a neutral tone. 'Not much can surprise you when you've been on this side of the desk as long as I have.' She left it at that.

Shaw didn't look as though he'd been admonished so Jack took up the slack of the sudden pause. 'How did Bruni know about the other incidents?' he asked, following his own line of thought.

'Rumours, I guess. Best to ask him.'

'I will.' Jack looked to his chief. 'How is that going to work?'

'We'll get to that. Do you have any other questions for Mr Shaw, here?'

'Not immediately,' Jack replied, getting the distinct feeling his boss wanted Shaw gone. 'Perhaps we could stay in touch.'

'Discreetly, yes, of course,' Shaw said, reaching into a breast pocket and withdrawing a matte black card with gold lettering on it. He turned it over – it was white on that side, and he'd penned a phone number. 'Reach me here. That's a private number I've set up for this matter. Mason has given Bruni a new phone with an untraceable number. I've already given that to you,' he said to Rowland, who nodded. 'He's expecting your call.'

A burner phone; that was a wise move. 'Thanks,' Jack said, pocketing the card.

'Mr Shaw, thank you very much for helping us today,' Rowland said, standing and offering a hand. 'We're grateful.'

'Good luck,' he said, shaking her hand and then Jack's.

'Perhaps hold off on the private detective for now,' Jack suggested.

'Okay, but you'll need to keep me briefed.'

'We'll let you know as much as we can.'

Shaw nodded. 'Right. Are we doing the same car swap for the way out?' he asked.

'Yes, my assistant has organised everything and will see you downstairs,' Rowland said. 'We can't let you go into the car park unfortunately – just protocol – so she will walk with you to the back of a nearby shop. I hope you don't mind her accompanying you arm in arm?'

'Not at all. I'm grateful.' He pulled a hat out of his briefcase and pulled it low over his face. 'Thanks.' He departed.

Rowland turned to Jack. 'Even we've gone Secret Seven,' she said. 'We had him brought here in a car with shaded windows from Waterloo Station. Now he's leaving in a van and being dropped off at some random Tube station. They're all very spooked, but Bruni has thrown a grenade into the situation.'

'What if they're watching Shaw's house?'

'Doubtful. The incident with his own athlete was four years ago, but we're cooperating with their caution to make them feel more secure. No, I believe the criminal eyes will be squarely focused on Luca Bruni and his agent. My instincts tell me Shaw is a fair way into the background for the perpetrators these days, which means he can move around without them bothering too much. He's a good choice for intermediary.'

'So, how do you want me to approach this? I want to meet Bruni face to face.'

'You decide. Work out how you can talk to Bruni easily and without being picked up by the watchers. Let me know what you need.'

'Is it an op?'

'Let's see. Once you've spoken to him, I'll let you call it.'

'Time is our enemy here, right?'

'No. Bruni doesn't seem to care if they're selling his sperm on the dark web. I should know later today if any activity to that end has been picked up.'

'So their ace is breaking it to the media and his girlfriend learning the hard way.'

'Exactly.'

'How much time do we have?'

'They've given him a week to come up with the money.'

'Generous.' Jack raised his brows.

She nodded. 'Yes, my puzzled thought too.'

4

'Hi,' Jack said carefully. After the meeting with Rowland, he'd taken a walk to collect his thoughts, but he couldn't put this call off any longer.

'Oh, hello,' the sarcastic reply came. 'I guess you've had a busy morning.'

'I have, actually,' Jack replied. 'I want to tell you about it.'

'Sicko.'

'Can you meet me, Kate?'

'So you can gloat?'

'About what?'

'You've never slept with one of my friends before.'

'I have never slept with one of your friends.'

'Until now,' Kate snarled.

'Not ever,' he said firmly. It wasn't really any of her business, but her friendship meant more to him than the principle.

This remark was met with a tense silence. 'You didn't—'

'No.'

'Why not?'

Stupid question. 'I'm not a robot, Kate. I choose for myself as to when, where and with whom, and she's not my type. Besides, what a cad I would be to take advantage of someone who was all but passed out on the dance floor.' Jack sensed that this was obviously all making sense to Kate now and the anger had winked out.

'Shit, I'm sorry.'

'For which part? For the accusation? For the presumption? For the unnecessary attack without any evidence? Or for really not knowing me all that well?'

'No, the problem isn't you.' She groaned. 'I know Bella too well.'

Jack remained silent and let her squirm.

'I'm sorry, truly. I feel humiliated.'

'Humiliation is what you deserve, not black pearl earrings. I had to leave, and she was all over me. I made sure she got home safely, that's all.'

'Oh, Jack, forgive me. I'm disgusted by myself now.'

'Good.' His tone was lighter now.

'Will you still meet me?'

'Yes.'

'Where? Your place?'

'Absolutely not. Can't have people jumping to conclusions, can we?' He wished he hadn't said that. 'There's a pub called the White Cross at Richmond. Can you meet me there?'

'In a heartbeat.'

'See you at twelve sharp, or we won't get an outdoor table. I'll be the one near the heater with the sneer on my face.'

'I'll be the one crawling in on my knees.'

When Kate arrived, Jack was already there, near one of the overhead heaters on the deck, sipping a beer, looking thoughtful and very attractive in navy track pants and a sweatshirt in a mid-denim hue. The small collar of a polo shirt was white against his skin, still tanned from his late summer yachting. It wasn't yet out-and-out cold, but when the wind blew she could feel the wintry promise not too far away.

'Hi,' she said tentatively.

He gestured to the bench opposite. 'Can I get you a drink?'

Kate kept it simple. 'Sparkling water will do me after last night.'

He stood up and walked into the pub. Normally she'd watch his slim, lanky legs because he had a distinctive, ever-so-slightly bow-legged walk that only added to the attraction. Instead, still burning within at her stupidity borne out of jealousy, she busied herself positioning her bag between her feet and putting her phone on the table. She couldn't tell yet whether he'd finished with her punishment or planned to make her suffer a little longer. She deserved it. If only she'd taken a moment to think clearly, she would have reassured herself that of course Gabrielle Ferrari wasn't Jack's type. Jack fell for women because of their intelligence and wit; the ones she'd met wore little make-up and had no pretensions, and definitely not Bella's kind of overt sexuality. She had to acknowledge that the description fit Kate; she always had been the opposite of Bella, who gave off heat any time of the day, any season. It was actually part of her armour to behave like that; Bella needed attention to survive. Without it, Kate reckoned she'd wither.

Jack was back with a tall glass, a small wedge of lemon bobbing in it. 'I've ordered some food, too – it will take too long if we wait to be served out here. You can see how quickly this place fills up. They do a good roast on Sundays.'

Kate nodded, still too wary to speak. He stared at her and she found that incredibly unnerving. She knew him. Knew him so well, and still her jealousy had got the better of her. When he switched on that laser gaze, she was never quite ready for its effect on her, which if she was honest could be anything from fear to desire. Right now it was more like hesitancy. 'Jack,' she began, apology in her tone.

'Forget it,' he said. 'Think better of me next time.'

'Will there be a next time?'

'Not a birthday party in a bar, that's for sure.'

'I thought you looked quite cute when you were dancing, though,' she risked.

He chuckled. 'Shut up.'

'So what's going on with work?' she asked, relieved that he'd laughed and they were moving on.

Jack told her what he'd learned that morning. As he spoke, Kate felt every mote of curiosity she possessed switching on; she could sense she might soon be working alongside him on a new operation.

'Interesting,' she said when he stopped speaking.

A waitress came to their table with two plates. 'Here we go, fish and chips with mushy peas?'

'That's us.' Jack smiled at her. 'Thank you, Sarah.'

Sarah obviously liked that he'd taken the time to read her badge and beamed back. 'Would you like some tartare sauce?'

'Please,' he said, and Kate watched him deliver his usual charm without any oiliness. It was the reason he was so popular; she wished she had a small portion of what he possessed, because life would certainly be easier on her. She knew how prickly she could be, but still couldn't stop herself. 'If this is just midday, how are you going to be in the thick of lunchtime?' he asked the smiling waitress.

She laughed. 'Sundays are murder. But the time goes quickly and I get paid double. Back in a sec.'

After she'd left, Jack gestured to the plates. 'I got us fish and chips, because you need all those carbs and oil to soak up last night's alcohol. You'll feel better. Tuck in.'

Kate knew he was right. Before she could take a bite, Sarah was back with two ceramic pots. 'I've given you some mayonnaise too. Nice to dunk the chips into.'

'Perfect, thanks.'

Kate felt Jack's attention return to her and become focused. He picked up a chip, encouraging her to do the same. 'Chief Rowland is expecting me to come up with a plan.'

'And have you?'

'Not yet, but two heads are better than one.'

'Does this plan involve me?'

'Perhaps.' He grinned. 'I'd like you at my side.'

'It's where I like to be, Jack. Tell me.'

He looked around to check no one else was in earshot. 'V lives around here, so we have to be super cautious.'

Kate understood he was using shorthand to avoid any eavesdroppers getting the full gist of their conversation, but he was speaking so quietly that she didn't think it was a problem. V meant 'victim', P meant 'perpetrator'; it wasn't hard to follow.

'So, I have to get in to talk with V. I want to look him in the eye, see him in his world, get a proper understanding of him and his life. I've also got to force his hand to tell his wife what's going on. It's going to be hard enough trying not to catch the attention of the P without having to tiptoe around his other half.'

Kate shook her head. 'It's pointless trying to keep it from her. She'll find out and it will go much worse for him.'

'Agreed. So access is our priority,' Jack continued. 'I want to see him either later today or first thing tomorrow. Just need to work out how to do it without being clocked.'

'Simple.'

'It is?'

Kate shrugged, taking a bite of the fish. 'Arrive like an old friend, lots of hugs. I imagine P is fully expecting activity at V's house, but P is only concerned with making sure there are no police. You also can't look like a stranger suddenly appearing. They'll know some-thing's up.'

'Almost certainly. Doesn't it smell off though? What's my reason for arriving?'

'Moral support. They're allowed to tell family, close friends. Not too many. P will expect V's agent, a parent or two perhaps, a mate. You'll be in that last category. Mmm, this is very good,' she said, cutting again into her beer-battered fish.

As they ate, she could see Jack rolling the idea around in his mind, testing it. She picked up a chip, dunked it deep into the mayo and then held it up like a warning. 'Of course, you'll have to be extra careful,' she said.

'What do you mean?' He joined her in dunking his chips.

'Your face is known to the media.'

'I haven't been on TV since—'

'Mirror, I know, but some journos are very cunning. You just need one wily one to make the connection.'

'I thought we were worried about P. You think the press will be staking out their house?'

'Why not? He's a big deal. The paparazzi are always watching people like him.'

'I wasn't planning to flash my warrant card.'

'I'm just saying.'

'No, you're right. If I'm caught in a photo, there is that risk.'

After a few mouthfuls, she tried again. 'How can I help?'

'This may turn into an op.'

'Okay.'

'Care to join if it does?'

'Of course. Will they let me?'

'I'll square it away with your boss.'

Kate smiled. Other people might struggle to get what they wanted at work, but never Jack. 'So what do I do for now?'

'Wait for me to meet with V.'

She dropped her fork abruptly. 'Jack, I've got a better idea!'

'You do?' he said, putting his knife and fork down too, then dabbing at his mouth with a napkin.

She nodded. 'We go in as a couple.'

His forehead creased in concern.

'No, listen, it's perfect. It means I can help with the wife, especially if there's going to be arguments, drama, et cetera, which I suspect there might be. Do you know much about them?'

He shrugged.

'Right. Well, while I don't keep abreast of the Premier League, I do read magazines at the hairdressers.' She began to tell him all she knew about one of England's most 'darling couples'. Kate made sure to speak barely above a murmur. 'She's been very outspoken about how faithful they are to each other, and how their relationship would be over the second he cheated.'

'She said that?'

Kate nodded. 'Apparently. Do we trust everything we read in gossipy celebrity mags? No. But there seems to be some truth to the idea that they're devoted and faithful to one another – it certainly comes up enough. I would guess she meant it.'

'She's a soap actress, right?'

Kate nodded. 'Mega star power in her lane. I take it you've never watched *Brighton*?'

'No,' he admitted.

'Well, you should go in knowing this stuff. It's a bit like *EastEnders*, but set on the beach.' She leaned in closer to all but whisper beneath her breath. 'Her character was Shelley Dawson, and she owns a hairdressing salon. She was a beloved character.'

'Got it.'

'But I wouldn't be fooled by any of that TV stuff. I think V's wife has her head firmly screwed on.'

'Why do you say that?'

'She's always been a straight shooter in interviews and very natural – you know, none of the pouty lips or looking for where the camera is.'

'Okay. And V, by all accounts, is much the same in terms of being seemingly unaffected by all the attention and adoration.'

'Not to mention his earnings . . . what kind of money are we talking about?'

Jack shrugged. 'Probably twenty-five to thirty a year.'

'Million?' she mouthed and he nodded. Kate's jaw opened in astonishment. 'No wonder he's a target,' she murmured. 'So, we'll go together?' she asked.

'Both of us observing is useful, and I agree, it seems less suspicious to have a couple turn up.' He shrugged. 'All right. I need to make a few calls. Let's see if we can get in this evening.'

'Has someone checked their phone lines to make sure they're clean?'

'His agent has given him a new mobile, but Rowland is having checks run as a matter of course.'

'Good. Go dressed like that.'

Jack looked down at his outfit. 'Really? I just changed after my meeting with Rowland.'

'Definitely. You're casual, sporty. He's a footballer. We have to fit in. I'll go home and change. Where do they live?'

'Not far from me.'

'Which is where? The last I knew you were living in Lauren's rental. You don't tell me anything.'

'I finally bought a place,' he said, sounding like he didn't want to make any more of it.

'Wait, what? *Bought?*'

He nodded. 'Felt like it was time to settle in somewhere again. I haven't had my own front door since I left Greenwich.'

'Wow. Are you going to tell me where?'

'Not too far away. Around Kew.'

She gave a mug of appreciation. 'Congratulations.' She desperately wanted to ask if he was going to invite her to see it, but now was not the time to ask anything of him.

'Do you want something else?' he asked, looking at her unfinished food.

'No, it was delicious, but I got sidetracked by the case and I'm still full of birthday cake.' She wanted to say, 'And I'm thrilled to be working with you again,' but left that alone as well.

He nodded and stood. 'You get going, I'll settle up here and then start making calls. I'll be in touch later.'

She stood. 'Jack?' He turned back. 'Are you ever going to smile at me again?'

He sighed, took a step towards her and surprised her by leaning in, clutching the top of her arm gently and kissing her cheek. 'See you later.'

She left the pub, grinning with relief and helplessly touching her face.

It was several hours later, as afternoon fought against the lowering light, that Jack picked Kate up at her new rental in Islington in a sporty Mercedes.

'What's this?'

'You said we have to look the part. We can't turn up in a Mazda hatchback.' He didn't admit he kind of liked it.

She laughed. 'Cool. And I brought clutter,' she said. 'We can put it in the boot, just in case.'

'No one's going to check.'

'If they do, we're covered.'

He opened the small boot and Kate dropped in a holdall filled with two squash rackets, an old water bottle and some gumboots replete with mud. To finish, she dropped a creased magazine on the passenger floor. He gave her a sideways glance.

'What?' she said. 'Now it looks more authentic as our car. I didn't know you were borrowing this, and yours is always pristine.'

'Hop in,' he said and held the passenger door open for her.

'I can't believe Rowland stumped up for this,' Kate said, looking incredulously around her as Jack settled into the driver's seat.

'She thinks your idea to go in as a couple is sound and agrees that looks are everything right now. Can you believe they had this in the car pool?'

'I can't, no. Have the Brunis been briefed?'

'Yes, they're expecting us and ready to play their welcoming roles.'

'Good. This will be fun.'

'It's not meant to be,' Jack said, easing out into the main traffic.

'Go on. It's a nice change from bodies on the ground.'

'Yes, but I don't think Mr and Mrs Bruni are going to be a bundle of laughs.' Jack was already dreading the conversation in front of them.

He was essentially driving home. The Brunis' penthouse flat sprawled over two storeys of an elegant luxury development on the Richmond side of the Thames. It overlooked the water at a wide and pretty stretch and was only minutes away from Jack's newly acquired townhouse. When he climbed up to the small roof garden he'd set up at his place, he too could see the river straight across to the Chiswick side. His house was closer to the old Mortlake Brewery site, where they used to make Watney's beers, a fact he had enjoyed hearing from the real estate agent when he'd been shown around. Even though his townhouse was relatively new, he was able to look past its young life in favour of its old-style under-stated elegance and its proximity to Kew Gardens.

The Bruni penthouse was far more 'blingy' than his own place, as he'd expected, and it was gated, which he'd also anticipated. So the paparazzi – if they were around – would have to get up onto the towpath that flanked the river and try to get a long shot from between the trees. It was possible.

Jack gave Kate his phone with the number already entered as 'V'. 'That's the clean line – you can speak freely. Let them know we're imminent, so they can get ready to perform.'

She dialled. 'Mr Bruni? This is DCI Kate Carter. I'm working with Detective Superintendent Jack Hawksworth.' She paused. 'Yes, that's right.' Waited again. 'About . . .?' She looked at Jack, who held up his hand with splayed fingers. 'Five minutes,' she confirmed. Again she paused. 'Okay, if you could come out and greet us as old friends down below, that should convince anyone who may be watching. Encourage your wife to do the same. Yes. Yes, okay thanks. See you shortly.'

'How is he?'

'Sounds aggressive.'

Jack shook his head. 'I think just eager to be proactive and not allow this to happen to him without some sort of fight. That's the impression I got earlier.'

He made a series of turns until they reached wide wrought-iron gates. 'Here we are.' He undid his seatbelt, but Kate was faster.

'Let me,' she said, ducking out of the car. Jack presumed she'd been told which number button to press because he heard her say, 'Hi, darlings. We're here!' in a sunny but concerned voice.

He smiled, glad to have Kate back at his side and to have shown his forgiveness. He hadn't enjoyed punishing her, short as it was, but her behaviour had not improved, no matter how many times he told her that they could never be an item. She seemed to understand each time, but her heart just seemed to override her head. It was the only chink in her armour and he hated being that weakness.

She was back in the car, buckling up again. 'All good. Let's do this.'

The gate swung open. With no sign of any lurking photographers, they purred through it, making sure it closed behind them. They found a visitor's spot and, as they got out of the car, they heard a whistle and both looked up.

'Hey, losers!' a young man called from the penthouse balcony.

'Here we go,' Kate murmured as Jack raised his arm and waved.

'Hello, brat!' Jack replied.

A blonde woman joined Luca, looking over the edge. 'Hey, you two,' she said, waving. 'Got anything to bring up?'

'Just this,' Kate said, pulling a bottle of wine from her handbag.

Luca grinned. 'I'll come down.'

Jack locked the car and put his arm around Kate's shoulders.

'Oh, this is cosy,' she said.

'We stay in character,' Jack said.

The door sighed open and Luca Bruni emerged, immediately pulling Jack into a bear hug. The men held their embrace slightly longer than usual to suggest it was an emotional moment, before Luca broke away to hug Kate in much the same manner. She kissed his cheek softly as though commiserating.

Inside, as soon as the door closed, awkwardness prevailed. 'That was excellent, Mr Bruni. It would have fooled anyone watching.'

'Good. Listen, call me Luca.'

Jack introduced them properly. 'But we're Jack and Kate to you, okay?'

Luca nodded. 'Thanks for coming. It's two floors up.'

'Lead the way,' Jack said.

'Luca,' Kate said, 'your wife did a good job just now. Does she know why we're here?'

He nodded again, unhappily this time. 'I told her this morning. It's all still very raw; you'll have to forgive her.'

'Perfectly understandable,' Kate said.

Luca shifted uncomfortably in the lift and eyed them both. 'I didn't do it.'

'We're not here to judge,' Jack counselled.

'That may be, but I need to know you trust me. I'm not lying about this.'

'Our role is to help you with the threatening—' Kate began, but Jack spoke softly.

'I believe you,' he said, hoping his sincerity was shining through the firm but gentle tone. He ignored Kate's surprised grimace. 'But Kate's right, it's irrelevant what we think, what anyone thinks. This is blackmail.'

'Yeah, but it's not irrelevant to me that you believe me, and it's not irrelevant to me whether my wife trusts me. The photograph is clear evidence that I was in that room, half naked with that woman. That alone is enough to have her saying we're over. But I didn't cheat. I know I didn't.'

The lift stopped. 'We're going to take this slow and steady, Luca, and we're going to do our utmost to avoid fallout or any further talk of separation.'

'Good luck,' Luca said sadly, as though he'd already resigned himself to a break-up. He gestured for Kate to go through first, which Jack liked; old-fashioned manners were not always present in men Luca's age and especially with his lifestyle.

5

They found Luca's wife, Ally, staring out of the large windows in the vast living area that overlooked the river. From her vantage point, Jack reckoned he would be able to pick out his house.

'Ally?' Luca prompted.

She turned. Far prettier than the photos Jack had seen during his swift research, Ally was a small, slim woman, heavily pregnant and wearing a baggy velvet tracksuit. Her blonde hair was bright and her eyes were light brown, almost like honey.

'This is Detective Superintendent Hawksworth and his colleague, DCI Carter.'

Jack stepped forward and offered his hand. 'Jack's fine, Ally.'

She gave him a wan smile.

Kate also shook her hand. 'And I'm Kate. Thank you for inviting us in and playing along with the charade.'

'I'm not sure I had any choice,' Ally said, shooting a glare towards her husband.

'Shall we sit?' Jack kept his tone light. He needed her to cooperate, at least for the time being.

'Can I get you folks anything? Tea? Coffee? Wine? Something harder?' Luca offered.

'Tea's good,' Kate said. 'Here, let me help.'

Jack slid her a small smile of thanks. They were a good team. As Luca and Kate clattered quietly in the open kitchen, Jack returned his attention to Luca's wife, who looked entirely tuned out.

'Ally, I've mentioned to your husband that we're not here to judge, simply to help. We want to identify the blackmailer as eagerly as he does.'

'There's only one judge here and that's me,' she said, sounding sour. 'We made a pact.'

Jack gave a small nod. 'I'm aware of it. If it helps, I am prepared to believe your husband.'

'You've seen the photo, right?'

'I have.'

'On what planet, detective, do you think that is a man being faithful to his wife?'

Jack gave a shrug. 'Luca claims he was drugged.'

'The photo shows him naked, and with a woman!' she spat as if that said everything. 'Apparently he went to his room around nine thirty.'

'Hardly a party animal.'

She glowered. 'That's my point. It was probably to meet her.'

'Who else was there who might be able to confirm this?'

'Luca's agent was there. Jonathan Mason. He told Luca that he saw the woman walking down the hallway towards his room.'

'And he didn't say anything?'

'Why would he? You blokes stick together, don't you?'

Jack looked back at her with a neutral expression. 'Why do you think Luca would tell you that, if he wasn't being honest? How did Mason know which room was Luca's?'

'He was staying in the one at the end of the hallway.' She made a sound of disgust. 'To think he took me there not long afterwards for a special weekend. Makes me sick.'

'I can completely appreciate how upset you are, Ally, but Luca's being awfully candid, given he risks hurting the person he loves most in the world. It's why I believe we should give him our trust. He is being courageous by defying his blackmailers.'

'He's never lacked bravery. Watch him tackle. Watch him run down the pitch with all the defenders prepared to win themselves a red card to take him out. He doesn't care. He thrives on danger.'

'This is a different sort of danger though, isn't it? This situation is threatening the woman he loves, the children he's soon to welcome, the life he's built . . .' Jack shrugged.

'What are you saying?'

'I'm saying that life would be a whole lot easier for him if he'd said nothing and simply organised payment.'

She blinked. 'You mean because we're so rich we can buy our way out of anything?' Her curiously honey-coloured eyes blazed their fury, only adding to her elfin beauty.

'Yes,' he agreed, deliberately blunt. 'Let's face it, Luca could take the easy path out of this mess. Any man about to marry one of the country's most eligible women, about to have twins with her, could be forgiven for taking such a way out.'

'That's just it though, Detective Hawksworth, I don't think I can.'

'Forgive him?'

Ally nodded, high spots of colour appearing on her cheeks. 'And if you so much as murmur the word "hormones", you can leave.'

Jack schooled his features to neutral. He could hear Kate chuckling with Luca in the kitchen and decided to try again while she had him distracted. 'He didn't take the easy path. He's taking the scary one, the destructive one, the humiliating one, and so I believe it's the honest one.' His tone softened. 'Luca says he was drugged – in other words, set up. I hope you might be able to at least appreciate that possibility. Give him a chance to work with us so we can hunt down those who want to ruin your life, and that of others.'

'Others? What do you mean?'

'Here we are,' Luca said, arriving back with Kate. 'I know you mentioned tea, but I've been trialling some sparkling fruit punches since Ally got pregnant, because everything else seemed to make her feel sick. This one is a fresh lemon, lime and mint.'

To prove his point, Kate pushed a sprig of fresh mint into each glass while Luca tumbled ice cubes and a pale greenish liquid on top of each sprig, releasing the oils of the herb. A bracing aromatic scent seemed to brighten the mood momentarily.

Luca lifted his glass and instead of saying cheers, said, 'To you guys. I need you to catch these bastards.'

On the last word, Jack heard Luca's Aussie accent push through. 'I'll drink to that,' he said and sipped. 'This is delicious, thank you.'

Ally turned to her husband. 'Luca, the detective is saying others have been targeted.'

Her husband began to pace, his lean but muscular frame prowling like a cat. 'Yes. Plenty before us, babe. Everyone thought they were just rumours, but Jon Mason confirmed that it's happened quite a lot. Not just footballers, but lots of sports stars. We're not the first. But I'm going to make sure we're the last.'

'Right,' Jack said, feeling that was a very good mood and leaping-off point; he also realised he'd already finished half his fizzy fruit drink. 'Luca, we'd like to hear from you exactly how that day at Lark's Hill went. Everything you remember, no matter how small the detail.' Before Luca began, Jack looked at his wife. 'Ally, are you okay to listen to this?'

'I want to. Luca's only given me the short version.'

Jack watched the couple glance at each other and felt a small surge of relief that at least she could look at Luca now. The hot rage that had been in her eyes on their arrival was gone.

'Luca, we need everything,' Kate counselled. 'As we were just discussing.'

The young footballer nodded, paused a few beats as though gathering his thoughts and began.

It was Jack's turn to pace. 'Just for clarity, Luca, you let this woman in?'

'Yes,' he said firmly.

Jack was impressed with his candour.

'Why?' Ally asked before either Jack or Kate could.

'Ally, I'm answering the question. These guys need facts. I did let her in, but I didn't know who she was.'

'Because the phone call beforehand had primed you,' Kate said.

'Yes. The front desk rang and told me there was a gift being sent up.' Luca shrugged. 'Look, we get sent gifts and promotional stuff all the time. You know that,' he appealed to Ally.

She nodded unhappily.

'I knew I was considered a special guest at the launch because I was the only player from our club seriously interested in the car.'

'Only fifty rooms, you said?' Kate clarified.

'Forty-eight,' Luca replied. 'They hadn't taken any reservations that night from the public; it was only guests for the Bentley event. I was in the room called Blackbird, right at the end of the hallway of the second floor.'

Jack knew Kate had deliberately tried to trip up Luca with the number of rooms. She was good – very slick at her tricks as she tested his tale. But the young man seemed sure of his story.

Jack picked up the questioning, aiming for his own subtle trip. 'Okay, so you thought the knock at the door—'

'No,' Luca said, frowning, unaware that he was being tested. 'There was a doorbell, which even I thought was odd, but they seem to do things differently there. It's a soft *ding-dong* sort of chime. She rang it once. I answered, expecting some sort of package, but she was holding a tray with champagne and two glasses.' He frowned again. 'Not the flute kind, but those old-fashioned ones.' He used his hands to form a cup shape.

'Bowls,' Kate offered.

'Yeah, like the ones they make a pyramid with, pouring champagne down like a waterfall.'

'Tell us again exactly what she said,' Jack urged.

Luca shook his head as though it was trivial. 'I asked, "Is this the gift?" and she smiled and said, "It certainly is." She went on to explain that this was a nineteen-something-or-other bottle of Grand Cru . . . I guess it was meant to impress me.' He shrugged. 'You know how you think you're listening when someone's been introduced and then you can't remember their name in the next minute?'

Jack nodded.

'It was like that. I was a bit surprised, not really paying enough attention; hearing her words but not listening.'

'Why?' Kate asked. 'Champagne seems like a reasonable gift for a guest at an event like that.'

'I suppose,' he said, 'but not for a Premier League player in the middle of the season. I don't drink alcohol at all in season, and not that much out of it. Bentley would know that – they would have been briefed not to have champagne for the players even during the proceedings.'

'He's telling the truth,' Ally said, nodding. 'He doesn't drink much alcohol and the club wouldn't want that anyway.'

Jack saw her husband thank her with a soft smile and put his hand on her knee. Ally looked down at it but didn't remove it. Progress.

'Go on, Luca,' Kate said. 'What do you recall happening next?'

'Er, well, on the tray alongside the glasses was a set of keys. "We'd like you to have a drive in the countryside tomorrow and experience the ride for yourself," the woman said. I mean, they already knew I was interested, so this was just straight-out selling disguised as a gift.'

'She said this as though she represented the car firm?' Kate clarified.

'Yes. But the champagne suggested she didn't, or maybe they were just doing it because it was visually appealing to have expensive French champagne next to a set of car keys.'

'What then?'

Luca sipped his drink. 'I thanked her. She offered to pour the champagne and—'

'Was it already open?' Jack interrupted, thinking it would be odd if it had been.

'No,' Luca confirmed and before they asked, he answered their next question. 'I said I'd probably take it home and share it with Ally, but only because I really didn't want it opened.'

'So why do you think she didn't just leave the champagne and go? Wouldn't that have been normal?'

'Of course. But before either of us could move, the phone rang – it was you, Ally – so I took the call.' Luca looked at Jack and Kate as though asking what might be wrong with that.

'And what time was that?' Kate asked.

'Must have been close to ten, I reckon,' he replied. 'I'm not certain.'

Ally sighed. 'It was just after ten, actually. I had been napping, waiting for Luca to call, and when I woke up and saw how late it was, I decided to call him. We talked for maybe fifteen minutes, because it was nearing twenty past when we said goodnight.' She looked at Jack as though she knew he'd ask for details and obliged. 'He said he wished I was with him, he told me about the huge room, the lovely view, and that he was going to bring me back to that same room so we could share it. He even told me about the champagne and car keys. What he didn't say is that this woman was standing there, that she'd never left the room.'

Luca looked down. 'I honestly didn't know she was still there.'

It was the first time Jack had heard any note of desperation in Luca's tone. The young man looked back at Jack and Kate. 'That room has this huge balcony and when I excused myself to take the call, I stepped outside the glass doors to chat. I just assumed she'd leave.'

'Why did you go outside? For privacy?' Jack queried.

'No, er . . .' He ran a hand through his hair. 'She was sort of lingering, and I thought if I moved to the balcony, she'd get the message. But when I finished the call and walked back in, she'd not only cracked open the bottle, champagne fizzing in both glasses, but she was undressed down to her underwear.'

Ally made a hissing sound.

Kate moved in swiftly. 'So, as you said, you expressed your shock and asked her to leave. How exactly did you say that?'

'When I first walked back in, I laughed, I think. Yeah, I did. I was embarrassed – for me, for her, for the people throwing the party. I said, "You've got the wrong idea, darlin'. I don't want the champagne or whatever else you're offering."'

'And her reply? Her exact words,' Kate pressed.

'"No man should drink champagne alone." That was her first response. I said, "Put your clothes back on now." And . . . er, I asked who'd sent her, because I felt a bit cranky now and planned to have a word with her boss. She said it was all part of the weekend, though.'

'Did she say she'd been hired specifically to deliver the champagne to your room?'

He shook his head. 'No, I don't recall her saying anything like that. It was more like she presumed I knew it would be happening.'

'How long did it take before she believed you were serious about her leaving?' Jack asked.

'When I picked up her uniform and threw it towards her, I reckon. I said again that I wanted her gone.'

'Did she look offended? Shocked?' Jack asked.

'Surprised, definitely. She immediately stepped back and put her clothes on in silence.'

'Did you watch her dress?' Ally demanded.

'No! I turned away to show my disgust and turned on the telly.'

'But she still didn't leave, did she?' Ally asked.

Luca gave a sheepish look, appealing for understanding from all of them. 'Look, I felt a bit sorry for her by then. She asked if we could at least pretend to drink the champagne.'

'Tell us again why and use her exact words if you can,' Kate urged.

'I explained why I didn't really want to drink – to stay in shape for the season, and that my wife is pregnant and it wouldn't look good if I was out getting drunk. She explained that she might not get paid if she failed to deliver the champagne properly, and she didn't want to leave the room so quickly with it so obviously undrunk.'

'It wasn't so quickly though, was it? I mean she'd been in the room since before Ally's call?'

He nodded. 'Yes, that's true.'

'So, let's say two minutes and then the call lasted about fifteen, so it had been at least seventeen minutes.'

Luca shrugged. 'I don't know how long they'd have expected her to be with me. Perhaps all night.'

No one had any response to that, other than Ally, who gave her husband another sour look.

'I wasn't paying much attention, but she seemed to feel that the length of time in my room wasn't sufficient.'

Jack sensed Luca was being honest. Talking so frankly about this embarrassing experience in front of his wife, who could now tear apart his life, was about as vulnerable as it got and yet he wasn't flinching. 'What was her demeanour?' Kate asked. At Luca's puzzled expression, she added, 'She was obviously flirtatious and confident to begin with. What about at this point?'

'Oh, I see.' Luca shrugged. 'By then she'd become herself. I mean, just a normal, nice girl. She probably hated having to earn her money that way. That was my impression. She'd dropped the flirty manner, if that's what you mean.'

Kate nodded. 'You said she was attractive?'

Luca nodded, carefully avoiding Ally's gaze. 'She was very pretty and although she had dark hair, she was not unlike Ally in her build.'

'You think she was chosen specifically for that reason?'

'I don't know,' Luca admitted. 'Maybe.'

'Do you think she was suggesting that she was paid by the hour?' Kate asked.

'I don't know that either,' Luca said, sounding humiliated. 'I've never used escort services before.'

Jack took over. 'All right, so what did you say to her request?'

'I said she could have a drink, but that I wouldn't. She said she didn't want it either but if I would let her pretend, they would believe she'd done her job.'

'And you agreed?' Ally erupted, her tone full of disgust.

Jack looked on uncomfortably.

'I felt sorry for her. Anyway, she got me a bottle of sparkling water, and I remember drinking some of that. The rest is a blur, really,' Luca explained.

'Do you still feel sorry for her?' Ally demanded.

'No. I hate her. I want to find her and expose her.'

'She's not the person to hunt, Luca,' Kate counselled. 'She was just the—'

'I don't care. She's the reason I'm dealing with this crap now, when I should be focused on next week's game. If this woman didn't win me over, make me feel sorry for her, none of this would have happened. I want her found. I'll hire a private detective if you guys don't think she's important.'

'Did she ever give you a name?' Jack asked quickly. He wanted to calm Luca, whose ire was up for the first time, giving them their first glimpse of just how fiery the striker could be. Jack still felt the young man was deeply distressed about the situation, and he knew he'd have to trust his instincts that this show of anger was genuine.

'What?' Luca blinked, before refocusing. 'Er, I'm not sure she did.'

Kate had already picked up on Jack's tack. 'Was she wearing a badge of any sort?'

'I can't remember,' Luca admitted.

'Could you describe her accurately?' Kate asked.

'No. I mean, she could have been wearing a wig for all I know. I remember she was small, had dark eyes and was pretty. But I could recognise her easily.'

'Why?'

'She has an accent. European, I think.'

Jack and Kate gave each other a sly glance.

'Anything else?' Jack pressed.

'Yes. She has a tattoo.'

That caught their attention.

6

They'd left the Brunis' flat around six, as Luca wanted to get to weight training. Despite Ally's protests, Jack had suggested that this was a good move; keep life as normal as possible.

Jack and Kate joined the traffic around Kew Gardens, first moving in the slipstream of an arterial road before Jack turned off to zigzag through some residential streets. He pulled into a car space and they waited for a few minutes. Kate watched Jack use the mirrors to study the traffic flowing around them.

'No one following?' she asked.

He shook his head. 'No, we're good.'

'Or perhaps just not interesting enough for any of the black-mailers.'

'There can't be that many in on this job, so chasing us would spread them too thin.'

'Agreed. What now?'

'Do you want me to drop you home?'

It was the last thing she wanted but she needed to tread with care. 'Not particularly,' she answered breezily but then became more serious. 'Actually, I want to talk this all through, work out our next step – what you need me to do. Shall we head to a café?'

Jack looked at his watch. 'It's quite late.'

'You mean for your bedtime?' she said, her tone light, risking some levity.

She won it. He laughed.

'It's after six. Pub?'

'I'm hungry.'

'Pub meal, then?' she offered tentatively.

He shook his head. 'I'll take you to my place.'

She paused before answering and neither could ignore that hesitation. 'Er, are you sure? I didn't mean—'

'No, I know you didn't. It's my idea. I've got a couple of salmon fillets in the fridge I don't want to waste. Are you up for fish and salad?'

'Are you kidding?' she said, as if he was mad to even ask. 'Stop by the off-licence – let me grab some wine.'

'I've got wine.'

'No, I insist.'

Within half an hour they were back in the Brunis' neighbourhood once more, but this time in Jack's small and elegant complex of houses.

'Wow,' she said, noticing the towpath and the river opposite as he reversed the car into an empty garage. 'This is really lovely.'

'Thank you. We can go in through the garage, but you might like to see it from the outside.'

'Please.' She stepped out of the car, clutching the wine and chocolate she'd bought. 'Lead the way.'

He walked her around to an entrance of the Burlington Riverside complex; his was the corner house. She felt captivated by a long, wide pond that ran the length of the avenue of homes. The oblong pond was still; barely a breeze today. Outlining the pond like soldiers on parade were deciduous trees, their autumnal uniforms lying around them in a mass of earthy colours as they undressed and stretched their bare branches. Small bushes clustered around them.

'Jack, it's brilliant.'

He sighed. 'I do like it here.'

'It's very you.'

'Really? I thought it was the antithesis of me.'

'No.' Kate laughed. 'Look at this elegant architecture,' she said, sweeping a hand and her gaze in a full three-hundred-and-sixty turn. 'It may not have historic weight, but it feels old and magnificently planned, like a fabulous old Georgian terrace in Bath or Brighton.'

'Now you're stretching it,' Jack remarked.

She shook her head. 'I'll bet these trees look amazing at any time of the year.'

'Yes, in winter, they apparently look very stark and rather lovely, all frosted on bare branches.'

'Very architectural, you see,' she said, ramming home her point.

'Come on,' he said, unzipping the pocket of his track pants for his house keys. He led her to the house, which wrapped around to the view of the river courtesy of bay windows and three storeys. 'Plenty of stairs,' he warned.

Inside, it was a study in neutrals but Jack had kept it warm with dove greys and rich creams punctuated by light Scandinavian pine and some exquisite antique furniture, also in a light, honey-coloured timber.

'Guest room and bathroom, visitor powder room and a sort of sitting room I don't really know what to do with. I guess if I had drinks with the neighbours that spilled onto the street, we'd start here.'

'Is that likely?'

He laughed. 'No. I'm a hermit, you know that.' He led her up to the middle level. 'This is where I spend most of my time when I'm home,' he admitted, shrugging at the well-kitted kitchen. It was twice as big as hers, but probably saw twice as much action under Jack's domesticity. A small dining space led into a compact, comfy living area that was lined with bookshelves and home to an exquisite old French rug and a pair of comfy, down-filled sofas. The television was small and unobtrusive, but she noted it was the latest tech.

Windows let in maximum light throughout. It was truly cosy, but she imagined it was sun-drenched by day.

'And upstairs is my space – bedroom, bathroom, another sort of den. But it also leads out onto a small rooftop garden.'

Her mouth fell open slightly. 'You're joking.'

He shook his head. 'I'll show you.'

Upstairs, she was horribly aware of being in his private area and was nervous when he waved a hand at his bedroom, which echoed the neutral palette with a petrol-blue linen quilt cover.

'Did you go to boarding school, Jack?'

'A few years, yes. Why?'

'Explains the made bed. If I walked you through my place I'd have to kill you afterwards for what you'd seen. You'd never think of me the same.'

'I don't believe that, not going by how immaculately you put yourself together.'

'Hmm, appearances can be deceiving. You've seen my desk when I'm working, right?'

'That's true,' he said. She had no doubt he was recalling the messy landscape of their operations room in past investigations. 'I wonder why that is?'

She tapped her temple. 'I tell myself that it's okay because I'm tidy up here,' she said, looking away from the bedroom to get past the blush it was surely causing at her cheeks. This was getting too personal. 'Your place is all very lovely, and quite spacious despite how it appears from outside.'

He nodded. 'Probably too much room for just me. And here's the rooftop garden,' he said, leading her through double doors from his study onto a square patio, made pretty by pot plants.

'You are not growing vegetables!'

He grinned sheepishly. 'Trying a few under glass through the cold months. Just some cherry tomatoes and fresh basil, some snow peas climbing around there. Other herbs.'

'Brilliant,' she said, feeling inadequate. 'And this!' She swept her hand across the vista of the River Thames. 'Blimey, I'd be out here in any season.'

Jack smiled. 'Right, I'm going to start prepping. Could you collect a few of those tomatoes before you come in? Then you can pour us a wine and we can start hatching a plan.'

Kate enjoyed watching Jack move confidently around his kitchen; he'd oiled the salmon and seasoned it, letting it sit in that mix while he chopped salad vegetables to add to the jewel-like cherry tomatoes. They were like tiny explosions of sugar. 'I ate at least that many before I came in,' she admitted, sipping the deliciously dry pinot gris she'd bought. 'Do you like it?' she asked, holding up her glass. 'It's French.'

'Very fruity and floral at once; it's magnificent. I know that label from around Alsace; hardly cheap.'

'As if I'd insult your cooking with cheap wine. Besides, we won't get a headache. All right. Walk me through your thoughts on the Brunis.'

Jack tumbled thin crescents of red onion on top of the salad, put a cast-iron fry pan on his induction hob to heat and began to download his thoughts, starting with Ally.

'I agree she's no airhead,' Kate said.

'No, she's much smarter than she seems,' he cautioned.

Her eyes widened. 'Do you think she's involved?'

'I'm not saying that, but I won't count out anyone. I don't see what she'd get out of it, though, if she is involved.'

Kate thought about it. 'Yes, it's a pretty elaborate method of achieving a separation. She'd get half of everything anyway. And then there are the babies.'

'I wonder if they're not his,' Jack suddenly said, turning back from the salmon he'd just placed in the hot pan. The fillets were hissing and sizzling as their skin shrivelled slightly in shock.

'No, they're his all right,' Kate confirmed. At Jack's quizzical look, she explained. 'It was one of my first thoughts – whether this was all connected to an affair. So I wandered up to that point while we were making the punch. These are IVF twins – apparently Ally miscarried early in three previous pregnancies and it was destroying them. Surprisingly, and happily for them, they got pregnant in their first round.'

'Do we agree then that this adds some clout to Luca's story?' Jack asked. 'He clearly wants these children, if they went through that process, which is really tough on couples,' he said. 'I learned that last year,' he added.

'Yeah, and while it's full of horrendous stress for the woman – I have a friend who has gone through it too – I think the man often feels helpless.' She shrugged. 'Once he's given his sperm, which is confronting for a lot of men, I gather, then he has no further part to play but has to participate in the angst and drama. My friend said she went a little mad during this time and her husband didn't know how to help her.'

'Exactly so.'

Kate thought about her interactions with Luca. 'Yes, I do believe him. His body language matched everything he was saying about Ally, wanting to be a father – all of it.'

'I do too.'

They both knew this was simple instinct at play, backed up by their years of experience, and Kate was secure in her trust of Luca. She sighed. 'So, dark net?'

'I haven't heard anything yet, but Rowland may have news on that for me.'

'When will you know?'

'Tomorrow, I hope. I'll go in,' he said, deftly serving the salmon onto plates. 'Ready?'

'Suddenly famished.'

'Because you barely touched your fish and chips.'

'I was completely stressed, that's why,' she said.

'Deservedly,' he remarked in an arch tone.

'I am really sorry about that.'

'We won't talk about it again. Happy to eat outside? I've installed a heater.'

She nodded.

'Can you grab the wine and salad? I'll bring the plates and glasses.'

Jack arrived behind her with a tray and set down the plates, glasses and a small jar of dressing.

'Of course it's homemade,' Kate said to herself, but loud enough to make him grin.

'Tuck in.'

They clinked glasses again and began eating. Kate gave a groan of pleasure. 'Perfect,' she said. 'Thank you. And it's beautiful out here, Jack. I think I'm a bit jealous.'

'You know you're grown up enough to buy your own place now, Kate?'

She rolled her eyes. 'Shut up and eat. I will soon. Would it be stalking for me to look around here?'

'Definitely creepy,' he said, but she knew he was joking from his amused tone.

'Listen, is this becoming an op?'

He chewed and swallowed. 'That's what I have to recommend to Rowland tomorrow. But it's a lot of manpower for one victim being blackmailed.'

Kate shook her head. 'But it's not one victim, is it? It's really about all those athletes who already have coughed up. We'll probably never know how many, right?'

'I think that agency network is being deliberately tight-lipped. They don't want this to be common knowledge.'

'Well, if we don't get the blackmailer, it's just going to continue.'

He nodded.

'But something's off, isn't it?'

'It is. And it's not my fish.' He didn't laugh.

Kate took a sip of her wine and looked out towards the river. 'I've been thinking about the deadline for payment. A week! What blackmailer would be that considerate?'

'No one who was serious.'

'We have to find out what the deadline was in some of the previous incidents. I can imagine it's about forty-eight hours at best for payment before they follow through on their threats.'

'Maybe. Certainly not a week.'

'We need to be sure we're hunting the same perpetrators – if this is different, it could be a copycat.'

'You think?' Jack asked, diligently chewing and not watching her. She knew he didn't disagree, but wanted her to think it through. Typical Jack. He liked his team to reach worthy conclusions before he told them his.

She took another bite and paused to chew. 'Well, there's the difference in timeline for starters. And it was quite a public place for the event to happen – risky. I think if we learned more about the other incidents, we might find out that they took place in more private surrounds; perhaps those other guys were picked off at parties but taken somewhere – a hotel, a private home, their place.' Kate shrugged. 'Very daring to enter the victim's room in such a shrewd manner – and relying so much on chance.'

'I agree. The blackmailer had to know a lot beforehand to pull it off.'

'So, an insider,' she pressed, putting down her knife and fork.

'That would be my contention and why I'll be recommending to Rowland that this does become an op. We need a team working on it around the clock. We've got less than a week before Luca's privacy is potentially fully blown.'

'Potentially?'

Jack finished eating, put his utensils together on the plate and reached for his wine. 'Well, if Luca's blackmailer is not the same one as the others, then who knows if this opportunist actually plans to carry out any threat?'

'You think they'd drop it after all that effort?' Kate shook her head. 'Doubtful.'

'The op is going to be necessary just to establish if we're dealing with the same party or we're chasing two different ones.'

'Well, I'm all in, Jack. If you can get me seconded, I'll get busy assembling who you need as soon as you tell me.'

He grinned. 'You already know who I need. I'll be formally seconding you tomorrow as soon as Carol Rowland signs off.'

'Thrilling,' she said, feeling delighted, and raised her glass to him.

After chocolate and an impressive macchiato handmade by her host, she kissed him goodbye, careful to keep it casual with a swift lips-to-cheek. She inhaled his cologne and closed her eyes briefly, trying to commit it to memory, although she'd spotted the bottle earlier in his bedroom.

Later that night she googled it: Y by Yves Saint Laurent, designed for men who were children of the eighties, as he was.

She couldn't help herself, digging deeper into the description – apparently it had notes of bergamot, ginger, mint, lemon, sage and even violet. But deeper still lurked ambergris, incense, cedar and, her favourite on a man, vetiver.

It was an intoxicating mix on an intoxicating man, and she wished with all of her heart she could rid herself of the hangover he caused whenever she spent time with him.

Jack had enjoyed his dinner with Kate, feeling like they might have turned a corner on her misguided fascination with him . . . but then he always wished for that. Deep down, he knew she was everything he might look for in a woman, but he'd made a pact with himself that he'd never encourage a relationship with anyone from within the police force.

It happened all the time, of course, but he'd seen the repercussions over and again. Kate and his old friend Geoff were a perfect example of how wrong it could go for two detectives, both stretched thin, both facing stressful situations in their daily grind of investigating anything from murder to child pornography. It wasn't a nine-to-five job that one could leave at the desk; Jack couldn't set aside all that he'd experienced, which at times had pushed him to the edge of his tolerance. It was why many in the police force lost themselves at the pub, or in lone pursuits like fishing. But that escape could also be offered through family and solid partners who brought chatter and experiences that had nothing to do with crime.

Jack could admit readily that it wasn't easy for a partner from outside the force to understand some of the stresses he and his colleagues dealt with, but he knew it could be horribly destructive if both people in the relationship were trying to balance it with their duties for the service.

Jack was sitting opposite Carol Rowland, whom he knew was single. Once again, he was feeling assaulted by the amount of teak veneer in her office; it never failed to astonish him. She had indicated he should sit while she finished up a phone conversation.

She put the phone down and buzzed through to her assistant. 'Hold all calls, please, Shirley. Sorry about that, Jack. I had to take the call.'

'No problem. Everything okay?'

She made a sour face. 'So much red tape! Now, to our footballer. You've spoken with him?'

Jack outlined the meet, finishing with his and Kate's thought that it was likely an inside job.

Rowland gave a frown. 'Do you think the agent could be in on it?'

Jack took a moment to answer this, searching his thoughts. 'Potentially, yes. Any agent would be well placed to be the inside man, so to speak. However, that agent would have to be in an enormous hole to be shitting in his own nest, if you'll pardon my phrasing.'

She waved it away. 'I think it bears exploring.'

He moved on. 'We need to talk to the football manager at the Huxley Arrows, the coach, and maybe players from other clubs.'

'How? We're meant to be keeping this under the radar.'

'My impression is that Luca Bruni doesn't care about that – he's willing to take the risk to take these guys down. If we're cautious and we brief the Arrows to be vigilant and tight-lipped, I'd like to speak with some of the execs, see if we can tease out any previous attempts, and then I'd like to cast the net a bit further via the agency network on their stars who have paid up.'

'If they'll talk to you.'

'Quite. Anyway, I don't plan on revealing anything beyond our small team and an even smaller circle at the Arrows.'

'So you're recommending an operation.'

'I am, ma'am.'

'Right.' She sighed, but sounded resigned and ready to act. 'You do know who owns the Huxley Arrows, Jack?'

He nodded.

'Well, Roger Tallis has far-reaching connections, including within the Metropolitan Police − the commissioner is a personal friend.'

Jack gave a sigh as Rowlands continued.

'He's very well connected through various parliamentarians and is, I might add, on first-name terms with the prime minister.'

'Okay.' Jack's tone made it clear that he understood she was giving him a warning.

But Rowland decided to press her point. The eyes he had once compared to concrete now gave him a hard, impenetrable stare. 'So we tread carefully, because the reverberations of any investigation rattle far and wide . . . and right back to this office. I do not relish any heat being put on me via the Home Secretary, who, incidentally, Tallis went to college with.'

'I thought he was Australian.'

'He is. A Rhodes scholar as well, so he was nice and cosy in Oxford with the home sec.'

'I understand,' Jack said. 'So, I can get busy setting up?'

'Keep it tight in terms of people, but whatever you need, brief it through Shirley and it will be done. Anything I need to know about immediately?'

'I need to second DCI Kate Carter from Anti-Corruption. I trust no one else more to captain a team.'

'She's been on all your major ops hasn't she?'

Jack nodded. 'She's as good as it gets, ma'am.'

'Anything else?'

'I'd like Joan Field. She keeps us all on the straight and narrow.'

'I thought she was retired.'

'No. Soon, sadly, I'm sure.'

'Okay, no problem. Is that it?'

'I need your permission to contact freely across our divisions. I may need to pull in some favours.'

She hesitated but he didn't lower his gaze, hoping he was giving a steely enough one of his own to make a dent in the concrete. She finally nodded. 'With care.'

'Always,' he said.

'Find this sod, Jack.'

He gave her a tight smile as he stood.

'Quickly. I don't want this turning into a media circus.'

7

Roger Tallis was a proud West Australian. He'd grown up in the salubrious suburb of Dalkeith, which sat in the prime region of Nedlands, about six kilometres outside of the Perth CBD.

He'd had the good fortune to be born into wealth, and defied the adage that it takes two generations to make it and one to break it. So far, Roger was doing an extraordinary job of building yet more wealth on the existing riches earned by his grandfather, who, after returning from the First World War, thought he was looking for gold but ended up staking a claim for iron ore in the northernmost region of the Pilbara and the Kimberley. Frances – Frank – Tallis built an art deco mansion with the proceeds in the early 1930s and to this day it remained the house that Roger considered home. Its location was in the brightest, most desired part of the richest belt of Perth, overlooking the Swan River.

Roger's father had capitalised on Frank's initial fortune, taking them into oil and nickel when generous deposits were discovered in the region. But it was Roger who diversified, with great swagger and success, into diamonds, various minerals and even salt, helping to supply nearly ninety percent of what Australia consumed. He had become a billionaire and invested in everything from property and resorts to shopping centres and now an English football club.

The police likely knew all of this, for his backstory was public and, given the time he'd spent mixing with the rich and powerful in England, he was hardly inconspicuous. And certainly not since he'd purchased the struggling Huxley Arrows and turned the proverbial ugly duckling into the bright swan it had become. Even he had recently admitted in the media that his acquisition of and relationship with the Arrows was akin to a fairytale.

There were no stains under his leadership, which was why Roger Tallis now blinked, astonished by the conversation he was having with the neatly dressed, plain-clothed policeman seated before him. When he'd been asked to meet first thing Monday, he'd expected a big-footed plod or a grouchy old guy in a rumpled suit and a tie that clashed with his shirt. The man across his desk was a tall, slim, well-spoken fellow with an annoyingly seductive smile that seemed to have charmed his middle-aged assistant. And although the man's suit didn't shout in its sombre navy, Tallis could tell it was not off-the-rack; it was also not rumpled. The white shirt, daring yet austere chocolate tie with a thin white stripe and a rich brown pair of polished brogues made up a sharp but modestly quiet ensemble that Tallis appreciated. He prided himself on being a canny judge of people and, while others might not, he noted that the policeman wore his clothes with a sort of nonchalant confidence, as though he didn't need anyone to approve of them anyway.

'I'm sorry, Detective Hawksworth. My assistant told me this visit was in connection with some general enquiries into football security. I've got my security guy joining us – should already be here.'

'No need, Mr Tallis,' the detective said. 'I'm sorry for the vagueness but it was necessary, as you'll see.'

'So you don't want him here?'

'Not really. Not yet anyway, if you don't mind.'

Tallis frowned, trying to get a read on the situation.

'What I have to say I'd rather keep between us, just until I can get your opinion.'

It was a polite and respectful response. It was even made to sound perfectly reasonable in its appeal. Tallis nodded and buzzed his assistant. 'Carol, can you let Peter know that he doesn't need to be in on this meeting? You might just catch him before he leaves the clubhouse – he's probably over at the training grounds this morning. And if he's already left, apologise for me.'

'Will do,' she said through the speaker. 'Coffee, anyone?'

Tallis glanced over at Jack and said, 'We have our own barista in-house.' He watched the detective's eyes light up.

'Thanks. Flat white, no sugar.'

'Hear that, Carol?'

'Yes, Mr Tallis. And your usual?'

'Perfect,' he said and flicked off the speaker.

'This is a very impressive stadium, Mr Tallis,' his guest said.

'Should be, it cost enough,' he quipped.

The policeman smiled as expected. 'So I gather. I've been aware – distantly – of the club's impressive rise. When did you buy the Arrows?'

Tallis could tell this was just chit-chat, knowing the man across from him would have done his homework, but he didn't mind; he quite liked talking about the club. It was an achievement he took great personal pride in and, besides, he imagined the detective was not going to talk shop until the coffee arrived. He would play along. 'In 2003. They were rubbish back then, but I've

wanted to own my own club since I worked out that I would
never make it as a professional football player, despite my best
efforts.'

Now his visitor nodded in amusement. 'Yes, I know you
schooled in England and had a good left foot as a winger at
Oxford.'

'Among other things. You've been reading up on me?'

The man shrugged. 'I'm a detective,' he said, as if that answered
all questions.

'Well, yes, I did get bitten by the bug. I mean, I love Aussie
Rules too, don't get me wrong, but this game . . . It's the game
the world plays, and it's so tribal in this country.'

'It's certainly amazing what you've done with the team.'

'Thank you,' he said. The coffee arrived and was served.
'Enjoy,' he said, as his assistant left with a long glance at his visitor.

'So, Mr Tallis . . .'

'Listen, what's your name? I was only given your surname and
I hate all this formality.'

'It's Jack.'

'Right, Jack. Call me Roger and tell me what this is all about.
One of our lads been playing up? I doubt it; they're a focused
bunch of boys this season. Maybe fans upsetting others?'

'Nothing like that. Let me explain.'

Tallis listened, not interrupting, the coffee souring in his throat.
His first response was to offer an expletive, which his guest didn't
seem to mind, nodding in fact, in agreement.

'Have you any idea what this could ruin?'

'I could take a guess.'

Out it came in a helpless rush. 'I don't think anyone realises
what the December-to-February period is like for a team like us,
contesting three major competitions in one season.'

Jack stayed silent, which he appreciated.

'Luca's my boy. I hand-picked him so I could build a team around those fabulous feet of his. Are they deliberately trying to sabotage us?'

Jack blinked, eyes widening. 'That's an interesting comment.'

'How so?' Tallis asked, putting his cup down.

'Until now I've only considered it a personal attack on Bruni, but it's intriguing that your mind leaps to the team and that it could be to disrupt your season.'

Tallis shrugged. 'My first thought is always about the team. We're on the cusp of pulling off something truly extraordinary.'

'You already have by getting into the Premier League,' Jack said, smiling.

'True.' Tallis nodded, helplessly flattered. 'We have. We've shown all the critics. But we want to go all the way.'

Jack leaned back in his seat. 'Who are the obvious critics?'

'You name them, mate! The media, the commentators . . . every bloody voice on the street has something to say about the Arrows. But other team managers are now sitting up and taking notice. They actually fear us. Who's your team?'

'The Blues.'

Tallis smiled. 'Well, we intend to bring your run to an end.'

Jack laughed. 'You probably will at the rate you're going.'

'I reckon this could be the work of a bastard who wants us to stumble just before we can make our run for the main prize.'

'Well, it's a new thought that we must now consider.'

Tallis cursed again, unable to help himself. 'Pardon my Australian. The timing is just so frustrating.'

'Any thoughts on who might be so moved as to take such dramatic action?' Jack took a notebook and pen from his pocket.

'No one in the industry. It will be from one of the fan bases – they can get pretty extreme.'

'Dare I ask who hates you the most?'

'Well, Man United is stinging from its loss, but they're up north and they've won a few since, so no, I reckon, if it is a fan or fans, then they'd be from one of the London clubs. Crosstown rivalry is vicious at times.'

'Can you list those, please?' Jack asked.

'Sure.' Tallis began counting off on his fingers. 'Arsenal, Spurs, your boys, West Ham, Crystal Palace, Fulham, Brentford, Chelsea, Millwall. They're not all in the Premier League right now, of course, but most are.'

'Okay,' his guest said, quickly jotting them down before looking up and blowing out his cheeks.

'Needle in a haystack?' Tallis asked.

Jack grinned. 'I have to find the haystack first.' His features straightened. 'What about here at the club? Anyone wishing Luca any harm? An injury, a red card, a benching?'

Tallis shook his head. 'I know it sounds like a cliché, but this club is run like a family. Luca is probably the most popular player within the team and with the staff – he's such a good kid. He's generous to everyone, he's polite and punctual, he doesn't break the rules, he's always working hard, and he's exceptional with the fans and the youngsters at the Academy. One of the reasons our acquisitions team had him as their number-one target is his attitude.'

'How do the transfers work? It always seems so frantic.'

Tallis nodded and sighed. 'See these grey hairs?'

Jack laughed.

'It begins with professional scouting. You can't find that talent about to erupt if you don't have the talent in the club to see that potential.'

Jack nodded. 'Get them early.'

'Right. Let's use Bruni as an example. I've watched him since he was playing in local boys' teams in South Australia. I put my guys onto him the moment he was recruited into the Adelaide Reds, and they've watched him ever since. And our team would have built a vast database on him. Not just stats – but what he's like, as a player, but also as a person. Every time we're thinking of recruiting a player, we want to know, are they impetuous? Are they decision-makers? Are they as confident off the pitch as they are on? That sort of thing doesn't always go hand in hand. The mildest guys can be absolute demons on the field. Do they party? Have they a steady relationship? Are they close to their family? What sort of lifestyle are they leading in these early days before they know we're watching them?'

Tallis shrugged. 'Most importantly, we build a snapshot of their mindset – this helps us work out their on-pitch character. Will they support others? Are they a selfish player or a selfless one? That's on top of their sporting prowess – right footer, left footer, both? Good header? Great corner crosser or fabulous set-piece taker? Are they a cunning player? A creative player? Do they follow the script that the head coach has set up? Do they dive? Do they lose their nerve in penalties? What's their attitude when they're fouled? What's their attitude when they're booked? What happens when they lose the ball or get yelled at by the coach from the sidelines?' He held up his palms and let out a breath.

'On and on it goes, Jack, until we have a bible on each potential transfer. It's all the good and all the bad – we have to take this approach, because the money we're talking about for a top player from a top club is anything from twenty to fifty million pounds these days. We need that big picture to make a big spend. And only then do we start to work out their valuation – what the transfer will cost if they're agreeable to signing. And then of course, will they sign?' Tallis steepled his hands. 'That's going on for maybe a dozen targets simultaneously, which we'll whittle down to perhaps four or five that we feel this club needs. So a defensive midfield might be our yawning gap, but then we really need a right winger and a fearless striker. We work out who we need to be as competitive as we can, and we go after them.'

Jack let out a low whistle. 'Intense.'

'It is. And that's not the end of it. Now comes the emotional part. I need my head coach deeply invested in these new players or it's a waste of everyone's time. Once he's bought into a player purchase, we hold our breath and hope our offer is attractive enough. It often isn't . . . and so we begin again. The final hurdle is the medical. We need to feel fully assured that a player's not carrying invisible injuries or a nagging issue that's going to haunt us. So the transfer windows add enormous strain to the recruitment team and the coaching staff, always when you least need added pressure.' Tallis grinned. 'Ah well, all part of being in a footy club.'

'And afterwards?' Jack asked. 'I gather the Arrows have a high reputation for the care of newly signed players.'

'The best, I like to think. Look, I'm a blow-in and I know how it feels.' He watched the detective smile at the Aussie term; was impressed he understood it. 'We have to make a stranger feel like part of the family as fast as possible, so we need a Rolls-Royce player care division. They help with accommodation, relocation, family, schools if necessary. Mum, Dad and kids could be uprooting their lives from one side of the world to the other. Luca didn't bring his family, but he had to make that big leap at a very tender age, so we put a lot of effort behind embedding him into his new life here. Helped that he was born here, but even so. He's made me very proud. I went out on a limb to get him here, so he's returned that faith spectacularly.'

'I've noticed. He's the poster boy for the team, right?'

Tallis nodded. 'Yeah, no doubt. He's our number-one striker, by a country mile. He's a bit like the lead singer of a rock

band . . . everyone's darling. All the kids wear the number nine
with Bruni's name on their backs on match day.'

'So no jealousies, no petty rivalries?'

'Oh, look that's part and parcel for a footy team. Other
guys here fancy themselves as offensive attackers and want that
number-nine jersey to wear, but I reckon our head coach would
encourage that competitiveness . . . you have to in order to keep
everyone sharp. But I know all these boys, and I can't see a single
one of them getting involved in something this low. But you
should probably talk to the head coach and also to Harry Taylor.'

'Your former captain?'

Tallis nodded. 'Harry was our former number nine. He's
probably Luca's closest pal, too. There are a few years between
them, so Harry treats Luca like a younger brother – they're
certainly tight enough to be considered so. And their wives are
very close.'

'Yes, Luca and Ally mentioned the Taylors when we interviewed them. That period – when Harry was injured, I mean – is
coming back to me now. An accident, right?'

'Absolutely, and not Luca's fault as some have claimed. It was a
freak accident, and Harry maintains his knee had been wobbly for
a couple of weeks.'

'And no one knew?'

Tallis pulled a face of uncertainty. 'I think deep down they did.
It wasn't noticeable enough for our staff to make much of, especially with Harry feeling so confident about it. It had been sore
for a couple of days, he told the coach, but he continued training
at full pelt. He didn't mention it to the conditioning guys either –
and they tend to be onto every niggle. We were too close to our
prize, and he didn't want to let the team down just when we were
about to qualify. But it all went pear-shaped when Luca did a
sliding tackle.'

Tallis watched the detective nod sadly. 'I remember watching it over and over and wincing. The opponent was from Man City, was it? He just seemed to leap out of the way in that split second.'

Tallis sighed with a helpless shrug. 'That's right. Anyway, the resulting dislocated knee and broken leg took more than a year to heal and then there were a further three months of conditioning and training to build him up, by which time even Harry felt it was too late to come back into the side. Bit of a sad way to end such a stellar career, but he works here now as one of our top trainers.'

'No hard feelings?'

Tallis gave a snort of disdain. 'No. They're tighter than ever. I mean, Harry was at the real pointy end of his career anyway – he acknowledges that publicly. The average age of retirement in this sport is around thirty-five, and he was thirty-four when it happened, and on his way to thirty-six when he had recovered enough to consider his future. He knew it would be the shortest-lived comeback, and perhaps that notion of getting battle-ready felt harder than the work he'd been doing in recovery. It was public knowledge that we'd already begun having discussions about his future at the club. I'd assured him he had a trainer position here and, you know, Harry's got the chops to become a senior coach for a club, so his future is really bright. Anyway, he managed to find perspective on it real fast.' Tallis shrugged.

'And how do you think he can help with the investigation?' Jack asked.

'Well, he knows Luca really well, as I mentioned. But he also knows everyone in the team. They look up to him as former captain, and they often go to him with their problems. If anyone knows of any rumbles, Harry will.'

'I'll definitely talk to him.'

'Why hasn't Luca come to me with this?' Tallis asked. He could admit to himself that that hurt.

'That's our fault. We cautioned him against telling anyone. As I explained, they've threatened him against any police or media involvement, so we've had to contain this situation.'

Tallis listened to the smooth detective explain how he and a colleague had interviewed Luca by posing as old friends.

'So we can't talk about it in-house?'

'Walls have ears. I would ask you to be especially cautious. His wife is deeply upset, as you can imagine, and we're trying to avoid the humiliation it would cause if the photo got out. The fallout for Luca would be huge and—'

'At a time when I need him on top of his game,' Tallis interjected with exasperation.

'Indeed. For now, they're staying tough and together, but they could easily come unstuck.'

Tallis nodded, putting his palms on his desk. 'All right, how can I help? You must have come here wanting something?'

'I do. I want free access to the club staff and the team itself.'

'You've got it.'

'But I don't want any sort of memo going out as to what this is about. I'll work out a vague reason for any interviews,' Jack said.

Tallis met his eye. 'You know this has happened at other clubs, don't you?'

Jack nodded. 'And in other sports. I don't have enough information on that yet, but we're setting up an operation to discover more.'

'Okay, well, if I can help connect you, just ask.'

'That's good of you, thank you.'

Tallis shrugged as if to say it was a given. 'Do you know how many competitions we're contesting this season? Three! Have you any idea what that looks like?'

Jack shook his head.

'We have to face something in the order of twenty-three matches in eighty-five days, some of them overseas, most of them not at home. That's endless travel, endless training, constant physio and conditioning, not to mention handling the inevitable injuries and the rollercoaster of emotions associated with potential losses, and the tendency to get cocky after wins. Plus snow, sleet, rain, freezing temperatures when no one wants to be out training on a bastard Tuesday night. Imagine telling all your staff they can't have Christmas or New Year like everyone else – no indulgence, no overeating, no alcohol, no merrymaking, no time with your kids or your wives and partners, and full training to boot. And,' Tallis said, landing on the word like he was punctuating his deep frustration, 'it's the effing winter transfer window coming up. The stuff of nightmares for the executive staff and legal team because it's so distracting. These next three months are unpleasant for everyone, from players to fans and everyone in between down to our canteen staff.' He shook his head helplessly. 'Now this.'

'I don't know what to say,' Jack said, sounding sincere, 'other than I imagine it's the same in other clubs.'

'Only for those playing across so many competitions,' Tallis growled, then softened. 'Look, I'm not complaining,' he said, even though he knew it must sound like he was. 'We want to win the quadruple. No one's done it in the modern era. Man United came close with its treble in the nineties – even that is a near-impossible task for most clubs these days – but we've got a sniff, detective, of the treble so I like to dream big. Imagine it,' he said, sounding suddenly dreamy. 'The bloody Huxley Arrows lifting silverware out of nowhere across the four major competitions, which has never been achieved since perhaps the 1960s and that was a whole different landscape. No Champions League, for starters.'

Jack smiled. 'What are your chances?'

'When I'm of the right mindset, I say they're good. If I'm being more realistic, I say they're slim, because we've got a few niggling injuries at present. But even to lift one cup – the Premier

League feels like our number-one target – then I need Luca solid,' Tallis said, tapping his temple and returning them to the original conversation. 'I have to ask myself, Jack, why he didn't just write a bloody cheque! He could have come to me, and I'd have organised the money.'

'I think that's the whole point, Roger. He can afford to pay it but that would have been capitulation . . . even a demonstration of guilt. He's angry. He's also defiant. He point-blank refuses to cooperate with the blackmail threat, because he assures us he did not do what the photo shows, did not agree to a sex worker visiting his room, let alone have sex with anyone while he was at Lark's Hill.'

Tallis nodded. That sounded like the Luca he knew. He gave a sad smile of understanding. 'Right. I shouldn't be surprised. The lad possesses a great sense of justice. I once saw him admit to a ref that a goal came off his arm and not his head. We drew that match instead of winning it. His coach was furious. The fans were vomiting. I was livid, but I wasn't shocked.'

'Well, that just adds yet another reason to why I believe his story.'

'The boy's no liar.' Tallis sighed. 'I've never questioned his ethics in the time I've known him. I just wish he'd told me first and allowed me to make it go away. He wouldn't have had to think on it again. And it wouldn't have been him paying the money or being made to feel complicit.'

'He did call his manager,' Jack noted. 'What do you think of him?'

'Mason? I don't know him all that well, but then I don't have a lot to do with the agency folk. You can learn more from our recruitment team – Dick Johnson and Ron Miller – and our scouts, John Farmer and Andy Marsden. Dick is probably your best bet. Mason delivered Bruni to us but he rarely gets involved in club doings. Some agents can be irritating in their interference, but Mason seems to take a more hands-off approach that we appreciate. He handles a couple of the others in the club and he's got a good list, generally, around other clubs. Respected.'

'Good to know, thanks.'

Tallis glanced at his watch. 'Well, look, all of that was a very long-winded way of assuring you I'll help in any way I can. Let me know what you need. My PA is very reliable and will take any secret to her grave, so you can tell her anything and she will not whisper it anywhere but in my ear.'

'Okay.' Jack stood up.

'Next time you're here, I'll give you a tour,' Tallis said, reaching out to shake the detective's hand. 'I can't help but show off what's been achieved here.'

Jack smiled. 'They're lucky to have you.'

Tallis waved the compliment away. 'Some people just invest, and that's fine. Their wealth allows a club to bring in new talent and improve facilities, and in return they get status and a much wider public profile. I'm not interested in all that, the media commentary or being invited to the right parties; I love football and I love what we've done with this club. It's an emotional thing for me, and to know my input is part of the reason that a tiny, unknown club is now contesting the treble is one of my private successes. I'll always consider it important in here,' he said, tapping his chest. 'This isn't about money. It's about winning against the odds.'

Jack nodded, and Tallis hoped the senior detective could tell he was being heartfelt.

'Thanks for seeing me at such short notice,' Jack said as Tallis opened the door of the office for him.

'No worries. Keep me posted, Jack,' he said and lifted a hand in farewell as the fellow strode away.

Roger Tallis felt the squirm of anxiety. He was known for his ruthless approach to business, but when it came to his beloved football team he was, beneath the calm and cool surface, as emotional as any fan. He was not going to let some blackmailing bastard of an opportunist take the possibility of winning the Premier League away from him and his squad. He was setting up some major sponsorships too – big global brands were about to sign on and that would mean enormous prestige and financial support for the club, taking the pressure off his own wallet. The next transfer window would be tantalising in terms of who they might be able to afford, and he was not about to risk that.

He might need to do some invisible digging of his own.

Jack left the home of the Arrows, a vast building that had gone up beneath the flight path of commercial jet aircraft bearing airline insignia from all over the globe. British Airways was just screaming away to somewhere, the nose of the 777 about to push through the clouds, probably on its way to the US.

He lowered his gaze and looked back at the stadium, an edifice of modern glittering glass. Some of it was mirrored, some transparent and some green or almost blue, with the rest of it translucent to form a patchwork design that echoed the fields from where the Arrows had risen. The semi-neutral span of colours was punctuated by the odd outline colour of pillar-box red, used sparingly against the grass-green glass. Old-fashioned arrows fletched with feathers that looked like they had been shot out of a medieval bow formed their recognisable logo in a cross and were emblazoned on each of the many entrances and exits that ringed the huge oval stadium. Jack had learned it could seat approximately twenty-five thousand singing, cheering, hysterical fans. The cost of this modern temple to the religion of football was unimaginable, and it was a result of the dream and drive of the man he'd just met, chief executive officer and chairman Roger

Tallis. There was no doubting his commitment to the success of the Huxley Arrows.

Jack could hear Kate's first query forming in his mind. *'Could Tallis be behind it?'*

He couldn't fathom why that might be; it would be the proverbial killing of the golden goose. No. He didn't believe so, but stranger things and all that. He'd keep an open mind, but for now the CEO was not in his immediate sights.

Jack began turning over in his mind how potent the man's remark about hobbling the team might be. Given the team's strategy had been designed around the golden boots of Luca Bruni, maybe there was some weight to the notion that if the blackmailer brought this one key player down, it could upset the balance of the whole team.

Jack frowned, coming out of his musings and wondering how best to get back into the city. The Underground would be efficient using the Piccadilly line to Green Park, but it would be faster by taxi at this time of day. He might even clip ten minutes off the journey.

Except, his mind reasoned, there were no taxis about and he could likely spend the next ten minutes waiting for one to drive by or trying to find somewhere to hail one from. He turned towards the Huxley Town Underground.

As he began descending on the escalator a minute or so later, his mobile rang. He expected it to be Kate, but it wasn't a number he recognised. 'Hawksworth.'

'Hi. Er, Jack?' A woman's voice.

'Yes?'

'It's Lou.'

'Lou?' he repeated, baffled.

'Bella's friend,' she added, sounding a little self-conscious. 'From the other night.'

'Oh, hello,' he said, vexed he'd been so slow. 'I'm so sorry, I'm racing down into the bowels of the earth to get from west London back into the city, and my mind is far away and lost in work. Forgive me. How are you?'

'I'm good, thanks. Look, I wanted to extend that invitation again so you know it wasn't a hollow one. We'd like to cook you dinner if you're agreeable. To say thank you.'

He smiled. Lou in her funny pyjamas had run across his mind a couple of times since they'd briefly met. 'That would be lovely, but you don't need to—'

'We want to,' she insisted. 'Besides, Bella owes you. Is Wednesday night any good for you?'

'It should be fine,' he said, mindful of potentially losing his signal any moment.

'Oh, great. Well, you know where we live. Shall we say six? Is that too early?'

He laughed. 'No. Never too early for a glass of wine and good food, good company.'

'Perfect. Wear something comfy. We're just as likely to morph it into a boozy picnic.'

'Okay, lovely.'

'Oh, and listen, I can imagine police work doesn't follow convenient timelines. We can rearrange at the drop of a hat. Don't feel bad if something comes up.'

She was so easygoing. 'It will be fine. Thank you.'

'Bye, Jack.'

He could hear the smile in her voice and he could feel his helpless internal response to it within.

8

Jack was back at Scotland Yard. The busy ops room looked as familiar as if he'd never left it.

'Good morning, Mother,' he said, his voice filled with affection.

Joan smiled from behind a reception desk. 'Glad you got my message.'

'I had to interview someone.'

'Oh, is that what they call it now?' she said in an arch tone.

Jack began to stammer an explanation and then realised the woman now in her mid-sixties had lost none of her wit. His alarm dissolved into a chuckle and she grinned.

'It's lovely to see you, Jack.'

He leaned over her desk and kissed her cheek. 'Mmm, Chanel No.5.'

'Never leave home without it,' she said and, if he didn't know better, he could forgive himself for believing she was wearing a Chanel suit to boot on her trim figure. He knew Joan wouldn't tolerate paying such an outrageous price to sit behind a work desk, but she had an uncanny eye for style – always had. He had no doubt that her heels would be expensive, because she had a thing for shoes in the same way he had a thing for coffee.

'I like your hair like that, Joan.'

'Grey?'

'Swept up. It's elegant and intimidating at once.'

'Get on with you, Jack! Would you know what I mean if I said I'm thinking about a pixie cut when I finally retire?'

'I do. And you'd rock it.'

'I should bottle you and carry you around with me.'

He grinned, then looked around. 'I see you wasted no time,' he said, marvelling at the activity.

'Years of experience – everything must always happen by last week. Anyway, I was thrilled to get the call from Carol Rowland. I thought my ops days were done.'

'Never,' Jack said. 'And I don't like running one without you keeping us on the straight and narrow. Kate here?'

'Yes, she's somewhere, probably taking out her fangs for the day after scaring the two young DCs you wanted. Their names are Natalie March – Nat – and, would you believe, Matthew Lowell – Matt?'

He laughed. 'I did know their names but I'd never put them together as Nat and Matt. And as for Kate, they'll realise she's all bark and no bite soon enough.'

'Sarah's setting up, and we've got Ari Varma from Vice. Kate knows him, says he's smart.'

'That's it?' Jack asked, his tone neutral rather than accusing, as he adjusted the box he was balancing.

'You said keep it tight,' Joan said, confident as ever in her arrangements. 'Why, did you buy too many cakes?'

He grinned. 'Perhaps. Well, more for us.' He noticed her concern. 'No, I was told to keep it tight by upstairs, so you've followed the brief, Joan, and it's important we keep this quiet. We'll be fine.'

'I'll put the kettle on and make a cuppa. Can't miss your first Yard briefing as a high and mighty Detective Superintendent,' she said, raising an impressed eyebrow. 'Oh, by the way, are you ready for the op's name?'

He gave her a look of mock disdain. 'What is it this time? Flowerpot? Cucumber? Hedgerow?'

Joan grinned. 'Nearly! Stonecrop.'

'Stonecrop,' Jack repeated. 'As in the succulent?'

'Well, you know more than me. You should be on one of those quiz shows.'

Kate breezed towards them, waving at Jack. 'Ah, there you are. So, do detective superintendents keep special hours?'

He feigned vexation. Clearly she was past her cringing moments of apology. 'I met with Roger Tallis this morning.'

'Did your antennae pick up anything?'

He smiled at the confirmation of how well he knew her. 'His shock seemed genuine and his anger grounded in how inconveniently timed it is. He posed a good question, but let's get to the briefing and keep everyone in the loop.'

'Go put your cakes down, and I'll get everyone organised.'

'Try not to scare everyone, Kate.'

'Too late,' Joan said, turning away to take a call.

'Me, scare people?' Kate said, feigning injury and turned back to Joan. 'Anyone important?'

'No, they're just bringing up the pinboard you requested.'

'Okay. By the way, Jack, do mention Sarah's new anorak,' Kate said.

He couldn't help but crack a smile. 'She's finally switched?'

Kate nodded. 'It's a rather racy olive green now.'

He gave a tutting sound and followed Joan out to the kitchenette to give her the cakes, listening to Kate gathering everyone together in the next room.

★

Inside the ops room, it was all about functionality. The bare, blandly kitted-out space rarely changed. Wooden desks were arranged in blocks, while old, bulky-looking computer terminals defied the slimline look of the tech shown on the crime TV shows. There was, however, a new partitioned meeting area with two small sofas. That was a most welcome addition, Jack thought. Even bulkier than the normal computers were the HOLMES terminals, of which there were four that he could see. One would be for Sarah as head HOLMES operator, but Nat and Matt had been hand-picked for their ability with the invaluable database system, so they each had one on their desks too. The last one he could see in a partitioned-off area that was presumably to be his office and new home for a while.

Kate confirmed the equipment that Joan had ordered, looking at a checklist. 'So that's all there, plus a PNC terminal, which I gather Nat is trained in?'

'She is,' Jack confirmed. 'And fast too.'

'I've already given everyone their new log-in details.'

'Excellent.'

Through the large windows, Jack could see the tall, familiar buildings across Victoria Street. The reflective coating he looked through meant the people in those buildings could not see inside to where he and his team were. He was sure he'd heard somewhere that the coating also helped to reduce shattering if a bomb exploded outside.

The two young detective constables looked slightly wide-eyed, and Jack assumed this was probably their first time at the Scotland Yard ops premises. He remembered his first time here and how overwhelming it had been; the big stage, finally his. He smiled at their eagerness. DI Sarah Jones was beaming at him and a glance towards the corner, where an olive anorak was draped over her chair, told him Kate was right – as catty as her running joke seemed, it was amusing and in good fun, really. They both respected Sarah immensely.

'Good morning, everyone,' he said. 'Sarah, thank you for saying yes to this.'

'I couldn't let Kate have all the fun, sir,' Sarah said, and that told him Sarah's elevation to detective inspector had given her the public confidence she'd lacked in previous ops.

'To the new faces, you do not have to address me by my title. It's a mouthful and I hardly recognise myself being called detective superintendent. So it's Jack, please.'

'Sir will do nicely, everyone,' Kate suggested.

He smiled. 'Welcome to you, DC Natalie March and DC Matthew Lowell. The Nat n' Matt team.' He gestured to the others with a sweep of his hand, which made them chuckle. 'Both of these new detectives have shown great promise on some tasks they've handled for me on previous jobs. Thanks for joining us.'

They gave each other congratulatory sideways grins as Jack continued.

'This is a very small team, so we'll be relying on you both to be the arms and legs for us in a lot of instances.'

They nodded as one.

'And DI Ari Varma, we're grateful to you for being on this op. Ari joins us from Vice.'

'Wild horses wouldn't keep me away, guv. Your reputation is gold,' Varma said.

Jack was delighted by the unexpected cockney accent.

'Besides, I'm scared to say no to DCI Carter.' Varma shot Kate a grin.

Jack watched Kate return a mock scathing look. 'And I know you've already met each other, but this is DCI Kate Carter, who I have worked with on most of my major operations. I couldn't imagine a more reliable or whip-smart wingman, or should I say wing-person?'

Everyone smiled.

'Please, if Kate's making a request, it's me making that request. Follow her instincts and don't worry too much; she only drinks blood at weekends.'

She cut him a sarcastic sneer, but only he could read how chuffed she was by his praise before his vampire remark.

'And standing behind me is Joan Field. She's actually the one to be frightened of; she will hound you relentlessly for your diary sheets'—that drew the groan he anticipated—'and your expenses claims. She will also fine us for poor word choices, so watch your language please.'

'No formal expense claim, no payment,' Joan said. He glanced behind just in time to see her waggling a finger.

'Joan keeps us all moving forwards and is the hub through which all messages can be routed. She will farm information out to all who need to know, so please consider Joan as our central nervous system for this op, which I've discovered just moments ago is called Stonecrop.'

The name won the groan he was expecting.

'Don't shoot the messenger.' He grinned. 'Anyway, please keep Joan fully updated on everything, even if you're just nipping out to grab a coffee – and I'd recommend you avoid the hellish gutter water that's on offer in the kitchen.'

Another round of chuckles from all.

'Right, get comfy, and let me tell you why we're here.' Jack removed his jacket and gestured a shiver. 'Joan, what's happening with the heating?'

'I've already spoken to the guys downstairs; they're fixing it. Wear a jumper for now, everyone.'

Fortunately, Jack had rolled a jumper into his messenger bag, and he now pulled it on over his shirt and tie, knowing his suddenly more casual appearance would relax everyone. He took up his customary position, leaning back against a desk, legs crossed at the ankles, and glanced around the room at his small team. He walked them through what he knew.

'I can't reinforce strongly enough how tight-lipped each of us must remain on this. I don't want to say lives depend on it, but a marriage, two new babies, reputations and a major football club's profile all depend on us keeping this within our walls. Do not discuss this at the pub, with friends, even with family. This is a secret op, in other words.' He watched that land on them heavily and be absorbed.

Kate jumped in next. 'We've already interviewed Luca and Ally Bruni. Is everyone familiar with this power couple?'

Everyone but Sarah nodded. Kate filled her in on the two darlings of the football and TV world. 'Britain will not like one of their favourite romances being shattered.'

'Why would that happen?' Ari asked.

'Because Mrs Bruni feels betrayed,' Jack replied.

'He believes it's a set-up though.'

'It is a set-up – Luca denies his part in it.' Jack ran a hand through his hair and answered the frowns. 'The semen exists.' He pointed to the board, where the photo of Bruni with the mystery woman had been blown up, looking grainy. 'But we don't know that it is his.'

'It could be condensed milk,' Kate suggested and won a round of disgusted groans. 'Well, even classroom glue looks much the same, let's face it,' she reasoned.

Jack cast her a look that conveyed an amused '*Really?*' before continuing. 'So, it could be glue, it could be his semen, it could be someone else's. Whichever it is, Bruni denies participating in the most obvious way, though he agrees he was likely drugged.

He is so insistent he's innocent that he's prepared to blow open the blackmailer's demands for secrecy.'

'The mere fact he's brought us in suggests he is defiantly opposed to the blackmailer's demands,' Kate added.

'This morning I met with Roger Tallis,' Jack said.

Everyone leaned forward, impressed. That was a name everyone knew.

'The casual swagger you see in the media is hidden when you meet him in person. I found him as shocked as Bruni, candid, charming and helpful.'

'That doesn't mean he isn't involved, sir,' Sarah remarked, and once again Jack was impressed. She'd certainly found her voice since previous ops.

Kate gave him a sly glance, obviously impressed too.

'But why would he?' Jack countered, happy to have this discussion; it was necessary to explore this idea as a team. 'Anyone got any thoughts on that?' He'd make them earn it, rather than putting forward his own theory.

'He doesn't need money,' Sarah said.

'He personally brought Bruni into the Arrows, and paid well over the top price to get him out of his contract with the Irish League,' Ari said, and then looked around at the soft surprise. 'What? So I'm a football addict.'

Jack grinned. 'Very handy. What else do you know?'

'That I'm impressed with the Arrows. For those of you who don't know much about football, until Roger Tallis, only locals would even know the Huxley Arrows existed. These guys flopped around in the lower tiers, and they started pushing under the helm of Tallis. When they got to the top tier, you'd have thought they won the FA Cup.'

'Tallis bought them in 2003 – he's a football fanatic like Ari here.' Jack took over again. 'He's an Oxford boy, a Rhodes scholar no less, played at university and was good enough to fancy himself a player but it never went any further. I suspect what he didn't tell me is that his father probably trampled on that dream and made it clear what his future held.'

Sarah put a finger in the air.

'Sarah?'

'I did some sleuthing, sir. May I?'

'Go ahead.'

Sarah began to read from a page of notes she'd made on the Australian. Much of it was common knowledge, but Jack was impressed she'd taken the trouble and it would help the team to have this background. 'He's been married twice. Has four children, two from each marriage, all grown up now. Two of them, one son, one daughter – one from each of the wives – now work in the mining operations. Another son is an artist and writer living in a lovely villa in Santorini, funded by his father, and the youngest daughter, now thirty-one, worked at the Huxley Arrows as the public relations director.'

Sarah paused. Jack knew it was unlikely to be intentional or for dramatic effect but it highlighted her final remark nonetheless. 'That daughter is rumoured to have had an affair with the former captain of the Arrows, Harry Taylor.'

That caught everyone's attention.

Jack looked at Kate. 'Onto it,' she said.

He nodded. 'Good work, Sarah, thank you. So we were listing why Tallis would not likely be involved. He doesn't need money. He is personally invested in Bruni, who is a fellow Aussie and like a lucky charm to the team. Tallis is also personally invested in the Arrows – no doubt to an eye-watering amount – so to hurt Bruni is to hurt himself. He has, however, suggested that this is a deliberate disturbance to the team's equilibrium.'

The team around him nodded. 'They could win some silverware this year, guv,' Ari said. 'I doubt Mr Tallis would be doing anything to rock those chances. It's everything they've spent the last few years working towards, grinding through the divisions. They've knocked off so many major clubs this season, I'll be betting they win the Premier League and give the FA Cup a nudge too.'

'Maybe even a clean sweep with the Champions League?' Jack asked.

'Why not?' Ari replied, giving a shrug. 'They're on a roll. It would be senseless to upset the team at this stage.'

'And that's my impression from this morning's meeting, too, but someone else might want exactly that. It was Tallis's first thought and not mine, I must admit. When Kate and I interviewed the Brunis, we were focused on the personal attack, but Tallis has widened my area of interest to consider that this might be about destabilising the team.'

'Sabotage,' Kate murmured. 'Okay.'

'To be honest, I'm not buying it, but my opinion doesn't matter. To be diligent we have to consider both theories. If it is someone trying to disrupt the team balance, then it's going to be coming from the fan base of one of the London-based clubs. He was quick to say that he couldn't imagine it was club-led, even though the rivalry is strong. His opinion is that it was most likely a fanatic . . . like Ari here.'

That won some amusement.

'Sir,' Sarah said, forcing them all back on task. 'What about the other incidents of blackmail?'

'Yes, that's our third strand that it's vital we look into. I'm going to put you exclusively on that, Sarah. See me later and we'll talk it through.'

She nodded, blinking behind her owl glasses.

Jack cleared his throat. 'So, Kate, if you'd oblige . . . Your writing is neater than mine,' he said, handing her a whiteboard

marker. 'We need to gather up the other cases of similar blackmail'—he tipped his head towards Sarah—'with a particular
emphasis on other Premier League players. Most of the top-paying
sports have suffered, I gather. Next,' he said, beginning to pace
as Kate's pen squeaked on the plastic surface, 'we need the staff
at Lark's Hill interviewed. I want everyone on duty that night
questioned. Kate, you take the lead on that, please.'

'Right,' she said from behind him, her pen still squeaking.

'Nat and Matt, I want one of you backing up Kate, and the
other will back up Ari, who will be going to the Huxley Arrows
training grounds – that's where the actual headquarters are. You'll
need to be talking with the key executives there, especially
security.'

Jack watched Ari's smile break widely. Clearly a perfect task for
him.

'Right, guv,' he said cheerfully.

Jack glanced at Joan, who was watching him from the doorway.
'I think Joan has some welcome-to-the-op cakes for everyone,
but'—he moved to the whiteboard and tapped it—'I want a
report back on all your tasks in the next forty-eight hours tops.
Time, as always, is against us.'

Natalie raised a palm tentatively, as though she was about to
swear an oath. He was glad to see her fear was overcome by her
curiosity. 'Is it me, sir, or is the length of time the blackmailers
have given the Brunis a bit odd? Don't they usually want it
right away?'

Jack nodded. 'It's not you, Nat. It's seriously odd, and one of
those questions we've already raised with our bosses and the agent
who brought the case to light with the Yard. Ah, that's something
that I meant to put on the list, Kate, and another task for you.
Can you have a chat to two fellows? Keep it casual, just routine,
but I'd like your take on the agent who represents the group who

have put money forward to hire a private detective. For now that's to the side while we're involved, but even so, we need to know what they'll tell us. His name is George Shaw. The other is Jonathan Mason, who is Luca Bruni's agent. I'm not expecting anything much from these two, but let's see what we learn when we press them.'

'On it,' she said.

'Right, cake and then heads down.'

Joan beckoned. 'Follow me, children. I'll show you around our make-believe kitchen, which is really a sink, and I'm going to be like your mothers and nag about tidiness, cleanliness and leaving the place neat. I am not your maid, and I will not be cleaning up after you. But I will make sure you have plenty of tea and coffee . . .' Her voice trailed away as the others traipsed after her.

Kate looked at Jack. 'And where are you headed?'

'I think I need to find out which escort service, if any, was used to set Bruni up.'

'Of course,' she said dryly. 'How silly of me. Let me put that on the board.' She wrote *Escort services/Prostitutes* and Jack's name next to it.

He gave a droll sigh. 'Just can't help yourself, can you?'

She laughed. 'Come on, nasty coffee and cake is on.'

9

Michael Evans looked into eyes the colour of a pale lime, noting how they reflected the enormous pain she was in.

'She'll need an opiate,' he said to the concerned thirty-something man nearby. 'In fact, I think we'll do that right now,' he decided, reaching for the right syringe from the kidney dishes on his bench. He opened the fridge and removed a vial of buprenorphine, puncturing its surface with a wire-fine needle and drawing out the right amount of the drug. 'Little sting,' he said to the patient, as he always did. She barely noticed the additional discomfort because there was already enough from the burns to keep her occupied. 'She's a miracle,' he remarked, prompting a sad smile from the guy, Nathan. 'The smoke alone should have killed her, by the sounds of things.'

'That's what the firemen said. They refused to let me go in because the roof was collapsing. I had to just watch the house burn.' He began to tear up.

'So, how . . .?' Michael trailed off, leaving the question hanging.

'It was the only policewoman there. Made the men look like softies. She kicked in a window and jumped in. I have no idea how she found Poppy, but she got her out and flung her into the neighbour's house. I discovered hours later she's a cat owner and said to my neighbour that if her house was burning down, she'd like to think someone would save her cat.'

Poppy looked back at Michael with a baleful grimace and, given the attitude that seemed to exist in this tri-colour breed, he half-expected her to hiss at him, perhaps give him a bat, but her paws were hurting too. She likely didn't have the energy right now, and as if answering him she gave a sneering cough.

'Hmm, that doesn't sound great, does it?'

Nathan shook his head. 'The smoke was black. The fire melted all the plastics and the fumes were toxic.' His voice sounded shaky.

'Okay, let me just look at her eyes for ulcers. I'm just going to stain them. Do you want to hold her?' Michael asked, flicking off the lights and reaching for the special fluorescent liquid.

Poppy squirmed and gave a low moan, but her owner held her gently, tears helplessly running down his cheeks. Michael snapped off the lights and used a UV torch. 'No ulcers, all good,' Michael finally said, and turned the lights back on. 'Well, Poppy, you've used up another of your lives,' he said, dragging a tissue from the box behind him and handing it to Nathan, who let go of the cat and took it gratefully. 'She's going to heal and be just fine, but it's going to take time.'

'Thank you, Dr Evans. I didn't know if the burns were too bad and you were going to advise putting her down.'

Michael shook his head. 'I'd fight as hard as you for her life, you know that. Her ears aren't great – they're going to take the longest to heal – and her paws are singed, but her fur is all good, no scorching, which is amazing,' he said, finishing his inspection of Poppy's already less tense body.

Nathan self-consciously dabbed at his eyes. 'So what now?'

Michael gave a soft sigh. 'It would be my recommendation that she go into an oxygen cage for a little while. We have to be sure about smoke inhalation. In animals, the effects only show up about twenty-four hours later, so I imagine they'd keep her overnight, possibly two nights, just being careful and doing obs.'

'They?'

'It won't be here, I'm afraid.'

'Why? You're the best vet in the region.'

'We don't have that specialist equipment in my clinic. The animal hospital I'm suggesting she be transferred to is really not too far away.' Michael reached for a card and handed it to Nathan. 'They've got staff round the clock. Is that okay?'

'Whatever she needs.'

'This is not going to be cheap, though.'

Nathan shifted uncomfortably. 'What am I looking at?'

'Probably around two thousand with all the meds.'

He gasped. 'I . . . I don't have that.' Nathan's voice wobbled and gave way. 'I've lost everything.'

Michael could see how genuine the man's fear was. 'Okay, look, Nathan, please stop fretting. You've had the most massive shock. If I understand what you're saying, you got out with the clothes you're standing in and, by some miracle, your cat is here too. Let me see what can be done about the costs, and you worry about giving Poppy her meds diligently once you get her back.'

'I will. I will, I promise.'

Michael had always had a soft spot for this client, a gay man who'd had some ups and downs but had recently won himself a terrific new job as a clinical lead in his specialty as a speech pathologist. He was now also lecturing at uni. He had upgraded his car and had admitted on the last visit for Poppy's annual injections that he had just negotiated with the owner of the house he rented to buy the property at the end of the year. It seemed just as life was coming good, he'd been given a massive blow. 'I need you to stop worrying about Poppy and save some strength for yourself. Have you got somewhere to stay?'

Nathan nodded, banishing his tears. 'With my sister and her family.'

'I'll speak to the hospital about minimising costs, and I'll take Poppy there myself. Is someone around to drive you home?'

He pointed over his shoulder. 'My friend.'

Through a small window at the side of the consulting room, Michael could see a tall, handsome fellow scrolling through his phone. 'Someone special?'

Nathan grinned. 'Yes. I feel very lucky to have him in my life right now. It's early days. Once you start living together, it changes. I want to enjoy this lovely time with David, getting to know each other. You understand better than most, I imagine . . .'

'I do. I've been with Paul now for nearly two years, but we're living together now and it still feels wonderful and shiny new. Enjoy it.' Michael smiled. 'And you have a good sister. I have one of those too,' he added. 'So go home, Nathan. She's out of it now anyway,' he said, directing his client's gaze to the cat, who had closed her eyes while they'd been talking. He lifted her into a cradle. 'When she's released from the hospital, I'll transfer her back here and you can pick up the medication she's going to need.'

'But the money . . .' Nathan began.

'We'll sort it,' Michael said in a tone of finality. He bustled Nathan out of the surgery and into the care of his new boyfriend. Michael glanced towards his receptionist and shook his head so she knew not to say anything about payment.

Returning to his consulting room, he carefully lifted Poppy into a pack for transfer. 'Rest up, Pops,' he said, gently stroking her and winning a soft mewl.

Mel tapped on the door. 'We're all done for the day. Anything I need to do before I leave?'

'No, Mel, that's great. You head off.'

'Have a lovely night.'

The door closed and he was finally alone, apart from the sleeping cat. He was glad he was in a position to help Nathan and Poppy out, though he was still brooding on his financial windfall and whether his decision had been wise; his mind never stopped nagging that it was all somehow going to catch up with him.

His sister's illness and long-term care had backed him into a corner. With their aunt no longer able to cope, he'd needed to hire a full-time, live-in carer, or have another horrible conversation about moving her into a home.

It wasn't Cathie who resisted this; she'd never had anything but an objective view of her awful, degenerative disease. The diagnosis of Huntington's had only come a few years ago. The fact that all the clever medical people hadn't nailed it down earlier often made him angry, but Cathie, ever mild and sensible, wondered what possible good that could have done.

'I preferred ignorance, to be honest,' she'd quipped when he'd pushed past his tears into anger. 'Now I know what it is and how bad it's going to get . . . and that we can't fix it. You have to accept this, Michael, and not rage against it.'

'It's *his* fault.'

'No, it's not.'

'He's given it to you!'

'Michael, I know he was a pretty lousy father, but he died with this and he didn't ask for it. He got it from one of *his* parents.'

'Not that we'd know which.'

'Look, you chose to have nothing to do with him when he left us, but I don't hate him as you do. I never felt anything much towards him, but I was happy I didn't cut him off entirely.'

'So he could blubber his apologies at the end.'

'Everyone deserves their chance to confess to their short-comings.'

'He did it on his death bed, near enough, Cath. He was simply making himself feel better. He treated Mum and us abominably.'

'I know. I just don't have enough room in my heart to hold hate.'

'Yep, as we all know, you're the good twin. I'm the nasty one.' He made a face at her.

She had laughed at that, their oldest joke. That's how they'd been since they were born – great friends – and they had adored their mother, who had died too young from breast cancer, while their no-good father had lived on for too long, in Michael's opinion. He'd given his children nothing except his legacy of death for Cathie.

'I know you're frightened,' Cathie had said to Michael often enough, 'but you must come to terms with this before I lose the ability to recognise you, or even move. You have to learn to live without me. Make some friends, find someone special. Put me in a home and stop feeling so fucking responsible for my problems.'

'Your problems are my problems too,' he'd grumbled just as often.

'Well, if you don't watch out, you're going to be left a very lonely old man. I don't want that for you. Find yourself a good bloke and get on with life. Nothing would make me happier before I lose mine.'

She'd always been blunt, which was alarming for some, but he'd always found it endearing, given he was someone who lived in the greys, never fully confronting issues.

It had become obvious that she could not live independ-ently. With his work, and if he was to have any sort of future for himself, then he had to take her advice and find her a good nursing home.

'It doesn't mean you can't see me. It doesn't mean we don't get to have all the same fun and laughs, Michael; it just means I can die knowing you have a life beyond your clients and their animals.'

When he'd finally relented, a place had been found at Robin Hall, a beautiful heritage residence on the outskirts of Tunbridge Wells in Kent. They offered Cathie a place that masqueraded as independent living but in fact had one care worker per two clients, and provided full support throughout each day and night, including public holidays. The grounds were impressive, taking full advantage of the beautiful Weald. Cathie was yet to need her wheelchair full time and assured him she could still take assisted, albeit shaky, walks around that stunning countryside. 'And I'm still just a one-hour express train from you,' she gushed.

He agreed. Their family home was yet to be sold – they were renting it out for the moment, the income welcome – but when it was he'd already decided all proceeds would go towards Cathie's new home. But there were so many other costs, not that he'd bothered her with them. He'd hoped his clinic could support it all, but a new vet clinic had opened up a couple of neighbour-hoods away and the animal hospital was beginning to encroach on the sort of regular services he offered, and he was feeling the effects of both.

He'd tried upping his fees, but that caused blowback from customers, so he'd increased his hours instead, hoping to maintain his cash flow. For a while that worked, but Cathie's bills had increased. She'd already used her cash inheritance from their mother. Now his was being eaten into, too, and his lovely, light-filled two-bedroom flat in Wimbledon was under serious threat. If he had to give that up, it would be a crushing blow.

The approach from the guy had come so unexpectedly, had been so exquisitely timed that he knew it had to have been orchestrated to take full advantage of the financial crisis he was facing. But how had they known? Only a few of his clients knew about his sister's illness. His present receptionist knew nothing of her.

The original request had sounded crazy. He still felt deeply awkward, even regretful, about agreeing to it, but the cash had paid off his mortgage and other bills in a blink. That sense of security had felt like no other rush he could remember experiencing. If the very worst happened, he could bring Cathie back to his flat and she could see her days out there, miserable though they might be. But knowing he had a roof to put over their heads felt like he'd stayed true to his dying mother's wish that he always provide for Cathie.

'. . . to the end, son,' she'd croaked.

He'd kissed his adored mother's cheek and given her his promise — and because of this clandestine business, he'd been able to keep it.

Increasingly, though, the illegal doings — whatever they were; he was not privy to them — weighed heavily on his conscience. The man who'd approached him had been good-looking and he'd fallen for the offer for a drink. They'd got on well enough, but he quickly suspected the guy was either after a quick lay or something else. It turned out to be the latter, catching him in a deeply vulnerable moment when his accountant had just laid out some bare and chilling facts for him.

He recalled the weird conversation. 'Can you freeze sperm in a domestic situation?' the man had asked without much of the usual polite conversation on their first date. He called himself Daniel, but Michael had sensed guile and no longer trusted the name was real.

'Sure,' he'd answered, surprised by the question, but it was within his wheelhouse to answer it.

'How?'

'That may well be the oddest question I've ever been asked, I think.'

'Really? As a vet?'

'No, I mean while in a bar, drinking a cocktail.'

The fellow ignored his jibe. 'But don't vets do this all the time? You help people knock up their pets?'

'Perhaps if I was a specialist who had clients with a horse stud.' He laughed. 'So no, I don't.'

'But you know how to do it?'

'I do. I'm a qualified vet with ten years of working experience, five of them with my own clinic.'

'So tell me.'

Michael had frowned, taken a sip of his cocktail and then laughed. 'All right. Er . . . well, there's a thing called a swim-up process.'

'Okay . . . What does that mean?'

'Are you sure you want to know this? I'd rather talk about your favourite book or television show.'

'I'm sure that I want to know this, yes,' the man replied; his cool manner was disarming and just a bit addictive for Michael.

He sighed. 'Right. Well, let's see. You add egg yolk and glycerol to the sperm sample, which is then gradually frozen using the vapour of liquid nitrogen. Then you dip it entirely into liquid nitro, keeping it submerged so it remains frozen. Liquid nitrogen is not available domestically, but I presume by domestic you mean outside of a full-scale lab.'

The man nodded, looking impressed. 'Interesting. And if I *was* at home, how would I do this?'

'At home?' Michael asked, incredulous. It seemed his companion was not jesting, from his answering expression. 'Well, at home, I suppose you could keep the liquid nitrogen temporarily in a foam cooler.'

'Like the kind we use for beer and soft drinks, you mean?'

'Exactly. In Australia it's the esky, in New Zealand it's the chilly bin. I suppose we just call them coolers. Are you thinking of preserving your sperm? Because—'

'Something like that,' the man who called himself Daniel replied.

Michael stopped talking. 'You're not really interested in a date, are you?' He wasn't offended; he just didn't like being used, and he was convinced this strange conversation was exactly why the guy had asked him out.

To his credit, Daniel shook his head. 'But I promise you, it's better than a date.'

'Oh yeah? How's that?'

'Twenty thousand times better.' He rubbed a thumb and finger together in the universal sign of money.

Michael had to swallow carefully for fear of coughing. He looked at his companion as though he had just explained he was from Mars. 'What does that even mean?'

'It means that I can make you rich. All I need is a little help.'

'Help with what?' Michael said, sounding affronted.

Daniel shrugged. 'Nothing more complicated than what you've just explained.'

Michael laughed. 'Well, you didn't allow me to explain that to keep the sperm frozen, you'd need a lined and insulated tank, plus other—'

'Presumably,' Daniel cut in impatiently, 'with the right equipment you could build all that you need? And instead of home, you could even keep it within your clinic, where it would not look out of place.'

'Why would I want to?'

A smile stretched lazily across Daniel's symmetrical, generous mouth. 'Okay, let's say I could give you thirty thousand reasons.'

Michael's stomach plummeted. That kind of money was insane. 'What?!'

Again Daniel shrugged, as nonchalantly as if he'd said, 'Do you want another Pimm's?'

'Why do you need me?' Michael demanded.

'I need to freeze sperm.'

'Your own,' Michael said flatly.

'Not necessarily.'

'I'm sorry, Daniel, if that's even your name, but I don't think I'll stay for the rest of this drink. It's gone a bit sour on me.'

'It's not.'

'Not what?' Michael was gathering up his wallet, feeling angry now.

'It's not my name. My name is Aslan.'

Michael paused. 'As in the lion from the CS Lewis story?'

Aslan laughed. 'I don't know. I didn't read English storybooks as a child.'

Michael thought he looked like his heritage might be Eastern Mediterranean, Turkish perhaps. He sounded English though, as though he'd been to a public school. 'Suits you better than Daniel.'

'My mother thought so,' he said and risked a smile. 'But call me Daniel anyway.'

'Why don't you tell me what this is all about?' Michael felt impatient; this was sounding dodgier by the second.

'I need to know I can trust you.'

'I don't know if you can,' he said honestly, shrugging. 'Are you planning to break the law?'

'Is it against the law to freeze sperm?'

'No.'

'Then you have nothing to fear.'

'I'm not talking about me. I'm talking about you. It *is* against the law if you plan to sell it on the black market.'

'Ah,' Daniel said, 'you may have me there.'

'Why would you need to do that?'

He gave a long, deep shrug that answered nothing. 'I don't. It's not my sperm.'

'Dan . . . Aslan. Listen, I don't know you . . . but whatever this is, I have no intention'—Michael crossed his heart like a child—'of mentioning it to anyone. I'm not intrigued, or even keen to learn more – I'm actually worried for you and where this is going.'

'That's curious,' Daniel replied. 'I'm worried for you.'

'Why?' Michael gasped, suddenly alarmed.

'Well, given the financial state you find yourself in, what with your sister's needs and your business costs . . . You're very good to her . . . at the expense of your own security.'

An uncomfortable warmth passed through Michael, like the sensation of being anaesthetised.

'But I can help,' Daniel continued. 'I can put forty thousand pounds into your hands within days.'

Michael could only blink, speechless and frightened at the amount but also how it kept escalating. How could this stranger know so much about him – so much that was private? And he was throwing the words 'forty thousand pounds' around as if he'd said 'forty pounds'.

'And your part of it is so very simple,' Daniel continued. 'Just say yes and I'll tell you more. Imagine what that money could do for you.'

Michael did imagine it. That amount of money would be life-changing. He blinked and out it came; he was unable to stop it. 'Yes,' he said, sounding robotic but emphatic, already mentally distributing the money across the debts that were threatening to swallow him.

His companion grinned and explained what would be required of him. His smooth, conversational tone was relaxed and strangely soothing. Michael waited for a heartbeat before the warning came. 'Of course, this is highly secret. We need your assurance that you'll go to your grave with it.'

'Why?'

'Why is it secret?'

Michael shook his head. 'Why are you doing this?'

Daniel tapped the side of his nose. 'That's the secret. Now, as we've discussed, what I'm asking you to do is not against the law. It happens up and down the country in lots of human fertility clinics and is a legitimate practice.'

'Then ask one of them.'

'You already know I can't.'

'Because of the secret,' Michael repeated. 'So why ask a vet who does not have the sort of rural practice that adds legitimacy?'

'It's a good question, Michael. It's because we need someone who feels beholden.'

The man paused, and Michael couldn't believe he was being so open about the situation.

'I use that word respectfully,' Daniel continued, 'and I simply mean you might be invested more acutely than any other vet we approach, because you have a specific need for this money like no other. We believe you will protect our secrecy because the money can change your life and your twin sister's life for the better . . . for as long as she may have,' he said, his tone not lacking in sympathy. 'We feel we can rely on you. Shall we say cheers?'

Michael felt slightly stunned. He cleared his throat. 'I have questions.'

'Fire away.'

'How long would I keep the, er, product?'

'A few days — a week max.'

'I'm presuming this is not a single event. You'll be back for more?'

'You'd be right in that presumption. Let's say a maximum of eight separate events for now. We'll pay you each time.'

'Eight!' Michael repeated, staggered by what that might mean to him financially. 'And you're not going to tell me what this is about?'

Daniel shook his head. 'But you'll get fifty thousand pounds for each occasion we ask you to do this.'

It was staggering. Four hundred thousand pounds. Michael shrugged. 'Before or after I freeze it?'

'After. Listen, I know you probably have more questions – I can guess them. The next are probably "Do I get paid no matter what happens at your end? Can I destroy the contents in the freezer if I get asked questions?"' He looked at Michael smugly. 'Do I need to go on?'

'Of course I have more questions.'

'You don't need to worry about that, Michael. We'll take care of everything. I will deliver the first fifty thousand pounds to your flat at Wimbledon by the end of next week.'

As he stood in his treatment room, staring at Poppy's tri-coloured fur, Michael remembered how he had slowed his breathing, begging himself to take a moment to consider that this sort of money did not come anyone's way without some kind of terrible illegal activity. And unless he spoke up now, he was about to become part of it.

Instead he had said, 'Cheers,' and raised his glass.

That had been around three years ago. Now he owned his flat and had paid for Cathie's care a year in advance, so he hadn't minded when he'd received word there wouldn't be any more jobs, at least not for a while. He'd managed to work entirely with cash, meaning no one was any the wiser. Everyone loved cash these days, especially as it was so hard to come by with online banking, credit cards and so many other ways to digitally transfer money.

Life was good – no, better than good – in the rarefied atmosphere that was being debt free. His new relationship had deepened. Paul worked as a paramedic, so they had complementary skills and both understood that a bad day wasn't just long hours or no milk in the lunchroom but loss of life, holding someone's hand as they cried, or delivering bad news. The way Michael felt when Paul looked at him was intoxicating; to know that someone thought he was the most handsome and desirable person in the world was seductive, and Michael had helplessly begun to think about their relationship as long-term, maybe even forever. Paul had admitted the same. And their combined wages brought even greater freedom as much as security.

Michael dealt with Poppy, confirming with the hospital that he would cover her fees. Maybe he could set up a payment scheme for Nathan, or just waive it entirely.

Michael headed home, feeling in a very good place. He and Paul had just decided that it was time for a short holiday somewhere – Malta or Cyprus – away from the cold. Neither could stop grinning at each other over the dinner Michael had cooked.

When the doorbell rang, Michael held a hand in the air to stop Paul moving. 'I'll get it, finish your meal.'

He died wearing the new designer track pants and sweatshirt that Paul had bought for him last week. The knife whipped so cleanly and keenly across his throat that he did not feel the slash, but he felt the rush of hot blood, his severed carotid like an opened spigot that gushed and painted a wall, his door, even the ceiling, with his life.

Paul, still eating and watching the news on the nearby television, didn't hear anything. Looking over his shoulder a few moments later, he scrambled to the door where Michael was now on the floor, gasping his final breaths, and realised with horror that none of his brilliant emergency skills could save the life of the man he loved.

10

Harry pushed the sweet potato wedges towards Luca. 'Eat your carbs,' he urged.

Luca shook his head. 'Don't feel hungry.' It was true; the whole blackmail situation had taken his appetite away almost entirely.

'I don't care. Tomorrow the Gunners are coming for us.'

'I'm not scared of them.'

Harry smirked. 'You should be.'

'Our Luca's not intimidated by anyone, least of all Arsenal,' Harry's wife, Gina, said, coming back to the table with some freshly cut sourdough. She tousled Luca's hair. 'Now, eat your carbs. We want you in tip-top condition and frightening them with your golden boots.'

Luca grinned. 'How's Ally?'

'I'm letting her rest, sweetheart,' Gina said. 'Most mothers only carry one at a time, and I can tell you from watching other friends and relatives, when you're as close as she is, you just want that child – children – out. She's pretty exhausted.'

Luca frowned. 'She's been complaining of reflux, too.'

'Very normal at this stage,' Gina assured him. 'You have to stop worrying. Her body knows what it's doing, but yours won't if you don't eat all the good stuff to keep you strong and fuelled for game day.'

'You sound like my mum, Gina,' Luca teased, leaning over to kiss her cheek.

'I hope these babies come either early or late,' Harry said.

Gina chuckled. 'You can imagine what Tallis would say if his number-one boy wasn't playing.'

'I would play though,' Luca assured them. 'It's not that I don't put family first – Ally would understand. What we're trying to achieve this year feels impossible.'

'Are you saying you'd miss out on your babies being born if Ally goes into labour on a game day?' Gina asked.

Luca gave a shrug. 'We've talked about it, because we know full well that she could. They're due any day, and if we're still in the hunt for the FA Cup we could be playing that day. I couldn't let the team down.'

Gina looked at Harry, astonished. 'But others have taken time off, and even you took a holiday when we were pregnant that time.'

Luca didn't know about that, but felt it was wise not to ask; his friends did not have children and, given they were talking so openly about it, they'd obviously made their peace with that pain. He didn't want to inflame it.

Harry shook his head. 'It wasn't critical eight years ago, babe. We were nowhere near the Premier League. But we need Luca playing ninety minutes in every game right now. They've all but built the team around his boots.'

'I hate it when you talk like that.' Luca sighed. 'We're a team.'

'I don't say it publicly,' Harry said, 'but no one understands more than me what's expected of you. It's unfair to put so much pressure on you, but you handle it better than anyone I know. Better than

I did, when it felt like the weight of the whole team and all the fans' expectations were on my right foot. But you do have to eat,' he insisted and gave Luca a gentle cuff.

'Have you heard any more from the blackmailers?' Gina asked. At Harry's scowl, her expression turned from concerned to pinched. 'What?'

'He doesn't want to talk about that now.'

Luca shrugged. 'I don't mind. I've no secrets. We're family. Has Ally said anything more to you?' He reached for the sweet potato and grudgingly took a bite.

Gina shook her head. 'Not really. She's pretty much dried up on the topic. I mean we talk as girls do, but I'm getting sort of mixed messages.'

'What do you mean?'

'Well, she's angry, you know that. And I'd be lying if I didn't say she sort of blames you.'

'Gina!' Harry admonished.

'Let me finish,' she said. 'She blames you for being naïve and for being too kind. But she's determined to support you through this, because I think she trusts that detective you mentioned.'

'Hawksworth,' Luca said absently.

'Yes. She likes him and admits she found him reassuring, because he believes you. I think she's glad you've brought the police in. Makes her believe your story that you didn't, er . . . you know, participate.'

'It's not a story. It's what happened. Could have happened to any of our players. Could have happened to Harry. We've all heard the rumours of other players being blackmailed over the years.'

'Do you trust this guy to have your back?'

'I do. Detective Superintendent Hawksworth accepts what I've told him – so does his colleague, Kate. They made us feel . . . oh, I dunno, sort of safe that they were involved now.'

'So what are they doing to find these guys?' Harry asked, tucking in to the lean steak they'd recently barbecued on Luca's balcony.

'No idea. I think they want us to sit tight.'

'It's so frustrating,' Gina remarked, reaching for a potato wedge and dipping it into some mayonnaise. 'Mmm, these are good. I must tell Ally.'

'Should we make her up a plate or something?'

Gina covered Luca's wrist with her hand. 'Don't fuss. She'll eat when she feels like it. I did offer, but she couldn't face a meal. We can make her a smoothie if she still doesn't feel like eating in an hour or so, and I promise to pump it full of good stuff.'

They finished their meal, fully balanced as it needed to be for Luca with protein, carbs and salad.

'That was great, Gina,' Luca said, smiling at her. 'Thanks for coming over.'

'You're most welcome, sweetheart. Can't have our star player going hungry.'

'No chance,' Luca replied. 'Ally's just not up to cooking at the moment, but I would have rustled something up.'

'It's fine,' Gina said. 'I was free tonight and now I've had a lovely steak, so I should be thanking you. Anyway, you boys chat, I'll just clear up.'

'You don't have to do that, love, we'll—'

'No,' she said with a look of long-suffering at her husband. 'I am well acquainted with how this goes, Harry my darling. You'll start talking about the game and then nothing gets done. I'll have it cleared and cleaned in a jiffy. Anyway, I can go and keep Ally company. Go on, you two go outside. In another week or so it will be too cold.'

They did as they were told, moving to the balcony and closing the sliding doors behind them. 'Gina's amazing, Harry. She's across everything and so in control. I hope you know you're a lucky guy.'

'Yeah.' Harry sighed and couldn't quite make eye contact with Luca.

'You know what I mean.'

'I do, Luca. Don't go there.' Harry shook his head.

But he did. 'Is it over?'

'Yep,' Harry said tightly. 'Done and dusted.'

'Good. You're crazy, man. If Tallis knew—'

'He doesn't.'

Luca stared at his friend. 'Others may know.'

Harry shrugged. 'Well, if they do, it doesn't matter now – Gina knows.'

'She does?'

'Yeah. It hasn't been pretty, but Gina's too pragmatic to throw everything away. Unlike your wife, who would shatter everything for her principles, my wife puts her money, status, house, car, holidays, jewellery and what's left of her reputation as a soapie goddess well ahead of her standards. I don't judge either way,' he said, holding a hand up so Luca couldn't jump in to defend her or Ally. 'I'm simply making the point that Gina, perhaps because she's older, with more at stake with her business, chose not to risk us for principle. She's had my balls for breakfast behind closed doors, but the rest of the world wouldn't know.'

Luca moved the conversation on. 'And are you both okay? Money, I mean? Things must be pretty different without a big player salary.'

Harry nodded. 'Yes, mate. It was hard at first for Gina when I retired. I mean, she was used to . . . well, you know how it is, all the fawning and special privileges at clubs and restaurants, the clothes, the cash, the sponsorships.'

'But you've made some investments, plus her business is going great guns, you said.'

'We have and it is, according to Gina. I leave it to her. She's the business mind – I'm not part of the day-to-day running of her cleaning firm. I was just the number nine . . . until I wasn't. But I'm not moaning, my trainer salary is hardly rubbish. I'm earning my share.' Again he held up a hand. 'Don't start, Luca. I've reconciled with my playing days being over, and you did not cause my injury, which was already niggling, or my retirement . . . or even the accident. And that's what it was, mate.' Harry actually hugged him, kissing his head. 'I love you. And I don't say that to many blokes.'

They both laughed.

'No others actually,' he added, and they laughed louder. 'I'm happy in my new role, you must believe that.'

'I do. We all really enjoy being under your training.'

'You're a good lad. I'm proud of you standing up to these arseholes, whoever they are.'

'Thanks.'

'No, really. Someone had to, and I'm not surprised you're the one who's flipping them the finger. Even Gina agrees you'll be the reason they find themselves behind bars.'

'I hope so. I hope she's explaining that to my wife. The cost of my pride is taking its toll on me and Ally. I love her so much and I've not cheated once, not even been tempted, and yet it counts for nothing in the face of this. I have to get these sods and somehow clear my name in her mind.'

Harry nodded. 'I admire your commitment.'

'We took vows. So did you. I meant them.' Luca paused, looking his friend in the eye. 'Try harder, Harry. I mean it. You can't lose Gina.'

Harry grinned sadly. 'It's probably hard for you to understand because you're so starry-eyed about Ally, but somewhere we lost the passion, Gina and me.'

'Finding it in someone else's arms is hardly going to make your marriage stay strong.' Luca looked over his shoulder to check Gina was still well out of earshot.

'No. And I've resolved to make it work. I told you, that's over.'

'Well, I'm glad you're trying. I'm being selfish, really. I don't want our foursome breaking up.'

'That's not going to happen. Gina and I love you guys, and we're looking forward to babysitting and all that stuff, going on holidays together. I promise, you don't have to worry about us. We'll be okay. At work I have to keep my distance – you and I have talked about that – but when training's over and we're away from the club, like now, you're like my brother and I'll always be here for you, okay?' Harry stared intently at him.

Luca nodded. 'Okay.' Harry had been his rock since he'd first arrived at the club, had taught him plenty, encouraging him to be even more daring on the pitch, and even from the sidelines of a match he could feel Harry urging him on. He often wished they were still playing side by side. Those days were magic.

'So what do you think they're going to do with Eric?' Luca asked, changing the subject and the mood.

'I think they'll play him . . . but you didn't hear that from me.'

'Really? Good. I always feel safer when he's at my back, you know?'

Harry nodded. 'I used to have Tommy Kojo behind me years ago; he was brilliant.'

Their conversation, as Gina had predicted, drifted quickly into football, the club's prospects and strategies for how Luca was going to hold off Arsenal's sublime midfield defender, who would be wearing Luca like a second skin in the upcoming match.

In the bedroom, Ally and Gina were having a similarly close conversation.

'Oh, we're okay, Ally, don't worry.'

Ally slowly moved her legs to the side of the bed. 'I do though. You and Harry are our closest friends.' She hated the idea of the couple splitting up, even though Gina said things weren't that bad.

'Here, let me.' Gina helped haul Ally to her feet and they both laughed.

'I'm like a sack of potatoes at this time of the day. I feel twice as heavy. I think I'll take a quick shower.'

'Do you want me to leave you to it?'

'No, stay. I won't be long.'

Ally was used to dressing and undressing in front of others from her years on the television show. Without any shyness, she pulled off her sweatpants and T-shirt and moved into the bathroom.

'You look like you've been pumped up with more air – the babies have grown in the last few days.' Gina chuckled.

'I'm like a blimp!' Ally called from the huge ensuite as she pulled the handle on the shower. It was a double shower, as Luca loved being alongside her. It would be a while before they got back to that sort of fun, she thought.

'Ally, you look beautiful and you're going to be such a good mum.'

'Oh, I hope so!' she called out. 'Two at once, though. That idea still terrifies me.'

'We'll be here, you know that. We've got your back, and I'm longing to get my hands on those bubs. Harry and I will babysit all the time, I promise.'

Ally didn't really need a shower, so she was soaping up out of habit. She just wanted to revive herself, and the warm water calmed the babies, stopped them being so active together. There were times when it felt like they were rolling around in concert just trying to make her feel ill and tired.

Gina appeared at the doorway and leaned against it so they didn't have to shout over the water. She had her back to Ally. 'Everything's going to be fine.'

'This shitty blackmail stuff couldn't have come at a worse time.' Ally turned off the tap and grabbed a towel, wrapping it around her swollen torso.

'Listen,' Gina said, turning. 'Do you trust him?'

Ally nodded helplessly. 'I know in my heart that Luca doesn't look around, only at me. His fidelity is honestly all I've ever asked of him. I've never put any constraints on our marriage, just that one non-negotiable. I don't believe he would risk breaking his word – he knows it would cost him dearly, and I don't mean money.'

'Then reassure him, sweetheart, because that guy out there is hurting. He's so worried about losing you that everything's going to suffer and we don't need Luca Bruni off his game. I know it's not all about the Arrows, but we're all invested in the club's success. It's giving our husbands their incomes, and us our lifestyles, our futures. If Luca loses his mojo, everyone in the club suffers, including you and me.' Gina paused, handing Ally a smaller towel for her hair. 'Look, I know that's a lot on a young man's shoulders, but he chose it, he wants it and, let's face it, he's good at it. But that's only because he's got you at his back, loving him and supporting him. If he loses that, who knows what will happen?'

'He won't lose me,' Ally said, squeezing water out of her hair. 'It just scares me that we're bringing these two precious babies into our lives and they're going to be photographed and scrutinised and we'll be hounded even more. We can handle it, but we need to be strong together, you know? I don't want my children to have any of this swirling around them. I want them to have parents who are totally together, and to have their dad every day of their lives. I do love him madly . . . I'm just angry that anyone would do this to us.'

Gina smiled. 'Then tell him all of this so he knows it's not his fault and that you're staying right by his side. It'll do him a world of good, and it will make you feel stronger too.'

Ally hugged her friend. 'I know you're right.' She sighed. 'Thanks, Gina, for being the wise woman in my life.'

Gina pulled back to look Ally square in the eyes. 'We'll get past this crap together. It's happened to others. Luca's just the next victim on their list and an obvious target – that's the way to look at this. It could have been any of the top twenty football players in England.'

'They chose him because he's vulnerable.'

Gina frowned. 'What do you mean?'

Ally gave a shrug. 'He's about to become a father to twins, has the weight of three, possibly four trophies riding on his ambidextrous feet, all these massive sponsorship deals. They've done their homework, all right. For them it's the perfect time to strike, but what they don't know is that when Luca feels vulnerable, that's when he is usually at his bravest. His mother told me that years ago. He won't bend, Gina. He won't give in to them.'

'I'm glad to hear it. I hope we all get the chance to watch those fuckers get their arses caned in court.'

Ally laughed. 'Ooh, you potty mouth.' She put a protective hand around her belly. 'My babies can hear that.'

'I hate thieves of any kind, Ally.' Gina grinned. 'Makes my blood boil.'

'I can tell. Come on, let's join the boys.'

11

Jack raised his glass of sparkling water with a wedge of lemon. Across the table, Claudia Lenkas smiled lazily and followed suit with her gin and tonic, clinking his glass. She was a former sex worker and had been instrumental in helping him hunt down a monster responsible for a series of crimes that the media ultimately dubbed the 'beautiful deaths'.

'Mmm, this is nice.'

'You look tired, Claudia . . . and thin.'

'I work hard.' She grinned. 'You should try me.'

He smiled. 'How's Hanna?'

Claudia gave a sound of exasperation. 'Never have children, Jack, or at least don't have a daughter. They grow up much too fast. She's nearly eight, but going on eighteen.'

'Eight already?'

She nodded. 'She's great, of course. Defiant but smart. She won't make the same mistakes as her mother.'

'Her mother will see to it that her daughter never has to make the same choices.'

Claudia gave a sad smile. 'Thanks. She's doing well at school, popular too, which is helpful.'

'Hanna's more like you than you care to admit. And how are you doing?'

She swept out her hands, palms up. 'As you see. Older.'

'Life is better, though, right?'

'Thanks to you, yes.'

'So why do you look drawn?'

'Drawn?' She frowned.

'So pale,' he clarified.

'Ah, I thought you were talking about crayons. Drawn ... I must learn to use this word in this way.' She realised he was waiting for an answer. 'Probably pale because I wear a lot of make-up for my work every day, and I choose not to wear it when I'm with someone I like to be with.'

'Well, I'm glad we're eating. You need some fattening up.'

She laughed. 'This is a bit posh,' she said, looking around.

'I feel bad that I haven't done more. You helped us catch the bad guys,' he said, remembering the terrible case of a few years back when he'd met her. 'We couldn't have done it without you.'

'All those poor girls who died.'

Jack met her gaze. 'But you saved more from dying.'

He watched her pull herself out of a dip of melancholy. 'You haven't changed,' she said. 'Do men ever age?'

He laughed and the waiter arrived. 'What would you like, Claudia?' Jack asked.

She gave her order and he followed, opting for the grilled salmon, at which she pulled a face. After the waiter had gone, she shook her head. 'You need good red meat, Jack, for your loins.' She raised a fist at table height. 'How else are you going to—?'

'My loins are fine,' he assured her.

She gurgled a delighted laugh. 'I'm sure. Are they getting any action?'

'You know a gentleman never discusses such things,' he said, leaning on the final word to amuse her more.

'You're so . . . how do you say . . . conservative,' she said, her Polish accent as attractive as her looks. She was on the far side of her mid-thirties and Jack felt a private ripple of gladness that he'd got her away from the day-to-day business of catching the eye of men on the street. It had taken him seven months or so, but he'd finally helped set her up as front of house for a high-end brothel in the city. No more 'marks' for Claudia, and although she still worked nights, it meant she could take her daughter to school, meet her afterwards and afford a decent flat and a better life for them. Curiously, though, dark circles showed under her eyes, and while she no longer looked like she carried an invisible weight on her shoulders, she looked some-how burdened in a different way. He didn't want to press; it was likely connected with family. Claudia was very private and only shared when she chose to.

'Did you get back to Poland as you threatened?' Jack asked.

'Yes!' Claudia said, delighted. 'My daughter has met her grand-mother. We've made a pact to get back to Poland regularly and for my mother to visit us here each year. It's good for Hanna; I want her to learn about her home and culture. She's learning the language, even talking about spending the summers there.' She gave a happy sigh. 'Maybe we'll move back there . . . She can grow up a little Polish princess,' she said, laughing.

'I'm really pleased for you,' he said. 'And work's going well?'

'Actually, the fellow who owns it wants me to consider being the hostess at a new, glitzy restaurant and nightclub he's opening in Mayfair.'

'Wow.' Jack grinned. 'What do you think?'

'It will be longer hours, but it's also a lot more money. Hanna's used to me working, and she likes our neighbour and spending time with her. I wouldn't mind taking on the challenge for as long as I can survive it.'

'You should do it,' Jack encouraged.

She shrugged, as if to say she'd think about it.

A glance at the clock on the wall over the bar behind Claudia told him it was nearing seven-thirty. 'Do you mind if we talk shop?' Jack asked.

'I know we're not here because you're romancing me, handsome Jack.'

He gave a single nod, like someone being found out.

'It's okay. This feels nice. Not quite a date, but close enough. Ask away.'

His phone pinged to let him know a text message had arrived, but he deliberately ignored it to let Claudia know she had his full attention. He began to explain about the woman who'd visited Luca Bruni at Lark's Hill, pausing while their meals arrived and were set down. 'Bon appetit,' he said, picking up his knife and fork before continuing. He told her all that he knew. 'So I need to find her.'

Claudia had listened carefully. 'Well, the first thing is that despite what she told this fellow, she knew she wouldn't get into any trouble. It wasn't a normal job, right? It was a special one that she was specifically hired to carry out.'

'Right.'

'So she was lying to him about getting into trouble with the *promoters*.' She emphasised the final word in an ironic tone.

'It certainly wasn't Bentley who hired her.'

'But she convinced him otherwise, which means she's clever at acting, and if she lied about that, then she's capable of lying about all of it.'

'All true.'

'But,' Claudia said, chewing her forkful of steak, 'she could be a victim too.'

'How so?' Jack could guess but he liked talking things through.

She shrugged. 'These girls don't get much of a choice. They're given a job and expected to do it; presumably she's somehow on the payroll or the pimp has control. She could have been threatened . . . I don't know the word. You know when someone has something against you they can use?'

'Leverage?'

'Ah,' she said, pointing her fork his way. 'Yes, this is what I mean. Even if she worked independently, they could have threatened her.'

'Okay.'

Claudia gave a twist of her mouth as if to say, 'Who can know?' 'Either way, she's just doing the job that was briefed and what she's paid for.'

'She wouldn't have a conscience about this?'

Claudia leaned her cutlery against her plate. 'You must understand that this girl is owned in some way – money or that leverage – by someone. Women don't go into this line of work because they're wealthy. They may become so – though not many of them – but her conscience would not come into this arrangement. It's an exchange between her and the pimp or the employer. The mark, as she would think of him, is not relevant. Besides, she doesn't care about him – he's rich. He can afford it. They would have told her he would not be hurt, not even financially.'

Jack nodded. 'I get the impression she's not a regular girl from the streets.'

She shook her head. 'No. The girls I knew and worked alongside on the street might have looked and sounded confident – and they were, in their environment – but not this. No way. This girl is from somewhere else.'

'Where, do you think?'

She gave a dramatic shrug. 'She would be used to higher-end clients and would think of them as clients, not punters. She wouldn't feel weakened . . . you know, overwhelmed by the surrounds you describe, this fancy place.'

'Okay, so she's not intimidated by the job, you mean.'

'Yes. I'm not saying it's usual. I just mean she would have visited fancy hotels before; she has probably kept a wealthy man company for a night in a five-star hotel many times.'

'So, she works for an escort service?' Jack asked.

'If I had to bet my week's wages,' Claudia said. Her long fingers reached for the side serve of thick, evenly cut chips, and dipped her selected fried potato into the garlicky sauce she'd specifically ordered. She bit into it, her burgundy nail polish gleaming; one nail studded with three diamantes glittered. 'I would bet she came from an expensive escort service.'

'Any thoughts on which it might be?'

'Where is this bird place?'

'Lark's Hill? It's near Maidenhead, about thirty-five miles outside of London.'

'The most upmarket escort services are close to the city, and around W1. So she didn't get out to this place herself.'

'Why do you say that?'

Claudia pointed two fingers towards her eyes. 'Your country's CCTV nosiness. She would have been driven.'

'Taxi?'

She shook her head. 'I doubt it. A private car. They would have delivered her precisely to where she needed to be, on time and organised.'

'And driven her away, too?' Jack asked.

'I would think so. They wouldn't want to risk her lurking around even at a railway station or taxi rank. It makes her too easily noticed and later recognised – and more cameras to look at her.'

'Claudia, have you heard any rumours at all about this sort of set-up?'

She picked up her cutlery and stared at him. 'I have to be careful, Jack.'

'I know.' He held her gaze.

Claudia sighed. 'Not recently.'

'How far back?'

She cut into the remaining morsels on her plate. 'Early last year. But nothing to do with football. It was a golfer.' Claudia began chewing. She swallowed and put the final mouthful neatly into her mouth. Her plate was clean; no waste.

'Okay. Well, will you call me if you learn anything?' he asked, writing his private number on a piece of paper he pulled from a pocket. He had never given it to her before. 'That's not a work number.'

She cut him a wicked smile and he laughed in return.

'It will probably reach voicemail, but if someone else finds it, it gives nothing away.'

She nodded her thanks.

'Dessert?' he asked.

'No. I need to be careful these days. How was your dull salmon?'

'Actually, quite delicious. Coffee, then?'

'Coffee, yes, and no more shop talk. I'm going to the bathroom and when I get back and my strong coffee with milk is here, I want you to tell me how good I look for my age.'

He laughed. 'That won't be hard.'

'Sorry about the wig,' Kate said, pulling off the chocolate-coloured, short bob and allowing her golden hair, dark like cooked honey, to topple out. She immediately wound it up and held it in place with a hair claw.

'Kate, these are our buddies, Harry and Gina Taylor. You can speak freely in front of them.'

'Hi, I'm Detective Inspector Kate Carter.' She nodded at the strangers. 'Harry, nice to meet you,' she said, noticing his limp as he stepped forward to shake hands. She raised a hand in the direction of the pretty auburn-haired woman pouring boiling water into a teapot behind the kitchen bench.

'Hello,' Gina said, holding up a mug. 'Fancy a cuppa?'

Kate shook her head. 'Thank you, but I'm not staying. You've explained how careful we're being?' she said to Luca.

'Yes, they know everything – we updated them over dinner tonight. Don't worry, they're family.'

'Good.' Kate smiled. 'I didn't mean to interrupt your evening, everyone, but I just wanted to bring you up to speed.' Luca nodded. 'A full operation has been set up at Scotland Yard to investigate the blackmail. We're keeping the ops team very small for reasons of security; Jack or I have worked with all the people chosen, so everyone's reliable.'

'Great. What happens next?' Luca asked.

'Well, we do what we do. You sit tight. I presume you've heard no more from the blackmailer?'

He shook his head. 'Not a peep, but we've still got a few days. Do you think you can crack it open by then?'

Kate didn't but she gave a reassuring grin. 'We're working hard and fast.'

'So what are you actually doing?' Harry chipped in. 'I mean, where are you beginning to look?'

It was a fair enough question, Kate thought, but she wasn't going to give much away. 'I'm really sorry, but I'm not at liberty to explain exactly what the ops team is chasing down. I want to assure you, though, that we'll leave no stone unturned.' Her sympathetic gaze took them all in, asking for their patience.

'It's just that we've got some vital matches coming up and Luca's our key striker,' Harry continued. 'We need his head in the game, not worrying about—'

'I realise that, Mr Taylor,' she began gently, trying in this moment to be Jack and not Kate, who might bristle at being told the obvious. 'We're very sensitive to Luca's responsibilities for the Arrows, and the pressures on the whole team, yourself included. Hopefully none of the others know of it?'

Luca shook his head; so did Harry.

'So it's about keeping Luca informed and, more importantly, keeping him and Ally confident that we're across everything.'

Gina put a tray on the table with the teapot, mugs, milk and sugar. She moved to put an arm around Ally. 'We'll just let it finish brewing. So do we know any more, other than what Luca's told us?'

'I can tell you that interviews have begun with key people. We're building a clear picture of Luca's life and the people around him, and moving out from there.' Before any of them could jump in, Kate continued. 'Lark's Hill, of course, is taking up our attention, and we'll begin interviews at the hotel from tomorrow.'

'You mean with the staff?' Ally asked.

Kate nodded. 'Yes, particularly with security. Mercifully they have cameras outside, so we'll be poring over all footage to see every newcomer who enters and exits the building. Inside, they don't have cameras, for the obvious reason that a lot of their guests would claim invasion of privacy. Look, I know you want to know as much as possible, but we are deliberately keeping this all very tightly held to protect you both. The less we reveal, the better, but I came here to reassure you that there's plenty in motion.'

'What about this woman? Do we know anything about her?' Gina asked.

Kate shook her head, though she wouldn't have told them even if Ops did know something. 'Not yet.'

'Nothing?' Gina replied, sounding deeply offended. 'It's been days.'

'To be fair, it's been two days, Mrs Taylor. And in that time we've set up a full operation.'

'But she's the linchpin to this blackmailer. Find her, find them,' Gina said, as if it were as simple as that.

Kate remained calm, channelling Jack. She wished he had come along to watch her perform precisely how he'd want her to; he'd be proud. 'You're right, of course,' she said, trying to smooth the woman's feathers, but then Kate poked through the Jack façade. 'That's why we're following a loose lead,' she said. It was a lie and she didn't mean to say it, but in the past she'd discovered that throwing out a hollow line as bait could often deliver unexpected rewards. She watched their faces.

'What do you mean?' It was Harry who grabbed at it first. 'What sort of lead? About the woman?'

She nodded. 'I can't say anything else.'

'There you go, Luca,' Gina said. 'They've probably found her on CCTV. We're going to get this bitch.' She gave Ally's shoulder a squeeze. 'That's good news, Detective Carter. Thank you.'

'Anyway, I'll be on my way. Do you need anything, Luca? Ally?'

'Just make it end,' Ally remarked, closing her eyes.

Kate nodded. 'Er, Luca, will you see me out?' He obliged and stood. 'Goodnight, everyone.'

She watched Gina kneel to pour the tea and Harry come and sit next to Ally; the Brunis had good support. She mentioned it at the door.

'Yeah. Harry's like a big brother to me and Ally's known Gina a long time from the TV show. Gina and Harry introduced us to each other, actually. I had just arrived at the Arrows and Ally had been on the show with Gina, and although she'd been out with a couple of footballers, it hadn't gone anywhere.'

'And then you came along.' Kate smiled.

'Yeah, I remember Harry pointing her out when I accompanied him once down to the studios to pick up Gina. I was infatuated with Ally from the moment I saw her. He said he'd set us up, and we've been tight ever since.'

'That's nice. I don't have any friends like that,' she admitted, although Jack came to mind. 'And what happened to Harry to end his career?'

'You don't know?'

Kate shook her head: another lie.

'Long story short, he had a bad injury on the pitch and he retired afterwards – I mean, he was due to retire soon anyway, but it came a few months earlier than he expected.'

'He's now one of the new trainers . . . coaches, right? I've seen his name on the staff list.'

'Yeah. He works with us strikers and some of the midfielders. He'll be a senior coach within a year or two, and a head coach within three or four, I reckon.'

'That good, eh?'

'He'll be amazing, not that I want him to leave the Arrows. But his future is really positive.'

'And how long has Gina known Ally? They look close.'

'They're inseparable. Gina took Ally under her wing and as Harry's been a brother to me, she's a big sister to Ally. It's why she's taking this whole thing a bit personally. I hope she didn't sound too angry?'

Kate shook her head. 'Just protective. I'd be disappointed if your close friends didn't feel like that. Don't we all love someone to have our back? I'm glad you've both got people around you.' She squeezed his wrist. It probably wasn't appropriate, but she liked him, and wanted him to stay strong. 'Good luck for the game. Feeling ready?'

'Always,' he said, but his smile was modest. She returned it, turning to leave. 'Kate, I've remembered something else.'

She swung back, her expression full of urgent enquiry. 'Yes?'

'The tattoo,' Luca said, his forehead wrinkling. 'I told you it was a heart.'

She nodded, holding her breath.

'But I realise now it was a heart featuring the French flag,' he continued. 'Here, on her arm.' He gestured at his own.

Kate blinked with surprise. She almost didn't want to believe him. This was huge. 'You're sure?'

'Yeah, I am. Could be anything though, right? Maybe she just loves France.'

'Had a great love affair in Paris . . .'

'Loves croissants . . .' At least he smiled, even if it was sad.

'Or she might just be French,' Kate said. 'You did say she had an accent. It's something, Luca. We'll take every clue we can, no matter how small.'

'Well, I've got one more.'

'You're kidding.'

'I think her name begins with F.'

'What makes you say that?' she asked, trying to sound calm and professional, even though she was feeling a little wild-eyed.

'That night was a blur, but I've been trying so hard to remember it in detail. It only came to me this morning at training when the coach was moving us through the game plan. He likes to give us little stories to remind us of moves, and he called this particular one "Fifi" because he'd nicknamed it the "French Maid".'

She knew this was going somewhere; she just had to be patient. 'Okay.'

'When I answered the door, this girl said, "Good evening, sir, I'm . . . ,"' and Luca started saying a name that began with F before cutting it off. 'And then she stopped, giving me a smile, and looked down at her badge.' He shook his head.

'So she *was* wearing one.'

He nodded. 'Clear as day now. I can't believe I couldn't remember that. But yes. And the really stupid thing is that I read the badge and said it with her – "Sandy" – and that made her laugh. But in that moment, I can now clearly remember my mind tripping, telling me something, but I ignored it. I think she nearly told me her real name, stopping herself just in time. Just a little stumble and then she came into the room with her tray.'

Kate beamed. 'This is brilliant, Luca. So now we have the name Sandy, though that might not be her real name, and a France tattoo, and her name may begin with F.' She might as well push. 'Nothing else?'

He shrugged. 'No. Unless a feeling counts?' He gazed at her awkwardly, and she was struck by just how young he was. He still looked like a boy and he was about to have twins, not to mention the thousands of fans who counted on his feet to strike gold every few days. All it would take was a missed penalty or even a lost opportunity to get them howling for blood. A few bad games on the trot would get tongues wagging in the pub that he might have been a flash in the pan. In the meantime, the media hung around him and his wife like hungry piranha, and now he was dealing with a criminal situation and enormous pressure. A lot for a young man to shoulder. So many at his age were getting pissed every Friday and Saturday night with little responsibility. She had a fresh respect for these young athletes, who might be paid eye-watering fortunes but were

handling the kind of pressure that most people likely would
never fathom.

'Feelings are important in our line of work, Luca. Instinct plays
a big part. What was it?'

'I hope I'm not making this up, but I think she hesitated.'

'When?'

'Before coming into the room.'

'Why do you think that?'

'I think maybe in that moment she was weighing up whether to
go ahead with the plan.'

'Okay, Luca. I appreciate it. You'd better get back inside and
get an early night.'

He nodded. 'Will you be watching tomorrow?'

'Of course.' She grinned. 'Miss an Arrows game? You must be
joking,' she said, using an ironic tone to make him smile, given he
likely could tell she'd never watched an entire match in her life.
'Does anyone know at the club about the blackmail?'

'Just Harry, and perhaps Mr Tallis. My phone went off not so
long ago.' Luca thumbed over his shoulder. 'I didn't take the call
because we were talking, but it was him. I'll call him back in a
minute.'

'Jack was speaking to him today.'

'Ah, well, just those two at this stage, then.'

'Keep it that way,' Kate said sternly. 'Luca, can you keep what
you've just told me about the girl between us? Don't say anything,
even to your closest folk.'

'You don't trust them?' He sounded surprised.

'It's not that. I just know from experience that the moment
something is shared, it's no longer protected information. Harry
could make a vague remark to someone at the club. Gina could
say something – even supportive – to Ally in front of other people.
Ally might mention something vague to her hairdresser. It's all very

innocent, but it has the potential to spark and catch fire from there, and suddenly you're reading about it in the media.'

'Well, I have no intention of discussing that woman any further with Ally. She just about blows up at any mention.'

'Thank you. Keep it to yourself for a few more days and give us a chance to work this out. And if you have any more flashes of recall, you have my personal number. Anytime, Luca. Okay?'

He nodded.

'Good luck tomorrow. Kick a bag of goals.'

Kate left, eager to see what knowledge the ops team had acquired on their opening day and to pass on Luca's revelations. It was just past eight. Before she pulled her gloves on, she rang Jack. The smooth tone of his voicemail message answered. She had his personal number too, but in a moment of sensibility decided she wouldn't ring it. He was seeing Claudia this evening, and it probably wasn't appropriate to disturb him. This could wait.

She walked to Kew Gardens Station, part of the District line that moved overground on its way into London. Using her warrant card, she pushed past the turnstiles and headed upstairs onto the breeze platform. It was dark, with only three others and herself waiting, stomping their feet to stave off the cold. Even so, she was reminded of how much she liked these late Victorian stations; this had to be one of the few remaining on the North London line. She shivered, thinking about Luca's game tomorrow, how his coach would have to keep him focused; presumably Jack would have signed off on briefing the head coach, especially as Harry Taylor was in the know.

She considered the Taylors. Gina was a bit aggressive, but Kate could see she was being protective of her pregnant best friend. She wondered if the Taylors had children. Gina was in good shape and dressed expensively, but then she was an ex-soapie star and married to a former star athlete – she could hardly dress as a slob.

She seemed like the ringleader of the quartet. Harry was a bit quieter – broody even – though he was the fastest to jump in and make the first demand.

She gave a groan at how frozen her toes felt, despite her boots, and wished she'd worn the ones with fur inside. The next train was still minutes away. Impatient as always, she pulled out her phone again and, using her teeth, pulled off her gloves. She'd text him instead. *Luca remembered something. The girl has a tattoo of a heart in striped red, blue, white like the French flag. Name might begin with F.*

Claudia returned from the ladies' room, smiling seductively. It wasn't deliberate, Jack knew; it was just her smile . . . a little lazy, but added to her slightly hooded, smoke-eyed gaze, it was very effective.

'Have I told you how good you look for your age?'

She smirked, sinking into her seat in the booth. 'Now what?' she asked.

The coffee had arrived just seconds before. Jack answered her question with one of his own, prompted by Kate's text. 'Do you know any French escorts?'

'Wow, Jack, you know how to chat a girl up.'

He gave her a pleading look.

'Yes, of course, plenty of French girls working in London. I don't know them all, don't claim to know any of them,' she said, making inverted commas over the word "know".

'Come on, Claudia. Help me, please? Look, this woman, whoever she is, is just a small cog in a bigger machine. I want the machine, not that cog.'

'Not you, maybe, but your bosses will. They'll want to clap everyone behind bars and make a big, how do you say, song and dance with the media to show how clever they are.' She took a swig of her coffee. 'You know, Jack, this girl is probably newly arrived, maybe new to the game, and she was probably pressured by her pimp, or blackmailed herself. She could even have been trafficked, or have a child or two she's supporting.'

'I hear you and I understand,' he said gently, not disagreeing with her but privately believing this girl was making her own cunning decisions. 'I just need to know what she knows.'

Claudia wasn't smiling any more. 'What if it gets her killed? They've been chasing big money, Jack.'

'How do you know that?'

'The golfer, for a start. We hear things, you know that. You say it's a crime ring of some sort? Well, they don't bother with small gains. There's going to be big amounts at stake. They could snuff her out simply for knowing what she knows, and get another girl for the next time.'

Jack matched her serious tone. 'Yes, they could.'

'You can't protect her.'

'No, but you can,' he said, and waited for the inevitable roll of Claudia's eyes. 'Just ask around your own circles,' he cajoled.

She shook her head very slowly, almost imperceptibly, as though she couldn't believe he was asking this of her. She wasn't refusing him though.

'She has a heart tattoo, here on her arm,' he gestured. 'And we think it denotes the French flag.' He drew three vertical stripes on the table as though he was drawing the three colours. 'Blue, white and red.'

'That's it?'

'We think her name might begin with F.'

'You're going to owe me a lot more dinners, *Mr Jack*.'

'Gladly.'

She finally smiled again. 'You need to mean that.'

'Cross my heart,' he said, drawing two different lines on his chest. 'All right.' She nodded. 'I'll ask.'

12

It was down to business this morning, and the ops room sounded hushed as one by one the team arrived, took off coats, made a cuppa and fired up computers.

Joan was at Jack's doorway, passing on a message, waggling a finger. 'You'll need to sign that form for me before lunchtime.'

'Will do. They're quiet in there.' He frowned. Were they working as hard as he needed them to?

'They're listening to the live reports about that murdered vet.'

Jack shook his head. 'How does that happen in Wimbledon?' He almost wished he could be assigned to that case, but he was busy enough as it was.

Kate arrived. 'Ugh, have you watched the BBC reports of that killing in Wimbledon?'

'We were just talking about it,' Joan said. 'Lunchtime, Jack. Don't forget,' she said, with a raised eyebrow of warning before she left.

'That's like a gangster killing, don't you think?' Kate continued.

Jack nodded. 'Mmm, the Met will be buzzing with that.'

'Handsome guy, too.'

'Your sort?'

'Don't be tacky, Jack. Anyway, he's gay. His poor partner was sobbing so much, he could barely speak; it was cruel to put him in front of the camera. You got my text?'

'I did. Well done.'

'I'm hoping it doesn't lead us on a wild goose chase, but it's something, isn't it?'

'It is. I've asked Claudia to see if she can find out more.'

'I thought you might. How is she? I know you're fond of her.'

'I am. She's a strong, brave woman ... Life's dealt her some blows, but she never complains and she risked so much to help us on the Panther operation. She's understandably unhappy that I'm leaning on her, but otherwise her life seems to be in a good place right now.'

Kate smiled. 'Right, come on. What do you want to focus on? It's game day at Huxley, so I doubt any of us will be welcome.'

'Let's hope they win, because I suspect they'll be chatty. Lark's Hill then?'

'That's what I was thinking. I sent the team a message last night. Make a mention of how good they look, will you?'

He stood and followed Kate into the ops room, his curiosity piqued. Ari flicked off the TV and everyone fell quiet.

'Morning, everyone.' Jack was met by a chorus of replies. 'What a smart-looking bunch of detectives. I presume this is for your visit to Lark's Hill?'

They shared a round of smiles.

'You all look great – just like important guests. Right, let's get to it. Kate, do you want to kick us off?'

She briefed the team on all the latest news from Bruni.

'He seems to be responding to you well, Kate, so I think you should be our conduit for the Brunis.'

'I met the friends. Former captain Harry Taylor and his wife, Gina. They're a tight foursome; the older couple are super protective.'

'So no hard feelings, clearly?' Ari piped up.

'What do you mean?' Kate frowned.

Ari looked around, seemed to realise he was dealing with mostly football Luddites and explained. 'So he doesn't subscribe to the notion that his catastrophic injury was Bruni's fault? Half the fans would dispute that.'

'Not according to Roger Tallis,' Jack offered. 'I spoke to him about it.'

'I believe it too. One of those freak things,' Ari said. 'I've watched that accident in slow motion, and Bruni doesn't make the original contact – it's the guy from the other team who creates the foul on Bruni, who then falls awkwardly on Taylor. But in spite of that, a lot of people blamed Bruni; I mean, he's won their trust and faith since, but it was hard on him. The press helped to stir up some resentment.'

'How long ago was this?' Kate asked.

Ari didn't hesitate. 'Two seasons back, about ten games out, and they were in their first exciting year of having left the Football League Championship.' At Kate's blank stare, he continued. 'First Division in old money,' he qualified. At her frown, he added, 'They were in the Premier League when this went down.'

Jack could see where everyone's minds were collectively shifting. 'It's good to question this, whether there's motive there, but Tallis is confident there's no friction between these two guys.'

Ari shrugged. 'Taylor was due to retire anyway.'

'Doesn't that make it worse?' Sarah asked. All eyes turned her way. 'I don't pretend to know anything about football, but don't elite players all want to go out in a blaze of glory?'

'As opposed to announcing retirement from the injured side-lines?' Kate looked thoughtful.

'Of course,' Ari said. 'But life's not always neat. And football doesn't go to plan.' He looked around and Jack saw his youth showing in his lack of empathy. It wasn't malicious; Ari was simply stating a fact of life, but the fifteen years that separated them meant that Jack could take a more sympathetic approach and imagine himself in Taylor's boots.

'No, but he was a beloved and popular captain whose stellar play, excellent marshalling and right foot helped take that team from near invisibility to the contender it is right now. He was a local hero,' Jack said.

Ari shrugged. 'He still is. Some of those supporters still wear shirts with his name on.'

'Okay.' Jack nodded at Kate. 'So maybe he does have motive.'

Kate took the whiteboard marker and added Harry's name to the list of potential blackmailers. 'I didn't sense anything off when I was with them. I know I wasn't with the Taylors that long, but there's no doubting the close ties between Harry and Luca. It's like a tangible spirit between them.'

Jack nodded. 'Okay, Kate, the tattoo.'

She explained to the group. 'So we're now looking for a girl, potentially from a high-end escort agency, who may be French and whose name might begin with F. We know she's young – around twenty-two, Luca guessed. Dark hair.' Kate waved a hand horizontally at her shoulder to signify the hair's length.

'Could have been a wig,' Sarah offered. 'I'll start looking through the network and see if anyone catches my attention,' she said.

'Meanwhile,' Jack added, 'I've been in touch with a contact from a previous case we worked on. She now fronts a Mayfair escort service and is putting some feelers out for me.' He couldn't help but catch the sly glance Kate cut his way and wished he'd phrased that better. He cleared his throat and moved on. 'And as I mentioned, Roger Tallis wondered whether this has more to do with the team – stalling their success by distracting their star player – as opposed to it being a genuine personal attack.' He looked around at the expressions pondering this notion. 'It's a theory we must explore, although the clock is ticking.' He saw Sarah's expression had become deeply thoughtful. 'Sarah?'

'Er . . .' she began, looking surprised that he'd picked her out for comment. 'I was just thinking that it doesn't add up.'

'What doesn't?' Jack encouraged.

'Well, the history of these blackmail events, according to the agent group, is that it is just that . . . targeted to a specific victim for monetary gain. The blackmailers disappear the moment the cash is provided. I spoke to George Shaw and he confirmed that to the best of his knowledge there's been no second bites. So the blackmailers kept their word, including destroying the semen, as far as they could trust the video evidence. That suggests that it's about who is the most vulnerable for extortion; these guys pick someone with wads of money to spare, and then put as much distance between themselves and the victim as they can.'

Jack wanted to cheer. She'd thought through the problem with that theory in a heartbeat. He certainly agreed with her reasoning.

'A conundrum,' Kate offered. 'We'll have to follow both pathways.'

'And there's not even an inkling, Sarah, on who might be behind the other cases?' Jack pressed. 'A rumour?'

She shook her head. 'All very clinical, invisible and swift. Also,' she added, 'well spaced out, though not consistent. Sometimes six weeks, sometimes eight apart, sometimes two.'

'No rhythm,' Jack said, thinking aloud.

'No. And I think that points to the cunning of the blackmailers. By not having any sort of regularity or even a particular sport for their hunting ground, it meant no one ever thought it would happen to them. When it did, it was a shock and, in my opinion, they probably paid up just to be rid of the nuisance and potential embarrassment.'

'How have the blackmailers collected the money?' Kate asked.

'The usual . . . an overseas account. No one cared, I gather. They just paid and wanted to forget the whole thing.'

'Has Luca received details of how to make the payment, even if he wanted to?' Jack asked, turning to Kate.

'Not yet,' she replied.

Jack met Sarah's gaze. Yes, they were definitely thinking the same thing.

'Anything else yet?' His phone pinged. He realised it was his private phone and dragged it out, frowning. *Call me*, the message said. 'Ari, anything from the club staff?'

'The head of security will not be available until later in the week. I managed to talk with the canteen staff, the online team and the gang who sell tickets at the gate. Nat spoke with all the shop staff. So far no red flags. We've got the admin, executive, fitness and coaching teams to go, but with today a game day, that'll be tomorrow.'

'Right. Good luck today at Lark's Hill. Kate, let me know how you go.'

'Okay, everyone, let's go,' Kate said. 'Joan's organised a car – who feels like taking the wheel to Maidenhead? Matt?'

'Sure,' he said, eager to have a star role.

'Sarah, a quick word,' Jack said. She nodded and followed him to his office while the others pulled on coats and made their departure.

He gestured to a chair and took the one behind his desk. 'Are we thinking the same thing, Sarah?'

'Probably, sir.' She found a rare grin of confidence.

'Why don't you tell me?'

'I don't believe we're dealing with the same blackmailer as the previous athletes.'

He smiled, relieved to have his own suspicions supported. 'I agree. Why do you think that?'

'The timeline for starters. A week to gather the money? I've checked with the agents, who confided that it was more like two days in the other cases.'

'Okay.' That was a good surprise.

'Each of the agents was equally reluctant to share . . . why are all football agents male?'

'I'm sure they will feel outnumbered soon enough. Look at us – not by design, but we're pretty much balanced in the op.'

'If you include Joan, it makes it weighted towards us women,' Sarah said, blinking.

'There you are. If it can happen in a major op, it can happen in sports agenting. What else?' he said, getting them back on track. In past ops, Sarah would never have let them stray, but she'd started the wandering and it was a genuine sign of her maturing; she was beating her shy, slightly obsessive nature.

'There are no specific instructions for payment yet from the Bruni blackmailer.'

He sat back, his chair squeaking from the sudden movement. 'It's only been a couple of days, though.'

She lost no momentum. 'I don't have the other notes for forensics to look over, unfortunately, so we can't compare the ransom letters, but I managed to find out from these other agents – unhappy as they were to give me the information – that a clear deadline for payment was posed in each one.'

Jack frowned. 'Were all of those letters destroyed?'

'So they assured me. Annoying. I did try several ways around to see if I could get a sniff that perhaps a couple had kept them in their safes or just for posterity. But it seems they shared a collective desire to be rid of the thing. A lot were burned, I'm told.'

'All right, tell me more.'

'I don't subscribe to the team disruption theory. I feel this is wholly targeted at Bruni.' She paused to let that land before adding, 'And I would hazard that it's extremely personal.'

'I need you to support that with some hard facts, Sarah.' Jack wanted to say, *Feelings aren't evidence.* But she already knew that and wouldn't be airing a hunch without something more substantial to back it.

'It's the tone of the letter.'

That was also a surprise. Unexpected and intriguing. He leaned forward, regarding her. 'Are the others that different?'

'I can't say for a fact, sir, because as I said, I haven't seen them, but a few of the agents have told me what they recall. They all support the same memory. The notes were short and aggressive. They were far from friendly and left them in no doubt of the threat. This note to Mr Bruni, though, is almost chatty. I wouldn't call it playful, but it's not so far off that. Almost like a cat teasing a mouse.'

'Enjoying it, you mean?'

'No, sir. The previous ones had no care factor. *Do this or we'll do that.* Like they were saying, *We don't care. We'll find a new target and leave you a smoking ruin,* kind of thing. This one is just a fraction more conversational – in its length, its explanation, the way it urges Bruni to take the note and potential consequences seriously.' She frowned as though considering whether her next concern carried sufficient weight. He watched her blink and presumably decide that it did. 'And one more thing stands out for me.'

'Yes?'

'They name Ally. If this is the same person or persons who threatened the others, then I think this note would have followed suit; they'd know those notes had worked and should continue to work. The previous wording was "We'll send your girlfriend the photo" or "We'll send your wife the picture".'

'Luca and Ally are very well known as a duo. They could easily know her name.'

Sarah shrugged. 'Even so. Bruni's note feels very personal because of the double reference to Ally, its length and the amount of time that's being extended.'

Jack sat back in his chair. 'So, Sarah, what is your conclusion?'

Sarah eyed him through her owl glasses with a hard stare. 'There are two different perpetrators.'

Jack nodded. 'I agree.'

'And I'm guessing now, sir, but this blackmailer is most likely known to the Brunis,' she said, her voice blunt.

'Because of the reference to Ally?'

She nodded. 'That, but also because of the use of the word "I". The previous ones, to the best of the various agents' memories, used "we". Now, whether the former situations were perpetrated by one or more people, that gave them some distance. But this blackmailer, whether they mean to or not, is taking ownership of the crime.'

Jack nodded, privately impressed by her observations. 'Do you think it's Harry Taylor?'

Sarah twisted her features into a look of uncertainty. 'He's an obvious choice – perhaps too obvious. But yes, motive does exist, although he's taken his time to come to this plan. His anger must simmer gently, if it is him.'

'He's a calm bloke, for sure. Look into him.'

'I will.'

'Any other suspicions?'

'Security at the hotel has to be in on it, wouldn't you say?' Sarah was speaking confidently now.

'Kate will sniff that out. So, to clarify, you think we have a copycat bribery scheme underway.'

'Well, that, or the money is irrelevant, sir, and someone is simply using it as a cover to bring down Luca Bruni.'

Jack blinked in surprise as she left. Sarah had opened up a new pathway of thought in his mind.

13

Lark's Hill was like a small crown on the head of a ridge of the Chiltern Hills in South Buckinghamshire. The property sloped down to the banks of the River Thames, and a little online digging had told Kate that the mansion had been built in the mid-seventeenth century. It had been home to many aristocrats and even royalty in its time. Today it was a listed building, protected by the government, and was leased to a five-star hotel.

Kate was surprised to see ramblers and curious members of the public roaming around its gardens, and she discovered the building itself was open on certain days for visitors as a tourist attraction. The rest of the time it functioned as a private retreat for paying guests.

Lark's Hill management, though understandably nervous, were keen to cooperate with the police, and Kate's team were met by the front of house manager, George Kalis. His charming manner and perfect English were spiced with a soft European accent.

'I was born in Poland to Dutch and Lithuanian parents,' he explained. 'I speak about six languages.'

'Impressive,' Kate said. She turned away from the tall man with close-cropped blond hair to take in the surrounds, and helplessly sighed. 'Wow. How beautiful this is.'

They arrived onto the gravel drive, doors were opened for them and apart from the lack of suitcases, the four detectives looked like two couples arriving for a weekend of indulgence. George noted this, murmuring, 'Thank you for looking the part. The staff know you're coming but I don't want to alarm any guests.'

'Actually, we always dress like this,' Kate whispered with a grin.

'Come into the warmth,' he said, and led them through the Italianate portico, past a colonnaded walk and into a massive wood-panelled room with a huge stone fireplace that was burning merrily. Small groups of armchairs and tables sat near arched mullioned windows, where people were taking pots of coffee. Velvet sofas were positioned around the main fireplace, and yet more faced the main reception and the glorious staircase that led up to the accommodation. These sofas were separated by elegant tables bearing softly lit lamps and decorative pieces of china or bronzes.

It was as though she'd stepped into a grand but inviting drawing room of an old-world aristocrat. Cigars and pipes would not look out of place. However, feminine touches lightened the effect: Corinthian-style columns and swags of carved flowers, as well as two enormous oil paintings of beautiful women – former residents, no doubt. Small dogs seemed welcome, as at least two guests had brought theirs. The colours were rich, muted, regal.

'Yes, George,' she sighed. 'I could live here.'

He smiled his pleasure at her comment and offered them all refreshments. 'As we offer every new guest on arrival, how about some piping hot coffee after your journey? And then we can discuss how to proceed?'

The four members of Operation Stonecrop murmured their gratitude and made themselves comfortable, sinking into soft sofas stuffed with feathers and plumped with extra cushions. The coffee soon arrived in silver pots, accompanied by tiny almond biscuits, no doubt made in the famed kitchen.

'Just relax and enjoy,' George urged. 'Soon enough, I will come and fetch Mr and Mrs Smith,' he said, taking in Kate and Ari with a smile. 'We'll be heading up to your room, Blackbird'—this was the room that Luca had stayed in when the incident occurred—'after a peek into rooms you might enjoy,' he said pointedly, and Kate was grateful that he was making sure to show them all the key spaces. 'My colleague will fetch Mr and Mrs Johnson,' he went on, looking at Nat and Matt, 'for a tour first of the spa,' which was code for the younger detectives beginning their interviews with the beauty salon, swimming pool and spa people.

'Lovely,' Kate said and settled in to enjoy her coffee and biscuits as George withdrew.

'You all got that? Ari and I will go with George and take a look upstairs, while you interview the salon and fitness staff. Then we'll join you back of house and we can all work through the kitchen and auxiliary staff.'

Everyone nodded.

'Take notes, trust nothing to memory,' she reminded them. All of this was said conversationally, with frequent smiles so, to all intents, the quartet looked like they were on a mini break together. 'Okay, drink up and let's begin,' she finally said. 'Mmm, good coffee. The boss would be pleased.'

George seemed to have timed himself perfectly, arriving in that moment. 'Ready? This is Alexis, who will take Mr and Mrs Johnson for a tour of the spa and fitness areas.'

Nat and Matt stood and followed Alexis across magnificent Persian rugs to a small doorway.

'And if you'd like to follow me, Mr and Mrs Smith.' George gestured with a welcoming hand pointing towards the staircase.

'Your bags have already been sent up,' he said loud enough for anyone nearby in the alcoves, darkened by velvet drapes and the overcast day outside, to hear. 'You're going to love Blackbird,' George continued. 'Is it a special occasion?'

'Our anniversary,' Ari chimed in, giving Kate a cheeky wink.

'You may like to see our French dining room, as it is known.'

'Why not?' Kate said.

'It's so called because the rococo panelling came from a chateau near Paris, which King Louis XV and his mistress Madame de Pompadour used as a hunting lodge and private place to rendez-vous.' George grinned. 'It was purchased and installed at Lark's Hill around 1901,' he said, flinging open the doors to a room that made Kate gasp as she stepped inside. It was a vast room with grand, gilded panels and tall gilt-framed mirrors that reflected the light coming through the enormous arched windows.

'I've brought you in here,' George said, his tone immediately less obsequious now they were alone, 'because this is where we held the main promotion for Bentley on the night of the alleged incident.'

'Right,' Kate said, her own tone indicating they were down to business. 'How many people were invited?'

'Two hundred, of which ten were guests overnight.'

'May I have a list of those guests, please?' At his hesitation, she tipped her head. 'I don't need to insist, do I, George?'

'No. I just need the police to be aware that one of the key reasons people come to Lark's Hill is for privacy.'

'You've got the general public wandering around out there,' Ari mentioned with a look of puzzlement.

'Only on certain days.'

'Your guests don't mind?' Ari said.

'They're not all so privately minded. I can assure you that those who wish for total privacy ensure they arrive on the days when no outside visitors are permitted.'

Ari nodded. 'I assume they pay for that privilege.'

'Of course,' George said, with a small dip of his head. 'Six of the ten were Bentley executives.'

'And on that day, there were no public visitors allowed?'

George shook his head. 'We had closed off the building three days beforehand to prepare for the event. It was lavish and required extra staff. No reservations other than Bentley's guests.'

'Where did you need the extra staff? In the kitchen?' Kate began to wander around the room, admiring it.

'Across all areas.'

Ari took up the conversation. 'So you had some new staff that day?'

'Yes. We brought in some staff from the stables – they now form a casual dining experience for our guests. Being rich doesn't mean you don't enjoy a pizza or burger like the next person. We also brought in some extra help from surrounding villages, but they were mostly to help out as parking attendants and porters.'

'Did they have access to the rooms?' Kate asked.

'Absolutely not!'

'Who did?'

'Alexis and I were in charge of showing each overnight guest to their room. And I was responsible for showing Mr Bruni to his.'

'Is there a lift?' Ari wondered.

'No.'

'Not even a service lift?'

'No.'

Ari nodded. 'So the only way to the guest rooms was via the stairs just outside?'

'Correct.'

'Were they guarded?'

George looked puzzled. 'Not guarded, no, but our security team certainly had eyes on, so to speak. Put it this way, no one who was not staff or booked in to a room was permitted to move upstairs. Room service staff were allowed access, for obvious reasons.'

'You knew these staff?'

'Yes. None with access were new to us – not on a night like that.'

'We'll need to talk to your security manager.'

'Of course. Shall we head upstairs?'

They followed him. 'Were many women employed that night as additional staff?' Kate asked.

'Several. All of them as waiting staff, downstairs with no access to the rooms.'

'And those people's names are on the list you gave us?'

'Yes.'

George closed the doors of the grand room and led them up the stairs. 'We employ new people and lose people all the time, of course. It's a high-turnover industry.'

Kate nodded, feeling like they were moving around blind. Without a photo or a more solid description of this woman, she could be anyone. An approximate age, dark hair that could be a wig . . . it wasn't much to go on.

'Sir Winston Churchill stayed here several times,' George said, as they reached the top of the heavy, dark-timbered staircase of three short flights. 'And, of course, royalty has visited many times over the centuries.'

'I heard there was a fire?' Ari said, continuing the pleasant conversation.

George nodded. 'Very sad. We lost one wing back at the turn of the previous century, but it was rebuilt.'

They were again clear of being overheard as they walked down the carpeted hallway to the end guest room known as Blackbird.

'The rooms are all named after local birds,' George explained unnecessarily while he found the right key on his large keychain.

'How many master keys are there?' Kate asked.

'This one, two keys per guest during their stay, and another set kept in the safe. I checked. None were tampered with as far as I could tell. And this set never left my side,' he said, lifting the chain to show they were secured to his clothes. He unlocked the door and pushed it open, letting Kate and Ari enter first.

Kate managed to stop herself gasping this time, but who couldn't fall in love with a room like this, she thought, especially if you came with someone you loved . . . or fancied. She halted those thoughts, tuning back in to George's commentary about the large stone balcony that overlooked the Thames and the pretty woodland surrounding the house.

The furnishings were plush, a medley of soft blues and dove greys, and the oak panelling in this room had been painted a rich parchment colour. Wall lamps like old-fashioned sconces punctuated the walls alongside old masters–style paintings. The bed was made with exquisite linen and hung with pewter-coloured velvet drapery behind the gilded headboard. At the end of the bed, a velvet chesterfield-stye sofa in a darker hue, like a stormy sky, was patterned with gold thread.

It was a lavish scene and Kate could imagine spending an entire weekend in the bed, let alone the large, ridiculously comfortable room itself, without ever wanting to leave it. 'Did Mr Bruni order any room service?' she asked.

'No. We served a lot of finger food of a substantial nature during the event. I daresay no one was hungry after that.'

'Did anyone else order room service that night?' Kate pressed.

'Er, that's something I'd have to check.'

'Thanks, George, if you would do that now, it would be helpful.'

George's gaze narrowed, but he didn't drop his helpful expression. 'Of course, excuse me,' he said, reaching for the guest phone and dialling.

Kate and Ari inspected the posh marble bathroom.

'It's bigger than my flat,' Ari remarked, before they headed onto the balcony, facing the sweeping views. 'Bruni's story matches up in terms of layout.'

Kate nodded. 'So he was outside having a phone conversation with his wife, presumably his back turned, while the woman delivering the champagne undressed herself.'

Ari swung around and Kate copied him. 'He turns back when he finishes his call and, according to him, is shocked and steps back in, demanding she get dressed and leave.' They both returned to the room, tracing Bruni's steps.

'Except she persuades him to let her stay a bit longer, saying she'll be in trouble otherwise. She opens the bottle,' Kate said.

'But then, according to Bruni, she realises he is not going to share the alcohol and she fetches him a bottle of sparkling water instead,' Ari narrated. 'If we're assuming that's how she drugged him, she'd have needed some moments to drop the tranquilliser in. Presumably liquid.'

Kate could see George had finished his phone call. 'Ari, check the fridge. Let's check that they do offer bottled sparkling.'

They stepped back into the room.

George looked up expectantly. 'One couple had room service – food, that is. Another couple had a pot of tea and biscuits delivered.'

'Who were they, please?'

He looked at his scribbled note. 'Mr James McSwain and his partner, Ms Lesley Dimbleby, had the tea.'

Ari looked up from the fridge, impressed. 'He's a top international golfer,' he said to Kate, assuming she wouldn't know, she guessed. 'And that's his wife, a top barrister.'

'And the other couple never actually attended the event. She was not feeling well, so they ate in their room. An odd pair. They asked for separate twin beds.'

Ari held up a bottle of Perrier from the fridge, catching Kate's attention. Before she could ask more of George, there was a knock at the door. It was Nat. 'Kate, can I have a word?'

'Yes, of course. Excuse me.' Kate heard George asking Ari if they were all done. 'What's up?' she asked, following Nat out into the hallway. 'Have you got something?'

'It may be nothing.'

'It may be something,' Kate countered with an encouraging grin.

The men had arrived behind them, and Kate could tell Nat would rather not speak in front of George.

'George, thank you. Ari, can you continue? I have to make a phone call.'

'Has something been found?' George asked, looking defensive.

Kate smiled. 'No, apparently our detective superintendent needs to speak with me urgently. Nothing to do with Lark's Hill,' she assured him, the lie delivered smoothly. 'We'll meet you downstairs.'

Outside on the gravel path, holding the phone to her ear but listening to Nat speaking beside her, she wished she'd put on her gloves.

'Well done, Nat. When did this new member of staff begin?'

'Just over twelve weeks ago, a couple of weeks prior to the Bentley event, ma'am. It caught in my mind because they said she was European. As I said, it may be a false trail.'

'Nat, you did the right thing; always follow your instincts,' Kate counselled. 'If I told you the number of times in my career I've gone down a pathway that didn't look at all promising and it turned out to be a major clue forward, you'd be surprised.'

Nat grinned. 'The salon manager believes she's French but said she couldn't be sure. Apparently this new girl was always talking about Switzerland, so she presumed she was Swiss.'

'They speak French there too. Does she have a tattoo?'

'Not that she's aware of.'

'Doesn't mean there isn't one, though. Nail polish?'

'I did ask about that. I was assured they have a strict policy of never having long or painted nails in the salon.'

'Well, she could have stuck them on for the night,' Kate reasoned. She hated that kind, personally, but plenty of women swore by them.

Nat nodded in agreement. 'She wasn't scheduled to work in the spa on that day. But then neither was the manager. It was the other senior salon person. So, the French woman could have easily come into work without other staff being in any way curious, because they were apparently pulling in staff from all departments.'

'If anything, I imagine everyone was so busy on that day, that any extra pair of hands would have been welcome. What's her name?'

'Sylvie Toussaint.'

'No F in there. But Luca said she wore a different name tag – maybe that's an alias. Good work, Nat. Come on, we're freezing our tits off out here.'

14

Francoise Laurent took a nervous drag on a cigarette and blew the smoke out almost immediately. She didn't inhale at the best of times, but today the cigarette was simply to keep her shaking hands busy rather than for nicotine. 'They're onto me!' she snapped.

'Stay calm,' Frank ordered, glancing at his sister to indicate she should join in.

When Francoise had first been introduced, Sophia, the sister, had said his name was Franco. 'After Franco Nero, the movie star,' she'd said, chuckling, but Francoise couldn't care any less. 'I told you our mother was obsessed with film stars. But he prefers Frank in England, don't you, Franco?' She'd ruffled his hair and he pulled away, looking exasperated at having his fashionable style using wax tampered with.

'It's easier to be Frank in London,' he said, finding a polite smile. He flicked away his cigarette to shake Francoise's hand.

That was then.

Right now, a few months on from that first get-together, there

were no smiles from any of them. They were meeting in a local
park, well off the main street, in a dingy neighbourhood around
Brentford.

'Listen, Francoise, they don't know anything. They're prodding.
It's what they do,' Frank assured her.

She looked at him as though he was speaking a language she
didn't understand or, rather, he didn't understand hers. 'No, you
both listen. They're looking for a French woman whose name
begins with F.'

'How do you know that?' Sophia asked, shocked.

Maybe she'd said too much. Francoise guiltily rubbed the tattoo
on her arm. They'd never seen it. 'Word moves fast in my game,
especially where police are concerned.'

'But how the hell would they even know that much?' Frank
asked, astounded. 'Did you ever give your—'

'I'm not an idiot,' Francoise said. 'I used only the name of
Sylvie Toussaint as we all agreed. I worked there for two weeks
under that name.'

'And you didn't slip once?' Sophia demanded.

'Not even slightly,' Francoise said, her tone full of disdain.

'Then how?' Frank asked.

Francoise shrugged dramatically. 'I don't know,' she replied,
aware that her tattoo had likely been noticed. To be honest, she'd
forgotten about the distinguishing mark in that moment at Lark's
Hill. It was easy to forget after years of having it. On previous
occasions, she'd never had to strip to force the situation. She'd had
them all out cold after just a bit of foreplay, having drunk their
laced drinks, with her still only slightly dishevelled, long sleeves
still covering her arms. Having to get creative with Luca Bruni
meant taking her clothes off – not that he was remotely tempted –
and that made him interesting. She liked that he wasn't so easily
coerced; she especially liked that he was clearly loyal to his wife.

'Maybe you slipped up,' she said, deflecting by turning suspicion back on them.

Frank groaned. 'Who told you this?'

'As I said, it came down the line, through various networks.' She shrugged. 'I'm an escort, Frank. Girls talk.'

'Oh, is that what they call it?'

'Who started the chain?' his sister cut in to get them back on track.

'I've already told you – I don't know,' she said firmly. 'But it must be someone in the game, at least within the escort industry, because it reached my last place of work in Knightsbridge. Friends passed it on. I haven't worked there in a while, so luckily it would have lost any, er, friction.' She wasn't going to give them more information than they needed.

'You mean traction,' Sophia corrected.

Francoise shrugged.

'So you don't believe the police are involved then? They didn't start asking questions?' Frank said.

Before Francoise could answer, his sister cut in again. 'I'm pretty certain it can't be the police,' Sophia said with confidence. 'So it's back on you, Francoise. Who have you been speaking to?'

'No one, I'm telling you,' she answered, genuinely furious. 'I did exactly what you told me to do. And I got you what you wanted. You are presumably already blackmailing the guy. And I have laid low, as you instructed, ever since. Now you owe me forty-five thousand and I want my money.'

'Wait until we—'

'Non!' she said, breaking angrily into French. *Putain!* she cursed inwardly at the amateurs. 'We agreed. My fee was not part of the ransom. We had a deal.'

'You're too hot now,' Frank said, shaking his head. 'You don't know who knows anything. It could well be the police.'

His sister sighed, but Francoise believed he was right.

'Give me my money and I'll disappear. Neither of you will ever see me again.'

Sophia frowned. 'Where will you go?'

Francoise shrugged. 'Not France,' she replied, knowing it would be their first thought – and that of the police. 'Switzerland, probably.'

'Who do you know there?'

'No one,' Francoise sneered. 'Isn't that the point? The language is no barrier, and I can disappear.' She saw the way Sophia looked at her brother. There was something sly, even sinister about it. Francoise wished she could see Sophia's face for real, but the other woman insisted on remaining in disguise whenever they met. Today's wig was straight, black and shoulder-length, over which Sophia had pulled a cloche hat, and the obligatory sunglasses were black as tar and so big they sat halfway down Sophia's cheeks. She was desperate not to be recognised, not just by Francoise, but by anyone, it seemed. Was she that recognisable that she'd worry about being spotted in this park in the middle of nowhereville? And how come Frank didn't seem to care who saw him? The questions were mounting and Francoise's gut twisted.

'Okay, we'll pay you your money,' Sophia finally said.

Frank looked astonished, casting an angry glance at his sister.

'It's fair,' Sophia said, giving a shrug before he could object. 'She's right, she did her bit. It's all in play now because of her.'

Frank looked between them in disbelief. 'Then it's your half it comes out of. She's compromised us.'

'She hasn't. Frank, this was my idea, not yours. You haven't even done that much, except be a chauffeur and confidant, so be grateful that I've agreed to give you anything.'

He glowered at her and she looked away, standing to stomp her feet in the cold. 'Listen, they don't know any more than they did a few days ago. So, what – they're looking for a French girl whose name begins with F? How they know that much is a mystery but'—she tipped her chin towards Francoise—'she'll be long gone before they find her.'

Frank waved a finger. 'You need to be very gone, very soon.'

'Give me my money,' Francoise said, as if it were obvious, 'and I'll leave the same day.'

'All right, tomorrow, at the other place,' Sophia answered. 'Four o'clock. Don't be late. I shan't wait and then you'll never see the cash.'

Francoise nodded. She couldn't wait to be rid of them and to be on her way. She had no intention of going to Switzerland, of course. She would head south. She was sick of this cold.

Jack was with Claudia again. 'That was quick, thank you.'

'I really shouldn't risk being seen with you, handsome Jack. Your face is quite well known in our circles, after the last time.'

He nodded his understanding. 'I'll be gone as soon as I finish this tea.' It was an excellent cuppa.

'You English certainly know how to make tea. But coffee . . .' She didn't finish.

He grinned. 'Don't get me started. So, tell me what you have.'

'What will happen to her? I'm not telling you anything if you plan to arrest her.'

Jack had suspected he would meet this hurdle and had already made peace with his decision. 'I will not arrest her. You have my word. She's a pawn, Claudia, we both know it. I'm not after her, only who she knows.'

'What about the victim? I can't imagine he's too thrilled. The mere fact he's brought the police in tells me he's angry, wants revenge. He'll want her, because she's the one who, in his mind, has hurt him.' Claudia waited, watching Jack with a ruthless, unblinking stare.

Jack didn't look away. 'I will keep her safe.'

Claudia held his gaze. 'I don't trust the police force. I do trust you, though.' She softened, finally looking down.

Jack tried to cover his anticipation by picking up his teacup and sipping. The brew was undeniably hot and strong in this tiny café that might have been an old greasy spoon in its previous life. It was in Hammersmith, crowded and noisy with plates and cutlery clanging constantly with the turnover of customers. It was obviously very popular with the locals, serving plain, everyday food from fried eggs to cheese and chutney sandwiches at lunchtime. No pretence at gastro wizardry here, and probably why it was a hot favourite with people who didn't care to spend more than a few pounds on their midday fare. None seemed interested in the couple by the window.

'Her name is Francoise,' Claudia said.

Jack nodded, feeling a punch of satisfaction. They were finally onto something.

Claudia plucked a thin paper napkin from the holder on the table, which sat next to the salt and pepper and a small plastic pot of fake flowers. 'May I have a pen?'

He reached into his jacket inside pocket and withdrew one.

She smiled. 'Still warm from your nice body, Jack.'

He gave her a look of soft despair that made her chuckle as she wrote down an address.

'She was working at an escort agency in Knightsbridge for a while. I met her only once. Our two agencies were each asked to send a girl to do a particular job together. It was for a very wealthy and extremely private client with specific tastes. I organised our girl, but we all met briefly to ensure we'd selected the right pair. Francoise is still very young, extremely attractive, with a fabulous body.' She shrugged. 'She struck me as ambitious. Hates her job but loves the money. Very single-minded. She was professional when we met: asked the right questions, and answered directly and candidly when I asked mine.'

Claudia slid over the napkin, and as Jack reached for it, she covered his hand with hers. He noted that her nails were not natural – too identical – but nor were they claw-like or overly long. They were painted in the French manicure fashion with the tips a toothpaste white.

'Jack, she's not the enemy,' Claudia warned once again.

'I know. I give you my word that I'll protect her.'

Claudia nodded and let go of his hand. Without looking at the napkin, he quickly folded it and put it in his pocket. 'May I ask two more questions?'

'So long as it's not about her,' Claudia said, giving him a slow blink.

'It's about fingernails, actually. Is it possible to stick on long painted nails for a few hours and take them off easily? I know a lot of women have long salon appointments for these types of things.'

Claudia laughed. 'Do you ever visit Boots?'

'The chemist? For prescriptions and things, yes.'

'Well, Jack, wander over to the women's beauty section sometime. It will blow your mind what you can buy and do for yourself these days, including press-on nails.'

'Press on? How? You glue them?'

'Exactly. And if you use a quality glue, then they're as easy to remove as they are to apply.'

'For a night?'

'For a night, for a week, for two weeks . . . that's probably the maximum for a working girl. We use them all the time. Some men like long red nails, some love black, others like pointed talons, and some prefer them natural, elegant. We please our clients.'

'Right. Thank you. Final question?' he asked, his tone sheepish.

Claudia sighed. 'Sounds like this one won't be so easy . . . or innocent.'

'The other girl – your girl, whom you paired with Francoise. Can I talk to her?'

Claudia looked instantly wary. 'Jack.' It was said with an admonishing tone.

'I'll pay for her time, but I don't want to ambush her. Can you organise it?'

'Set her up with a policeman who can arrest her?' Claudia said, sitting back and folding her arms across her chest.

'Who will *not* arrest her. Who will pay for her services while off duty, and book her through the correct channels. Who will protect her if she gets dragged into this scenario unwittingly and—'

'What do you mean?' she interrupted.

He pursed his lips. 'Claudia, your girl knows Francoise better than you. Professional bad guys don't leave any stone unturned, you know that. If they get even a whiff that someone else is in on the game, they'll consider blotting them out. Right now they don't know about your girl, but they might soon. I can throw a ring of protection around her.'

Claudia considered this. 'Let me speak with her first. I'll text you.'

'Thank you. Let me pay for this.' Jack pulled out his wallet and took out two fifty-pound notes and a fiver.

Claudia stared at him, baffled. 'Two cups of tea do not cost that much.'

'The five should cover it. The rest is for you to spend on Hanna. Go do something nice, until I can treat you both properly. We can share a picnic near where I live.'

Claudia shook her head. 'What a heartbreaker you are.'

Jack grinned and stood, leaning over to kiss her cheek. 'Thanks. You have my number. Call me.'

Jack left the tiny café, his hand in his pocket clutching the

serviette. His phone rang just as he was legging it to the Underground station. 'Hawksworth.'

'Hey, Hawk.'

'Geoff? Good to hear from you.'

'Where are you?'

'Just about to dive into the Tube station at Hammersmith.'

'Are you on your way to the Yard?' Geoff asked.

'Yes, should be back in about twenty-five minutes or so.'

'Yep. District line. Call me when you're on top again.'

Jack paused. 'Everything okay?'

'Just need to ask you something.'

'Okay, talk shortly.'

He re-dialled Geoff as he walked from the Tube to Broadway.
'It's me.'

'I'm outside the Yard. Can you spare a few moments?'

'Sure.'

Jack found his old friend chatting to one of the security guards.
Geoff noticed his arrival and finished up, walking towards him.
'Hi,' Geoff said, raising a hand in welcome.

They gave each other a brief hug. 'Too long,' Jack said, shaking
his head. 'Bloody hell, what's happened? You look fit! Must be a
woman.' He grinned.

Geoff cut him a baleful look.

'Do you want to come up?' Jack asked.

'No, I know you're working on a new op, Stonecrop, right?'

'I see our terribly secret squirrel methods are working,' Jack
remarked in a sarcastic tone.

Geoff chuckled. 'You know I know everything.'

Jack followed his friend's lead, walking towards Whitehall
Garden. 'Are we on a date? Going somewhere special?'

It made them both laugh. 'No, I didn't think Kate would want
to see me,' Geoff said. 'This is easier.'

'She's okay,' Jack reassured him.

'Yeah, but I'm not,' Geoff said, sounding momentarily sad.

That surprised Jack. 'You've never really spoken about it.'

'No.' He pointed to a bench and the men sat down. Geoff scratched gently at his beard, a new shape, more closely shaved than his fuller beard of years gone. It suited him. 'That's because I've never really got over it. We were good together.'

Jack nodded. 'You were.'

'Anyway, Hawk, that's not what I'm here to discuss. I need your help. You know a thing or two about reproductive stuff, don't you?'

'I do. Let me explain. You see, when a couple fancy each other – doesn't matter what species for the most part – the male produces sperm, and he delivers that via—'

The frustrated glare from his friend lightened what had become a painful atmosphere. The break-up with Kate had always been a sad outcome in Jack's mind; he'd thought them a brilliant pairing despite being such opposites.

'You loser,' Geoff said, helplessly grinning. 'How about I explain?'

'Go on.'

'You heard about the murder of the vet at Wimbledon?'

'Yes, shocking. Sounded like an execution.'

'That's exactly what we believe it is.'

Jack frowned. 'What had he got himself into?'

'No idea. But while he hasn't been splashing money about, he's certainly been shoring up his financials. From what we can tell, he's paid off his mortgage and some business debt, and has been financing his invalid sister's stay in a top care establishment.'

'Vets earn well.' Jack shrugged, as if to say there was nothing too suspicious in all of this so far.

'Mmm, yep, but everything I've mentioned happened in a short time, as though he'd come into money fast and hard.'

'Had he?'

'No sign of it in a bank account. He comes from a modest family, parents both dead – mother quite recently – and the family home hasn't been sold yet. It's been rented. He and his sister split the income. They're twins; very close apparently. We can find the rent trail in his bank account, but no sign of the sort of money that has financed the rest.'

'Cash, then,' Jack said. 'Do people pay vet bills in cash? I gather from friends it's always more expensive than you imagine, right, and not many people have pet insurance?'

'Indeed. But the expensive nature is all the more reason that people might pay on credit.'

Jack nodded. 'Could he be doing consultancies on the side?'

'He could, but we can't find any sign of it – you know, drugs and disposable equipment. If he had suddenly begun consulting, say on every third animal, for cash, we'd see some reflection of that.'

Jack nodded. 'And he'd have to be doing something substantial to be generating enough funds to finance what you're suggesting.'

'Precisely. We're talking around a quarter of a million, at least.'

'Well, that's not coming from vaccinating cats and bunny rabbits,' Jack said. 'So how can I help?'

'Well, there's this one oddity discovered this morning by a switched-on young detective in our team whose brother happens to be a country vet.'

'Go on.'

'The deceased, Michael Evans, had a small set-up for storing reproductive material. The detective asked his brother, showed him photos, and although the brother recognised what it was, he was surprised. Said it was unusual.'

'Why's that?'

'Because you wouldn't have this gear in a city vet clinic, he says. It's the sort of thing you have at studs, or if you're a vet who services a farm – the gear you need for artificial insemination of cows and so on. Evans was dealing with hamsters and the like. No big animals, just your common pets like cats, dogs, bunnies, gerbils and so on.'

'Putting that together, you're wondering if Evans was executed because of that equipment?'

'Well, not exactly, but it's an oddity. I need to explain it for our own peace of mind, to make sure we've covered off everything. As I said, we believe it was an execution, so I can't leave a stone unturned.'

Jack wasn't surprised. His friend was very good at detail.

Geoff continued. 'Can you think of any reason why he would have a set-up for freezing reproductive material when he doesn't need it? Or why a local vet might be executed in Wimbledon on a Monday evening over dinner with his partner?'

Jack rubbed his chin. 'Did you get any samples of the material?'

'No. It was empty. All cleaned out.'

Jack blinked. A distant alarm was sounding in his mind and although he was aware of it, he couldn't understand why it had gone off. 'So not in use even recently?'

'No. But I still have to satisfy myself as to why he had it.'

'He could have been looking after it for someone.'

'Maybe.'

'Geoff, if I follow your line of thought, you're suggesting it might not have been used for animals?'

His colleague nodded awkwardly. 'It's incongruous, the only oddity in his otherwise perfectly normal suburban clinic. I'm hopeful it's not a clue to his death and we can put it aside and move on. But you know me . . .'

'I do. The odd equipment and him being cashed up are both red flags here.'

'Yes. They're my puzzles.'

Jack nodded. 'Okay, so how do I fit in here?'

Geoff sat forward, and Jack realised his friend's coat had been disguising how much weight he'd lost. He'd always been a cuddly guy who loved his beer, eating well and living generally larger than Jack, with a busy social life and plenty of friends. Cuddly or not, it would have been wrong to presume that DCI Geoff Benson was not fit. A former back rower for his university rugby team and still playing for one of the police clubs, he pursued active pastimes of rambling, trekking and his latest, fell running. The new sport had probably been the one to change his appearance. His face had lost its previous rosy-cheeked Father Christmas chubbiness and Jack now saw the younger Geoff from their days at Hendon and police training. He also suspected his friend had been forced into investing in a new wardrobe. He looked smarter.

Geoff launched in. 'Your Australian case gave you a solid grounding, I gather, and now you're working on Stonecrop, which isn't so far away from—' Geoff halted, words seemingly backing up in his mouth as Jack stood up suddenly, staring at the ground, deep in thought. 'Hawk?'

'Bloody hell. What if he's the link?'

'Evans? You think he was involved in your case?'

'What if Evans is the guy in the middle who can store the semen?'

'He *can* store semen, with the gear we found, including liquid nitrogen. It has to be kept cold in the fridge, alongside half a dozen eggs, would you believe? Who would keep their breakfast eggs alongside semen?'

Jack began to pace, a gust of a laugh disappearing as soon as it arrived. 'The eggs are part of it!' He couldn't believe his luck.

'Now you've lost me, matey.'

Jack went through what he'd explained to Carol Rowland, watching the same look of disgust pass across his friend's face.

'You're joking . . . egg yolk?'

'I'm not. I think this guy could have been in the middle of my case. If I'm right, I wonder why they'd kill someone who was integral to the success of their blackmail operation.'

Geoff looked thoughtful. 'It always comes down to money.'

'That's what Kate believes.'

'She's right – her time in Vice would have showed her that over and again. It's always, "He asked for more, he asked for too much, he spent it too openly, he drew attention to the new money he was earning."'

'Maybe this vet threatened them?'

'Maybe, but why? He was onto a good thing. The money was making a huge difference in his life, and the partner tells us all was great. He was happy, they were planning a future together.'

'And the partner knows nothing about this other business?'

Geoff shook his head. 'No. And we barely do. You're the one leaping onto it. I've been scratching my head over it as a curiosity – really, I just wanted to rule out its involvement in his murder, but now you've suggested a whole new angle.'

'If my theory is right, they've destroyed a key link in the chain. That means they've either replaced him or stopped needing him. There was no reproductive material in the unit itself?'

Geoff shook his head. 'All clean. Dust on its lid.'

'So that doesn't make sense either, given we're in the midst of a blackmail case. They would be storing someone's semen right now.'

'Maybe he's not involved.'

Jack shook his head. 'No, there's something here. We need permission to share information.'

'I'll send you everything we can on Evans.'

'Do you have any leads? Evidence?'

'We have a cigar butt that was left near the scene, and through going door to door around the flats we have established that no one smokes cigars. It could have been a visitor, of course, to another flat.'

'Or just a passer-by flinging it away?'

'Well, passers-by would be more likely to toss a butt towards the gutter. This was caught in a small bush just outside the main door to the flats.'

'And no one saw anything?'

'Ah, well, there is a witness. Not to the murder, but potentially to the killer.'

'You have a description?' Jack was pulling out his notebook.

Geoff nodded. 'Better. We have a photo.'

Jack's head whipped up.

'In fact, we have a photo of two men. One who kept a lookout, and another who presumably did the ugly deed. We can't see the lookout's face, but he's wearing a distinctive cap. The other guy we can see, but we don't know him.'

'We need to go upstairs,' Jack said, grabbing his phone. He dialled Carol Rowland's office.

The Chief Superintendent of Homicide and Serious Crimes regarded the two senior detectives. She didn't know whether to be impressed by the two friends comparing notes or whether to consider them irresponsible for doing just that. It would be easy to criticise them and walk the line of enforcing correct protocol, perhaps even cautioning Hawksworth for sharing information about such a sensitive case. However, people were beginning to learn that while Carol Rowland looked like a stickler, she was just as ambitious as her peers. If bending the rules was the only way to catch the bad guys and add to her reputation, then she was far from the goodie-two-shoes she knew many had her pegged as.

She could tell Hawksworth was trying to read her. He probably couldn't guess that she would be the first to defend him on the basis that Benson had contacted him for advice. What's more, neither of them could have had even a hunch that two such random events may have connections before their chat. There would be no reprimand, even though she sensed that Hawksworth felt it was coming . . . and still he'd brought it to her. She admired that.

Much as she had wanted to keep him at arm's length, it was true that Hawksworth had a curious manner of getting under the skin. Her predecessor had warned her that she'd like him, but she didn't like being told how to react so she had tested it for herself. She had wanted to be sure that Hawksworth's charm wasn't contrived. He didn't, she now firmly believed, set out to win attention, and she saw no evidence of him flirting with female staff. If anything, it was the opposite. Her personal assistant always seemed to touch her hair and smile a lot when Hawksworth walked in, and find reasons to pop in. But he was polite, respectful of the women he worked with, and still this trail of destruction seemed to yawn behind him . . . either dead women or broken hearts.

She considered the other man. While Hawksworth had pipped his pal to a promotion, she suspected it wouldn't be long before Geoff Benson was a detective superintendent too. He was a reliable, exceptionally smart operator.

'Good work, you two.' She saw the flash of surprise in their eyes. 'You realise what this means, DCI Benson?'

'Ma'am?'

'I'll need you to open up your case to Hawksworth's team.'

'No problem,' he replied.

'Er, ma'am, perhaps DCI Benson should come to briefing sessions at the op?' Jack offered tentatively.

She gave a nod. 'You okay with that?' she asked Geoff.

'Of course,' he said, cutting Jack a look she couldn't read. Their friendship was old; it had its own language. 'I don't mean this to sound rude, but does the sharing go both ways, ma'am? Perhaps the team working on this murder could benefit from Stonecrop's information.'

'If it's relevant, definitely,' she answered. 'My reservation, and I'll let Hawksworth brief you, is that there is some sensitivity surrounding the case.'

Geoff nodded. 'Okay.'

'I'll explain,' Jack said to him. 'Thank you, ma'am.'

They stood and made their way to the door, but she called Jack back. 'I'll need an update. I've got upstairs to brief.'

'Is tomorrow all right? Everyone is out and about interviewing and gathering info for a briefing first thing tomorrow.'

'Tomorrow evening, then,' she said.

'Absolutely, ma'am,' he answered and departed.

Yes, Hawksworth understood her.

'Thanks a lot,' Geoff growled in the lift, looking miserable.

'I've done you a favour. You can't keep avoiding each other,' Jack appealed. 'Plus, meeting in a professional capacity means you can't get your head ripped off.'

'Don't be so sure, Hawk.'

'Kate's one of the most confident and brilliant women I know, but she still suffers insecurity when it comes to men . . . at least I think that's what it is. I don't imagine she dared allow herself to believe she was in love with you.'

'Because she's crazy about you, do you mean?'

Jack gave him a doleful look. 'No. I don't mean that, and I don't want to hear that again from you. I think with Kate it's habit, and I'm a habit. I'm safe to be around, because she knows there's nothing more than friendship to it. But you took her by surprise. She didn't expect all that she found with you – and maybe she too regrets breaking up.'

'We'll soon find out.'

Jack gave him an encouraging grin. 'If nothing else, Joan will be pleased to see you.'

15

Baris Celik took a long drag on the cigarette he'd just lit from his pack of Camel Blues. Given his propensity for chain smoking, he'd traded his preferred oriental tobacco flavour in the Yellow Camels for the lighter Blues, which had less of everything except bitterness. But the slightly lower amount of nicotine quietened his daughter, who had convinced him to consider changing his habits. She was only seven and had been regularly pleading with him to stop; she'd finally worn him down. They'd made a pact that he would do as she asked the day she started Year 3; in the meantime, he had ten months to quit. He had to. His son was just two. Becoming a father again had changed his mind about a lot of things, including the blackmail scheme that he and his brother, Eren, had set up and done extremely well from over the years.

It had amazed them both how easy it had been. These athletes had so much money, they'd rather pay the ransom than be bothered with the hassle and potential publicity of not going along with the demands. Baris had insisted they remain 'honest'.

'If they pay without fuss, then we destroy what they want gone. And they never hear from us again. Is that clear?'

His brother had nodded. 'Sure, but—'

'No buts. We let them keep their dignity by keeping ours, Eren. When you make a deal, you stick to it. Promise me you understand that and will abide by it, or I won't be a part of it.'

'Okay, okay, big brother. I'll stick to the plan.'

The first time had been a slick triumph that had given them tremendous confidence, and they were instantly half a million pounds richer, minus costs for the vet and girl. It would have been so easy to up the payload, but Baris had cooled Eren's burners.

'If we don't get greedy, they won't flinch at paying.'

'But if we make it a million, it's still—'

'It's still a million. A bit of a magical number, even for these high-earning guys, who probably throw money like that around. Imagine what it takes to make a million pounds, to pay tax on a million,' Baris said.

'You know how our grandparents struggled after the war. And then our parents; if not for their sacrifices we would not be here today living comfortably.'

'Exactly!' Baris pointed at his brother as though it was all so obvious. 'Your words! Living comfortably. Right now, our families are expanding, growing, being educated and living well. Greed will not help them to keep enjoying this good life we've built.'

'But I want it faster. I don't want to struggle like our parents and grandparents did. Comfortable is good, but I want easy for my wife and my children. These guys earn millions a year. They won't even feel the loss of such a tiny amount.'

Baris shook his head. 'The trick is to stay modest in our demands. Why can't you see that?'

'You want to be a gentleman about it?' Eren laughed.

'Why not? We make it easy for them to flick us away with a bit of cash. But that cash can change our lives, while to them it's just another fucking Ferrari.'

Eren had laughed, probably because Baris rarely cursed and it always sounded weird when he did. 'Okay, brother. We'll stay small, think small.'

'I didn't say that. We act small so no one sees us or what we're up to, and then soon we go clean. I don't want to be a criminal. I just want to set our children up for a good life – an honest life – in this country.'

So they'd picked their marks with great care, putting many months of research into learning as much as they could about each target. It had always been a man; neither of them felt comfortable targeting a woman. And besides, men were easy to entice with the right woman, especially if they were young and single, with huge egos and bank accounts to match. They had spoken about faking the semen, or even using their own, but Baris had believed they needed to be genuine in their threat, just as they would be genuine in their destruction of that threat.

They had followed that path eleven times now.

From the outside, it looked like the brothers were spearheading a successful, ever-growing network of barber shops. Their childhood had begun in Turkey and they'd been brought to England to start a new life with their parents. These days they looked and sounded like a pair of Londoners, going by Barry and Eric professionally. Both men were very tall, and Eren was broad-shouldered as well, adding to his commanding stature.

Baris had worked out during his twenties that he, like most young men, no longer wanted to go to a standard hairdresser – even a men's hairdresser. What these guys wanted was to go to a salon that looked like a club, painted black with fancy chairs and a lot of chrome and timber. They wanted a shave, hot towels, nose hair plucking, ear hair removal. They wanted fashionable cuts and sexy product – they were as susceptible to the appeal of an expensive shampoo or conditioner as any woman. And the tiny, excruciatingly expensive tins of hair wax, styling foam, lotion and now beard oils made them as vain and interested in their appearance as their female counterparts. Baris knew this, and so that's what he'd created, with his brother's help. In his barber shops, good Turkish coffee was served while clients waited. Non-dog-eared, flashy magazines about cars, boats, investment made them feel even more pampered, as did the young woman who came out from the back only when asked to give each customer a head massage while their hair was shampooed. Part of the expensive service and much enjoyed.

Newly introduced was nail trimming and grooming, plus a dedicated waxing room in the back for men interested in having their backs and chests groomed too.

Baris now employed dozens of people across their barber shops around southern England, and they never told the managers when they'd be dropping in. They each visited a different shop daily and had a roaming pair of collectors who would gather up the takings each evening and bring them back to base. Discreet cameras were installed in all shops to make sure the staff were not misappropriating funds, because most blokes still paid for haircuts in cash.

Recently, they'd invested in a bar in Soho as well, and it had become so popular it looked as though they might be taking on another; luckily they had reliable managers to oversee most of the day-to-day business. They'd each be responsible for running one but share the profits across both. They'd also dipped their toe into the world of brothels, acquiring a high-end escort service run out of Kensington Gardens, not too far from the Victoria and Albert Museum. Their aunt, an experienced businesswoman whose design firm had run aground during the global financial crisis, had taken over its management. She ran a tight ship but looked after her workers as well as they looked after their clients. Already the brothers had their eye on another in Mayfair – a little more upmarket, but still competitive, because the neighbourhood had its share of high-class agencies. The idea was to keep it below the radar, no soliciting of any sort, strictly word of mouth, and to work with regular clients who ran accounts. And then there was the blackmail.

None of the women in their lives knew of their lucrative criminal activity; not even the wives suspected there was any darker underbelly to their successful salon and bar businesses. Only their cousin, Davut, a cunning and talented accountant with his own accounting firm, knew the truth and joined in with the spoils. The salons, the brothel and the bar, which he had advised should be joined as soon as possible by some laundry outlets, were the perfect vehicles through which to clean cash and minimise tax payments. Davut earned enough through them to not demand a penny from the blackmail jobs, and was now guiding their earnings into wholly legitimate businesses.

They'd stopped shy of a dozen blackmails. Baris had finally brought their run to its end. Eren, unhappy to lose the seemingly easy injections of cash, railed at his brother but, as usual, Baris had won through with his calming, ever sensible caution.

'Enough is enough. We've made nearly three million pounds each from the venture. More than we could have dreamed of, and now it's time to stop. For our children's sake, let's just have everything lawful.'

'We've had to pay the vet and the woman, and Aslan, who found the vet,' Eren reminded him.

'That's still negligible compared to what we've earned. In a way, Aslan's accident has done us a favour.'

'You weren't even upset, Baris.'

'He was your friend. He was good,' Baris said, putting up his hands in surrender, 'but he lived a little dangerously. Snorting and injecting all those drugs, well, let's just say it was a bad way to go. I am embarrassed that our money helped him to afford that crap.'

'He was an idiot, but everyone loved Aslan. It's such a waste.'

Baris nodded. 'My point is, when you push your luck, that's when it all goes wrong. Another job would be pushing our luck. We don't need the tension of the ransom demands and laundering that amount of cash any more. We're businessmen now, and we're going fully legit soon before we come to the attention of the authorities. Let's not draw attention to ourselves – that's always been our way, right? Let's enjoy our lives, our families, no tension.'

Eren had agreed. And the blackmail operation had been halted for good; everyone involved was to be paid off, including the girl who'd lured their marks and the vet who stored the semen.

Which is why they sat in their bar now, staring at each other. It was not due to open for hours so they were alone. They'd met to go over all the final details, make sure nothing would trip them up.

'Really? Murdering the vet was the only way?' Davut, the accountant, asked in genuine dismay. He sounded frightened.

'Had to, Dav.' Eren shrugged. 'We agreed to tie up the loose ends.'

'Not fucking kill them,' Davut replied, disgusted.

'Look, I was just going to warn him, but he's an emotional guy – we knew that – and I stupidly mentioned when I sent our guy to his flat that if the police ever questioned him, he'd fold.'

'He liked the money too much,' Dav said. 'He wouldn't have done that.' He sighed out his cigarette smoke.

It was a full-strength Yellow Camel, Baris noted, and he quietly inhaled the strong burnt smell, all but tasting the Burleigh and Virginian in it. He shook his head. 'Dav, Evans had a lot on his plate with his invalid sister. I gather he was newly in love but easily spooked. As much as I detest what happened, Eren's right. He wouldn't have stood up to any interrogation. This way they can't get anything from him.'

His brother cut him a grateful nod.

Davut was yet to be convinced though. 'Think of what the police might find! There's a trail of money, for a start.'

'Why would they look?' Eren appealed, looking baffled.

'Because of the way he died!' their cousin yelled. 'It wasn't even made to look accidental. I drove by his place. It's a full-on fucking crime scene with guys in those forensic suits crawling all over it, tape everywhere.'

'Calm down, Dav,' Baris said. 'Look, I did think we were just warning the vet, but the guy we used . . .' He hesitated.

'What?'

Honesty was best. 'He went rogue. Eren shouldn't have said what he did, but he didn't actually order a hit.'

Eren slowly shook his head, looking ashamed too.

'I don't know what happened,' Baris continued. 'I wasn't there. The fact is, the vet is dead. I don't like it any more than you, but like Aslan's untimely death, it does tie off a loose end. Evans can't be connected back to us, because his only contact was Aslan. The police may find Evans came into money that was beyond his earnings, but how will they trace that to us?'

Dav nodded, blowing smoke silently from his nose. 'They won't. I was careful.'

Baris gave his shoulder a congratulatory, gentle slap. 'There you are. You took the precaution.'

Dav turned to the younger brother. 'But were you careful, Eren?'

Eren frowned. 'What do you mean?'

'Going into this place in broad daylight. Anyone could have seen you.'

'Nah, I told you, I didn't go into the building. Our guy wore a courier uniform. No one would have noticed him. I was in a coffee shop opposite, watching,' Eren said, looking like he'd just called 'Snap!' and taken away all of Dav's cards. 'Just another café-goer reading his paper over tea and toast. I even wore a baseball cap.'

'There's too much distance between us, Dav,' Baris said. 'There are no clues to connect,' he said, pretending to link imaginary dots in the air. 'Eren says the guy who did the job is solid, and anyway, we're done with that business now. We've all agreed no more targeting of the athletes.'

'All right, so why are we here?' Dav asked, finally reaching for his Scotch. 'Why are we even talking about this?'

Baris gave a sigh. *Here it comes*, he thought. His cousin would choke on his whisky. 'Because we think someone else has picked up where we left off.'

Dav stared at him in disbelief; the mouthful of Scotch was swallowed loudly. He gave a small cough. 'What do you mean?'

'I think some bastard has decided to do exactly what we did.'

'How do you know?'

'Through the brothel. Aunty Dil heard on the grapevine that enquiries were being made about a girl involved in a blackmail scheme out at that fancy-pants place near Maidenhead.'

Dav frowned. 'Which place?'

Baris looked at Eren. 'What's it called again?'

'Lark's Nest or something.'

'Lark's Hill,' Dav corrected.

'That's it.' Baris nodded. 'Apparently it was identical to the process we used with our girl.'

'Shit! You sure it's not your girl, flying solo?' Dav asked.

'She's meant to be in Australia, where we sent her to lay low with a lot of money. We've had a couple of messages from her, just to confirm her arrival and that she's in Melbourne. Another with her address. But she doesn't plan on staying in touch, for obvious reasons.'

'She could have come back,' Dav said.

'Could have,' Baris agreed. 'But why would she?'

'Any number of reasons. She's French, you said?' He nodded. 'Homesick, maybe, or a sick relative. Maybe she needed a proper croissant!'

'I don't think we have to worry about her,' Eren echoed, though he didn't sound convinced.

'So what are you not telling me?' Dav looked as though he was about to lose all patience. 'Tell me.'

Eren obliged. 'Someone is hunting a French woman who was part of this blackmail scheme through the escort services – the copycat scheme, I mean.'

'Fuck! It's her! Francoise.'

Baris shrugged. 'Not necessarily,' he said, no longer sounding convinced himself. He'd liked and trusted Francoise. She was smart, dependable, and she had done her job perfectly each time. She'd never demanded more from them. She'd never had any wobbly moments where he might begin to question her loyalty. He'd found it easy to pay her the final fee and let her walk off safely with the promise that she would never speak of their connection again. And so far he'd had no reason to question the trust they shared.

'Who did they target?' Dav asked.

'We don't know exactly who the mark is, but I hear it's a footballer. Probably from the Premier Division for him to be able to pay that kind of money.'

'And you know this how?'

'I did some snooping at the hotel,' Baris answered. 'Guess who works at this place?'

'Who?' Eren asked.

'Remember that little toe-rag Ronnie?'

'The one we called Ronnie Corbett?'

Baris nodded and saw Dav looking exasperated. 'He was a little bloke,' he explained.

'What was he doing working in a fancy hotel?' Eren asked.

'Essentially he's an errand boy, as I understand it.'

'Why are we talking about Ronnie Corbett?' Dav demanded.

Baris had to control his desire to laugh as an image of the real Ronnie Corbett came to mind. He'd always thought *The Two Ronnies* was hilarious. Made him think of his father; his father's English had been well honed through the war days, and so when the family had come to England, he'd understood all the subtle jokes and wordplay that the two comedians batted back and forth. He sighed. 'Ronnie Barrett is his name. And we're talking about Ronnie because he's now working at the same place where the copycat scam occurred, Dav. He worked for us first.'

'We couldn't prove it, but we always suspected Ronnie of playing both sides. He's lucky we didn't give him a cement-shoe send-off in the Thames.' Eren laughed. 'Just a joke, cuz,' he said, holding both palms up in mock surrender.

Dav gave them both a look of despair. 'I thought we were all working towards the pair of you going straight?' He gave a sound of disgust.

'We are, Dav,' Baris assured him. 'We've come a long way.'

'And yet we're sitting here, just accepting that your thug killed the vet – who wasn't in our way – just because he *might* have got in our way.' His frustration couldn't be disguised. 'And now little brother reckons you should have bumped off someone who may or may not be a snitch. That's the attitude of a hoodlum, Baris.' He tapped his temple. 'It's thinking like gangsters, not like businessmen.'

Baris sighed, knowing his cousin was right. He moved the conversation forward to deal with the problem at hand. 'Anyway, the staff were being interviewed about a special event that was held there, some kind of flashy car promotion. Something went down that night with one of the special guests. Ronnie, who works as a porter and general hand, said the only famous person he knew who was staying overnight was that superstar kid who plays for Huxley.'

'You mean Luca Bruni?' Dav asked, astonished.

'Yeah. Maybe. Sounds like he'd be the right sort of mark.'

'Sure is.'

'So our worry is that although we've tied up our loose ends, the joker who's behind the copycat scam might cock it up and then we risk exposure,' Eren explained.

'Why?'

Baris tried not to show his exasperation. But then Dav was a details man and needed to know every in, every out. 'All it will take is a more extensive enquiry that loosens the lips of one of the people we've targeted and'—he shrugged—'you know, bang. We've got a full-scale investigation.'

'But you said you've been careful.'

'We have,' Baris said. 'Never as careful as you though, Dav.'

Eren sighed. 'Look, we got away with it so many times. And then we quit,' he said, as though it had been his idea to be careful. 'We're mostly legit now.'

'As legit as money laundering,' Dav said, unable to help himself.

'That too will stop, cousin,' Baris said. 'We have families to protect, yourself included, and kids growing up that we want to go to university and live good lives without the worry of the tap on the shoulder. We're set up well enough now that we can probably look at an entirely clean business in less than a couple of years. It's what we all want.'

Dav nodded. 'You know I want that too. I only help because I promised your parents I'd keep you both out of trouble.'

'I know,' Baris said, aware of the family pressure put on his older cousin.

'Oh, come on, you like the money, too,' Eren quipped.

'Not saying I don't,' Dav replied. 'But I'll be happy when we just earn and live off the barber shops and the bars, without needing to clean any cash and worrying about it.'

'Us too, cousin,' Baris assured him. 'So this enquiry that's reached us is worrying. Potentially dangerous. I want to nip it in the bud.'

'How? Do you know who's behind it?'

'No. But whichever girl they used does. So if the police are involved, I want to get to her before the police do.'

Eren sighed with boredom. 'I'm going to fire up the coffee machine. Anyone want one?'

'I will,' Dav said and Baris knew he'd accepted in order to keep Eren busy for a bit longer; he clearly had something to say.

The two men waited until they heard Eren move through the door at the back of the bar.

'You know it's your girl, don't you?' Dav said.

Baris hesitated. For the first time since the alarm sounded he was prepared to admit that yes, it had to be Francoise. He nodded. 'Only she knew the role and how to play it. She'd become so good at it, why would you use anyone else? But how would they have known her to use her?' he asked, and in doing so admitted his true worry.

Dav sighed. 'I don't know, but you need to find out whether she's moonlighting on you. Got any leads?'

They could hear the mechanical sounds of Eren drawing water through the coffee machine and flushing it.

Baris nodded. 'Yeah, I do. I'm hearing there's a photo.'

Dav looked back at him, puzzled.

'Whether it's Francoise or not, I think this girl worked at this fancy Lark's place for a while as a spa girl or something. That's what Ronnie told me.' He explained about her two weeks of regular and reliable work, and then her disappearance the day after the incident.

Eren arrived back, balancing two small cups holding the viscous, bitter coffee that his family brewed. They used modern technology but tried to achieve the taste their grandparents had grown up with. Their mother still preferred to boil her coffee in a copper pot and insisted that whenever her boys travelled to Turkey, they brought back coffee so finely ground it was just short of talc and looked like Dutch-processed cocoa.

'I've put in two lumps of sugar for you,' Eren said, handing Dav his steaming cup.

Dav sipped, being polite, and it was obviously tasty because he nodded. 'Good coffee, Eren. Go on,' he said to Baris. 'How do you know this girl's disappeared?'

'She wasn't scheduled to work on the night it happened, but she was meant to be working the following five days straight. No one's seen her.'

'Let's talk to this Ronnie fellow, shall we? I mean now, by phone. Can you call him, Eren?'

Baris noted from his brother's expression that he didn't like being instructed to do anything by their cousin but Eren did nod – it made sense. He took out his phone and looked for Ronnie's contact details. 'Dialling,' he said unnecessarily, and Dav nodded, sipping his coffee again. Baris looked at his shoes, waiting.

'Hey, Ronnie boy,' Eren said. 'Yeah, I know you're working, but listen, we want to know more about this girl you mentioned.' He waited while Ronnie obviously whined about something. 'This is not actually a question, Ronnie.' Eren switched the call onto speaker.

Baris spoke. 'Ronnie, you know who this is?'

'Hello, Baris.' The man's voice was tinny.

'Good. Tell us about the girl.'

'Look, I have a photo I took at a work social.'

'Pretty, is she?'

'Yeah, well, I do fancy her.'

'So you sneaked a shot?'

'Yeah,' Ronnie admitted, sounding nervous.

'Can you send it to us?' Dav asked.

'Who's that?'

'Our cousin,' Baris said. 'He's interested in her too.'

'Not in the same way you are, though, Ronnie.' Eren laughed.

Ronnie hesitated. 'I changed phones. My photos aren't in this one.'

'I see,' Dav said. 'You can get it though?'

They could almost hear him shrugging, maybe wondering if it was too dangerous to ask them what it might be worth. 'Er, yeah, somewhere on the computer at home.'

'Find it, Ronnie,' Baris said. 'And send it. Right away. What about an address?'

'Er . . . maybe. I'm working at the moment,' he said tentatively, no doubt expecting them to threaten him.

'Soon as you can, the photo and the address,' Dav said in an attempt at a soothing tone, but Eren grinned at how menacing the accountant could sound.

'Yeah, yeah, okay. Soon as I can. I gotta go . . . er, bye.' He hung up.

'After we get the photo, then what?' Dav said.

'Well, then we'll know if it's Francoise or not. Either way, we'll find her,' Baris answered.

'And?' Dav asked.

'Question her before we silence her.'

16

Luca took the risk, feeling bold after last night's win. Ally had her back to him, the shower's heavy pattering of water muting other sounds, so his barefoot steps were silent. He stepped into the shower and put his arms around her. She stiffened momentarily, surprised, and then relaxed against his hard, muscled body.

They let the warmth of the water and the feeling of skin on skin say plenty.

'I've so missed you, Luca,' Ally whispered, sounding sad. 'I'm sorry I've been so difficult.'

'I don't blame you,' Luca said. 'This has been frightening.' He meant it.

'It's not just that. I'm not frightened with you next to me. I'm frightened of loving you so much and you not being here. I was so angry – I still am – that another woman has touched you.'

'So am I,' he said, turning her around so they faced one another, blinking in the hail of warm water. 'I swear on the life of my parents, my sister and these unborn babies that I did not cheat on you. I failed you by showing pity to someone, and she took advantage of that and put us in this mess. But whatever she did to me, under the influence of whatever drug she gave me, I did not touch her back.'

'I believe you. I'm sorry for making you feel so bad – I just had to come to terms with what she did.'

'I'm here, Ally, I always will be,' he said, enjoying holding her close. One of their babies stretched at that moment and he felt a foot – or was it an elbow? – push against him.

'Tell me you felt that?' Ally said.

Tears welled in his eyes; it was as though one of their precious children had reached out to help keep them close. He'd always been a romantic and liked to look at life through the most optimistic lens. 'I felt it. That was our child letting us know all will be well.'

'You mean that you'll win the triple or quadruple or whatever it is.' Ally laughed, kissing him.

He grinned. 'No, I'll do that anyway. For us. He or she is telling us that this thing won't hurt us.'

Ally kissed him again, more deeply this time, and he felt her love as though he was feeling it for the first time.

'Thank you,' he said. 'I so needed that today.'

She put her head to one side; she knew him too well. 'Something to tell me?'

He hesitated.

Her smile faded. 'Is it them?'

He nodded. 'The letter's come with the payment details. Arrived not long ago.'

Ally switched off the taps, and Luca helped her step out of the shower, reaching for a huge bath towel to wrap around her. Then he turned her again to face him.

'I want to say something.'

She waited.

'I can instruct Jon Mason to pay off those arseholes tonight.' He snapped his fingers, making a loud clicking sound that reverberated around the bathroom. 'I can make this whole business go away like that. I don't care any more. All I care about is you . . . and them,' he said, pointing to her belly. 'I want you to feel safe again and not look as . . .'

'Miserable?' she suggested, with a sad smile.

He shook his head slightly. 'Vulnerable.'

She blinked.

'Ally, you've always been so strong, so direct,' he said, cutting the air with his hand. 'But this blackmail crap has made you seem, I don't know . . . defenceless. And I won't have that. You've been my rock since the day I met you. I play my best because of you. You're always there in the stands cheering me on, and even if we play badly, you always say the right things to help me get back up. But since this, I feel like you've withdrawn. I'm also feeling, you know, exposed. I don't like it, I don't want it and I don't have to put up with it, because we've got the money to make it go away. So now tell me. Shall I just pay the bastards?'

Ally dropped her towel and, naked, reached up to hug him. She whispered in his ear, 'You get them, Luca. No one does this to us.' Then she stood back. 'We've never hurt anyone. We've always looked after others. I know you give away plenty to charity, and you never say no when this fundraiser or that one asks you to help. I'll be damned if I let some scammer reduce us to prisoners in our home, or make you look down. You look them in the eye, Luca Bruni, and say, "Fuck you – go earn it like I do."'

He laughed. 'There she is. There's my Ally.'

'We won't be paying them a penny, because if we do then someone else might be facing this, and that's on us for being cowards. So you fight them, for me, and for that next victim.'

Luca nodded. 'So much to love about you, Ally Bruni.'

'I wish you didn't have to go to training.'

'I know, I'd like to have cuddled up with you in bed right now.'

'There's always tonight. But just a cuddle, mind!' she said, slapping away his wandering hands.

Harry yawned as he brought Gina's favourite china cup to where she was curled up on the sofa, flicking through a magazine. She always had been an early riser. He needed to try harder with her; patching up their relationship had been a slow journey.

'There you go, babe. Tea.'

'Thanks,' she said. 'You can leave it there.' She pointed to the coaster on the table. 'I'll let it cool a bit, because I know you didn't make it in a pot, right?' She gave him an accusing look.

He smiled sheepishly. 'I'm trying, babe.'

'Yeah. But you've got a way to go . . . babe,' she echoed the last word, making it sound insincere. 'I don't like being number two, you know that.'

He nodded. How was he going to make her believe it wasn't like that?

'You know, I didn't believe it when I heard you were sleeping with that Tallis tart.'

He winced.

'You weren't careful enough. You knew my girls cleaned at that property and still you risked it. Stole my master key so you could fu—'

'How many different ways can I say I'm sorry?' he interjected, working hard to keep his tone apologetic and tender.

'Sorry just doesn't cut it. You've humiliated me. I'm sure everyone knows.'

'No, they—'

'Harry, don't manage me. Manage the "children" in that footy club, but don't try it on me.'

'Gina, I want this marriage to work.'

'Really?' she shot back. 'You have a strange way of showing that. Listen, the only reason you're not with the slut right now is because she cracked on to something much, much better. You're a has-been. You're good-looking, no one denies that, and while she was there in the club playing at PR for Daddy, you were her plaything. But she's grown up and married into money as serious as her own. You were never more than a distraction for her, but you broke us.'

'How long will this go on?' It wasn't the right question; he could see that in the fury of her expression.

'This? This, whatever that means, will go on for as long as I choose.'

He sighed. She wasn't going to forgive him easily. He'd need to take Gina's form of medicine for the next six months, he suspected, maybe a year, playing slave and adoring partner until she deemed him worthy of her. She would come around. Gina was too sensible not to – it was just going to take a while.

'I'll stay patient then. I have to get to training.'

She nodded, beginning to turn the pages of her magazine once more. She grimaced. 'All these young hotties. They all wear the same vacant, gormless expression.'

'Not like in your time, eh?'

'You make me sound very old, Harry, with that remark.'

He moved behind her and rubbed her shoulders. 'Gina, you look amazing and you know it. Millions of women want to be you.'

'And yet you had your affair,' she said airily.

He stopped rubbing her shoulders and squatted by the arm of the sofa. When she didn't look at him, he touched her chin, tilting her face to regard him. 'However long it takes, I need you to forgive me. I will do anything in the world to make it up to you.'

'I have yet to understand why you did it. Clearly I'm not enough.'

'Do I need to say it again?'

She stared at him. 'Harry, you need to *keep* saying it and keep proving it.'

'You know how much I was hurting. I wasn't myself. The accident, having to retire before I was ready, giving up my whole life as I knew it . . .'

'And yet I was there, loving you, supporting you, taking care of you. But you turned to that Tallis bitch instead, and now where is she? Married, having children of her own. You couldn't give her that. You couldn't give it to me either, but did I complain? Did I shit in our perfect nest?'

He flinched. 'No.'

'I was loyal, even through my own anguish at not having children.'

'Gina, we should have adopted—'

'No. I told you, ours or not at all. I wanted to carry a baby in my belly, Harry. I offered you an option, but you weren't having anything to do with that.'

He looked down. 'I didn't want another man's baby inside you.'

She softened. 'It would always have been ours. Our love would have raised a child.'

'I've failed you, darling, in every way, but will you let me try again properly? Just let me in.'

'I keep thinking of her, smiling at me at the club, all the time she was fu—'

'Please! It was a mistake. I was dumb. A stupid, dumb man like all dumb men – easy targets.'

'Not Luca, though. Your apprentice isn't like that.'

'I might have been the master, but he was never my apprentice – he was a born bloody wizard.'

'My point is that Luca, as young as he is, resisted the charms of another woman.'

'So he says.' Harry had to say it.

'I trust him. He's still a boy. You've seen the way he looks at Ally, haven't you? You haven't looked at me like that in years.'

Harry looked down. 'Gina, darl, we've been together for ages.'

She poked his arm. 'I want to be looked at like that.'

He smiled. 'I have never stopped loving you or fancying you. You're just quite tough, Gina. You're so together, so strong, and you were determined for me to reinvent myself. You could see it, but I couldn't. I felt lost and you needed to let me feel a little lost for a while.'

'You mean I should have pandered to your self-pity?'

He gave a shrug. 'I think I needed a little time to get used to the idea of no longer being a Premier League god.'

'No one's a god, Harry.'

'Luca is. He's only going to get better, get tougher. He'll bulk up a bit more and no one will be able to push him off the ball.'

'I don't want to discuss Luca's attributes. I know them. He's amazing and so is Ally. She has more forgiveness in her heart than me. She is already moving past her pain, realising she has to be strong for him to come through this shit they're going through. That's all I was doing for you. But you didn't respond like Luca is now. He needs Ally's strength, but you turned away from mine. I just can't see how it is different.'

'The difference was me. I'm the weak one. Luca's not weak – he's defying those goons, whoever they are.'

'Can't you find out through the football network?' Gina asked.

Harry was surprised at the turn of conversation. 'I'm not even meant to know about it, really. The police are handling it. But I'd like to break their bastard necks for putting Luca and Ally through this.'

'I like his attitude, hitting back.'

'If I were him, I'd pay and spare the aggro.'

'You're not him, though, Harry, are you?' she said. It wasn't a question. Gina stood up. 'I better get going.'

'I didn't think you were going in to work today.'

'I'd better. I know you think it runs itself, but unless I'm there and cracking the whip, things don't go to plan.'

'How *are* things at work?'

Gina gave him a look of contrived shock.

'What? Can't I be interested in your business?'

'You can. You just haven't been for about a year. I didn't think you even knew I had a business any more.'

'Come on. Talk to me.' He stood, gave her a hug and she allowed it.

'Business isn't brilliant, and it might not survive.'

He frowned. 'But—'

'Don't worry, Harry, I have some ideas.'

'Why didn't you say something before?'

'Because you've got enough on your mind with the team. Listen, you're doing a great job. I have no doubt you'll laugh about this one day when you're head coach at one of the Premier League clubs.'

He gave an awkward grin.

'Until then, we do our best. I've got plans and I won't trouble you with them until they're close, but I promise you'll be the first to know. In the meantime, keep winning matches and earning the bonuses. Keep Luca scoring goals and let's win the treble, at least.'

'At least,' he murmured, looking at the ceiling exaggeratedly to make her smile. 'Have you any idea how hard winning a single one is?' The question was rhetorical. 'I know we both have work now, but can we have this evening together, Gina? Just the two of us?'

She hesitated. 'I was going to check in on Ally. She's so close now.'

He nodded, looked a little disappointed. 'Please, Gina. Let's make today day one of a new us. I'll work at it, and when you feel I've earned your trust, we can take our vows again or something . . . have a party and reaffirm our love for one another.' Harry thought she perked up at that. He was relieved to see her smile and not snarl with disdain.

'All right. I'll tell her we're on a date night, how's that?'

He looked up, delighted. 'Dress up and we'll go to Matteo's.'

'Ah, spoiling me?'

'This is how it's going to be from now on – if you'll let me.'

'Spoil me all you like.'

'I'll be home by six. Wear that red dress.'

She kissed him, but not lingeringly – even so, to Harry, it was a breakthrough; it was the first time in an age that she'd kissed him first, and it felt like she meant it.

'I'm sorry,' he said again when she pulled back. 'I'm sorry about us and I'm sorry about your business. But I'm going to make you feel like a princess every day from now on.'

This time she pecked his cheek. 'See you this evening.'

17

The air in the Stonecrop ops room suddenly thickened with collective surprise as a stranger entered. Heads turned and conversations muted. Kate had been securing a grainy photo to their board and paused; Jack noticed her upbeat mood as she beamed him a smile full of anticipation, but then her mouth opened with surprise as she saw who was following him. Her mouth clamped shut again and Jack imagined hackles rising. It was a normal response to alarm, but where most would want to turn and run, Kate was one of those who'd stop and want to face it.

'Morning, all,' Jack said, deliberately breezy, trying not to meet Kate's shocked gaze just yet. He knew her mind would be racing. She'd certainly feel ambushed, but he'd figured it was easier this way. Force them to meet. She was showing signs of loneliness. He suspected he knew what she needed in her life – and what she needed was standing beside him, also avoiding her stare of disbelief.

'I want to introduce you all to DCI Geoff Benson. Geoff and I go way back, and I trust this bloke with my life. He's here on the instructions of Chief Superintendent Carol Rowland, who anticipates that we will now share information with the investigation that DCI Benson is spearheading into the murder of the Wimbledon vet.' Jack hoped Kate wouldn't be upset he hadn't warned her about Geoff. 'I think it's best if he briefs you – all will become clear. I know we're keeping our ring of silence tight around Operation Stonecrop, but you have nothing to fear from him and can speak openly. Geoff?'

'Thanks, Hawk. Er, morning, everyone. Hello again, Kate,' he risked, clearly picking up on Jack's plan to push through in a professional manner. 'We're also old friends and colleagues,' he said, gesturing in her direction.

Jack wanted to cheer at the way his friend had effectively moved off the back foot and taken control.

'DCI Benson, what a surprise this is. Good to see you again,' Kate said, also staying formal and professional.

'Thanks, everyone. I look forward to meeting you all individually, but let me tell you why your boss has called me in.' Geoff cut a look at Jack before explaining about Michael Evans.

As he finished, Jack listened to the room grow quieter until they could all hear Joan, in the distance, at her keyboard, giving a light cough. The significance of the link between the two cases wasn't lost on anyone in the ops room. Even Kate seemed to have set aside her surprise and was now fully engaged with Geoff's details of the vet's death.

'So do we now formally believe that Evans was involved in Bruni's blackmail?' Kate asked.

Jack shook his head. 'No, that's not what we should believe. The only evidence we have is that Evans seemed to be storing reproductive material that his clinic had no professional reason to be involved with. So that leads us to question whether he was storing animal reproductive material on the side, or whether, more worryingly, he was storing human reproductive material as part of the blackmail scheme that's been happening over the past few years.'

'Evans died viciously. Do you believe it to be an execution?' Kate asked Geoff directly.

Geoff nodded. 'That was my first and only reaction. It certainly wasn't a break-in. The vet's partner says he was inside watching the news and eating dinner with his back to the door. The killer arrived, Evans answered the door, was murdered swiftly, silently – after only a couple of words exchanged, according to the partner. I would hazard those were the killer asking if he was Michael Evans before he slashed his throat. And then the killer was gone. His partner believes it might have taken all of twenty seconds once the door was opened.'

The ops team gave a collective sigh of dismay.

'So, it really does appear to be an execution. The manner was too fast, clean and clinical to be anything else.'

'What about mistaken identity?' Kate asked.

'It's possible, but then there's this reproductive material storage. That muddies the notion that he was an innocent.'

Ari piped up before Kate could ask another question. 'Why do you think he was killed?'

Geoff gave a mirthless smile. 'At this stage it's only a personal conclusion, but I've been in this game long enough to know that Evan's death was not a message, not a warning, or any kind of threat, but—'

'A close of business,' Kate finished, meeting his gaze properly for the first time.

'Exactly.' He nodded. 'I believe this was someone putting distance between themselves and whatever Michael Evans might have known, or been involved with, in the most conclusive manner.'

'So, if we're presuming Evans stored the semen, who else is there that they'd be worried about?' Ari asked. 'Do you think anyone else is at risk?'

Jack jumped in. 'Well, in this sort of game you'd keep it very small. I'd say the other potential liability is the woman – the escort they used to get the, uh, sample that gives them the ability to blackmail these guys.'

'So we can expect another execution?' Ari asked.

'I'd say so,' Geoff said, shrugging. 'If it's the same woman being used for Bruni's blackmail, perhaps this op has a chance to get to her first.'

Kate frowned. 'She'd go into hiding, surely, having heard what happened to the vet? That was all over the news.'

'She might not even know he's involved, though. The perpetrators wouldn't necessarily let one hand know what the other was doing. I certainly wouldn't if I was running a scheme like this. The fewer people who know of each other, the safer you are.'

'She could already be dead,' Sarah said from the background. Jack had noted her silently taking in everything, but he was pleased she'd spoken up now.

'She could,' Jack agreed. 'And to this end, we'll be looking into any bodies found of women, anything that's under even the slightest suspicion of foul play. Matt – can you get started on that today?'

'They might not even use the same woman each time,' Ari offered.

'True,' Geoff conceded.

Jack shook his head thoughtfully. 'No, as you say, the greater the ring of knowledge, the more exposed the perpetrators become. I would suggest they've been successful thus far by following that rule.'

Geoff shrugged, nodding his agreement.

'Which brings me to something I'd like to throw into our ring. Sarah, you might like to brief everyone on what you've discovered.' He watched her straighten, and although she still blinked nervously behind her glasses, he could see the glitter of pleasure at being asked.

'Right,' she said, grabbing some notes from her desk.

Jack gestured for her to stand at the front while he and Geoff retreated. Geoff sidled towards Kate, who angled a barrage of silent questions at him with her glare, while Jack leaned back against a desk to the side of the room. 'Go ahead,' he said.

'There are at least nine incidents of blackmail we know about, though we've had little information about them,' Sarah said, glancing Geoff's way. 'There are likely more. Unfortunately the sporting fraternity is not sharing what they know.'

'Not yet, anyway,' Kate said.

'But, um, there's a worthy case to be built for the Luca Bruni blackmailer to be a copycat.' Sarah paused and let that sink in before continuing. 'The MO *appears* identical, but there are actually quite a few differences, and they're not necessarily subtle.' She looked over to her boss. 'Sir, would you like to take it from here?'

'No, carry on, Sarah,' Jack said, noting that Geoff was now standing directly next to Kate, who had not deliberately discouraged him. *Good.*

'Right, well, first off, there's the note. Bruni's note was delivered by Donkey Express, whereas all the others that we know of came in via the post. Over the last couple of days and after a great deal of coercion we have fortunately been able to now view two of these historical ransom notes,' Sarah told the group. 'We believe these are the only two in existence, as the rest were likely burned. These notes, one to a tennis player, the other to a cricketer, were given to us through the agency cohort that first contacted the police, via George Shaw, and while they quite markedly resemble each other, neither resembles Bruni's. Shaw said all of the previous ones looked similar, if not identical, to these two.' She let that land. 'Moving on to the time frame. Shaw said the time given to the other victims was two days in every case. The classic forty-eight hours. And that ultimatum was delivered in the original and only note, which contained the information about payment – what account to send it to, all that. At this point, Mr Bruni is yet to receive those details, which are presumably coming in another note.'

'That all makes sense,' Geoff said, nodding. 'So Bruni doesn't know if they actually have his semen? Jack said he's denying any, uh, . . . indiscretion.'

Kate answered. 'He tells us that if it is his, he didn't give it willingly. He believes he was drugged, so he can't remember much at all, least of all giving the, er, sample.'

'So it could be someone else's semen, or . . .' Geoff began.

'School glue,' Matt said, with a look of embarrassment.

Kate had none. 'Or a mix of, you know, condensed milk and . . .'

As the others burst out laughing, Geoff held up a hand. 'Oh, stop, that's repulsive,' he said, trying to hold back a smirk of his own. 'Please don't explain that to anyone outside of this room.'

Jack grinned and saw that Kate did as well. 'Sarah, keep going,' he said and that quietened his team again.

'Er, thanks. So, as well as the differences I mentioned already, there's the tone of the note, which is probably the most compelling reason to question its source. The Bruni note is considerably different to the previous blackmail notes. It's just short of conversational, bordering on playful, if I can use that word, whereas the letters the agency group has shared were concise to the point of brutal,' she said, pushing her glasses back up her nose and glancing at Jack.

'Good. Thanks, Sarah. There is genuine merit in that scenario. We'll talk about how we address that once we've been briefed on your day at Lark's Hill. Anything helpful, Kate?'

'Yes. I think we might have something,' she said, clearly trying to temper her triumph by playing it down. 'And this is thanks to the focus of Nat here. Nat, do you want to brief us?'

Nat shook her head, looking too overwhelmed to speak in front of so many senior detectives, all turning towards her.

Kate didn't press her. 'Okay, well, while Ari and I were upstairs with the front of house manager, trying to get a measure of Luca Bruni's night there, Nat and Matt,' she said, cutting a look that said *Don't* at Geoff, 'were downstairs at the back of house interviewing staff.'

Kate moved to the front and pointed at the latest image she'd secured to the board. 'This is a member of staff known as Sylvie Toussaint.' She tapped the photograph, a standard staff ID shot.

Jack looked at the image of a dark-haired woman, perhaps in her mid-twenties, with an elfin cast to her face. She was halfway to beautiful in a movie star sort of way, but somewhere her features fell short and instead remained in the realm of simply pretty. He could only see the top of her body, clad in an off-the-shoulder blouse of engine red to match her lipstick.

'This, we believe, could be our girl. For the last few weeks she has worked in the Lark's Hill spa as a masseuse. According to everyone, Sylvie is bright, fun, never late and yet always prepared to stay late. The manager, Angela Wright, assures us that Sylvie's credentials were in order and that every client – and she emphasised *every* client – commended Sylvie's massages as worth coming back for. Angela tells us that everyone loves Sylvie's French accent'—Kate looked pointedly around at the room at the word 'French'—'and mannerisms, and that she was diligent in ensuring every client left happy.' Kate shrugged. 'A model member of staff. Now, this photo was taken at a colleague's birthday bash a few weeks ago. The guy who took the photo, coincidentally, is a porter at Lark's Hill and has had a crush on Sylvie since she began working there.' Kate paused to pin up another photo from the file she had sitting nearby. 'While Nat can take all the glory for finding out about Sylvie, Matt over here should get a beer at least for getting us a second photo of her. Thanks, you two — really good work.'

They nodded at her compliment and Jack watched them each take a deep breath of pleasure. Kate was doing them proud.

The second image was a candid shot, snapped in a moment of jollity. Sylvie was cheering as the birthday girl, another staff member from the health and fitness centre, blew out candles on a birthday cake. Sylvie's arms were flung carelessly in the air and she was smiling with genuine pleasure.

Everyone gave the same sound of awe. Clearly displayed on the underside of her forearm was a tattoo they all recognised. It was exactly as Luca Bruni had recalled.

Kate nodded, grinning. 'Exactly,' she said, tapping the tattoo.

'Where is she now?' Jack asked, not waiting for anyone else to ask the obvious.

Kate sighed. 'Unknown. She hasn't shown up for work since the Bentley gala. Angela's worried something's happened to her.'

'Judging by what's happened to the vet, that's a very real fear. Good work, all of you,' Jack said. 'Do we know where she lives?'

Ari jumped in. 'No longer at that address, guv. I went straight around. Her flatmate sounds shocked. Apparently Sylvie came in during the early hours after the Bentley event to collect her gear and then left. She didn't take much, left a lot of her clothes behind. No note. But she did leave two weeks' rent in advance, which is kind of decent, right?'

No one answered him.

'Well, she certainly matches the description,' Jack said. 'We need to do everything we can to find her.'

'Sir?' It was Sarah. Jack nodded to her, giving her freedom to say what was on her mind. 'If we subscribe to the idea that the Luca Bruni blackmail is a copycat event, do we think Sylvie was in on the original incidents? What about the vet? The other cases were quite a while ago.'

Jack met Geoff's gaze; he looked as grave as Jack felt.

'My work in Vice and Major Crimes would suggest that's highly likely,' Geoff answered. 'How long ago was the previous incident?'

'From what we can tell, the last one was about nine months ago, right, Sarah?'

She nodded.

'An international cricketer . . . English,' Jack clarified.

'And what's the regularity?' Geoff asked.

Jack shrugged. 'The agent would only give general answers. They're extremely cagey because they barely want to admit it's happened. Shaw reckons it happened every six to eight weeks, so it's unusual that it's popped up again after so long. That's another reason we think it's someone else this time.'

Geoff took a breath. 'So, in the intervening months, a copycat has latched on to their modus operandi, and the original perpetrators have got wind of it somehow. And now, concerned for their own invisibility, they're cleaning house.'

'It feels about right,' Jack said. It was all coming together.

'I think they'll be coming after her.' Sarah pointed to the image of Sylvie. 'She's a loose end, like the vet.'

'She may not be the same girl.' Ari frowned. 'What if we get distracted trying to protect her and someone else gets killed?'

'But she might be the same girl,' Sarah replied. 'Even if she isn't, we know she's involved in Bruni's case and probably in danger because of that. Why else would she have disappeared?'

'On the run?' Kate thought aloud for everyone's benefit.

'Or she's just laying low,' Jack said reasonably. 'If it's the same girl, she's done her part and is likely waiting for them to collect the semen and pay her share. I imagine she wants a decent cut, because she could hardly not know the wealth of the guy she was blackmailing. I doubt they paid her much up front. If they're copycats, it might be more a case of "Let's see if it works, and if it does, we all share the spoils".'

'All conjecture,' Kate warned, biting her lip. 'But certainly feasible.'

'Right. We need another meeting with our tight-lipped agent,' Jack said. 'I want to know if Shaw thinks Sylvie was involved in the original incidents. Sarah, you and I can tackle that.'

'Right, sir. I'll organise it.'

'Nat and Matt,' Jack said, 'get onto the porter that Matt discovered. If he has a crush on Sylvie, he might know more than he let on. Do we have a photo of *him*?'

Nat nodded and dug around on her desk. She walked up to the board and added a typical staff shot of a man who was not memorable for any visual reason, with close-cropped, darkish hair and regular features.

'This is the porter. He works as a casual dogsbody as needed, usually in porterage but sometimes running errands, picking up supplies,' Matt said.

Jack nodded. 'Good, bring him in for interview and feel free to scare him a little without giving the Met a bad name. Do the—'

'Hey, wait!' It was Geoff, who'd gone over to the board to get a clear look at the photo. 'This is the porter?'

Nat nodded, looking worried.

'Is his name Ronnie?'

'That's right,' Nat said. 'Er, Ronnie Barrett.'

Geoff gave a mirthless smile that didn't last. 'He's a slimy little toad, often nicknamed Ronnie Corbett because he's really short.

He's a small-time hood who used to work for the Celiks. Do you know the Celiks, Hawk?'

Jack shook his head.

'You must, Kate?'

Recognition showed on her face. 'Yeah, yeah, Turkish brothers, right? I never had much to do with them, but of course we heard about them in Vice.'

'Have we ever pinned anything on them?' Ari asked.

Geoff shook his head. 'No, they're smart and, above all, they're modest. They're not at all flashy. Seemingly nice blokes, good members of the Turkish community. They sponsor school events and I think they donated all the money required for that guy whose car was stolen last year at Putney – remember, he lost his special wheelchair and all those aids? Anyway, beneath all that, we believe they're in up to their necks. On the surface, they run barber shops and bars. Doing very well, always expanding. Both married with kids. But they're crims, open to all sorts, probably, getting into brothels, definitely laundering cash, and we'll get them for dodging tax if necessary. We have some evidence of that but have held off, hoping to get them on something bigger.'

'What kind of criminal activity?' Sarah asked. 'Do you think they're involved here?'

Geoff considered her question. 'Look, their crimes have been escalating, from what we can tell. We don't have confirmation of any blood on their hands – mostly white-collar stuff – but I wouldn't rule it out. Their cousin runs a successful accounting firm, and we believe he's the one helping them launder their illegal earnings.'

'A bit of creative financial management?' Jack wondered.

Geoff smiled. 'Probably. It's what several in our team are looking at now. If we can't pin them down for money laundering, as I hope, then we can get the Celik brothers on tax fraud.' He tapped the photo of the porter. 'But Ronnie fell out of favour with them some months ago, and he bobbed up as a police informer.'

'And now he's working at Lark's Hill, right at the heart of all this,' Kate said.

'He's worth looking at seriously,' Geoff said. 'If there's a scam about, Ronnie will know something about it . . . if he isn't already part of it.'

Jack looked at Matt. 'Let's get him in immediately. Get Angela Wright in too. We want every little detail they can give us on Sylvie. Keep in mind that we think that's a pseudonym, so we're also looking for clues as to what her real name might be. But, Geoff, Ronnie's link with the Celiks could open up a whole new strand here. Why don't you take point on that?'

'Will do.'

'Ari, we still need to talk to security at the football club – that's long overdue. Did the Arrows win, by the way?'

Ari nodded. 'Two–nil, guv. They'll qualify easily for Europe. This week it's a big game for the premiership against West Ham.'

'Right, well, big game or not, that security team is now under our scrutiny. Get onto it today.'

'Oh, bugger, bugger!' It was Kate.

'I heard that,' came Joan's distant voice and a tin rattling soon after.

Kate shook her head. 'I've just remembered something the manager at Lark's Hill said. It got lost in an interruption while Ari and I were in the guest room, which by the way he describes accurately.'

Ari looked puzzled. 'What did we forget?'

'The overnight guests,' she said.

'The golfer and his partner? He's a world-class competitor. American.'

She shook her head. 'No, the other guests.'

'Others?' Ari looked baffled.

Kate looked cross with herself as she shared her recollection with the team. 'There were two couples also staying overnight, but I heard from the manager that one pair ordered separate beds, and they didn't attend the event in the end, claiming the woman wasn't feeling well. Seemed a little odd. I never did check who that was, so I'll get onto it now.'

Jack nodded. 'Right, perhaps it's also time to interview the former captain of the Huxley Arrows and his wife – separately.'

'On it,' Kate said. 'And sorry it took me a while to bring that back.'

'Better go pay Joan,' Geoff offered.

She half-grimaced but couldn't fully disguise her amusement.

'And you might like to update the Brunis,' Jack added.

Her phone began ringing as he said this. 'Speak of the devil.' She headed for the door to take the call. 'Hello, Luca?'

Jack turned back to Geoff. 'I'm going to need all the help we can get to find Sylvie Toussaint. Can you circulate her photo through your networks? She's now our link to all of them and, if Sarah's right, she might also be in serious danger.'

'I'll get onto that now.'

Jack nodded. 'Good luck, everyone. Work fast.'

Kate stepped back in. 'I have news.' Everyone paused. 'The second note is in, the one with the payment details. Arrived at the Brunis' by Donkey Express just a few minutes ago.'

'Right, got your casual gear?' Jack asked. 'You and I had better get over there first. Tell them to meet us—'

Kate shook her head. 'He's going to training.'

Jack took a deep breath. 'Tell him we'll meet him at the grounds, then, and he's to keep up the pretence of old friends.'

Everyone started to move again and there was a frisson of fresh eagerness in the room. Even Joan noticed it when she walked in.

'Wow, have you all had too much sugar? Don't forget your diary sheets on my desk, please. Kate?' She shook the tin. 'Two pounds, please.'

'I only swore once.'

'But you said the naughty word twice,' Joan said sweetly, as Kate huffed off to get her purse.

Geoff caught Jack in his office as he was pulling off his jacket and digging around for sneakers. 'What's all this?'

Jack explained the ruse.

'Okay, look, can we plan to see each other this afternoon?' Geoff asked. 'There are still a few gaps to fill in.'

'Sure. One, one-thirty?'

'Good.' Geoff gave the universal sign for a phone at his ear. 'Give me a buzz.'

'Hey, Geoff.'

His friend turned back.

'I thought that went okay.' They both knew Jack was talking about Kate. 'The plaster's been ripped off. Time to make the wound heal.'

Geoff smiled sadly. 'I'll try.'

18

Jack and Kate were standing on the edge of the training grounds, arms crossed and gloved hands tucked into their armpits as they intermittently stomped their feet. Ari, now with the security team, had driven out with them, so they hadn't been able to talk freely in the car.

Dressed casually, they looked like typical visitors being given a tour of the stadium. Jack was watching the first and second goalies taking turns – six shots per turn – saving goals from their trainer. 'Wow, they hit that ground quite hard, don't they?' he said, thinking aloud. 'It must feel like concrete on a day like today.'

'I'm glad we don't have to do this every day. You look quite good in a beanie, though,' Kate said.

Jack tuned in and laughed. 'And you look good in anything.'

They were both in jeans, hooded sweats and thick coats. Kate's was fur-lined but she looked almost blue from the cold breeze dancing around their exposed faces.

'Ugh,' she whined. 'They all look so horribly happy and fit . . . and warm.'

'They are running while we stand around. I do regret the sneakers, I admit. I can't feel my toes.'

It made her chuckle. 'I'm angry with you, of course.'

'I know,' Jack said, giving her a soft sideways smile, knowing exactly what she was referring to. 'But it was not intentional.' He explained how Geoff had been dragged into the case. '. . . Carol Rowland insisted, and I had no chance to warn you.'

'It's okay, you're forgiven. It was nice to see him actually,' she admitted sheepishly. 'I've avoided him since—'

'So he tells me. And he feels as awkward as arse too.'

At this remark she burst into laughter. 'Oh, I must save that for future use.'

'My nephew taught me that one. I like it too – it's meaningless, yet funny, right? Anyway, I thought you were both pretty good, considering that was the first time you've had to be in the same room since you parted ways.'

'I won't lie. It was hard, Jack; hard to part, hard to watch him today. I can't believe how different he looks. I'm proud of him, though.' She paused, looking down. 'Geoff and I were good together.'

'You still could be,' Jack offered, waiting for the rebuff and getting a soft snort instead.

'I don't think so.'

'Why not? Time has passed, and plenty has happened in between. You've stared death in the face, and you've also had a meaningful relationship that—'

'Also didn't last,' she interjected with a sneer, more at herself than him.

'I don't mean to play psych, Kate, but maybe Dan didn't work out because of unfinished business with Geoff. You said you were the problem, not him.'

She shifted uncomfortably. 'I blamed work.'

'I don't doubt it, but it's also an ideal excuse. Plenty of people in the force have solid relationships and marriages.' Was it okay to fib if it made the person feel better, in a moment when feeling better was essential? Yes. He decided to abandon his personal creed on this occasion.

'That depends on whether your version of plenty lines up with mine. You don't look to be getting serious anytime soon.'

'That's true. But I have never chased it.'

'Why though? You seem to possess all the qualities of a guy who'd like to be a family man.'

'Perhaps. Maybe I'm too long in the tooth now.'

'Not true. I speak from experience. There are tens of thousands of women in inner London alone searching for a good man to share their life with. So many are disappointing. So many let you down after you've put in the effort, and then you've lost those good years you'll never get back. We age fast, if you haven't noticed. You blokes just seem to get better!' She gave a sigh of disgust. 'Plus time is cruel to women, because it can deny us children if we leave it too long, faffing around trying to find the right mate.'

Jack put an arm around her, knowing it was the right moment to do so; it would look convincing to observers, too, though that wasn't why he'd done it. 'Then don't leave it too long,' he said gently. 'Give yourself and Geoff a chance to work things out.'

'You think he wants to?' She sounded surprised.

'Kate,' Jack said baldly. 'He has never recovered from losing you.'

She shook her head. 'But he left me.'

'So did Dan. But in both cases I suspect they thought it was what you wanted, that it would make it easier on your heart. Geoff wants a family, you know that. I know your first response is to be fearful of that, but it doesn't have to stop you working. It will make it harder, but hardly impossible.'

'I don't want to end up in a desk job just yet, Jack.'

'Fair enough, but you also don't have to rush headlong into potentially fatal situations all the time. You're ready to run your own ops, and you don't have to view that as growing old and slow behind a desk.'

She smiled and nodded, clearly appreciating his advice.

They returned their attention to the training session, which involved a lot of shouting between the players, a fair amount of playful jostling and constant whistles from the head coach. Jack sensed Kate getting colder and more bored.

'Bloody hell, how many more times will they do that drill? They're not dimwits . . . or are they?'

'They're rehearsing what they call set pieces.'

'Oh, like the other team is going to oblige and all stand exactly where this coach wants them to.' Kate rolled her eyes.

Jack sighed and began to explain as though addressing a small child. 'There are corners, free kicks and even strategic set pieces, which run out of defence and go into offensive positions with crosses and passes that could result in goals. These are all worked out specifically to counterattack specific teams and talents, so what works against the Spurs doesn't necessarily work against Wolves or Real Madrid. These set pieces need to be practised repeatedly depending on the next team coming up.'

She blew out her cheeks. 'I'd rather just watch Federer.'

He laughed. 'Fair enough. Ah, here comes Luca.'

The striker had broken free and was loping across the pitch to reach them. He arrived with a streaming nose, sniffing, and breathing hard from his exertions, creating vapours around him. 'I've been given an early off. Thanks for waiting in the cold.'

They nodded.

'Well done on the goal last night,' Jack said as they fell in step.

He grinned. 'Thanks. So, I just have to do a quick cool-down with the physio. Would that be okay? You're welcome to come along.'

'Fine,' Jack said amiably. 'We won't discuss anything other than football. You can explain stuff to Kate, who thinks your training drills are extremely boring – she got it the first time and you must all be very dim.'

That made Luca laugh with genuine amusement and Jack saw again how very young he still was. Until now, Bruni had looked to be carrying the weight of the world on his shoulders. It was a pleasure to witness the delight in his features and unguarded laughter.

They followed him into the physio rooms as Luca tried to make sense of the drills for Kate, who was wearing her 'patient' face. Inside, Luca was greeted with a fist bump from one of the physios.

'This is Dan,' he said. 'Er, these are some friends of mine, Jack and Kate. They've been given clearance by the top man himself.'

'Ah, nice,' Dan said. 'Hop up, Luca.' He gestured to the physio table. 'How's the calf?'

'Actually, it's good. It was niggly a couple of days ago, but I didn't feel much today or last night – not even at the start of the warm-ups.'

'All hail the stars that are shining upon us,' Dan said loudly, attracting the attention of the other physios in the room, who smiled and yelled, 'All hail.'

Jack and Kate grinned.

'This boy is very important to our team, in case you hadn't already caught on,' Dan said.

'Never stops telling us,' Kate replied. 'He's quite the bore.'

Dan smiled, hearing the fun of the lie. 'We know he's modest,' he said, reaching for a bottle of liniment. 'Light rub-down, okay, nothing too deep. I don't want to wake it up.'

Luca nodded.

Jack and Kate put up with a stream of small talk before other specialists came to see Luca. He introduced them to his dietitian, his strength trainer and then Harry came wandering in. He gave Luca a brotherly hug.

'Hello again,' he said to Jack and Kate as though they were old friends. Jack was impressed. 'Come to see where the real work happens?'

'Yes – it's all very eye-opening. Luca's been telling us that he's been working to an individual training plan since he was twenty.'

Harry nodded. 'Each of our guys has a specifically drawn-up plan for every aspect of his football life, from which carbs he eats and when, to how much sleep he gets, which weights he lifts and how many times. They split upper and lower body gym sessions for different days. Lung capacity, stamina and, of course, any niggles like the young bloke's calf here. It's complex, but these fellows in the back room are across it all.'

Dan the physio grinned. 'Our boy's good, Harry. No tightness or soreness that I can tell, and I haven't seen him wince once – I tested him.'

Luca grinned. 'Didn't feel a thing.'

'Good lad. We need you in killer form.'

Jack and Kate watched Harry ruffle his mate's hair and it was so full of affection that the two detectives cast each other a look: *It's not Harry*. They'd prod at that thought later.

'So all this conditioning,' Kate wondered, acting deliberately dumb, 'does this happen every day?'

'Most days,' all three of them said together, making everyone chuckle.

Dan began to explain. 'So many reasons for physio intervention. Sometimes it's just for muscle conditioning, a chance for us to make sure everything's in tip-top health; other times for some light working – you know, if they have a niggle, and it needs attention. If a player is on his way back from injury, then we're nursing those muscles back to their best and that might be a six-month or nine-month program.' He gave Luca's leg a tap. 'You're good to go.'

'I'll just shower – ten minutes tops – and see you in the canteen,' he said to Kate and Jack, who nodded as one.

Luca hopped off the table and headed off, while Dan grabbed the liniment and moved away to pack up.

Harry smiled politely at the detectives. 'Did you ever play football, Jack?'

Jack shook his head. 'Not really. I was more of a rugby guy and then got into rowing and sailing.'

Harry raised his brows. 'Do you remember any of the guys jumping into ice baths?'

Jack nodded with a look of horror. 'My best mate, Geoff, used to tell me about it. I think he still does sometimes.'

Kate laughed. 'I've seen him fill up a wheelie bin with ice and jump in after a rugby match.'

'I remember it all too well in my days,' Harry agreed. 'But now these lucky boys have something called cryotherapy units. Mr Tallis swears by it, and he's installed a magnificent chamber. Want to see it?'

They did.

'Come with me. We've got a little time to kill while Luca showers, and then I'll show you back to the canteen. Thanks, Dan,' he said with a fist bump as they made for the door.

Jack and Kate thanked Dan too and hurried after Harry.

'If you're lucky, you might see some victims going in.'

They were indeed lucky and watched, mouths slightly agape, as two players donned masks and gloves and then, as the door of the chamber was opened and a plume of vapours escaped, unhappily stepped in, already with looks of dread.

'Help us!' one shouted in jest as the door closed.

Harry laughed. 'They'll do a couple of minutes in below-freezing temperature.'

Kate shuddered. 'How low exactly?'

'Down to one hundred and fifty below, sometimes.'

'Fuck!' she said and that made Harry guffaw. 'Why?'

'It aids fast recovery. It also shocks the muscles awake and out of their soreness. They all sleep well after a session.'

Jack shook his head in wonder as the pair was let out and another pair went in, grinning and joshing with each other as the vapours enveloped them. 'All of them do this?' Jack asked.

'From time to time. Not every player will come through straight after training, though.'

'All part of their conditioning plan, right?' Kate said.

Harry made a clicking sound and grinned as though cocking a pistol. 'Exactly. Okay, we'll let them suffer and I'll show you to the canteen.'

They dutifully followed. 'Seems like Mr Tallis is leaving no stone unturned for his team,' Kate commented.

Harry nodded. 'Truly, only the best. He's said to me that this way he can sleep straight knowing he's done everything he can within his power to give them the chance to win. He's an amazing guy.'

'And he has a daughter who works here?' Jack decided to see what that delivered.

'She used to. She's now married and living in Europe . . . very happily.'

'And you, Harry, are you happy?' Jack asked as they walked down the corridor that mercifully was empty, bar themselves. He stared hard at the ex-captain.

Harry hesitated, meeting his gaze. 'That's all in my past. It was a mistake – I was miserable about how my career ended – and now

I'm trying to be the best version of myself, make it up to my wife, and be a reliable, professional trainer and the best friend I can be.'

Jack nodded. 'We had to ask.'

'It's okay. Her father doesn't know, and I'd rather protect him from that – and her, to be honest. She deserves to live her life without my self-pity following her around.'

'Is that what it was?' Kate probed.

'Yeah, pretty pathetic. My wife knows and we're slowly patching things up. We've always been a good team . . . I let her down, but she's giving me a chance and I don't want to mess that up.'

'Our lips are sealed,' Jack said, appreciating the candour. Kate pretended to lock her lips.

'Thanks.' He smiled, clearly grateful. 'The canteen's just through here.'

Luca was as good as his word and walked in just as they did, his hair still dripping and a towel in one hand. He guided them to a private meeting room, showing them the new Arrows hoodie he'd changed into. Behind him came someone with a tray of food and takeaway coffees. Harry left them to their conversation with a friendly wave.

'Er, I've put milk in all, but sugar's there if you need. I've also brought in some rolls and pastries. Not for you, Luca,' the girl said with a soft smile. 'Only your guests get those. Don't get me into trouble, eh? Chicken soup and those sandwiches are for you.' She pointed.

'No worries, thank you,' he said as she left. He looked back at them. 'Please, help yourself.'

They did; the cold had made them hungry and it would have been rude not to partake, anyway.

'So these are just the training grounds, right?' Kate asked, reaching for a cup of coffee and placing another in front of Jack, who looked at it suspiciously. He couldn't help himself. Tallis paid for the best of the best, but did that extend to coffee outside of his stadium office? He'd risk it.

'Yeah. All the offices are here. Most of the staff. Our canteen, our training facilities, conditioning areas, gym, physio, laundry – all the backroom stuff. The stadium, on the other hand, is simply that – a showpiece. Our spiritual home and temple for the fans,' he said, no contempt in his voice at all. 'It's where we turn up for home games and where Mr Tallis has a more swanky office, but he and the executive team all work from here too in modest, normal spaces.' He paused to take a bite of his sandwich. 'Thanks for coming out here. I know it's a bit of a trek, but I didn't know how to fit it all in.'

'We understand,' Jack said.

Kate smiled softly. 'You've brought the letter?'

Luca nodded self-consciously and pulled it out of a backpack he'd put down beside him. 'I told Ally,' he said. 'I haven't told anyone else though.'

'How is Ally?' Jack asked.

'She's stressed. I don't want to add more to it. Gina's spending a lot more time with her. We're all a bit concerned it might affect the pregnancy if she gets too emotionally overloaded.'

'How much do Harry and Gina know?'

Luca looked surprised by the question. 'Most of it, except what Kate said to keep to myself. I don't know what we'd do without them. But they've got their own stuff to worry about.'

'What do you mean?' Kate asked.

Luca frowned. 'Just that Harry's at the club daily and under real pressure. You know we're going after three trophies this year. His performance is rated in much the same way that ours is.'

'And Gina?'

Luca smiled. 'She's got her own business to run, but she's been taking a lot of time out to help Ally.'

'What sort of business?' Kate asked. 'Isn't she an actress?'

'She was. She retired to help Harry after the accident, and then once he was back on his feet, she opened a cleaning business. We thought she was mad, but it's gone through the roof. She can barely keep up, but she never complains. She runs the house, the business and now puts in time with us. She's terrific.'

He pushed the letter forward, and Jack and Kate, who'd already pulled on gloves, opened it.

Jack scanned fast.

You've had time to think and hopefully you've decided it's easier to pay. I certainly think it is.

To make this go away, it's only going to cost you half a million pounds. That's nothing, right? It's not even a fraction of your sponsorship money.

You're too important to the team, Luca. Pay the money and this all disappears – you can get your mind back on winning.

One measly half million is all it takes, Luca.

Be careful. No cunning markings or trackers because we'll know. I do hope you're not involving the police. I've noted some new friends hanging around – we are watching you. Don't be tempted. Why blow your life up? Because that's what will happen. So much easier to pay this small sum and move on. You'll never hear from us again.

Tomorrow night. Ten thousand fifty-pound notes, wrapped in lots of plastic – Ryman's do a good quality – in a suitcase. It won't weigh more than about 11 kilos, Luca. You can carry that, a fit boy like you. Normal airline stuff. Do it carefully.

I'll let you know what to do next.

Remember this. If you don't follow our instructions exactly as we've asked, we'll hurt Ally. We can.

Smile – this is nearly over. And life can be safe again. And if you score some more goals next week, your bonus will wipe this fee out in a heartbeat. ☺

Jack looked at Luca, who shrugged.

Kate was still reading. She finally gave a sound of disdain. 'A smiley face?'

'Listen,' Luca began, 'I'm thinking of paying.'

'What?' Jack and Kate said together.

Luca put his palms up. 'I know I was angry and defiant before, but secretly I'm worried about Ally. I wanted to flip the finger at them. If I wasn't expecting babies soon, I'd do everything to help you hunt them down.'

'But that's the point, Luca,' Jack said, waving the letter. 'That's why you're the target – you're vulnerable. This person knows that, and I'd suggest they also know you've involved the police, or at least strongly suspect it, and so they're turning the screws on you. They're expecting you to give in and pay, because you can. It's easier.'

'It is,' Luca said. 'I've got so much on my plate. Our next game is going to be tough, and my coach wants at least one goal from me, probably two. He wants us to crush them convincingly. All those set pieces you were watching . . .' He flicked his thumb over his shoulder. 'Three of the four involved me scoring.'

Jack nodded, aware of the cracks appearing in not just the striker's resolve but the case right in front of him.

Luca shook his head. 'There's an even bigger game after that. They rely on me. I don't need this any more.' He flicked at the note. 'I can pay it and it can be done, and Ally and I can get back to our life.'

'You can't go back,' Kate said, echoing Jack's thoughts. 'Nothing will be the same. Ally's upset, and suspicions won't disappear. What *can* change things, however, and set them straight is when we catch these bastards and prove your innocence.'

'I *am* innocent!' he growled, looking around to check no one was listening. 'I don't need it proven to me.'

'Others do, though,' Jack said softly. 'And you want to clear all suspicion, don't you? I'm guessing Ally would prefer you to and not capitulate?' He could tell he'd hit on the truth from the relaxing of Luca's expression. Jack switched focus quickly as he wanted to ensure Luca's cooperation. 'Kate wants to show you a photo.'

It was Kate's turn to withdraw a page from her bag. 'Is this the woman who brought the champagne, Luca?'

He looked at the staff picture of Sylvie Toussaint and back to them, shocked. 'You've found her.'

'That's her?' Jack pressed.

'Yes.'

Kate feigned puzzlement. 'Where is the tattoo you mentioned?'

'Erm . . .' He looked at the photo again. 'You can't see it in this photo. It's here,' he said, pointing to his forearm. 'It's not very big, from memory.'

'Okay,' Kate said. Jack heard relief in her voice. 'We're going to take this,' she said, touching the ransom note.

'You can have it,' he said, sounding disgusted.

'Will you hold out for us, Luca?' Jack asked. 'Now we have this photo, we know who she is and we've got a good shot at finding her and everyone else involved in this scheme.'

'They're giving you time,' Kate said. 'There's another letter yet to come. They don't know how close we may be.'

Luca sighed. 'I suppose I can wait a little longer. What do you want me to do?'

'Go through the motions of getting the money. Who can help you with that?'

'Jon, my agent. He thinks we should just pay and get the hell out of it, so he'll be happy to help.'

'Easy for him to say, it's not his money,' Kate said, to support Luca in defying the blackmailers, Jack guessed.

'I really don't care about the money. I can pay this tomorrow and I will if you can't find her soon.' He looked hard at Jack and Kate.

'Between now and the next letter, we'll have her,' Jack said. It wasn't exactly a promise – more of a statement – but he felt Kate's gaze land heavily on him. 'And in the meantime, we'll keep our distance from you as they're obviously watching closely.'

'And Luca,' Kate said, 'you mentioned my caution about not mentioning what we discuss with anyone ... not even your friends?'

He nodded.

'Can we keep it that way, please? Do not let anyone beyond the three of us know that we've shown you that photo.'

'Even Ally?'

'Especially Ally,' Kate said and then added, 'It'll only fuel her anger. We want her calm and supportive, because that keeps you calm. Don't mention anything about this woman to anyone.'

'Okay.' He frowned. 'I've got nothing to fear from the people around me.'

'I know,' Jack reassured him, 'but we know from bitter experience that even an innocent remark can find its way to the wrong ears.'

'So, what we've shared today stays between us,' Kate said, drawing a small circle in the air to take in the three of them. 'We'll keep you fully briefed on progress.' She reached for her coat and bag.

'One more thing,' Jack said, causing Kate to pause.

'Oh, yes. May I see your phone, please, not the burner?' Kate asked.

Luca unlocked his phone and handed it over, and Kate began punching keys. 'I'm going to put in a number under the name of Charlie Jones. He's an old friend from Australia, okay? You haven't seen him in yonks. But he's moved to London and got in touch via the club.'

'It's so that our team can contact you and you can contact us,' Jack continued. 'Just in case the phone we gave you goes missing or is not in your possession in the moment.'

'Are they listening to my phone calls?'

He shook his head. 'No, we've checked. But just in case, or if anyone is nearby, you speak to us as if we're Charlie, all right? We'll keep it simple with yes and no questions if we need to check anything. Keep it chatty – it's just your mate, hoping to catch up.'

Kate handed the phone back.

'That one number is ours, just like the burner. Use it anytime, day or night,' Jack reinforced. 'It will be answered by one of my team and they can connect me or Kate in an instant – whichever of us you need, okay?'

Luca nodded and took the phone. 'So Ally mustn't know about this?'

'Not Ally, not your buddies, not anyone here,' Kate said. 'You can also text us on that number too.'

'My agent? Jon's going to help me sort out the money.'

'No one, Luca,' Jack said.

'Got it,' he said. 'Can you hurry up and find the girl?'

They stood, shook hands. 'Hope training goes well this week,' Kate said, unsure of what else they could say. They left.

19

Ronnie Barrett finished work at Lark's Hill, his insides still twisted like knotted string. Ever since the call from the Celiks, he'd felt like his skin was itching from the fear that they were back in his life. And why the interest in Sylvie Toussaint? How could they even know her?

What no one knew – not even Sylvie – was that before she'd disappeared he'd been following her, somewhat regularly. He knew it was creepy. If she ever discovered her shadow, she would humiliate him and reveal him to the rest of the staff, so he'd been exceptionally cautious, but he felt helpless. Sylvie was like a drug to him and since the day he'd first seen her, he'd believed himself in love. He had never felt like this before, never experienced having no control over an infatuation. And so, like a dog on a leash, he followed her near enough daily.

The occasions he drove her home were the happiest moments of his life, and he was very careful never to overstep the mark of friendship. As much as he wanted to be Sylvie's lover and could imagine himself in so many situations with her, like a movie montage as the couple falls in love, he sensed it was in vain. The mirror told him that Sylvie would have zero romantic interest in him, and yet he defied what he knew to be true and his heart pursued her nonetheless, until she'd disappeared after the Bentley event. He'd worried about her at first, but then he'd taken it as a sign that he wasn't supposed to be with her.

He hated that Baris and Eren even knew her.

Even so, Ronnie was nothing if not an opportunist, and he decided he would find out more, if he could, before he sent them the photo. Forewarned is forearmed, his father used to say. His father was always quoting stupid sayings like that. He was a drunk and a useless parent, but there was certainly truth in that phrase.

Ronnie had never seen Sylvie meet anyone associated with the Celiks or be involved in anything dodgy. She seemed to live the most normal of lives other than one oddity, which he planned to look into now.

He didn't want to put Sylvie in danger, but he would be in danger himself if he didn't comply with the Celiks' requests. He'd felt obliged to give them the address they wanted and had texted it through on his tea break. Now the Celiks knew where Sylvie lived, and he was sure they'd visit soon enough. He had to get there first.

After knocking on the door, he was surprised and relieved to learn from her flatmate she hadn't lived there for a while. Given she hadn't been at work, it was all beginning to make sense, but the fact the Celiks were chasing her only made her absence more sinister. She likely knew she was being hunted. What had she been up to?

'I used to drop her here, though,' he said to the flatmate, hoping to get a little more information from her. 'I'm a mate.'

'Oh, that's right. She did say a friend from work would bring her home sometimes,' the flatmate said. 'Well, she left in a hurry.'

'When?'

'Er . . . it would have been the night of that big event at your work. Some fancy car thing. She told me she was working that night until late and not to wait up. I didn't – I had an early start, but she had already cleared out by the time I got up. Didn't take much; said I could keep what I wanted and throw the rest away. She left rent money.'

This didn't sound good. Was she all right? 'She didn't say where she was going?'

'No. Bitch.' The housemate grinned. 'But I hope she's lying on a beach on a Greek island somewhere. It's what she used to talk about.'

Ronnie felt deflated. 'Okay, thanks.'

He left frowning. That did sound suspicious. How it was linked to the scary Celiks he had no idea, but Ronnie knew to trust his instincts for an opportunity. Maybe he could be the person to broker something here . . . Maybe he could keep Sylvie safe?

What he had never told anyone was that he often used to sit here on lonely nights and watch her after dropping her home. Sometimes he could see her moving around in her room upstairs. Other times, he'd hang around to see if she was home and if she left, he'd follow at a distance. He was lovesick, that was for sure. But the night of the event he hadn't dropped her home – he hadn't even known she was working. He'd remained behind to help return the rooms to their normal state for guests arriving the following day, but he had been surprised when he'd seen her earlier in the evening, as she hadn't been rostered on.

'They called me in at late notice,' she said, in answer to his query. 'Apparently they need everyone who's available.'

'But not for salon work?'

'No,' she said in a tone that implied he was being dim. 'I guess I'm waitressing tonight. I've done it before, no problem.' She took a familiar waitress uniform from a dry-cleaning bag.

She'd left before he could offer her a lift – if he had, or if he'd been able to follow her, he might have known she'd packed up and left. Damn!

And so to the oddity. It was the only option he had left. He didn't expect to find her, but he would try nonetheless, and then he would send the photo that he didn't want to send to the men he feared. He really hoped they weren't going to hurt her.

Once he had followed her to an unexpected place, close to Ockwells Park, where she seemed to know where the key was kept. All too aware of time ticking on, with Baris and Eren no doubt becoming more impatient, he decided to go there to see if he could find anything. The lights were on, he saw, and so he waited. All night and morning. Luckily he wasn't due to work until the next day. His heart felt like it flipped in his chest when his hunch was borne out and she appeared. There she was, his beautiful Sylvie, emerging from the tiny home. Who it belonged to he would never know. He left his car where it was parked and followed her on foot.

First to a café, where he watched from a distance as she ate a late lunch, his own belly grinding in hunger, and then he followed her down into the Underground, again from a really safe distance. With a peaked cap pulled low, he followed her for nearly an hour, changing trains, unable to work out where they were headed as they ducked around interconnecting motorways and areas with no residential buildings, until they arrived at an industrial park.

He dropped back even further as he watched Sylvie cautiously approach what looked to be an abandoned warehouse or some sort of unused car repair place. He didn't risk following her in. Instead he stayed in the shadows of a nearby shed and waited.

What was she up to?

He waited anxiously for more than an hour, and just when he wondered if she knew she was being followed and had perhaps come here to give him the slip, he saw a car arriving. He shrank back deeper into the shadows, grateful for his black clothes.

Two people emerged from the car, a woman, who'd been driving, and a man who got out first and opened the door for her. As they approached the building, Ronnie was close enough to hear them calling out to Sylvie.

Except they were calling for Francoise.

Who was Francoise?

Francoise Laurent was in position, trying to put the cold out of her mind and remain patient. She'd arrived one hour before she was scheduled to meet them but hadn't dared to so much as light a cigarette for fear of being discovered. She was hiding in an empty unit at the industrial trading region known as Park Royal, at Acton in West London. The front shutters had been securely padlocked, but she'd made her way around to the door on the side, which was open as it had been the first time they'd met.

Her eyes were now fully accustomed to the gloom and she could see well enough from her spot behind some crates, making sure there was nothing loose around her that she might accidentally bump or upend and create noise. She needed to be silent. When she crouched, she had a perfect view of anyone who came through those doors. And so she'd been waiting. She checked her phone. They were one minute late. She checked again that her phone was on silent and zipped it securely into her pocket so no light might suddenly flash and alert someone to her presence. Her feet were clad in sneakers so her tread was noiseless too. Nothing would give away her position if she remained still and watchful.

Why didn't she trust Sophia? It had been bothering her since their last meeting. Francoise had done everything exactly as they'd demanded, and she'd been successful in spite of the guy's reluctance. She wanted to fling it into their greedy faces: without her they couldn't have pulled this off.

She was the one with experience.

She was the one who knew how to bring a man to his knees.

She was the one who had done this nearly a dozen times before.

The Celiks had paid her generously and promptly, striking the deal and then keeping their word. They frightened her but, as they'd said, she had twenty thousand reasons to accept their offer; twenty thousand reasons *per job*. It was a fortune she'd never dreamed of. She'd used it to buy her mother an apartment in Cassis, the town of her birth. It wasn't flash, but it was roomy enough, with fresh breezes blowing through shuttered windows and a sun-drenched balcony where she could grow herbs and tomatoes. It was the first time her mother had owned anything of value, and she could now see out her years without worrying about a roof over her head or the abusive, alcoholic husband who had taken everything from her, including her self-respect. Francoise had given her that back. Watching her mother's tear-stained face as she took in each room, all hers, was worth every cent.

Francoise had used the rest of the money to buy a tiny apartment in Cyprus. Limassol was cheap, full of Russians on holiday who tipped well, and it was warm year-round. Her plan was to join the cruise ships and sail the world, using Cyprus as her base and calling in to Cassis to see her mother every few months. She wouldn't sail forever; five years, maybe. By then she'd be thirty and could think about her next move ... perhaps a small bar in either France or Cyprus, wherever she ended up, and most importantly, being able to take care of her mum.

It had all felt solid, exciting even, but she'd kept her head down after they gave up the scheme, as the Celik brothers had warned, and did a masterful job in fooling them that she'd left for Australia. She'd even sent letters via a friend who was in Melbourne. She wanted them to believe she was far away; that was why she had only done private escort jobs outside of London for the last year. Most of her work was on the far outskirts of London or more often reaching into Sussex, Kent and around Hampshire and Berkshire, with a regular clientele.

The Turks had no idea she was still here. Her aim was one more year of earnings and then to leave London for good. The plan was working. She lived her life with great care, not partying or making a name for herself around any of the usual haunts. And she hadn't troubled the Celiks. Although she'd sensed violence lurking within them, they'd been nothing but generous and indeed courteous towards her. Neither had sneered at her line of work, and they had behaved like gentlemen towards her, especially the older brother, Baris, which was more than she could say for most men she met, including that preening Frank, who liked to leer at her but also look down upon her. Neither of the Celik brothers made her feel awkward or inadequate, and they always congratulated her on a job well done. So she had given them her respect and not brought any attention their way.

But then the others had found her.

Her only real friend, Lyn, who worked for a different firm, had done a job and done it well. The client had asked her if she was interested in some other work . . . a very specific piece of work. Lyn didn't want to moonlight as she'd made that error before and was under close scrutiny, so she had passed the job to Francoise.

'You've worked for the sporting people before.'

'Putain!' Francoise had cursed. 'I didn't work *for* them, I worked *them!*'

'Whatever,' Lyn had said carelessly.

'What have you told them?' Francoise had reached and grabbed the lapels of Lyn's denim jacket.

'Nothing!' her friend said, shaking free and scowling. 'Ouch! That hurt.'

'I told you that in absolute secret,' Francoise said. She hadn't wanted to tell her anything. 'What have you said?' she demanded.

Lyn sighed. 'Just that you did some jobs for sporting people . . . that you were familiar with them.'

'Fuck!' Francoise gave the best translation of her French curse. It sounded more anguished in English and measured up to how she truly felt. 'You're an idiot, Lyn.'

'What?' Her friend sounded completely innocent of all wrong-doing, shocked that Francoise was reacting this way.

'I told you not to breathe a word.'

'I thought you'd like the work. You don't have the same issues as me doing stuff on the side.' She grinned. 'They promised it would pay well.'

Francoise shook her head. 'They'll kill me.'

'Who will?'

Francoise closed her eyes. *Maybe if I leave today*, she remembered thinking. If she just got out of her seat in the greasy café where they were sharing a coffee and went straight to London City Airport, she could be in Athens by the afternoon. She'd go to Greece so she could lose anyone who might even think of trying to track her movements, then take a bus to the port, to muddy that trail, then catch a random ferry and island hop as a final precaution until she could safely ferry to Limassol. No one knew about her mother or even where she came from in France, so she knew her only living relative was safe.

'Who'll kill you?' Lyn asked again.

Francoise shook her head and shrugged for her friend's sake. She didn't need to know; she was a liability. 'I'm just frightened that anyone knows.'

'All right. Well, she's meeting us here.'

'Who is?'

'The woman. I said we'd be—'

'No, no, I—'

'Oh, she's right on time.' Francoise watched with horror as Lyn raised a hand. 'Hi! Over here.'

A woman had walked in, the bell on the door announcing her arrival as though she'd stepped into an old grocery store. The café didn't seem her kind; she was overdressed, even though it looked like she'd tried to tone her look down. There was no mistaking those designer jeans.

'Hello,' the woman said, easing into the booth next to Lyn. 'And you must be Francoise?'

Merde! Lyn had given her name! Francoise nodded, feeling ill.

The newcomer held out a hand. 'Pleased to meet you. Call me Sophia.'

Francoise didn't want to take the woman's hand. She was not here to make any deal. It was impossible for Sophia not to notice Francoise's reluctance, yet her smile didn't die; if anything it broadened, but somehow never reached her eyes. She was as ruthless as the Celiks, Francoise thought. Years of working as an escort had honed her ability to quickly make a judgement call on someone, and she was usually right.

'Thanks, Lynney.' Sophia put a small fan of twenty-pound notes on the table. 'I know you don't enjoy fifties. Don't spend it all at once. You can leave us now.'

Francoise wanted to ask why but remained silent. Lyn grinned, snatched up the money, plunged it into her fake leather bag and blew a kiss at Francoise. 'I'll see you.'

'Don't lea—'

'It's okay, Francoise,' the stranger said. 'Just hear me out.' She took off her huge sunglasses to reveal large, dark eyes that might be hazel in the right light, but Francoise didn't want to meet them for long.

Francoise watched Lyn leave with a sinking heart before sliding her gaze back to the woman. Sophia wore an auburn wig – spotting

fake hair was another skill Francoise possessed – cut into a blunt
bob and no make-up. The naked face was, counterintuitively, a
further disguise, Francoise supposed. The quality of her clothes
suggested she would normally be made up, rarely seen without
mascara or lipstick, so the lack of make-up made her less recognisable. Francoise gave no smile and no inkling of what she was
thinking, but she'd already sized up Sophia as cunning. She'd have
to tread carefully.

'I don't want any side work,' she said firmly. 'I'm sorry to waste
your time.'

'Are you sure?'

'Very.'

'Your accent is very charming – flirtatious, actually.'

Francoise didn't reply. There was nothing to say to that.

'You're also perfect for what I need.' Sophia crossed her arms
and leaned back against the seat. 'You're incredibly attractive, even when you're unhappy. I defy any man, least of all a
handsome young footballer, to resist you.'

'I told you, I don't want the job. Now, thanks but—'

Sophia reached for Francoise's wrist to stop her leaving, but
was sensible enough not to grip it too hard. 'Will you just hear
me out? I have a lucrative bargain to offer you. If you don't
understand that word, it means you can name your own price,'
she said, eyes glittering at the way that remark halted Francoise's
movement. 'Let's order some brunch and just talk.'

Brunch. Sophia really was in the wrong place. And her insult
was not lost on Francoise. She knew very well what 'lucrative'
meant. For now she would play along until she felt confident
enough to extricate herself.

Sophia explained what the job would entail while they ate
toasted ham, cheese and tomato sandwiches that were not nearly
as good as a croque monsieur at home. Francoise had become

used to plainer English food, but she was already dreaming of Cypriot souvlakia in a taverna on a summer's evening.

'Lyn tells me you've worked with footballers before?'

'Performed sex acts, yes,' Francoise clarified, deliberately blunt. 'They're not my colleagues. I don't work with them.'

Sophia gave a small, embarrassed chuckle. 'Right. So if I could persuade you to . . .' She trailed off, searching for the right phrasing. '. . . do what you're good at with one particular person on one particular night, how much might that cost me?'

'You make that sound so simple, Miss . . .?'

'Just Sophia,' she said, smiling and catching a tomato seed from her lip with a paper napkin before it fell to her plate. 'It is simple.'

Francoise shook her head. 'If it was, you could use anyone in the game. Even you could do it!'

Sophia's gaze narrowed to an intense stare and she put down her sandwich. Francoise saw the flare of anger at her insult but also how quickly the woman managed to rein it in.

'You're right. I'm just cautious,' Sophia said. 'I need some distance from this.'

'So am I.'

'Good. Then we can be cautious together. I will tell you exactly what my plan is.' And she did.

Francoise was staggered. It was an imitation of the Celiks' scheme. Her breath became a fraction ragged as she listened with increasing alarm. 'That's not an original plan.'

Again Sophia regarded her with intensity. 'How do you know that?'

'I knew the girl involved in the original set-up.'

Sophia looked caught out. Stunned, Francoise thought. 'I . . . I don't understand.'

'I'm leaving.' This time she got away, but Sophia caught up with her outside.

'Wait!'

Francoise closed her eyes and wanted to scream, wishing she hadn't revealed so much. This woman was too smart not to use it against her. 'How do *you* know about the blackmail scheme?' she asked.

Sophia shrugged. 'It's well known in sporting circles.'

'So you're in sporting circles?'

'I . . . Yes, I am privy, you could say.'

'Well, I'm not and I don't want anything to do with this.' Francoise turned to leave.

'I could go to the police,' Sophia said. 'They would be pretty interested to hear about your involvement.'

Francoise swung around. 'And I could tell them just what you've asked me to do.'

Sophia smiled. 'So let's keep each other's secrets and help one another. Just name a price.'

'Listen,' Francoise said, 'for something like this to work, you have to pick your mark very carefully. The previous girl told me the blackmailer took months to choose their target, and it was all set up perfectly and worked without any problems.'

'So will this plan. It's only once. It's also guaranteed if you're on board. I've already chosen our mark. You know exactly what to do and when.'

'No, I don't. Hearing it from someone else and actually doing it are not the same thing.' Francoise knew she'd convinced Sophia of the fictional other girl's existence, but her anxiety was going to catch Sophia's attention if she didn't dial it down. She took control; it was the only way she knew to defend herself. 'Is the guy in a relationship?'

'Yes.'

'So how do you separate him from his girlfriend?'

'Wife. She's pregnant. Heavily. I know she won't want to attend.'

'Attend what?'

'A blokey sort of car promotion at a hotel.'

'You can guarantee he'll be alone?'

Sophia nodded. 'Easy.'

'And they're used to escorts just moving around their posh hotel, are they? No security?'

Sophia smiled. 'Ah, this is where it gets clever.' She gestured to an expensive car that looked wrong in this neighbourhood. It wasn't Sophia's, going by the rental car sign stuck discreetly on the back window. She was taking no chances about being recognised. 'Would you like to get in where it's warm?'

Francoise considered this and nodded. The more they talked about it, the more she realised this amateur and her one-off blackmail event could blow back onto her, ruining everything she'd cultivated since working the scheme with the Turks. She needed to know more about this plan in case she had to do something about it.

From the back seat, she asked, 'Where does your clever plan actually get clever, Sophia?'

The woman, who'd chosen to sit in the driver's seat, ignored her sarcasm. 'We get hold of a uniform and you pose as staff. The guest rooms are all upstairs and quiet. You just walk along the hallway confidently, tap on the door that I tell you to tap on, holding a bottle of champagne, and bingo.' She looked forward as she spoke, making eye contact in the rear-view mirror.

Francoise laughed. 'And you don't imagine someone will ask questions of the stranger with the French accent?'

'No, because you'll act like staff,' Sophia said, as though Francoise was the stupid one.

Francoise shook her head. 'I've been to places like that so many times with clients. Security is tighter than you think.'

'No cameras, I've checked. Discretion is everything at this

place, because it's frequented by film stars and politicians and celebrities the world over.'

That did help, Francoise had to admit. 'You say this is a special event evening or something?'

'It is. The launch of a new car.'

'I'm telling you, security will be even tighter then. Special event, VIPs, lots of money, lots of champagne . . . That means lots of stress for the staff – they'll be looking for people who shouldn't be there.'

Sophia's features, which had been full of excitement at sharing the plan now straightened as Francoise pressed home her point.

'You will be found out before you get what you need.'

'You don't know—'

'I *do* know. For something like this to work, you'd have to plant someone.'

'What?' Francoise could tell that Sophia had thought she was being shut down; she hadn't expected Francoise to provide an alternative. 'Oh. So what are you saying?'

'For this to work, I would have to become a genuine member of staff so I can move freely around the venue.'

'But that would take time.'

Francoise laughed, and began to light up a cigarette. 'I told you, the previous blackmailers were careful and patient.'

'Not in the car, please.'

Francoise, exasperated by the amateur in front of her, pushed the cigarette back into its pack. 'Listen, you'll get caught if you run this how you're saying. Then it's jail for you and whoever else is in on your game.'

'Just me and one other.'

'Who?'

'It doesn't matter. Totally trustworthy.'

Totally bent, more like, Francoise thought. She'd always liked these odd English expressions and enjoyed using them, even privately.

Sophia's brow hooded. 'Just say yes. We can work all this out.'

Francoise closed her eyes for a moment. She couldn't help herself; this was a golden opportunity and although Sophia didn't know it, there was no one better qualified to pull off the job. *No pun intended*, she thought, quoting her English friends, wanting to smile but instead sighing. 'It will cost you.'

Sophia's expression brightened. 'Try me,' she said, attempting to regain her previous control and nonchalance.

Francoise shook her head. 'Not try. Once-off price. That's it. No negotiation.'

'Let me hear it.'

'Fifty thousand.'

Sophia's eyes widened but to her credit she didn't flinch or gasp or begin to remonstrate. 'That's a lot of money,' she remarked calmly.

'It's a lot of risk. And I would need to get myself embedded in the staff a few weeks out.'

Francoise could see from the way her new client's mouth twitched that she really liked this idea. Yes, she was good at reading people; Sophia was on the hook. 'What sort of job?'

'I'm actually a qualified masseuse. I presume there's a spa in this fancy place?'

'Of course,' Sophia said, sounding more intrigued. 'A very good one. The hotel sells itself as a health resort.'

Francoise shrugged. 'Beauty salons and spas are notorious for staff turnover; girls being sick, being on holiday, arguing with their boyfriends, going off to have babies . . . There are any number of reasons that they would require a temporary member. Leave it to me. I'll expect five up front as working capital.'

Sophia began to shake her head.

'Or I don't do it,' Francoise added. 'No negotiation. That's my fee.'

Sophia now twisted in the seat, looking back at Francoise. 'You said you know how to make it look like the other people did this? I have to ensure it's a copycat.'

'Why? So they'll be blamed?'

'You catch on fast. Well?'

'I get the guy's squirt into a condom and take a polaroid, right?'

Sophia blinked. 'Your friend gave you all those details?'

'She's not a friend. I don't even know her name. We were booked from separate agencies to do a job together. She got drunk after the guy passed out and told me.' Francoise's lie sounded convincing even to her. 'I listened, didn't pay much attention but now you've confirmed she wasn't lying.'

'Where is she now?'

'How the fuck should I know? I think she went to Australia. That's what she said she was going to do with the money.'

'And it all worked easily?'

'I don't know. She didn't mention any problems. And if she could afford to get out of the game, I have to assume they used her repeatedly.'

'How much were they demanding?'

'I have none of that detail. Enough,' Francoise said and knew the way she lifted her gaze to Sophia's was the clincher. She wouldn't be able to resist that word, *enough*.

She was right. 'Okay, you're hired.'

'Five up front,' Francoise repeated.

Sophia nodded. 'I'll give you an address and I'll bring the cash. What happens after that?'

'Then I get myself employed. You'll have to give me all the details, and you'll have to be very patient while I set this up. Who's the mark?'

'Luca Bruni.'

'That's meaningless to me. He can afford your ransom?'

'Without his pulse even going up a beat.'

That would help. 'Why are you doing this, Sophia?'

'Because I can.'

'You don't look like you need the money.'

'Appearances can be deceptive, but I have my reasons.'

Francoise doubted she was going to get much out of this woman, but she tried anyway. 'Is Sophia your real name?'

'My mother's Italian. She named me, my brother and sister after Italian movie stars, and that's all I'm going to say.' Sophia got out a pen and wrote on a napkin. 'Here's where we'll meet.'

'When?'

'The day after tomorrow. I need a day to get your cash sorted. My brother will come too.'

Francoise had nodded, knowing deep down even then that it was a stupid, risky decision, but the money on offer was so big, how could she resist? That sort of money would allow her to open her bar immediately, skip working on a cruise line.

That's what had clouded her judgement: her greed. She had always been so careful. And the Celiks had taught her about moving slowly and cautiously. It's how they'd got away with their scheme – not getting greedy, not getting impatient and taking the time to study their mark. She'd done none of that, and she knew Sophia and Frank definitely hadn't.

And so, this was on her. She had known better and even now, crouching here, she was somehow hoping that the brother and sister would show.

But her instincts were screaming at her that Sophia and Franco were not going to come through with the rest of the money. An even baser instinct, the primeval one that drove fear, told her that not only were they going to renege, but they might decide to get rid of her, considering her a liability. That was why she was in hiding now, to observe them.

This was a lonely place.

Anything could happen.

Ronnie's phone rang and he quickly flicked the call to voice-mail. It pinged that a message had been left. All was quiet at the warehouse; he dared not sneak up to see what was going on. He checked the voicemail and was stunned to hear it was the police; a detective was politely asking him to assist with some enquiries into an event that had occurred at Lark's Hill and might involve a staff member, Sylvie Toussaint, who had disappeared.

Ronnie froze. This was getting too hot, even for him. Should he stay, and see whether the woman he'd followed here – he was sure it was Sylvie! – came out again? He couldn't tell if she'd slipped out the back. Or should he leave and just try to forget what he'd heard? But what would he tell the police? What would he tell the Celiks? It all felt impossible.

The man and woman paused outside the door. Curiously, now that he got a really good look at them, Ronnie was sure he recognised the bloke. He'd come to Lark's Hill that night of the Bentley event. And yes, the woman too, though her hair looked different; different colour, different length. A wig?

Ronnie's instincts began to twitch. Something was very wrong here and he needed to be clear of it. He'd go to the police interview, stay in their good books but evade their questions. And then he would go to the Celiks with an ace up his sleeve. He wouldn't tell them he had seen Sylvie, but he would give them the registration of the car this pair had arrived in. The Celiks had contacts and could soon find out who the car was registered to. Obviously this couple were involved in something connected to Lark's Hill. If the police were interested in it, it was likely what the Celiks were after Sylvie for.

They'd be grateful to him. He could earn their trust again – maybe make some money on the side for his intel. And, just perhaps, he might earn some gratitude from Sylvie . . . or was it Francoise? If he could set the Celiks onto this man and woman, maybe the heat would come off her?

Maybe. Either way, Ronnie had no intention of being burned. He left silently, texting the detective that he was on his way.

Francoise heard the car's wheels crunching on the small road leading down to the abandoned unit. Once again she checked that nothing around her could make any noise; she even quickly took the precaution of removing her puffer jacket, which tended to make a swishy noise if she moved. All was secured.

She waited, holding her breath at first and then forcing herself to let it out and breathe . . . silently. Footsteps sounded, and then voices.

'Francoise?' It was Sophia.

She didn't answer.

'And I thought we were late,' Francoise heard Frank say.

'She'll be here,' Sophia said, entering the gloom of the old repair shop. 'I hate the smell in here.'

'Nah, I love it. Oil and metal. Lovely old smell of a car workshop. Can't beat it.'

'I prefer the smell of a new box of shoes,' Sophia remarked.

'If you could afford it.' He laughed.

'Oh, I'll be able to soon, when Luca pays up.'

'I hope he will, for your sake.'

'He has to.'

'Doesn't sound like he intends to.'

'Frank,' she said in a tone that essentially said *Shut up*, 'he'll pay. It's already becoming too hard for him. We keep piling on the pressure and he'll cave.'

Francoise stayed hidden, watching from behind the stacked crates. The siblings' voices were carrying clearly across the space, but with the light of the doorway to their backs, the brother and sister were just silhouettes; she couldn't gauge their expressions yet.

'So where is she? I'm not going to stand around here all day.'

'She'll come because she's greedy for the money.'

'I'm surprised you agreed to pay it.'

'You really think I'm going to pay that French slut another penny?'

Francoise covered her mouth so no sound of shock might escape.

'Why the fuck are we here, then?'

'Because, Frank, we have to deal with her. If she doesn't get her money, what d'you reckon is going to happen?'

'She's got her five thousand.'

Francoise watched Sophia shake her head as she dug in her bag for a pack of cigarettes. After lighting up, she blew the smoke out in a long stream. 'She's a clever whore, that one. Far too smart for my liking. You know what I think?'

'What?'

'I think she was part of those first scams we heard about. Francoise just seemed to know what to do. She was in and out so fast it took my breath away. And she thought of things I would never have thought about . . . exactly how to set up the polaroid, the disguise, even working in the joint long before the Bentley event so she could move around unnoticed as one of the staff.' Sophia took a long drag and an equally long time to exhale the stale smoke. 'She knew more than she should.'

'So, maybe her being late means she's already onto you?'

'Why would she be? She wants her money. I gave her no indication that we wouldn't give it to her, and then she could move to fucking Switzerland.'

'She wasn't ever going to Switzerland,' Frank said, shaking his head.

'It's irrelevant anyway.'

'Why?'

'Because, Frank, and you can be so thick, we have to be rid of her.'

'Isn't that what Switzerland means?'

Sophia sighed, evidently exasperated. 'I mean we need to be *permanently* rid of her.'

Behind the crates, Francoise closed her eyes as a fresh trill of fear clawed up her spine.

20

Jack was seated with Geoff behind a two-way mirror, watching Kate and Ari interview Ronnie Barrett. Ari had just switched on the recorder, and he was going through the procedure of introducing everyone in the room, including Ronnie's legal aid solicitor.

Jack's phone gave a soft ping nearby. He glanced at it. Claudia. He opened the message: *She doesn't want to see u alone. Meet one hour outside Harrods.*

He tapped a reply: *OK thanks.*

One more message pinged back: *Told her she'd regret not seeing you alone* ☺

He couldn't help but smile, and Geoff gave him a knowing look. 'Some lucky lady?'

Jack shook his head. He told Geoff about Claudia's contact. 'I need to get some witness protection across Rowland's desk.'

'Want me to ask? I owe you one.'

Jack raised his brows. 'Oh, yes? For what?'

Geoff nodded towards Kate. 'She's meeting me for supper.

Nothing heavy – we've both agreed not to rake over the dead coals. Just friends, you know.'

'That's good news,' Jack said, smiling. 'I suspect Kate is in a more receptive mood than you think – she just needed you to make the first move.'

'If I'd known, I would have knocked on the door a lot earlier.' Geoff laughed.

'The timing is perfect. She probably also needed to meet Dan and experience a relationship outside of the police. He was a good bloke by all accounts, but I imagine he would have always struggled with her job. He tried hard to work around it, but Kate didn't make that easy for him, whereas she doesn't have to compensate with you. I have my suspicions she's never fully let you go, anyway.'

'Hope for me, you think, Hawk?'

Jack grinned. 'Try harder, Benson!'

It was an old joke. One of their senior tutors at Hendon Police Academy used to employ that line regularly, just subbing in the surname of whichever new recruit he was admonishing at the time.

Kate had just finished explaining to Ronnie that he could leave at any time and that Ms Anderson seated beside him had been organised on his behalf. He already knew this, but it was standard procedure for the benefit of the recording. She began the interview. 'Mr Barrett, thank you for coming in today. We just have a few questions for you.'

'So I'm not under arrest?' Ronnie looked between Kate and Ari nervously.

'No, absolutely not, Mr Barrett. Just as I've explained, you are free to leave at any time. I want to assure you that you are simply assisting with enquiries.'

'Then I'll go. I thought assisting with enquiries was police code for something serious.' Ronnie gave a low and nervous laugh.

'Oh, this is serious, Mr Barrett. We're looking into the disappearance of one of your colleagues.'

He frowned. 'Who? I don't have colleagues. I work with a couple of guys and we're just grunts. One of them is a recovered alcoholic and the other is a part-timer like me. No one's qualified at anything – we simply heft luggage around, upstairs to a room or back down to a car.' He looked bewildered.

'The person we're trying to find is Sylvie Toussaint, Mr Barrett, whom we think you know.'

Barrett looked immediately uncomfortable, shifting in his seat, his expression suddenly wary. 'I haven't done anything to her.'

Kate gave a soft smile. 'I wasn't suggesting that you had. What can you tell us about her?'

'Nothing.'

'Nothing?' Ari echoed. 'But you worked with her.'

'No, she worked in the spa. I was out in the cold most of the time – usually waiting in the driveway or in the draughty reception walkway where we hang up guests' coats and outdoor gear.'

'But you know Sylvie, right?' Kate asked.

'Yes. I know her. We all know her.'

'Good. What can you tell me that you know about her?'

Ronnie looked between them again as though they were idiots.

'Mr Barrett, you are not obliged to say anything,' his solicitor said.

'If you have nothing to hide, Mr Barrett, help us. You might help her,' Kate countered.

Ronnie sighed. 'She's French. She works in the spa. She does really good massages. Everyone likes her. She's one of the most popular members of the staff.' He shrugged, as if that was all obvious.

'Yes, but you like her just a bit more, don't you?' Kate asked.

'What are you suggesting?'

'That you had a crush on her, Mr Barrett. Am I right?'

He shrugged again. 'I fancied her, yes.'

'Did you ever ask her out?'

'No.'

'No?' Kate pressed.

'Mr Barrett has answered your question, DCI Carter. Please don't harangue him.'

'My apologies, Mr Barrett. It's just that if you wanted to ask her out, why didn't you?'

Ronnie looked down. 'I wasn't ready, didn't have the spondoolies. I'd like to have taken her somewhere nice.'

Kate gave an encouraging smile, and Jack was impressed with how she was leading Barrett to where she needed his help. 'That's nice. Would you say that you and Sylvie were friendly?'

'Yes.'

'How friendly?'

'I don't know.'

'Well, friendly enough to go out for a drink together?'

'Maybe. We never did.'

Kate ignored his answer. 'Friendly enough to go home with each other?'

Ronnie looked away. 'No. Not that friendly. Not yet.'

'Hang on though,' Ari now interrupted with perfect timing. 'Didn't you drive Sylvie home one night?' He began flicking through notes as though looking for the right entry. Jack knew it didn't exist, but Ari was experienced enough to play the game properly.

'Yeah, yeah, that's right,' Ronnie said. 'Once I did. But there were others in the car.'

'How many others?' Kate asked.

'Well, just one other. I dropped her off first and then I dropped Sylvie home. It was raining that night.'

'You live in Reading, is that correct?' Ari asked.

'Yes.'

'And you were going home that night?'

'Yeah, where else would I be going?' Ronnie looked at his solicitor, snorting a laugh as though that was a dumb question.

'I don't know. Perhaps you had plans to spend the night with Sylvie.'

'I was going home,' he reinforced, firm now.

Kate joined in. 'And Sylvie lived where?'

'Southall.'

'Southall, yes. So, that's distinctly out of your way, Mr Barrett, in fact—'

'It's only about ten miles from Lark's Hill,' he interrupted, again giving them the 'duh' expression.

Kate smiled and nodded. 'Yes, I gather. But Southall to Reading is close to thirty-two miles, so it became a much longer journey for you. And even if we add in, let's say, seven or eight miles for the other person you were dropping off, you were doing a fifty-mile journey . . . for what?'

Ronnie shifted in his seat. 'What do you mean, for what?'

'For petrol money? For conversation? For friendship?' Kate asked innocently.

'We were all mates. I didn't want those girls going home alone in the dark . . . in the rain.'

'But you don't drive them home every night, surely?'

'No, I don't,' he said, obviously frustrated. 'But it doesn't rain every night and we don't have birthday parties every night either.'

'Fair enough,' Kate replied.

Ari took over again. 'So you dropped her home at . . . is it Avendale Road?'

'Yeah.'

Both Kate, who was flicking through her file, and Ari, who had just consulted his notepad, snapped their attention up to Barrett as if a switch had been thrown.

'She doesn't live at Avendale Road, Mr Barrett,' Kate said. 'Sorry, DI Varma, you may have made a mistake there.'

'I did, I'm so sorry,' Ari said, deliberately overdoing his apology. 'It's not Avendale, is it, Mr Barrett?'

To his credit, the Lark's Hill porter looked chagrined. 'No, it's, er, Barnsley . . . no, Barndale Avenue. Number fourteen, I think.'

Ari smiled. 'Yeah, that's what I have here. Thanks, Mr Barrett.'

The solicitor gave Kate a scathing look. 'We don't need that sort of trickery, DCI Carter. May I remind you my client is here willingly to help you?'

'Of course,' Kate replied. 'All right, Mr Barrett. Did you drive Sylvie home on other occasions?'

He nodded.

'Why did that come about?'

'We became friends of sorts.'

'It must have cost you plenty in petrol and lost sleep.'

'Not really. Look, I told you − I fancy her. I thought if I was good to her and earned her trust and didn't try anything, she might agree to go out with me.'

'Doesn't usually work that way, mate,' Ari said, managing to look sympathetic. 'Then they only ever see you as a friend.'

Kate let that sit for a moment, then asked, 'On the day before the Bentley launch, did you take Sylvie home?'

Ronnie hesitated. They waited. He shifted around nervously, glancing at Ms Anderson.

'What's wrong, Mr Barrett? It's a simple question. Would you like me to repeat it?'

'Yes.'

Kate opened her mouth to make the enquiry again, but he cut her off.

'I mean yes, I took her home.'

Jack leaned forward behind the mirror, watching Barrett closely.

'And what happened?' Kate asked.

'Nothing happened.' Ronnie frowned. 'I dropped her off and waved goodbye as usual, then drove away.'

'Why were you reluctant to tell us that?'

'Because I feel like you're building up to accusing me of hurting her or something.'

'I haven't said anything about an injury to Sylvie.'

'But she's not been back at work. And you lot are sniffing around. What's happened to her?'

'We don't know, Mr Barrett. It's why we're talking to as many people as we can, including you.'

Ronnie sat back in his chair, folding his arms. 'Well, I hardly know her, to be honest.'

It was the right moment; Jack was pleased when Kate pushed deeply into it.

'But you do know the Celik brothers, isn't that right, Ronnie? May I call you Ronnie?'

He looked a little stunned at the sudden switch. He began gabbling. 'What? Why . . . why would you ask me that?'

'It's true, isn't it?'

'I know them.' Ronnie nodded, looking daunted.

'What does this have to do with my client helping you with information about the missing woman?' Ms Anderson interjected.

Kate turned to the solicitor. 'We believe Baris and Eren Celik have a vested interest in Ms Toussaint not being found.'

'I'm sorry, but I don't see how—'

'Your client worked for the Celik brothers, isn't that right?' Kate said, pointedly switching her gaze back to the quavering Ronnie.

'I . . . I . . .'

Kate ignored his stuttering and returned her attention to the solicitor. 'You see, Ms Anderson, this case could well turn into a murder investigation,' Kate said, voice as hard and unforgiving as granite. 'The investigating team has genuine concerns for Ms Toussaint's safety, as regards to Baris and Eren Celik, who also employed her.'

'No, no, they didn't,' Ronnie stammered. 'I would know.'

'Would you, Ronnie?' Ari asked. 'You see, we think they cut ties with you before they got Sylvie Toussaint to help them run a blackmail scam. And in a horrible coincidence, it turns out that you and Sylvie, unaware of that link, happened to find work at the same establishment.'

'Then ask your question, detectives, because this feels like an ambush, and I'm about to advise my client to give you no comment,' Ms Anderson said.

'One final question, then.' Kate smiled and it was so warm and sweet, Jack felt anyone would crack under her gaze. 'Ronnie, relax. All we want to know is whether either of the Celik brothers, or a representative, has contacted you since the incident at Lark's Hill and asked what you know about Sylvie Toussaint.'

Ronnie had a wild look in his eyes now. It was pure fear.

'What are you scared of, Ronnie? We're not pointing any fingers at you.'

His mouth moved but no words emerged.

Kate continued speaking in her calm, conversational tone. 'It's just, if we ask the Celik brothers to help us with our enquiries, I imagine you don't want your name to come up?' She looked concerned for him.

'DCI Carter, really,' Ms Anderson warned. 'Mr Barrett, you are not obliged to—'

'All I did was tell them where she lived. They said they'd break both of my knees if I didn't,' Ronnie spluttered, sounding close to tears. 'They never told me why. And I never asked.'

At his confession, Jack was off his chair and moving; so was Geoff. Neither of them needed to confer on the danger that had just erupted.

'I'll get some people down to Sylvie's address,' Geoff said.

'And I'll go make this meet with Claudia and her contact,' Jack replied, putting a finger to his lips. 'That's between us for now. Can you ask Rowland about that safe house? I think we're going to need it.'

21

Jack took a taxi and had the driver drop him slightly before Harrods.

'Cheers, mate,' the cabbie said through the window after seeing his tip.

Jack gave a low wave as the heavy black car eased back into the traffic. He turned to push through the fast-moving river of people who were already busy at their festive shopping. It seemed to him that Christmas came earlier each year, with retailers triggering the merchandising from late October. It wasn't exactly the panic buying to come of mid-December but, around here, at the iconic store, it was quite the crowd that he had to shoulder through.

The light was low on this murky autumn day, and the store was lit by thousands of illuminated bulbs that picked out its entire shape. When night fell, Jack knew it would appear as an enormous festive decoration for London, blazing with light and colour.

He passed the windows where Archie the Christmas Bear wore a red sweater, this year teamed with a red, white and green scarf.

He made a mental note to send one to his sister in Australia. He had been around fourteen when she'd opened a Christmas gift containing her first Archie Bear. It was his present to her, and his 'baby sister' had squealed, loving it on sight and triggering a collection that would span years. He wasn't sure if she bothered any more – not living so far away – but it might be a nice reminder of home.

An arm shot out and grabbed him. It was Claudia.

'Oh, hi.' He frowned. 'I'm not late, am I?'

'Three minutes to spare,' she said, casting a worried glance towards the rugged-up woman next to her. 'This is Lyn.'

He smiled at the nervous-looking stranger. 'Well, let's get you both out of the cold. Would you like to go in here? We can go to the Tea Room,' he offered.

They looked collectively daunted. 'Bit posh for us,' Claudia said, as Lyn shook her head. 'We're more Starbucks customers.'

Jack grinned. 'Okay. Starbucks is a bit of a walk, but I'm sure there's something similar closer.'

There was. He spotted the unmistakable Mediterranean blue awning of a Caffè Nero, and he tried very hard not to twist his mouth at the thought of their coffee as he opened the door for his guests. As if the angels were looking out for him, a family vacated a table at the back and by the wall. It was quieter here, away from the hustle and bustle of the counter and the front window, where everyone wanted to be looking out onto Harrods.

'Comfy?' he asked, clearing the family's cups and plates onto a tray he'd grabbed as he walked in. They nodded. 'Right, what are you having?'

Lyn was yet to say a word and looked to Claudia.

'Please have something to eat,' he urged. 'How about some pastries?'

Lyn still looked hesitant. 'Okay.'

'And to drink?'

'Hazelnut latte for me,' Claudia said and they both looked at Lyn.

'Er, the same,' she said.

Jack gave them an encouraging smile. 'I'll be right back.'

While the women took off their coats and got settled, Jack joined the queue. He finally returned with a tray of goodies.

'Two hazelnut lattes for two beautiful women,' he said as he placed them down, ignoring Claudia's expression of mock disdain. 'And I didn't know what you felt like, Lyn, so I chose a selection. I hope that's all right.'

'They look lovely,' she said, with a greedy glance at the pastries.

'All yours,' Jack said, sitting down and placing a mug of tea in front of himself, trying not to shudder at the tea bag that hung over the edge. 'Thanks for speaking with me, Lyn. Can I just say up front that I'm worried for your friend.' There was no point in hedging, he'd decided.

'How worried?' Claudia asked.

'Very,' he mouthed to her. Lyn, mesmerised by the treats in front of her, missed his caution, which he was glad for. 'Lyn, we're sending someone to Sylvie's flat to—'

'That's not her name,' Lyn said, biting into a Danish pastry and making a groaning sound of pleasure.

'That's fine. Will you tell me her name?'

She hesitated. 'I don't want to get her into trouble.'

'Lyn,' Jack said gently, 'She's not in trouble with me. I just want to help her.'

'That's what all the police say,' Lyn said through a mouthful of gooey apple and pastry.

'Except I'm not all the police. I won't lie to you and I will not trick you. Sylvie might be in danger.'

'You can trust handsome Jack. I do,' Claudia encouraged the younger woman.

Lyn blinked. 'She'll kill me.'

'I won't let her. And it's better to be threatened by your friend than know afterwards that you could have saved her life.'

Lyn's mouth fell open in shock. She took some time to process that, twisting off the tops of two sugar sticks and pouring their contents into her coffee and stirring. Jack remained patient, even as she paused to sip and reach for a third packet.

It was Claudia who stayed her hand. 'Let's help her, Lyn. He knows she's not the bad guy. He wants to catch the bad guy,' she said, nodding at Jack.

Lyn took another bite of her pastry while she thought through her options. 'All right. Her name's Francoise Laurent.'

Jack took a silent breath. He'd found her. He didn't interrupt.

'She took a job that I couldn't,' Lyn continued.

'Will you tell me everything you know, Lyn?'

'Tell me what you know first,' she challenged him.

That impressed him. She looked spooked and still she had the street smarts to not give too much away; either that or the pastries were far more interesting and she'd rather keep him talking while she ate. 'All right.'

'Can I have another one? I'm starving.'

'Go ahead, sweetie,' Claudia said, sipping her coffee.

Jack continued. 'Some prominent people have been blackmailed by someone, or a group, who drug the victim in order to collect semen, which they then threaten to sell if the person doesn't agree to pay their ransom.'

Lyn pulled a face of disgust at the word 'semen' but still reached for an apricot Danish.

'The victims are extremely wealthy and can't afford the bad publicity,' Jack continued, 'or they don't want their families

finding out, or their workplaces learning about a night of fun
with a hired woman. I believe the people behind this scheme are
known to police – the Celik brothers. They're Turkish.'

Lyn shook her head. 'The people who approached me aren't
Turkish.'

'That's because the people who approached you are actually
part of a copycat operation.'

Lyn licked syrup from her lips as she considered what he'd said.
Finally, she shrugged. 'So what's the problem?'

Jack remained patient. 'The problem, as we see it, is that if the
Celik brothers are indeed behind the original scam, they aren't
going to be impressed by someone playing copycat, especially
since it's attracted the police.' He turned to Claudia. 'You can see
where this is going, right?'

Claudia nodded and covered Lyn's hand as she reached for the
rest of her pastry. 'They'll go after everyone, not just the people
orchestrating the copycat scheme but the people they work
with.'

Lyn frowned. Jack didn't think she was dim; she just didn't see
herself as part of this.

'Lyn. If they get to Francoise, they'll know you passed the job
up.'

That registered. Shock flared in her expression. 'But I didn't do
anything.'

'It won't matter,' Jack said, but he could see that she needed
convincing. 'Did you hear about the killing in Wimbledon?'

'Yeah, some vet or something.'

'That's right. I probably shouldn't be telling you this, but
we believe he was killed simply for being on the fringe of their
operation, because he could recognise them, identify them to
the police. So if that was them and they're busy tidying up such
distant loose ends, as they likely see it,' he explained, 'then why

wouldn't they go after the escorts too? Sylvie – Francoise, sorry –
is just as much a loose end as the vet.'

'And if they can find Francoise, they can also find you,' Claudia
continued.

'You can't be fucking serious,' Lyn snapped, pushing away her
plate. 'I'm telling you, I didn't do anything. That's not fair!'

Jack softened his expression. 'We know. But they don't
consider fairness. They just want to shore up their position, and
that means the more mouths they can close the better. What can
you tell me about the people who tried to hire you?'

She really did look spooked now, and he knew he'd won her
cooperation. 'Er, a brother and sister. Frank and Sophia.'

'Surnames?'

She shook her head. 'No idea.'

'What else, Lyn?' Claudia urged. 'Describe them.'

'He looks Italian – you know, slicked-back hair. Walks a bit
like those guys in the American mafia movies. But he didn't strike
me as the leader; she wears the pants.'

Jack leaned in. 'Tell me more.'

Lyn relaxed slightly and began sipping her coffee again. 'Hard
to say. She wears disguises – wigs, big glasses, hats. I couldn't tell
you much else, to be honest. She's attractive, dresses expensively.
But she's a total bitch.'

'Car?'

'Uses rentals as far as I can tell. They're always slightly different.'

'Any accent or recognisable features?'

Lyn shrugged. 'Sounds like she's from here.'

'Anything else . . . any little detail about her you can tell us?'

'Not really. She jokes about her name. I heard her say it to
Francoise as well, that her mother loved old-time Italian movie
stars and all three children were named after them.'

Jack noted the extra sibling. 'Okay. Would you recognise her if you saw her again?'

'If she took off all that disguise? No, I wouldn't. But then you wouldn't recognise me in the street if I dressed like her, did my hair differently and spoke posh and wore different make-up.'

Jack looked at Claudia, who shook her head. 'I know exactly what you're going to say.'

'And?'

She scowled at him. 'I'll do my best.'

Lyn looked between them. 'What have I missed?'

'I need Claudia to take you out of action and keep you safe, Lyn, just until we can sort this.'

She closed her eyes, exasperated.

'And I need you to contact Francoise.'

She opened her eyes again and stared at him hard, reluctant to agree.

'Can you do that for me? Her life is in danger. So's yours. I want to keep you both safe.'

'No blowback on us with the police?'

'Scout's honour,' Jack said and meant it.

He watched with enormous relief as Lyn took out her phone and began tapping a message.

'Kill her?' Frank shouted. His shock stopped his pacing and he swung around. The sound of his shoes twisting on the gritty floor and his raised voice covered the tiny groan that escaped Francoise.

'What else could I mean?' his sister snarled. 'Don't be so naïve.'

'Hey, no way. I didn't get into this to go down for murder.'

'No one's going down. But we must get rid of this loose end. And there's no pulling out now, Frank. You're in too deep.'

'Or what? Would you kill me too?'

Francoise couldn't see Sophia's expression, but she assumed she was looking at Frank with total exasperation.

'Listen, darling brother. I'm not in the habit of killing anyone, but I don't know else how to make us safe. Did you hear that? Keep *us* safe. This whore knows too much, plus there's too much money involved for her to stay quiet. She'll want revenge.'

'Then just give her the money. Shut her up that way.'

'I don't have it! What don't you understand about this, Franco? I'm broke. I agreed to fifty thousand I didn't have to get the job done. That five thousand advance was the last of everything I could cobble together. The house is already mortgaged to the hilt. We lease the cars. Okay, I own some jewellery, but I won't get far on that.'

'Does your husband know?'

'He doesn't know what day of the week it is. He leaves all the money matters to me. But he put us in this fix.'

'That's not very fair, sis.'

She shrugged his protest away. 'The next fucking month of payments on the house and cars will break us. But if we can get the money out of Luca as planned, I can rebuild a life for myself. A dead street-slut found in an abandoned shed is meaningless,' she said, waving the hand with the lit cigarette in an arc.

She sounded genuinely anxious, Francoise noticed. It was the first time she'd seen so much as a crack in Sophia.

'They can't connect her to us,' Sophia snarled. 'There are no connections to us. But if she's left out in the wild, this could come back and bite us – do you understand? I could lose everything, including my freedom and, little brother . . . so could you.'

'When did you get this cold, Sophia? Did you always plan to kill her?'

'Not initially. But once I started thinking about it, I realised she was trying to fleece us – asking for more than I thought was a fair exchange. It meant upping the ransom.'

'But you agreed to it. And you said it didn't matter to the footballer – drop in the ocean.'

'It doesn't! But I resented her cocky attitude, like she had us over a barrel. Like this was her idea. She's just a shitty prostitute who gets paid for blow jobs. The idea was mine. I've made this whole thing happen, not her,' Sophia said, flinging her cigarette to the cement and grinding it out beneath her expensive shoe. 'And I'm not going to let her ruin everything.'

Francoise could see the heel of Sophia's shoe in the small amount of light from outside. She knew the signature red sole meant it was a Christian Louboutin; her grandmother had liked to tell stories about visiting the original store in Paris in the sixties, when she was an actress. Francoise still had her grandmother's Louboutin stilettos in immaculate condition, and although they were a little tight for her, she occasionally wore them for posterity as much as poise, to hell with discomfort. *Blisters heal*, she used to tell her mother. But there would be no coming back from what this two-faced bitch was planning. Francoise's instincts had served her right once again. She took her hands away from her mouth as the desire for vengeance overtook fear. She had to take control.

'So what now?' she heard Frank ask. 'What's your clever plan?'

'I've got champagne in the car,' Sophia replied. 'One bottle is clean, the other is laced with Rohypnol. As soon as she arrives, we pretend we're going to celebrate – we've just delivered the second note to Luca. I need you to pay attention and make sure she gets the glass of bubbles from the bottle laced with the drug.'

'Uh-uh,' he said, shaking his head. 'I came along to help finalise this deal, but not in the way you have in mind. No, Sophia. I'm not helping you to kill her; I'm not helping you to move her. I'm not so much as touching her.'

Sophia sighed out her frustration. 'Fine. Just keep her talking, and I'll get the champagne and serve it to her and make sure she's dead, okay?'

'No, none of it's okay. But I'd prefer it that way. I'll walk out the minute she takes a sip. And I'll tell you what, Sophia, if this comes back on me, I'll say I had no idea what was in those bottles. They won't have my fingerprints on them.'

'You always were a coward, Franco. Mum always said I was the strong one. "Look after him, Sophia," she used to plead.'

'Yeah, but she loved me more,' he replied, and Francoise was surprised to hear that it made Sophia laugh. This was obviously an old conversation between the siblings. He gestured towards the door. 'How late is she?'

'Nearing twenty minutes by my reckoning.'

'She's not coming. You know it.'

'She's coming. She thinks she's getting paid, remember?'

'Nah. She's onto you.'

'Let's give her another ten minutes.'

Hidden behind the crates, Francoise stifled an impend-ing sneeze, glad that her prospective killers had moved to the doorway to look out for her.

'And if she's still not here?'

Sophia shrugged. 'I'll let it slip somewhere that Luca Bruni is being blackmailed. It will get back to the guys who set up the original scheme and, if my hunch is right and she's known to those people, then they'll take care of her for us.'

Francoise closed her eyes with fresh fear; she knew Sophia was right. The Celik brothers would find her. With great care, she unzipped her pocket to check her phone, making sure to shield the soft blue light. There was a text message. It was Lyn, urgently pleading for Francoise to call her. She ended with the words: *I'm now frightened for my own life, babe. Please help!*

22

Jack left the two women after winning a promise from Claudia that she would keep Lyn close. 'I don't know what danger she may be in, but let's not wait to find out,' he murmured as he kissed Claudia's cheek. She'd simply given him a wink and a soft nod, and he knew she understood his concern and would act on it.

Out in the street, the crowds had not subsided. In fact their energy felt more urgent. Maybe because it was even colder now, maybe because it was almost evening, or maybe it was because the light had fallen into the winter darkness and everyone wanted to get inside Harrods; in any case, Jack had to fight his way to a long taxi queue and then decided he couldn't wait and would head underground. As he began striding towards Knightsbridge Tube station, his phone rang.

He pulled it from his inside pocket. 'Hawksworth.' Even he could hear how distracted he sounded. He expected Kate or Geoff.

'Oh, hello?' said a friendly voice. 'Sorry, bad time? It's Lou Barclay.'

'Lou!' he said, immediately cringing at the realisation of what she was about to say.

She was quicker than him. 'Did you forget?'

'No,' he said, trying to sound convincing. He was surprised and relieved to hear her laugh.

'You did. It doesn't matter.'

'It does. May I still come?'

'Of course, I've cooked.'

He shook his head, horrified that he would have gone back to the office, none the wiser.

'But honestly, we can leave it to another time.'

'I'm starving though.'

It made her chuckle again. 'Where are you? Sounds busy.'

'Would you believe outside Harrods?'

'I would, going by the noise. Um, it's nearly five now, so . . .' He could all but hear her calculating times and arrivals.

'I can nip home and—'

'Where's home if you don't mind me asking?'

Someone shouldered past Jack and he moved out of the way. 'Richmond area,' he said, deliberately vague.

'Oh, no, nightmare in the evening and then you have to get to us.'

'I don't mind the travel, but I don't want to keep you.'

'Come straight over.'

'I'm in work gear.'

'I promise I won't change.'

He nearly said, 'Wear your pyjamas,' but that would have sounded altogether wrong, despite the light-heartedness that was intended. 'Okay. What can I bring?'

'Just yourself.'

That wouldn't do. 'I'll see you in about an hour then.'

'Perfect.'

He rang off smiling and then sighed. Time for some shopping.

Luck was with him. Precisely where he stood, a taxi pulled in and disgorged its passengers and Jack was able to hop in, much to the disgust of two women who were desperately trying to catch the cabbie's attention. They rushed up to him, suggesting a gentleman would give up his taxi.

'. . . especially as it's about to rain,' one complained.

Jack grinned. 'Forgive me, ladies, but I'm on a mission to find the best roses in this city to give to a gorgeous woman. You wouldn't want me to be late for her, would you?'

One appeared to forgive him and smiled, but the other clearly found no amusement in his remark. He left her scowling by the roadside and winked at the other.

'Where to?' the cabbie asked, looking in his rear-view mirror.

'New King's Road, please. There's a florist I can direct you to.'

The guy grinned and swung out into the traffic. 'Might have to play dodgems for a while.'

'That's okay, I'm glad to be out of the rain,' Jack said, realising the downpour had begun.

'Just a shower. Be gone by the time I drop you off.'

'Actually, can you wait while I'm in there?'

'Sure. Where are we going?'

'Just south of Charing Cross, but I need to do flowers, wine and something like cake or chocolates.'

'Right, well, we better get busy then. Flowers first, because most florists, I'm told, close at five-thirty.'

Francoise waited them out. She watched the siblings grow more impatient over the ten minutes, which leaked away like slow-moving treacle. Every time she checked her Swatch, glad for its luminous hands and numerals, it didn't seem to have moved on a notch. Eventually though, Frank called it.

'She's not coming.'

Francoise heard Sophia give an angry sigh. She could barely see them now, as the evening had closed in, and she could no longer feel her toes from holding her crouched, uncomfortable position in the cold.

'Fuck her!' Sophia exploded.

'Just let it go,' her brother demanded. 'Take this as a sign.'

'Oh, okay, Franco. Sure. Do you really think she'll just let forty-five grand go?'

'Perhaps she'll be patient, if you tell her that you have to wait for Bruni to pay up.'

'No, if she doesn't trust me now, she's never going to fall for it again.'

'Well, maybe she's in the wind, fleeing to Switzerland.'

'If you believe that, you're dumber than I think you are.'

Again, Francoise was surprised to hear Frank laugh. 'Do you have to be so rude all the time?'

'You know I'm rude when I'm angry.'

'Come on, I'll drive you home. We'll have to hatch something else along the way.'

'Nothing to hatch. I'm going to hire someone to find her and deal with her.'

'You're colder than a winter's night, do you know that?'

'So you tell me, Franco. Let's go.'

Francoise squinted into the darkness and could just make out their shadowy forms leaving. They shut the shed door as best they could behind them. She straightened slowly, wanting to groan at the pins and needles that the movement prompted, but she stayed quiet, listening intently. Now was not the time to give herself away. She heard the car cough once and then start. Now she waited to hear it move, for that reassuring scrunch of the tyres moving the car away and into the distance. At the sound of it retreating she let out a breath silently, but was still not prepared to shift her position. What if one of them had stayed behind just in case?

She waited another hour, like a statue, and only then did she allow herself to breathe normally and ease out of her hiding spot. She tiptoed to the door and listened for even the slightest sound of grit underfoot or a giveaway whisper of a sigh.

Nothing. Well, she reckoned she could outrun Sophia anyway, even if her foe was wearing full training gear instead of heels and had a professional starter's block to launch from.

Go, she told herself.

Francoise flung the door open and ran. She ran faster than she'd ever run in her life until she was two blocks away and bent over double, sucking in air as tears leaked down her face. But no one was following her. There were no giveaway headlights suddenly switched on, no one laughing in the distance.

But the threat of Sophia burned bright in her mind. And her imagination didn't have to stretch too far to conjure up what the Celiks would do to her, or any hit man that Sophia could pay off, for that matter. She was trapped between the two sets of criminals. If she contacted the Celiks and gave them Sophia, they would know that she had gone back on her word and would punish her anyway.

Despite her fear and shaky breath, she was thinking clearly and quickly. It was obvious she had only one choice, but she needed to get away from here first and put some distance between her and her would-be killers.

With her breathing slowed, she began to jog. She told herself she'd stay on the move for the next hour and then surface from some random underground station and put her new plan – her only plan – into action.

★

'Glad I caught you.' Jack smiled at the woman behind the counter, who was clearly tidying up for the day.

'I'm glad you did too. It's been a quiet day. This is surely an apology, right?' She laughed at his raised brows. 'You look far too stressed for this to be a planned visit.' She walked to the main door and locked it, turning over the closed sign. 'That your taxi out there?'

'It is.'

'I'll be quick then. What can I get you?'

'I need something that does say sorry, but only for being forgetful. Something beautiful.'

'Romantic?'

Jack didn't know how to answer that, but his smile probably answered for him.

The florist walked back towards the fridges. 'Honestly, you can't go past this,' she said, and pulled out a single, exquisite red rose. 'These came in this afternoon from our farm in Hampshire. They'll all be gone by tomorrow midday.'

'Hampshire? I thought all the commercial roses come from overseas.'

'You're right, most florists stock long-stemmed roses from Ecuador or Kenya, perhaps Ethiopia.'

Jack was surprised. 'I thought you were going to say Europe.'

'No, to get those really long stems and perfect, almost fake-looking blooms, you need to be well above sea level.'

'I sense a *but* coming.' He grinned.

'But they have to travel such long distances and look amazing despite it that all those poor commercialised stocks have had their scent gene bred out of them.'

Jack looked at her in awe. 'Scent gene. Wow.'

'Our owner put in years of research, starting over, to make sure our roses have their scent gene intact. You won't find more naturally perfect, scented roses. How did you know about us?'

'I used to work around here,' he said, not entirely telling the truth. He'd seen the shop dozens of times, usually as he careered past in a squad car, and had always wanted to visit.

'Here, smell this perfume,' she offered, holding out the rose.

He leaned in and inhaled. It was headily sweet, with a rich, deep, classically rose scent that was both musky and fruity. The petals felt like velvet where they briefly kissed the top of his lip. 'Mmm.'

'When this opens, it changes from vivid red to a deep, delicious sort of imperial purple, and the centre offers up a flash of sunlit gold at its stamens. That fragrance you're enjoying now will be even more intoxicating, too.'

'My gosh, I'm sold,' he exclaimed. 'I want a dozen,' he said, feigning overwhelming excitement.

'Is a dozen too much for an apology?' she wondered aloud. 'Are you wooing this lucky woman?'

He shrugged, unsure. Such an old-fashioned, rather lovely concept too. 'I like her, and I forgot she was expecting to see me tonight . . . and she knows I forgot. She's cooked dinner.'

The florist gave a tutting sound. 'May I make a suggestion?'

'Go ahead.'

'A single rose speaks volumes. This will open beautifully in a vase and make its own statement. I think a dozen says something else, which perhaps you're not ready to say. Instead, how about a box of rose petals?'

Jack blinked, confused. 'Pardon?'

'Let me show you.' She reached into the fridge and pulled out a sage-green hatbox. When she lifted the lid, he saw a glorious tumble of pale petals from ivory to lilac, through to peach, pink and deep red.

He opened his mouth in delighted surprise.

'Stunning, right?' she continued. 'It's not actually saying anything too specific, but it's somehow wildly romantic.'

'The rose and the box, please, definitely. Now, there's another woman who might be at dinner.' At her widening gaze, he added, 'Er, it's her flatmate. I can't leave her out. Is there anything that isn't romantic but is lovely?'

'How about a small box of dried rose petals and some chocolates?'

'Perfect. Let's do that.'

Within five minutes, Jack was back in the taxi. 'Now a wine shop somewhere and we're done,' he said.

He arrived to knock at Lou and Gabriella's door after almost skipping up the flights of stairs to their flat. Lou had already called down that she'd leave the door open, as she was checking something on the stove. He hoped Gabriella would behave tonight and not make it awkward for him, but he could tell her flirtatious manner was part of her, and she was unlikely to switch it on and off.

He gently pushed open the door. 'Evening?'

Lou Barclay rounded the corner and walked down the hall wearing comfy jeans, an oversized lemon sweater and an apron.

'Hello, you.' She beamed as though greeting her oldest, closest friend. 'You made it then.'

'No wonder you're so trim,' he complained, looking back at the stairs. 'Here, these are for you.'

'What? I said bring nothing,' she said, reprimanding him gently.

'My mother said never to go to anyone's house empty-handed.' He gave her the tall, slim box and the hatbox.

She looked down at them, puzzled. 'How intriguing.'

'And this is for Gabriella,' he said, holding out the small, round box and chocolates. 'Is she . . .?'

'She got a better offer,' Lou replied. 'I hope that's not disappointing for you.' She raised her eyes back to his, watching for a reaction.

He knew she saw his eyes light up at this news. 'Er, no, not at all. Would you give this to her and let her know that I hope she's feeling brighter from the time we met?' He pressed the two boxes into her hands.

'I can assure you that Bella doesn't stay ill for long. She's met a man, so it's on for young and old.'

Jack smiled. 'And I found us a nice shiraz, although I'm now wondering if you even drink red wine. I don't know anything about you to be honest, other than . . . you're just lovely,' he said, as if that thought had been pent up in his chest since they'd met. He wasn't even embarrassed. 'I don't know where you come from, what you do, what you like.'

She cast him a look of surprised befuddlement in the hallway. 'Well, I'm originally from Oxfordshire – my folk live in the Cotswolds. I'm a designer and I like lots of things, including shiraz on a cool night and a polite policeman who says nice things about me.' She smiled. 'Come on in. My hands are full, or I'd offer to take your coat.'

'No, no, I'll hang it up here,' he said, glancing at the row of hooks on an old piece of misshapen timber. 'That's fun.'

'My brother made that in his woodwork class at school. I've always loved it for its wonkiness.'

He followed her down towards the end of the flat, which opened up into a huge living area. 'Wow. This is enormous.'

'Yes, these old places were built properly. More than enough space to swing a cat, eh, Bingo?'

Jack looked down to see a muscular tabby staring at him with large, accusatory eyes the colour of old depression glass.

Lou smiled fondly at the cat. 'I hope you're not allergic?'

'Not that I'm aware. Hello, Bingo.'

'May I open these?' Lou lifted the parcels he'd given her.

'Please.'

She put them down on the coffee table and opened the hatbox first, giving a soft squeal of joy, just as the florist had predicted. 'Oh, Jack, these are just ... oh my, they're beautiful.' She tenderly touched the petals and then almost buried her face in them. 'They smell intoxicating.' She leaned over and kissed him; it wasn't his mouth, but it wasn't far off.

He smiled. 'You're welcome.'

'Wow, how very romantic. What am I supposed to do with them? Toss them all over the bed?' She gave him an arch look.

He wasn't going to give an answer that would get him in any deeper. 'Do you know, I asked the florist just this question, and she gave me no satisfactory answer. What we agree on is that they're just exquisite and, frankly, even I would like that gift. If I'd had somewhere to hide them, I would have kept them for myself.'

Lou chuckled. 'Such a modern man! I'm going to scatter some on our table for dinner if you don't mind.'

He shook his head, thrilled at her delight.

'Now,' Lou said, reaching for the long, narrow box, 'this has me completely intrigued.' She lifted the lid and saw the perfect red rose and said nothing, staring at it, looking to Jack as though she was holding her breath.

He watched her lift the rose to her face and close her eyes as she inhaled the fragrance he could recreate in his mind. Her long lashes fluttered gently and he remembered the soft, plump touch of that velvety petal against his lips. He filled the silence. 'Er, I didn't know how to say sorry for almost forgetting tonight. Work is just—'

He got no further. Lou reached for him and this time kissed him gently and fully, as a lover might. He didn't resist, he didn't press his luck; he simply enjoyed the surprise and the lovely feel of a woman's arms reaching around his neck.

When they parted, he blinked in astonishment. 'I thought perhaps I'd upset you when you looked at the rose,' he said, sounding concerned and scanning her watering eyes.

She shook her head and smiled. 'I haven't had a single red rose ever from a guy who wasn't my dad. He used to give me a red rose from the garden every birthday. And since he died, no more single red roses . . . until now. And it smells like a rose should.'

Jack didn't know what to say, but she continued.

'I would have been happy with a block of Supermilk from Hotel Chocolat. But this . . . this is the perfect apology, Jack, though it wasn't necessary. Thank you.' She kissed him again and for longer this time, and he sank into it, all the drama of the day set aside momentarily.

This time when they parted, they leaned their foreheads together. Neither, it seemed, was ready to let go.

'Well, that was a lovely surprise,' he admitted.

She lifted a single shoulder in a careless shrug. 'Actually, that's how I welcome all my dinner guests who bring something, don't you?'

He laughed and hugged her. 'Lou, you're exactly what I needed this evening.'

She leaned back to look him square in the eye. 'Only this evening?'

Jack chose to reply to her question with a kiss of his own, and soon lost track of how long it lasted in the delicious abandon.

When he finally released her, she smiled lazily, her arms still loosely at his shoulders. 'Well, I guess that answers that.'

Neither of them was in a hurry to let go. 'And perhaps we shouldn't waste, um . . .' She looked down below his waist and back up to meet his gaze of admonishment.

'Saucy,' he said and that made her burst into laughter.

'That is such a funny turn of phrase. You're so old-fashioned.'

'So they say.' Grinning like a loon, Jack was happy to be led back down the hallway and into a bedroom lit by tiny white fairy lights, which wrapped serpent-like around a Victorian canopy bed of black wrought iron, giving it a lacy, featherlight appearance. He had just enough time to take in the attractive rug beneath their feet before he was toppling with Lou onto the soft grey stripe of the linen covering her billowy quilt.

'I wanted to kiss you the moment you came down the stairs in pyjama bottoms and the top that said "Don't think about it". It's all I thought about for hours afterwards.' Jack stroked her tumbling hair away from her face.

'Good. You took me entirely by surprise, I'll admit. I'm usually immune to charming men . . . for a while anyway. They need to stick around and impress me.'

'I don't remember trying. I didn't even bring a block of Supermilk, which I happen to admire very much myself.'

'You did impress though. You were very kind to Bella. She has a, well, shall we say *breezy* way about her, which a lot of men presume they can take advantage of and you look like the kind of guy who can get any woman he wants.' She gave him a wicked smile and pulled his shirt out from where it was tucked beneath his belt.

Jack shook his head, frowning. 'I'm not like that, I promise.'

She snuggled into his neck. 'So I've gathered, because I know Bella was fairly throwing herself at you. And I might add she has been quite sulky that you haven't called her. She's not used to that.'

'Not my type, I'm afraid.'

'What is your type?'

'Certainly not scary like Gabriella,' he said, making Lou laugh again. 'I like women who amuse me. Women who are so addictive I can forget my work.'

'It's that bad, huh?'

He nodded. 'At the moment, definitely.' Right on cue, Jack felt his phone buzz in his pocket.

Laughing, she rolled off him to lie next to him, and they linked hands. 'Your phone is talking to you, Detective Hawksworth.'

'But I don't want to let go. I'm happy right here, not thinking about work but thinking about what's making that delicious smell in the kitchen and just how beautiful you are from this angle.'

'Flattery, flattery,' Lou said, smiling.

'Besides, my phone is always nagging.'

'It might be important. You check it, and I'll turn our simmering dinner down and be right back.' She leaned down and pecked his lips. 'Don't move from this bed.'

Lou nimbly got up, even though he was reluctant to break their contact, and Jack leaned up on one arm to reach into his pocket, cursing the invention of the mobile phone.

It was a text message. *I believe you're looking for me. Francoise.*

He sat up, no longer relaxed, and swung his legs over the bed.

Lou returned. 'Now, I thought we were clear on the brief . . . Jack? What's wrong?'

Standing, he sighed, running a hand backwards through his hair, aware that he was dishevelled with his shirt hanging out. He didn't know what to say.

'Gotta go?' she offered, clearly trying to help him extract himself without hurting her feelings.

'I . . . er.' He gave a low sigh of frustration. 'May I make a call?'

'Of course. Something with your case?'

'There's a young woman in real trouble.' He looked at her, hoping she understood he didn't want to leave her.

She gave a small nod. 'What are you waiting for?'

'Thanks.' He tapped his phone and paused, deliberately not turning away from Lou. He didn't particularly want her to share this conversation, but he also didn't want to lock her out; it would be a dampener on whatever it was between them if he walked away for privacy, even though he probably should. He let it ring. 'I believe she's in terrible danger,' he explained, pulling Lou to sit next to him on the bed. Surprising himself, he put the call onto speaker and took Lou's hand in his.

'Hello,' said a woman.

'Francoise?'

'Yes. You're Jack Hawksworth?'

'I am.' He waited.

'What do you want?'

'You made the contact, Francoise, I presume you know you're in danger. Will you let me help you?'

'How can you help?'

'I suspect you know that the likelihood of two different parties hunting you is real. You're not safe on the outside. You need to come in.'

'Come in where?'

'To safety. Look, I'll meet you. Tell me where you are.'

'No, tell me where *you* are. But I'm not coming to a police station.'

Jack looked helplessly at Lou and muted the phone. She shrugged. 'I've cooked for three,' she murmured, kissing his cheek and standing to leave, but he didn't let go of her hand.

Jack unmuted the phone and gave Francoise the address, but not the flat number. 'This is a friend's place. I'll meet you outside. How long will it take you to get here?'

'I'll be there at seven-thirty.' She rang off.

Jack let out a breath he didn't know he was holding. 'I'm sorry,' he began, looking at Lou's hand still in his.

Lou squeezed it. 'Don't be. It wasn't what I expected though – she didn't sound very grateful.'

'I suspect she's incredibly scared.'

'How much trouble is she in?'

'The kind that would take her life in a heartbeat if I don't give my all to protect her.'

Lou looked shocked. 'Well, there, you've just given me another reason to like you, Jack. This woman, Francoise – she said one hour?'

He nodded sadly, aware that he'd ruined their evening and their mood.

She lifted his chin and looked him in the eye. 'Plenty of time before she arrives for dinner,' she said, pulling off her lemon sweater.

Jack had even had time for a quick shower, and he now stood behind the main entrance of the block of art deco flats, staring out at the rain that had still not let up. He was still in the glow of Lou Barclay's lovemaking and the feeling – just for a while – of being deliciously lost. It hadn't been slow and teasing, but at the same time it hadn't felt rushed.

It had felt like they were two magnets inevitably drawn to one another, neither of them able to resist the other, and being patient had not been required once he began to kiss down the length of her body. He was already daydreaming of the next occasion he could have Lou in his arms. She tasted as good as she looked, her skin unimaginably soft with lovely angles for him to explore. He began to imagine all day in bed with Lou; breakfast in bed, a picnic in bed, drinking tea in bed, reading the newspaper in bed, drinking champagne in bed . . . and perhaps the most seductive of all, falling asleep curled up around Lou. He could almost create that sensation of being pressed close against her back with his arms protectively around her.

Wow, he'd moved that dream along fast. Who was this woman, who had captured him so quickly? He shook his mind free and noticed a small smudge of a figure in the darkness. She was staring at him. He had zero doubt that this was Francoise.

He opened the door and beckoned.

She shook her head.

Jack sighed and looked around for something to wedge the door open with but came up wanting. There was nothing for it but to step out into the cold rain. Wishing he'd grabbed his coat and wasn't just in his shirtsleeves, he skipped into the street and ran gingerly across the slippery road into the darkness. 'Francoise?'

'Prove to me who you are,' she demanded.

He looked at her helplessly. 'I haven't brought anything down.'

'Then I can't trust you.'

'You can.'

'How?'

'We're getting drenched. Can we discuss this out of the rain at least?'

She shook her head resolutely. Her hair was plastered around her face and she was shivering.

Jack sighed. 'Okay, okay, er . . . Your friend is Lyn. I met with her today, and you probably got a call or a message of some sort from her giving you my name or we wouldn't be standing here getting colder by the second . . . would we?' He looked at her, hopeful. *Please let that be enough.*

She nodded, finally softening her expression, and he led her across the road at a brisk trot. He pressed the bell.

Lou answered quickly. 'Hi.'

'It's us.' The door buzzed open. 'Come on,' Jack said, gesturing for Francoise to go in. 'You'll like Lou.'

'Is this a police house, like a safe place?'

'No, but it is safe. It's the home of a friend. One we can trust.' Jack risked a grin. 'I'm afraid it's a lot of stairs.'

Lou was waiting with a towel when they arrived. She handed it to Francoise with a smile. The newcomer nodded and took it wordlessly.

'Lou, this is Francoise,' Jack said.

'The bathroom is down the hall and first on the left,' Lou said, her tone kind.

Jack and Lou watched her move into the flat. 'I'm sorry – this must be very odd.'

Lou shrugged. 'It's okay. It must be very odd for her too. We're strangers to her.' They looked at each other before grinning in a shared moment of awkwardness. 'Not to each other, though. You're drenched. I'll grab you a towel too.'

He hugged her first. 'Tonight has been lovely, and if you'll let me try again, I'll make our next meeting more special.'

'Promises, promises . . .' She laughed, and Jack felt relieved. 'I'll hold you to that. Come on, let's see if we can find something dry for you to put on – I think you'll look good in lilac. And Jack, I just know what you're going to ask next and yes, but for one night only.'

He blinked at her ability to read his mind. 'What sort of designs do you do?' he asked in wonder.

'Crystal balls, of course,' she quipped, waving a finger. 'She can stay here for one night.'

'Thank you. She'll be in a safe house tomorrow morning, I promise.'

'Where have you been, Ronnie?' Baris asked. They were in one of the barber shops and, given the late hour, had the place to themselves.

'Nowhere. I mean, I've been working as I told you.'

'You've kept us waiting for that photo.'

'I have it here,' he said, flicking through his phone. 'I loaded it from my computer,' he lied, hoping the tremble in his voice showed respect rather than the fear he was experiencing. He prayed they didn't know he'd been with the police, but he needed to be ready to answer for that if they did. 'Here, Mr Celik, this is Sylvie.'

Baris leaned in and looked at the image. He said nothing, but Ronnie watched him glance up at Eren, who blinked slowly.

'Sylvie, you say?'

'Sylvie Toussaint.'

'That address you gave us didn't work out.'

Ronnie played dumb, hoping with all of his heart that the flatmate hadn't dobbed him in. His short stature meant he was easy to recognise. 'What do you mean?'

'She doesn't live there any more.'

Ronnie's eyelids fluttered as he built his lie, and he guessed that gesture would only make him seem more nervous, which perhaps was a good thing. They, in comparison, looked relaxed, like cats, toying with a trapped mouse. 'That's the only place I know, Mr Celik. I took her home several times to that address.' He shrugged.

'And you've had no contact with her.'

'No, sir. None. You can look in my phone. The last text message was on that day when I wondered why she was at work on her day off.'

Eren took the phone to check, scrolling up and down the texts. Baris waited until his brother looked up and nodded.

'Have you any other information for us, Ronnie?' Baris asked. 'We'd be grateful.'

They were the words he'd longed to hear. 'Er, I'm not sure, Mr Baris,' he began. 'But I did see Sylvie meet these people once.' He gestured to have his phone back and Eren obliged. It was Ronnie's turn to scroll, but he'd already carefully put it in a folder so they wouldn't know it was his latest photo. They were very cunning and might check that sort of thing. 'Here. I can't tell you their names, but it's a man and woman and they were driving this car.'

Baris nodded at Eren, who made a note of the registration. 'We'll look into it. What do you know about them?'

Ronnie shrugged. 'Nothing, other than I think they were at the Bentley event at Lark's Hill.'

That won their attention. 'Is that so?' Baris asked.

Ronnie nodded. 'Good, Ronnie. This is a help and I'm sure we'll show our appreciation. We will look into this couple and be back to you.'

'Back to me, Mr Baris? I thought—'

'I think you might still be helpful, Ronnie, and you owe us that much. We can consider it a debt cleared.'

'Thank you, Mr Celik.' He looked between them. 'Er, I'll wait to hear.'

They let him get as far as the door.

'Oh, and Ronnie?' Baris said, as he opened the door. 'No more talking to police, now.'

Behind him, Eren drew a finger across his throat and smiled.

23

Claudia made up a bed for herself on the small sofa in Lyn's flat, admiring the hand-drawn flowers on the wall. 'This looks like something my daughter would want in a room,' she said.

Lyn looked surprised. 'Daughter? I didn't know you had a child. Where is she?'

'I've organised for a friend to stay with her tonight, so I can keep an eye on you. Tomorrow you might be on the sofa at my place – I'll get my revenge.'

'S'okay. I'll sleep anywhere. I never had a real room of my own growing up, so I got permission from the landlord to put up this plain wallpaper and then I got paints and made my own pattern.'

'It's fun,' Claudia said, keeping to herself the sadness that it looked like a child's fantasy, clearly achieved by someone who'd missed out on a proper childhood.

'Your daughter's lucky.' Lyn smiled, somewhat forlornly, Claudia thought.

'Is she? I wish I could do more for her.'

'You're a very cool mum, I'm sure, Claudia,' Lyn assured her. 'I wish you were my mum.'

Claudia gave the younger woman a hug. 'Well, for tonight we can pretend, okay? I know they've put police outside, but I want to make sure you're safe.'

'As if I could miss them. Anyway, I do feel safe. Thanks for looking out for me – and for organising the detective. I can be a bit funny at first when people are being kind, but he was nice.'

Claudia laughed. 'I told you that you could trust Jack. Come on, did you use my phone to order the pizza you wanted?'

'Yeah, shouldn't be long. It's from around the corner. Ham and pineapple okay?'

'That's fine – my daughter's favourite. So, shall we lay this table?'

'Lay the table,' Lyn repeated with wonder. 'But it hardly seats two people.'

'We can make it work. I insist my girl knows her manners and how to sit at a table and make conversation, and it won't hurt you either. You know, Lyn, you could probably get some higher-end jobs if you practise some of this.'

'Practise what?'

'Being less prickly around newcomers, learning how to make light conversation, how to put your knife and fork down in between mouthfuls and not speaking with your mouth full . . . Not gorging on one pastry after another.'

At that Lyn frowned. 'He said they were all mine. He didn't mean it?'

'He did, I promise. I'm just saying in polite company you wouldn't cram all three pastries down in less than fifteen minutes.' Claudia chuckled.

'Well, isn't wasting them worse?'

Claudia smiled. 'You're right. Here, sweetie. Forks and knives.' At Lyn's look of despair, she added, 'You don't have to use them.

Pizza is one of those things you can use your hands for, but I'd love to see you use some cutlery if—'

There was a ping on her phone. 'Ah, the pizza guy's here.'

'I'll go meet him,' Lyn said.

'Here, take some money.' Claudia rummaged in her purse and gave Lyn a twenty. 'Bring me a fiver back; he can keep the rest.'

'Okay.'

Claudia got busy putting plates out onto the small table by the kitchen window. She didn't hold out hope for paper napkins but found some kitchen roll and folded a couple of sheets into triangles. It made her think of her own small table by the window in her flat, where the sun streamed in each morning. She loved sharing a proper breakfast with her daughter before she walked her to school. It was the best part of her day.

Life was good . . . if too short. She hoped her plan for Hanna to fall in love with Poland was going to work out – it needed to.

'Claudia?' Lyn's voice shook her out of her thoughts. She sounded frightened, and Claudia swung around, sucking in a terrified breath as she saw Lyn in a man's grip. Clutching the pizza, she was so tiny against him, she looked like a doll.

Another man smirked from the doorway. 'Pizza smells great, girls,' he said. 'I might have that afterwards.'

After what? Claudia thought, her throat too choked to speak. She already knew, within a second of his statement, how this would end; she could see it in the man's smile of menace. She was glad for the tiny bit of luck that she hadn't taken Lyn back to her home where Hanna slept.

After changing into a dry shirt and sitting down to eat the meal Lou had prepared, a delicious casserole, Jack deliberately kept the conversation at a surface level for Francoise's benefit.

Lou hadn't lied; she'd handed him a sweatshirt in lilac to wear while his own was in the dryer. 'Largest one I have,' was her innocent explanation at his bemused silent query. He was sure she was fibbing.

He'd asked Francoise no hard questions and when she wondered aloud why he and Lou were talking about life in London or the new iPad released from Apple that she would probably never touch, let alone own, he sighed.

'Just trying to keep the chat light, you know, until you feel like joining in. Listen, I know you're suspicious and scared. You've clearly been warned by Lyn that they're hunting you—'

'They tried today.'

Jack glanced at Lou. He really didn't want her to be drawn into this conversation or the police investigation. Carol Rowland's warning to keep his personal life far away from work was klaxoning loudly in his mind. He'd finally met someone who had nothing to do with his case or his work, and the small voice in his head said: *so what do you do? You immediately invite her into the danger.* Somehow he'd managed to bring a woman who was being actively hunted by killers to Lou's dining table and invited her to stay overnight.

Well, it was too late now. He breathed in lightly to stop the thoughts, tried to focus on what Francoise was saying. 'What do you mean? Tried what?'

'They tried to kill me today.'

Jack desperately wanted to put his hand against Francoise's mouth to stop her from saying another word but she'd decided in that moment to become suddenly chatty. 'We met at a place we've met previously for handover.'

'Handover?' Lou asked.

'Money,' Francoise confirmed.

'Oh.' Lou glanced at Jack.

He could see this conversation now had legs and was going to run. 'Shall we save this until—'

'But I didn't trust them,' Francoise cut in, 'so I got there early and hid. When they arrived, they thought I was late, so they talked about how they were going to kill me with a bottle of champagne. My glass would be laced with Rohypnol and they'd finish me off once I was unconscious . . . leave me to rot and not be found for weeks . . . or not. I might not be found for years.'

Jack saw Lou stop eating. 'Who tried to kill you?' Lou asked, aghast, and Jack wished she hadn't.

'Sophia and her brother, Franco. He wasn't as interested to be rid of me as she is. But she's the boss. They're as bad as the Celiks.' Francoise glanced up from her meal at Jack. 'That's who I did the original blackmail with.'

Jack closed his eyes for a moment. 'Francoise, I need you to not speak of this until we can have the right team around you.' He reached out to touch Lou's hand. 'I can see you're upset—'

'Upset? I'm fucking horrified. People tried to kill her today and you're sitting here, calmly eating?'

Jack nodded and dabbed at his mouth with the napkin. 'I have to be. I can't—' His phone rang shrilly and juddered against the table. Kate. 'Sorry, excuse me.' He stood up from the table. 'Please, don't talk any more about what happened until I get back.'

'Hi.'

'Jack . . .' Kate sounded odd. 'Er . . . can you talk?'

He frowned. 'Go ahead.'

There was a silence so loud on the other end that fresh alarm moved through him.

'What is it? Are you hurt? Are you—'

'I'm fine, sorry. I'm with Geoff. We're at the flat in Southall.'

Jack glanced over at Francoise and moved fully away from the dining table into the hall. 'What's going on?'

'It's Claudia.'

Jack frowned deeper. 'Claudia Lenkas?'

'Geoff told me you were meeting her and someone called Lyn today, a friend of Sylvie Toussaint's?'

'Yes, that's right . . .' he said, trailing off, silent questions hanging on the line. 'What aren't you saying?'

'Jack, I'm really sorry, but Claudia and Lyn are dead,' she blurted. 'Police were called out to the flat by neighbours who heard screams, but it was too late. Geoff's team was immediately alerted due to the . . . well, due to the scene.'

Jack blinked rapidly, hoping against hope that he'd misheard her. The silence lengthened.

'Jack?'

He cleared his throat. 'I heard you.' And then he spoke his thoughts aloud. 'I thought I'd—'

'Yes, Geoff had sent people to watch the block of flats but—'

'But the killers were already there,' he finished for Kate. He shook his head; he had been too late after all.

'Yes, that's what it looks like. They used an old fire escape to avoid being seen and came into the flat with a pizza delivery guy. Geoff's team had checked out the pizza guy and became suspicious when he didn't come back out. He'd been locked in the caretaker's cupboard.'

Jack felt hot bile rising but had to stay focused and calm. 'Claudia has a daughter.'

'I remember. She wasn't there. Do you—'

'I'm on my way. I'll send some people to Claudia's place. Hanna's probably with a babysitter.'

'I'm so very sorry,' Kate repeated. 'I'll send the address. Geoff's called in all the right people.'

As Jack rang off, he walked back to the table.

'Jack, what's happened?' Lou said, reacting to his fallen expression and tense silence. 'Bad news?'

'What's going on?' Francoise demanded. 'Is it Lyn? She said they were coming for her too.'

Jack looked at the French woman, so small and yet seemingly so tough, but he could see the tears already welling. 'I'm afraid it is her, Francoise. And a friend of mine was murdered simply for accompanying her, for trying to keep her safe.'

Lou stood suddenly, her chair scraping the floor in a loud squeal. 'Fuck!'

Jack moved towards her but she put her hands up, shaking her head.

'Are they coming here?' Lou demanded.

'No!' Both Jack and Francoise said it together.

'Absolutely not,' Jack said. 'They don't know where Francoise is, that's the point. Right?' He stared at Francoise. 'You didn't tell Lyn where you were going, did you?'

'No, she had no idea.' Francoise was shaking her head.

'And you're sure you weren't followed?'

Francoise explained all the precautions she had taken. 'I promise you, no one knows I'm here but I'll leave immediately.' She stood up. 'Thank you for being kind.'

'No, wait,' Lou said, her tone calmer but her voice still shaky. 'I'm sorry . . . to both of you.' She gave a tight, mirthless smile. 'You both talk of death and murder as easily I might discuss where to hang a painting in a gallery.' At Jack's frown, she explained. 'It's what I do – I design exhibitions. I don't fraternise with gangsters.'

There was no time to enjoy learning about her work. 'We'll both go,' Jack said.

'No,' Lou insisted. She reached out and took Francoise's hand. 'I can't have you on my conscience. If Jack says we're safe, then we are. Please stay here.'

He put the phone to his ear. 'I'm organising for detectives to be sitting outside through the night. If anyone so much as walks up to the front door, they'll be all over them. Do you have a back or side entrance?'

Lou shook her head. 'I'll see if your shirt is dry.' She disappeared for a moment, returning with the only slightly damp garment.

'That'll do,' Jack said. 'Okay. I'll be back here at seven-thirty tomorrow morning to pick you up, Francoise, but I have to go now.' He looked at Lou, who nodded.

'Then what?' Francoise demanded.

'You'll be interviewed by my team, and we'll get you set up in a safe house.'

'Am I under arrest?'

Jack shook his head. 'Not if you cooperate and do what Lou tells you.'

She seemed to accept that, flopping back into her chair. Jack ducked back into the bedroom to change. He hated himself for putting Lou in this position. It was so wrong. What's more, it was dangerous. As he removed the lilac sweatshirt and shook out his own shirt, he searched every option available to him, but this was the only way. He didn't like breaking rules or protocols, but he had shown over his career that he'd disregard both if it meant protecting lives. If Francoise could stay here, in obscurity and safety, for just the next few hours, then he might have a chance at catching the blackmailers and protecting her. The self-loathing didn't dissipate with this thought though, and he wondered how he would ever justify it if anything happened to these women. Lou was an innocent.

Once he emerged from the bedroom, trying to disguise how sick he felt, Lou said, 'I'll see you out,' and walked with him to the door. As he opened his mouth to speak, she held up a hand. 'If you apologise again, I'm going to biff you. It's my turn. Sorry for going wobbly on you. I should have let you walk out in a lilac sweatshirt.'

He cupped her face and kissed her, putting everything he wanted to say into the kiss. 'What I'm asking you to do flies in the face of all the rules of how we operate.'

'Do you have an option?'

'Not one she'd agree to. I could carry her out of here in hand-cuffs, kicking and screaming, and—'

Lou shook her head. 'Don't do that. She'll never help. She's too hardened. From the little I've heard, I imagine her ringing you must have been a last resort, which means she's terrified.' She shrugged. 'If you can keep us safe, then I want to help.'

'I promise I'm going to make this up to you, Lou. Can you not let her out of your sight, please?'

'You'd better have a box of pain au chocolat in hand for break-fast when you arrive tomorrow.'

He somehow found a grin, then kissed her again.

She returned his smile through her fear. 'Stay safe.'

Jack arranged for Ari, Nat and Matt to be stationed outside Lou's building with firm instructions. He found a taxi easily enough now that the rain had eased and within forty minutes met Geoff and Kate, both looking sombre, outside the slightly grungy block of three flats that now looked like a TV crime scene with flashing lights, ambulances and plenty of police cordoning off the area.

'SOCO's in there now,' Kate said, taking one look at Jack's grim expression and knowing it was best to get straight down to business.

'Don't go in there, Hawk,' Geoff said. 'They obviously wanted information.'

Jack swore sadly under his breath. He knew that was Geoff's code for torture. 'Claudia was just—'

'I know, matey. No point in beating yourself up now,' his friend said, his voice firm and brisk. 'We have to let her folk know, but Kate says she's Polish, so her family is probably not in the UK, right?'

'She has a daughter here. Her mother's in Krakow.' Jack rubbed his eyes.

'Okay, it's all in hand; my guys are all over it. I can make a statement to the media that ensures it's kept separate from what we know is probably going on. I'll keep it general. But you can brief Rowland that all parties are now colliding.'

Jack nodded miserably. 'No one saw anything?'

Both Kate and Geoff shook their heads. 'Neighbours heard screams, but nothing so far in terms of witnesses, other than the pizza guy who is seventeen and so spooked he can barely talk. They clubbed him from behind, so he doesn't remember anything after arriving and heading upstairs to the first floor. He was left unconscious in the caretaker's storeroom and he's been sent to hospital,' Kate said, answering every question that Jack might ask. 'We've organised some door to door – that's underway, but in this area of town, they'll go silent on us. They won't want trouble, even if they did see something.'

Geoff stamped his feet in the cold. 'I'll stay here until pathology is finished, and we can safely have the bodies removed to the morgue. My number two will remain with the SOCO team until they're done.' He paused, looking at Jack. 'How did you go?'

'I've got her,' he said, uncontrollably blunt.

Kate snapped to attention. 'What are we talking about?'

Geoff shrugged, looking at Jack. 'Over to you. But I suggest you get out of here, because we don't want any cluey journos putting two and two together and making five as usual.'

'We'll head back to the Yard,' Kate said, obviously agreeing with his caution. 'See you later?'

Geoff nodded and mimed ringing her.

'Come on, Jack. We're no use here. You can fill me in on the way.'

He allowed himself to be led for the second time that night, but where Kate was leading him was only towards misery and self-recrimination. She had a squad car and drove in silence until they were about ten minutes out from Westminster.

'How bad was it?' he asked suddenly into the gloom.

Kate knew him well enough to be honest. 'Bad. They cut them.'

He covered his face with his hands. 'I promised them I'd keep them safe.'

Kate remained silent. There was nothing to say to that.

However, as they turned to go down into the Yard's car park, it seemed she couldn't remain quiet any longer. 'Are you going to tell me, or do I have to winkle it out of you?'

'Winkle. Good word,' he said absently. 'I've got Sylvie Toussaint.'

She turned and looked at him in complete surprise.

'Watch the ramp,' he said softly.

'How have you got Sylvie?' she demanded.

'It's a bit of a story, but let's just shorten it to the fact that her real name is Francoise Laurent, and she is the woman with the condom in the polaroid, involved in both Luca's blackmail and the earlier incidents.'

'Blimey. Where is she?'

'She is presently hidden, and I hope by tomorrow we shall move her into a safe house.'

'Don't tell me you've taken her to your place, Jack. The chief will absolutely—'

'She's not at my place. She's with a friend.'

Kate spotted an empty space and slowed down. 'Are you mad?'

'I had just met with Claudia and Lyn. I asked Claudia to keep Lyn safe, since I thought she might be in danger along with Francoise. Geoff's people were there to watch out for anyone who might come by. But it was too late, it seems. What a mess,' he breathed. In his mind he was using far more rank words, but he schooled himself to remain calm. If he lost that grip, then he might spook his team. 'I really believed they would be all right – after all, it was Sylvie who I thought was most at risk. So I was at a friend's for dinner when I got a message from a person calling herself Francoise, who said, "I gather you're looking for me." When I said I'd meet her, she refused. When I said come to the Yard, she refused. She demanded to know where I was and to meet me there – I think it made her feel like she was in control that way. I had to bring her in, primarily to keep her safe, but also to find out what she knows about our blackmailers. What would you have done? Let her remain out there where anything could happen? There was no way she was coming anywhere near a police station tonight.'

Kate finished parking and turned off the ignition. She didn't answer immediately, but when she did, she gave him what he wanted: exoneration. 'Okay. I can't see what else you could do in that situation.'

'I toyed briefly with a hotel, but I can't control all that public space. Where she is now, only three people know and I'm one of them, and she's another. So that keeps her safe.'

'You're not going to tell me who the friend is, are you?'

'No, and it doesn't matter.'

Kate sighed as if already guessing that it had to be a woman, but Jack didn't care. He couldn't get Claudia out of his mind. It was only hours ago that she'd winked at him.

Kate was talking but he missed it. 'Sorry, what?'

'I said I heard from Luca,' Kate repeated. 'He's got the money sorted.'

'The drop is tomorrow, right?'

'Yep, tomorrow night.'

'And we don't know where yet?'

'No.'

Nothing more was said until the lift doors opened on their floor. The place was in relative darkness, just one small light on in the corner.

'Sarah,' they both said softly and walked around to where she sat.

She jumped when she saw them. 'Crap! You scared me. I thought everyone had gone.'

'We had. We're back. We're miserable. I'm going to make tea,' Kate said.

'Unless you can find something stronger in Joan's hidey places,' Jack replied.

Kate cast him a sad smile. 'I'll see what I can do.' She disappeared.

Jack collapsed into a small sofa, let his head fall back and covered his face with his hands again.

'Oh, sir, something awful has happened, I'm guessing.'

From beneath his hands, his voice muffled, he sighed and answered. 'It has, Sarah, and it's my fault.'

She rolled over her desk chair and sat down. 'To do with the case?'

'Yes.'

'Will you tell me?'

He straightened in his chair and was aware of her dismay. He really must be wearing a broken expression, he realised, and as damaged as he felt, he shouldn't convey that to a team member who was still looking to him to lead. He took a deep breath and began to tell Sarah everything that had happened over the course of the day. 'I still have to contact Claudia's mother in Poland and'—he shook his head—'her little girl needs—'

'I've found something *you* need,' Kate bellowed, shaking a three-quarters-empty bottle of Scotch as she joined them. 'Here, have a nip and get it together.' She added 'Sir' to be respectful, but her tone brooked no argument.

'Where on earth did you find that?'

'Don't ask. Here.' She poured a slug into one of the glasses she was also clutching. 'Get that down you. Sarah?'

'No, but thanks.'

'Well, I will, because no doubt you've heard about our evening.'

Sarah nodded. Kate and Jack knocked back their drams and both groaned.

'Right, one more, a little one, to sip, and I'll take this back,' Kate said. She poured, then looked guiltily at the bottle.

'Don't top it up with water,' Jack warned.

She laughed sadly, already moving. 'I did think about it,' she called over her shoulder.

'How about that tea?' Sarah offered and Jack nodded with a fresh sigh.

They walked to the tearoom together. Jack leaned against the counter and tried his best not to look lost, although he didn't think he was succeeding.

'Will Claudia's mother take her grandchild?' Sarah asked.

'Yes, I'm sure she will. But Hanna is still so young. It won't be easy on either of them.'

'But that means she's still young enough to learn to be Polish.'

He nodded, unsure whether that was true, but there was no one else for the little girl. Maybe down the track he might find comfort knowing that she would be in a loving environment, but for now, he loathed himself for having involved Claudia in the first place. She had been reluctant, but she'd done it for him. And now she was de—

'Jack, come on!' Kate was back and clicking her fingers in front of him. She glanced at Sarah, perhaps embarrassed by the familiarity she was showing. 'You can soul search when we've caught the bastard.'

Jack shook his head. 'Well, we know it's not the person behind the Luca Bruni blackmail.'

'Do we? Let's talk it through. Three heads are better than one.'

He began to lay out his thoughts, both women listening without interrupting. Tea in hand, they strolled back into the ops room and took seats as Jack kept talking, arriving at the point where Francoise had started talking about her would-be killers.

'A Sophia and Franco, brother and sister?' Kate frowned and glanced at Sarah. 'Might be worth tapping HOLMES for that.'

Sarah nodded. 'Definitely. But they came to kill her, not pay her, you said?'

Jack nodded. 'Yes. But the brother seemed against it, according to Francoise. It was the sister who wanted to do it, but she planned to drug Francoise first.'

'Hmm,' Kate pondered. 'Not at all like the executions of this evening or the vet in Wimbledon.'

Jack agreed. 'It seems what we presumed might happen is happening, and the original party is now hoping to kill the person who can identify them . . . Francoise.'

'And Sophia and Franco want to kill her because they can't or won't pay her,' Sarah said. 'Sounds to me like the Bruni blackmailers, apart from being first-timers, are also desperate.'

'I agree,' Jack said. A new dark thought struck him. 'Kate, what about Ronnie Barrett?'

'Oh, shit! I'll call Thames Valley. They can bring him in for his own safety.'

'Right,' Jack said, inhaling audibly. 'I'm going to help sort out everything for Hanna, and then I'd better have a chat to the chief. Sarah, perhaps you'll have some news for us by tomorrow, but in a few hours I'm going to pick up Francoise and take her to the safe house, wherever that is.'

'I have an address, sir. DCI Benson sent it to me via our coded system.'

'Good, okay. Message me that and anything you find. I'll probably go to the morgue tomorrow morning as well. Kate, I think we'll debrief Francoise at the safe house, rather than here.'

'Okay.'

'You can handle that. She might respond better to a woman,' he said, thinking about how Lou had managed to get Francoise's trust more easily than him. 'She's a tough nut, so don't go hard. You have to get beneath her armour first. And put Ari and a team in that safe house, will you?'

'Will do.'

He sipped his tea. 'And then tomorrow evening, we need everyone positioned wherever the drop is going to be.'

'They obviously believe they can get away with it, sir,' Sarah said, frowning.

Jack gave a shrug. 'Hard to know if they suspect we're involved. But we have no choice. Kate, you'll be in touch with Luca?'

'All day long. I'll go over there as soon as I'm finished with Francoise.'

'Good.'

'Given the two unpleasant tasks ahead for you, do you want me to brief the others?' she asked.

'Yes, sure,' Jack said, not realising his mistake until later the next morning, by which time it was too late.

24

Geoff met Jack at the morgue just before six, with takeaway coffees and a box of cakes for the pathology team.

'Yes, the coffee's from one of your preferred haunts,' he said before Jack could ask, 'and the cakes are for our friends who have done us a great favour and worked through the night.'

Inside they met with Dr Norton, whose eyes lit up at the box. 'They'll appreciate it,' he said, gratefully taking a coffee from Geoff's cardboard tray. 'Come in, gentlemen,' he said, gesturing to the seats opposite. He rubbed his eyes. 'Sorry, long night.'

Jack grimaced. 'Our fault.'

'Anything to help get these guys off the streets. The sort of people who do what we confronted . . .' He didn't have to finish his sentence for Jack to know it had been a bad one.

Geoff slid Jack a glance, but Jack didn't return it, remaining stony-faced.

'Well, I'll keep it brief. Both women died of a single effective cut to their jugulars.'

Jack swallowed.

'Both women suffered blows and other deep but not life-threatening cuts prior to their deaths.'

Geoff nodded, reaching for his phone. 'Detective Super-intendent Hawksworth was not present at the scene,' he qualified, as though explaining Jack's silence.

Norton continued. 'Right, well, I can say with reasonable accuracy that the same knife was likely used on these two victims as was used on your vet, who we performed the post-mortem on recently.'

Geoff looked up from his phone. 'Sorry, Dr Norton, I'm just sending a message to my team to pick up some people who I believe could be responsible for these deaths.' He was busily tapping out a message. 'Please continue.'

'Er, well, you were at the scene, DCI Benson, so you would know these women were clearly tortured before they were killed. We found burns on the older woman's body that were made with a cigar, we think.'

'Cigar?' Jack repeated, looking at Geoff.

The pathologist nodded. 'Yes, messy business. This woman also has a nasty goose-egg on her forehead. The hematoma was caused not long prior to her death. We got some DNA material from under her fingernails, so that might be useful.'

'You think they beat her?' Jack felt his anger feathering up his gullet from his stomach to his throat. He had to swallow it down.

'Beat her or threw her against something hard, going by the bruising. And then, yes, the cuts and burns. The younger one was cut and, of course, killed as I stated but no burns . . . a bit of bruising around the tops of her arms where I'm guessing someone grabbed or gripped her hard.'

'Bastards,' Geoff said. 'And the DNA?'

'Gone for testing. I'd hazard it's flesh from the cheek.'

'Good,' Jack snarled. 'A marked man then.' He was proud that at least she hadn't gone down without a fight.

'Precisely. Uh, one more thing. It's not relevant to your case, but it's part of our job to note and report these things. The older of the two, Ms Lenkas? She had cancer. Quite advanced. If I had to guess, I'd say stage four. It had spread to other organs and it was definitely in the lymph nodes. She was dying, in my opinion.'

Jack had to blink slowly to understand what he'd just heard. *Claudia had been dying?* The dark circles, the weight loss and the fatigue suddenly made sense, as did her melancholy and that quip about Hanna going to Poland to be raised as a Polish princess. Had she already seen the future where her daughter would be raised by a grandmother?

It didn't help Jack's despair that Claudia had died horribly, brutally and unnecessarily. Perhaps in her last moments, she had known she would miss out on her final days with her daughter. It did, however, ease his heart a little that at least he could make sure that all arrangements for Hanna were made swiftly and properly.

Jack arrived at Lou's flat a few minutes after seven, balancing a box of croissants and pain au chocolat, as promised. At the buzzer, Lou's distant voice demanded to know if he'd remembered.

'I have them right here, and from a French baker too at Charing Cross.'

'Ooh, I know the one. Excellent!'

'How's your guest?'

'Moody. Showering. Should be ready by the time you struggle up the stairs.'

She was. Francoise's hair was dripping and her face was scrubbed, but she was alive. Thank goodness. Most importantly,

Lou sounded chirpy and welcomed him with an affectionate grin. It made some of the tightness in his chest relax slightly. Confronting the bodies of Claudia and Lyn had been one of the most difficult moments in his career.

'Ready?'

Francoise nodded and Lou opened the box of pastries. 'Don't go on an empty stomach,' she said, smiling. 'Take some. None for him though.'

Jack gave an obligatory chuckle. 'So, Lou, are you going in to work today?'

'I work from home. I haven't shown you my studio yet.'

'Oh, good. I'm going to keep some people in place today and tonight. Don't be alarmed. It's protocol.' Strictly, it wasn't, but after the morning he'd had, he was taking no chances. 'Meanwhile, Francoise will be in a safe house. I shan't tell you where, because that's how these things work.'

'Will I see her again?' Francoise asked bluntly.

'Of course,' Jack assured her, although he wasn't certain about that.

'Okay, then,' Lou said. 'I shall see you later, Francoise.'

Francoise surprised them both by giving Lou a hug. 'Thank you. You've been very kind.'

Lou patted her back gently. 'Come and visit properly when this is all over and you feel safe again. I speak fluent French and love to watch French movies.'

Francoise pulled back and grinned. 'Then we're already best friends. See you, Lou.' She started making her way downstairs.

'How are you doing?' Lou said to Jack, who held back for a moment.

'I have been better,' he admitted. It didn't feel wrong to share that with her. Normally he'd keep such thoughts to himself.

Lou looked at him gravely. 'When can I see you?'

'Tomorrow, I hope. May I call?'

She looked disappointed, but he didn't want to explain what was happening tonight. 'Well, if you end up being free, ring my bell,' she said. 'I'm not enjoying the cast of your face and how pale you look.' She blew him a kiss and gently shook the box of pastries. 'Thanks for these.'

He gave a nod, then set off after Francoise.

'Jack,' Lou called over the banister. He looked up. 'The early evening bit yesterday was lovely. Please be safe.'

He found a smile despite his glumness. 'I will. What are you doing today?'

'Working on a new installation – I have to have final sketches by Monday.'

'Hope the croissants give you strength.'

'Are you kidding?' she called down. 'They're like crack cocaine.'

'I'm not even going to ask you how you know that,' he said, looking up through the central atrium. 'I may have to arrest you.'

'Bring handcuffs,' she warned with a naughty grin, and he forgave himself for feeling happy just in that instant.

Kate had let Jack know she was conducting her interview at the safe house in Putney while he met with Carol Rowland.

'So she's there now?' Rowland asked, sipping her morning brew, which smelled both bitter and acidic at once to Jack.

'Yes. DCI Carter and DCI Benson are handling the interview. I thought it best not to be involved because she knows me. It may be too familiar.'

'I'm not even going to ask where you put her last night.' Rowland gave him a hard look.

'She was not at my place, ma'am, just in case you were thinking—'

'I wasn't,' she said in a clipped tone. 'Are we any closer to catching these scum? I must explain two more grisly deaths to a salivating media, and I feel as though we take one step forward and three back. And once they get wind of two investigations overlapping to become one, I'll need a personal bodyguard.'

Jack didn't know if that was an attempt at a joke and he was meant to smile; he didn't risk it.

She sighed. 'So what next?'

'Tonight. The exchange of money is supposed to occur, although we wait for news of how, where and exactly when.'

'Bruni's capitulated?' Rowland sounded surprised. Jack didn't think Rowland did shock.

'I don't blame him,' Jack said with a shrug. 'He's trying to remain focused on his job for the team. This weekend it's the Premier League against Man United.'

'You're not talking my language, Jack.'

He forced a mirthless smile. 'Huxley has something to prove, ma'am. This team who were nobodies, languishing in the depths of the various divisions, with probably no one to launder their strips except their mums and local volunteers, are suddenly in a position to do the clean sweep.'

'Clean sweep?'

'Premier League, FA Cup and Champions League, all in the same year.'

'I get the gist. Big deal, right?'

He shrugged. 'It's like a junior player just hitting the big stage at Wimbledon is upsetting all the other major players. That's what the Arrows are doing, thanks to Luca.'

Rowland nodded. 'So he's preoccupied, you're saying?'

'Yes. I think he may be wearying of remaining defiant with so much else at stake. While I get the feeling his wife is no longer threatening to walk out with their unborn babies, I think he must feel like the walls are closing in on him. His team is rightfully expecting him to score the goals that will carry them through – and keep in mind, ma'am, no one knows this ransom is underway. It's a lot of pressure for a youngster.'

'And I suppose you're going to say he can afford it and not think again about the money.'

Jack shrugged. 'They picked their mark perfectly.'

'Well, if, as you say, it's not the Celiks but a copycat, it has to be someone close to him or close to the club ... I mean, given the agents have been so tight-lipped about the previous blackmails, it has to be someone with very close access to this information to pick Bruni out as a perfect mark in that perfect time frame.'

Jack stared at her.

'What?' she asked.

'I agree,' he said, for the first time allowing himself to admit that the crime might be far closer to home than Bruni would like to think. 'Ms Laurent didn't know who they are beyond first names, but that doesn't mean Luca doesn't.' He stood. 'Excuse me, ma'am. I need to contact him and ask about any brother and sister pairs he knows.'

'The car was a rental,' Baris said without any introduction on the phone call, and Ronnie closed his eyes. 'All is not lost, though,' Baris continued, and Ronnie felt fresh hope. 'The stupid bitch hired it in her own name. So now we know who she is.'

'That's good, Mr Celik. And, look, I don't want to have anything to do with this. Whatever has been happening, you don't need to tell me; I'm just happy to have helped,' he said, knowing in his heart they were not finished with him.

'Not so fast, Ronnie,' Baris said and Ronnie could almost see him smiling lazily as was his way. 'We need you to do one more thing. Something you'd be good at.'

'What's that?'

'Playing one side off the other,' Baris answered and chuckled. 'We want you to meet this woman and convince her of something.'

'I don't know her—'

'Shh, Ronnie. We've got it worked out and we're going to tell you what to say. Be our puppet and then you're free. Now, pay attention . . .'

Ronnie listened carefully, already planning to leave London for good after this.

Luca was at home, heading downstairs to check his mail, carrying a mug of tea that Ally had made. They were doing all right, he thought, all things considered. He was grateful to Gina, in particular, for soothing Ally and being a good friend to her.

Harry had to keep it professional at work, but he and Luca spoke often after hours, with Harry suggesting Luca make it easy on himself and just get it over with.

'You'd pay?' Luca had asked, surprised.

'If I had your income, I wouldn't hesitate. Look, mate, you're about to have twins. And we're about to do something few others have ever achieved in the history of our sport.' Harry had tapped his temple. 'We need you clear-headed. I know how even little things can topple the house of cards. I've been where you are through a World Cup qualifier and then the finals. You need to be solid. Get rid of it – pay the fuckers. Move on.'

Luca had shaken his head. 'And they'll move on to the next poor bastard.'

'So what? It's not you, and this will all be forgotten when you're holding three trophies and two new babies.' Harry had squeezed his shoulder. 'You've got it all to look forward to.'

Luca had nodded. That conversation had been the tipping point. He loved Harry, respected him enormously. Maybe he was right; maybe he should just be rid of the problem, put it all behind him and get on with his life. When he'd told the police he could tell that Kate Carter hadn't been surprised. Disappointed maybe, but there was no shock in her voice. She'd simply changed tack and told him their team would now do everything to apprehend the blackmailers when the money drop was made.

He was anticipating details of that drop. He couldn't imagine the blackmailers would risk phoning, but he had recording equipment ready to go if they did. No, he suspected a note would come by courier again, probably a different one this time. The police could hardly be across every parcel and document delivery service in the UK.

He hadn't expected it to arrive like this though: quietly hand-delivered by the postman into the general box just outside the gates. One of the other residents had brought the mail in to the building foyer, where there was a table for sorting it into little piles for each flat. There were only ten of them in this tower. Luca had no pile today though, just a single buff-coloured envelope that he recognised instantly. His breathing changed and his pulse accelerated. He glanced around – no one else in the foyer. He picked up the envelope.

There was no stamp. The address was printed in felt tip in a hand he did not recognise. He tore it open and before he'd even read it, he was grabbing his phone from his pocket and dialling Charlie, the nickname he'd been schooled to use to reach Kate or Jack.

Kate answered and listened to him read the message aloud.

'Okay, sit tight, Luca,' she told him. 'I'm going to send someone dressed as a bike messenger. Allow them in when they buzz the gate. They'll go up to the fourth floor in the lifts in case anyone is watching and then use the stairs to come up to your floor. Please put that envelope into a zip-lock bag and give it to him. We'll be in touch.'

As Kate rang off, Jack called. Luca told him what had been arranged. 'Excellent. Stay calm now, Luca. We're getting to the pointy end of this thing.'

Luca grunted but said nothing. What could he say?

'Can I ask, do you have a brother and sister duo in your close circle?'

Luca frowned. 'In Australia, yes, but not here that I can think of.'

'Is anyone at the club tight with his sister?'

'No, not that I know of, but that doesn't mean there isn't,' Luca said. 'Why?'

'In our investigations, we've begun to hear about these siblings who may be involved. We think they're behind your blackmail attempt.'

'How do you know?'

'Because we've spoken to the girl with the tattoo.'

Luca felt like his heart was in his stomach. They'd found the woman who'd done this to him. He clenched his teeth. 'Where is she?'

'Safe.'

'Safe?' he almost snarled.

'Yes. There's been an attempt on her life. She's currently got what you might call a "hit" out on her, and not just by one party, we think. She's our link, Luca. We have to keep her safe so we can learn who is doing this to you, so please, trust me now. She is not the enemy. The people who hired her are, and I am going to bring them down as well as the bastards who began this thing.'

'What do you mean?'

'I'll explain later,' Jack said and rang off.

Jack had another call. 'Geoff? What's going on?'

'Hawk, she's escaped.'

He didn't have to ask who. 'How?'

'They'd done the first debriefing and she said she needed to rest, but what she did was hide. When no one could find her, it set off a panic and in the chaos they were opening doors and checking outside and she slipped out. She's a cunning one.'

Jack sighed. 'Tell me they got what was needed on the Celiks.'

'They did. Enough to arrest and charge, but . . .'

Geoff didn't need to say more. Jack knew that Francoise had to be found if they were going to make charges stick. 'Want me to set up all the alerts?'

'No, I will. Where are you?'

'On my way to give them a bollocking. They're my guys.'

'Okay, see you back at the Yard.'

Jack took the stairs down to the ops room, but paused, his mind racing. When he'd handed Francoise over to the team who would take her to the safe house, they'd taken her small bag, promising to return it once it had been searched. So he knew she had nothing to run with. Where would she go? She couldn't go back to her flat or any of the familiar places she frequented, because the Celiks would surely be hunting her. She couldn't go anywhere near the haunts of the copycat blackmailers, because they too wished her harm. She'd refused to come in to the police and, despite it being secure and in her own interests, she'd left the only safe place she had. Out in the open, penniless, friendless. She couldn't lie low for long.

Jack frowned. There was one place she could go. He dialled.

'Yes, she's here,' Lou said, and he could hear a furious Francoise distantly cursing Lou in French. 'Listen, Francoise, he's the only ally you've got right now. Just be quiet. And don't run. I'll give you money, I promise.'

Jack heard Lou sigh. 'What do I do? I can't physically restrain her, nor do I want to. Frankly, I just want to give her some money and let her go.'

Jack made a decision, closing his eyes as he said it aloud. 'Do it.'

'What?'

'She's not your problem or your responsibility, and she shouldn't have come to you. I've involved you enough already . . . My chief will have my balls if she finds out about this.'

'And she won't cut them off for letting her go?'

Jack spoke calmly. 'I didn't learn she came to you until after she'd gone, okay?'

There was a silence as Lou processed this. 'Okay, I get it. Listen, she has her passport and I've given her some money. She just wants to see her mother, to give her a bank account number.'

Again he heard Francoise yelling and Lou's response. 'We're helping you! I promise.'

'Right. I'd like to say this to her myself, but I can't. Please tell her to do what she has to, but on the understanding that my team will be talking to Europol and Interpol. We will alert the French liaison at NCIS, so they'll have the French police tracing her with a view to arrest. I'll only learn she came to you in six hours, because I've been ignoring personal calls all day. She came to you and threatened you. You gave her money and asked her to leave, and she fled the country. That should give her enough time to get on a train to Paris and disappear. Put me on speaker, please, Lou.'

She did so. 'So my best advice,' he continued as though he were still talking only to Lou, 'is that you suggest to Francoise that she turn herself in to the French police as soon as possible. It will go better for her if she does. Don't make us find her – the courts will not look kindly on this. However, she's already given us valuable information, and so if she offers herself up, then sentencing can likely be kept lean. We all know she is not the villain here.'

Although Luca Bruni might not see it that way, he thought.

'She's nodding,' Lou said and switched the phone off speaker. 'Thank you, Jack. Makes me like you more.'

'I'm sorry you've been dragged into this.'

'I'm a big girl. Besides, I chose to be involved. I could have flung you both out yesterday as soon as I caught the first whiff of trouble.'

'Get her going, Lou. I can't keep the dogs off for long.'

'She's already gone. Blew me a kiss a moment ago.'

Jack finished the conversation standing in the stairwell, shaking his head. If Rowland got wind of what he'd just sanctioned, he'd be sacked, certainly demoted.

But then rule followers were such a pain in the arse. He'd promised Claudia he wouldn't make Francoise the scapegoat, and she had given her life protecting a woman under threat. Risking his job was the least he could do for the women who trusted him. He continued down the stairs.

25

The whole team was gathered in the ops room, along with Geoff and a couple of his senior people, as it was now a genuine joint op under Jack's leadership.

He'd had Joan organise platters of food to be delivered, as well as a dozen takeaway cups of freshly drawn barista coffee, and he noted everyone had happily helped themselves. Even Joan was present, dangling a herbal tea bag into a mug.

'Afternoon, everyone – actually, perhaps I should say evening,' he said. 'It's going to be a long night, so eat now. We don't know when we'll need to leave, and we don't know where we might be sent. Thanks to Joan for the lovely spread.'

Everyone murmured thanks in Joan's direction. 'Your boss paid for it, and I don't mean the one upstairs,' she said, grinning towards Jack.

'Right, we need to go through what we know and briskly. But before we get onto that, I have something to let you all know. Our key witness, Francoise Laurent, was safely in custody as of this morning, but she has escaped the safe house.'

His news was met by astonished gasps and questions. He glanced at Geoff, who looked down in anguish, and Jack felt sick for him; it had not been his fault, but as a leader, you had to take the blame when things went wrong. 'Look, the whys and hows are irrelevant. She could be anywhere, but all is not lost; the team did debrief her and we now have sufficient information to formally arrest the Celiks.'

'Should we be alerting airports, ports, and sending it out across the networks?' Kate asked, looking dismayed.

'Yes, we'll get to that, but frankly we have far more pressing business just in this moment. The money drop.' He paused, looking around the room, meeting everyone's eyes. 'We move the moment Kate's or my phone rings. It will be Luca telling us where the drop is. Kate, perhaps you're best placed to take us through what we have.'

'Certainly.' Kate stepped forward, still shaking her head at the revelation. She pointed at the photo of Francoise. 'Just recapping . . . while we now know that there are indeed two separate parties who have blackmailed our sporting stars, Francoise has confirmed the Celiks as the original blackmailers. We also understand they are the ones behind the vet's murder. I believe DCI Benson has already set those arrests in motion?'

'We have,' Geoff confirmed. 'They'll be picked up for questioning as soon as we can find them.'

Kate nodded briskly. 'So we're now on the hunt for the copycats. As far as we know, they're proceeding with the ransom collection as planned.'

'Have we got eyes on Ronnie Barrett?' Jack asked.

'His solicitor was making arrangements for him to head out of town to his sister's place,' Ari replied. 'Apparently the Celiks have no idea about his family.'

'Good. And who is with Ally while this all goes down?'

Kate answered this time. 'Harry Taylor. Gina's got some family affair on, but he offered to sit with her, and I've had confirmation that our watchers have seen him go in. He must have come straight from training because he was wearing his Huxley gear.'

'Good. Carry on.'

Kate nodded. 'While Francoise Laurent could confirm that the Celiks were behind the original scheme, she cannot give us any information about the Bruni blackmailers other than them being a brother and sister. We know their names as Franco and Sophia – they could be aliases, of course. We know she wears disguises but he doesn't. Perhaps she is going to some length not to be recognised because she's recognisable to the public?' Kate shrugged. 'Or she's just more cautious than her brother. Either way, it's wigs, dark glasses, et cetera. They use rental cars, and meet at out-of-the-way, abandoned spots. A lot of vigilance on one hand, and yet quite amateurish in other ways when you look at how slick and direct the Celiks were in their blackmail.'

'So Ms Laurent couldn't identify the sister?' Ari asked.

Kate shook her head. 'She says not. Sarah, did you run the names through the system?'

Sarah nodded. 'A few hits on the name Franco, two of which are London based, but one's currently in prison and the other is in hospital after being beaten up a week ago. I don't think they're our guys.'

'We think these siblings could well have inside access to Luca somehow – through the club or a personal connection,' Jack added. 'I asked Luca if he has any brother-and-sister duos who are close to him, but he can't think of any in the club or otherwise.'

Sarah frowned. 'There was some rumour or connection between Harry Taylor and the owner's daughter, wasn't there?'

Jack exchanged a look with Kate. 'Yes, there was an affair, but Harry assures us that it was brief and that it's over.'

Ari spoke up. 'I did the call to confirm all that. She's presently in Europe with her husband. From what I can tell, there's been no blowback, no publicity. Not even her father knew. She said that Harry was trying to make things work with his wife, and she wants to get on with life as Mrs Durand – her husband's in television, so she doesn't want any contamination around her new relationship.' He paused. 'She also said – and I know this is purely subjective – that Harry would do nothing to hurt a hair on Luca's head . . . her words.'

'Thanks, Ari.' Jack looked at Kate. 'Finished?'

'Yes. There wasn't much more to get out of Ms Laurent other than what I've told you. She describes the woman in disguise as a "cold bitch" who was happy to do the killing when her brother refused, simply to avoid having to pay the rest of what was owed. Oh, one more thing,' she said, glancing Jack's way to apologise. He nodded for her to continue. 'It may not matter, but apparently there's actually three of them – Franco, Sophia and another sister, whom Francoise has not met and doesn't think is involved. She only knows about this sister because Sophia said on a couple of occasions that their mother named her children after Italian movie stars of old . . . though Francoise never did learn what the other sister was called.'

'Yes, I heard the same tale. Thanks, Kate,' Jack said. 'Any questions?' He saw Sarah move back to her desk and start rattling on her keyboard. 'Right, onwards to tonight's money drop. The ransom note arrived at the Brunis' building just after midday. We don't know how they achieved it, because CCTV shows only the usual flat owners and regular guests, including the postman.'

'It couldn't have come by regular post?' Ari asked.

'No stamp.'

'Could the postie have been paid off?' Ari asked.

'Possibly. We're looking into it,' Jack assured him and glanced at Joan. 'Any luck yet?'

'No. We should know shortly the name of the person who was on that route and they will be questioned the moment we do.'

'Look, even another resident could have been asked by a passer-by to leave it for the Bruni apartment. So, here we have it,' Jack said, turning to Kate.

She obliged by walking over to turn on the projector and immediately an enlarged copy of the letter appeared on the white-board. 'This was from a photo taken by Luca Bruni. You can see the immediate difference to the others,' Jack said. He gave them a few moments to quickly scan it.

The clock is ticking down. There's a phone hidden in the big plant pot at the gate. Go fetch it now! Say goodbye to your wife – maybe call her best friend to sit with her – and get on the Underground and take the phone with you. We'll tell you where to go.

Bring your suitcase of money. Come alone. If someone is with you or the police are involved, we will hurt Ally.

It's up to you. After you've delivered the money, you'll never hear from us again if you do as we say.

Jack continued. 'It's handwritten as opposed to typed, but the stock they've used is bog standard, so we're not going to get anything from that. What else do you notice? Nat?'

'Er, the writing on the envelope is emphatic, slanting top to bottom – perhaps a left-hander? Maybe that black felt tip achieves anonymity, but in choosing it, it feels like there's more tension than with the first two letters, sir?'

Jack smiled. 'Well done. All hypothetical but very interesting, especially the left-handed bit. What else, Matt?'

The young constable frowned. 'The letter's lost that playful aspect we noted in the first two notes. It's now sort of brisk and urgent, nothing like the previous.'

'Indeed,' Jack said, tapping the whiteboard where the image was projected. 'You can feel the tension and the urgency simply by the language. Sarah?'

'The actual threat is no longer couched in a friendly tone.'

'Absolutely. I think it's safe to say that not only are the black-mailers nervous, as we see through their shortened note and language, but, as Sarah notes, the threat is now real. It's spelled out for Luca so he can't mistake what's at stake. They've given him a burner phone and Luca is already in motion, but we don't know where he's headed yet.'

That caused a murmur to ripple through the team.

Kate spoke. 'He's rung us once already to say they've got him going in circles on the Underground.'

'I think they'll bring him to the surface,' Geoff said, and everyone looked his way. He shrugged. 'They can't rely on a phone signal without him being up on street level.'

Jack agreed. 'We must presume that they know we're involved and that's why they're giving him the run-around. They're only going to give him a short amount of time to get to wherever the drop point is to minimise our intervention.'

'Sir, if they know so much, it surely means they have to be physically close. Maybe they're watching through long lenses from another building?' Sarah offered.

Jack shrugged. 'We can't think about that in this instant. We have to be on the starting blocks ready to chase them down at drop time,' he said, almost in apology to Sarah's valid observation. 'I don't disagree, but we have to focus on what we have even minimal control over.'

She nodded and returned to her keyboard. It impressed him that she could research while still giving their conversation her attention, but then Sarah always had been an enigma.

Jack continued. 'In the previous note, they mentioned being

diligent about the plastic Luca used to wrap the money. What does that tell us?'

'It's going to be stored rather than transported?' Matt offered. 'Perhaps for a while . . . maybe in damp conditions like a deep hole in the ground?'

'Probably more like wet,' Ari said.

'In water,' Geoff agreed.

'I would say so,' Jack said. 'So, maybe they're leaving it in a drum of liquid, a swimming pool, a—'

'Or the Thames,' Kate said. 'The Serpentine. Any stream. Drop it in, weigh it down, who would know?'

'Doesn't make sense, though,' Geoff argued. 'If they've got their hands on it, why not just drive it fast out of London?'

'They say hiding in plain sight is often easier,' Kate remarked more than argued, and Geoff grinned at her. She looked away, but Jack could tell she was pleased. He felt a spike of hope for them yet.

'There would be nowhere more confusing than the River Thames, I have to agree,' Jack said.

'Or a garden pond,' Geoff chimed in unhelpfully. But Jack knew he was right. Everything was so hypothetical. 'The fact is,' Geoff continued, 'we just don't know. We have to be ready for anywhere they send Luca.'

'They'll want to do this—' Kate's phone lit up on the desk in front of her, silencing everyone. 'It's Luca,' she said, and Geoff gave the signal for everyone to move. Francoise's escape appeared to be instantly forgotten as collective adrenaline kicked in. 'Hi, it's Kate.'

Jack watched her face as he pulled on his warm jacket and a beanie.

'Sir? I've had a thought,' Sarah called across the room.

'Can it wait?' he asked.

She shook her head. Jack had learned over several ops to hear Sarah out, because her mind worked agilely in so many directions. He strode over, catching Kate's eye. At work they seemed to possess the rare ability to tune in to each other, to know what the other needed or was thinking. She stuck five fingers in the air and he nodded: five minutes before they needed to be in the car park. 'Everyone follow Geoff, be ready in cars. Kate and I are following. Sarah and Joan will hold the fort here. Go!'

The room emptied.

'Right, Sarah. What is it?'

'The movie star comment. I looked up the big Italian film stars of that time. Franco Nero, Sophia Loren and Gina Lollobrigida!'

Jack felt the familiar Tingler, as he liked to call it — taken from an old fifties movie, probably made around the time that this Italian actress was in her prime. It was a terrible horror film, about a parasite that lives in humans and feeds on fear, mostly felt in the spine with a tingling sensation. He had been nine when he watched it, and the notion of this creature living within and growing stronger with fear had stuck with him. He sometimes wondered if he'd gone into the police force to stop others from feeling it. It was certainly feeding on his fear inside right now.

'Kate!' he swung around. 'We have to check on Ally.'

'I told you, Luca said she's with Harry Taylor. Why?'

'Let's go. Sarah, get hold of Ally. Connect me when you do, and get that team sitting outside in the squad car to break down her door if they have to. They are to arrest Harry Taylor, and someone armed is to sit with Ally Bruni until I arrive, no matter how long that is.'

'Right, sir.'

'Good work, Sarah.'

'Er, sir, the alerts?'

'Stay focused on Bruni,' he called over his shoulder, not really answering the question, acting as though he'd barely heard her. He figured Sarah would take the initiative anyway and send out the bulletins. It was out of his control now, anyway, as he and Kate rushed off. Given the frequency of Eurostar trains, Francoise was likely already out of the country.

Trapped in the lift, unable to go any faster to the Yard's underground car park, Jack told Kate what Sarah had discovered.

Kate's mouth opened in shock. 'Gina! Shit.'

He nodded, knowing she was running through every coincidence that had already rushed around his mind. 'It's how they knew everything. If Gina wasn't in the room when we were around, then Ally was telling her all that we discussed.'

Kate's expression dropped. 'I suppose there's some consolation that we got to Luca early enough to tell him not to share everything – not even with Ally.'

The lift doors opened. Jack knew he didn't look convinced, but there was no point anguishing over what couldn't be changed. 'Our people should have her soon, if not already. What's the plan for Luca?' he said, walking briskly towards the cars where their colleagues waited.

'The drop is underneath Kew Bridge.'

'That's just a short walk from his apartment.' Jack couldn't disguise his astonishment.

Kate nodded. 'Maybe it's an easy pick-up for Gina, given she's always near Ally.'

'You know what I'm thinking?' It was rhetorical. 'I don't think Sophia exists. The elaborate disguises are because Gina is too recognisable. The name Sophia is part of the disguise.'

It was academic and Jack could see that reflected in Kate's expression. She moved on to the only topic where they had a tiny chance at control. 'They've given him twenty minutes to get there. He's en route via the Tube.' She looked at her watch. 'Three minutes have gone. But we can make it.'

'Seventeen minutes,' Jack muttered as he opened a car door. 'We'll have to push. All right, let's go.'

Kate got into the other car, no doubt already directing the driver to their target.

'Kew Bridge,' Jack told Ari, who was driving. Nat and Matt were in the back seat, quiet with anticipation. Geoff was driving Kate and two of his men.

Geoff led the way. Lights and sirens were switched on and cars began to slow or make way. They needed a clear path to Kew if they were going to make it in time.

They raced through Kensington and were moving at speed towards Hammersmith. Jack rang Sarah before he told the others the latest development.

'Sir. Bad news. I can't get onto Ally.'

'What about our people?'

'They saw Taylor arrive, and then they saw him leave with Ally. She waved, yelled that they were just going out for a quick pizza as she was suffering cabin fever. They haven't returned.'

Jack rang off and relayed the chilling news, which was met by silence. He ran through his thoughts aloud. 'Obviously the brother can pass for Harry Taylor from a distance, maybe by wearing Huxley Arrows gear, and all they had to do was leave the compound. There are lots of other entrances to the river and the towpath.'

'I'm sorry we missed that, sir,' Ari remarked.

'We all did,' Jack growled. 'We don't know for sure, but it fits. Hiding in plain sight, remember.' His phone rang again: Kate. 'Any news?'

'Luca's just arrived at the station and is now running down to the towpath, angry that this is happening all but below his balcony.'

'Did you say anything about Gina?'

'No. And I didn't mention Francoise's escape either. I need him clear-headed right now. He did say he can't reach Ally, but I said she's probably in the bathroom. He bought it for now.'

They rang off. Jack felt the Tingler become more insistent, jangling at his nerves. 'Faster, Ari.'

26

Luca's verbal instruction – from a bloke – was to go down the towpath to Kew Bridge. He knew the area well, and at this time of the year and at this time of night it would be muddy, slippery and potentially dangerous, but none of that was troubling him.

Two things were worrying him. First, the fact that he couldn't reach his wife, which was beginning to play a fearful game in his mind, given whoever this was had threatened to hurt her if he didn't obey. And the second thought, which seemed to grow dark and menacing, was that while Luca had given the impression of capitulating, his defiance was intact. He thought about the conversation with his agent while he jogged along the path, not going full pelt, because that meant getting tired or attracting attention. It was better to stay at a steady, brisk speed and he'd get there faster, more reliably.

'Why would you change your mind again?' Jonathan Mason had asked, aghast.

Luca had been resolute. 'Because they need to be stopped.'

'Leave it to someone else. Let the police find them.'

'The police haven't done much of a job of that so far,' Luca had sneered, carefully packing his bag with blank sheets of paper guillotined to the correct size to resemble money and hidden between wads of real pounds sterling. They were wrapped in quality plastic, as requested.

'For fuck's sake, just pay it and get out of this. Luca, listen to me. They probably know the police are involved and are pushing ahead anyway, which means they're pretty confident of getting away with it. And what's more, why would you risk you or Ally being hurt?'

'They haven't said anything about hurting us.'

He knew better now, of course, but now it was too late. He wished he could go back to that moment. Jon had persisted for a few more minutes, trying repeatedly to stop his plan.

'What, you think criminals brief you fully before they commit their crimes? Don't do this. Let them have their measly half-million.'

'Jon, it isn't the money. How many times do I have to say it?'

'If you say "it's the principle" to me, I'll stop being your agent. This is stupidity of the highest order. Let some other poor bastard deal with this. You're on the brink of greatness, Luca, and you are jeopardising that, big time.'

'None of it will matter if I'm a coward. If I don't stand up to these arseholes, I'll never run down the field again with confidence. I don't know how to explain that to you, I just know it. This is my test. This is all those trophies rolled into one. Do I have the nerve? Yes, fuck them! If they get away, then they'll only have a few thousand. That won't get them far.'

'And if they come back at you in retaliation?'

'They won't.'

Luca had been so sure of himself then, burning with a righteousness that felt long gone now, especially since Ally wasn't answering her phone. But she was safe, he told himself. She was with Harry. They'd have to go through him first.

The guy on the phone had sounded nervous. Good. Luca would like to take him on, use him like a punching bag for putting him through this. He wondered if the guy would have a weapon. Probably.

He arrived onto the towpath. Deserted, of course. The air was frigid, and he could hear the thrum of the great river moving beside him on his right. Lights twinkled around him from all the nearby buildings . . . people getting on with their small lives. He felt a moment's desire for a simpler life, but that passed as quickly as it came.

There was no overhead lighting on the long, snaking path that flanked this side of the Thames, just dim moonlight. Luca doggedly passed his own apartment building, not pausing but looking up longingly at his sweeping balcony, where the penthouse looked to be in complete darkness. Why? Rising nausea began to burn in his chest. He'd made a mistake. What if they'd hurt Ally? He couldn't defy them, couldn't trick them. His only hope was to delay them and pray that Carter and Hawksworth got here in time.

Sirens were silenced but the flashing lights remained on as the ops team exploded out of the two cars.

'Kate, Geoff, lead them down, spread out. I'm going onto the bridge. It might give us an angle,' Jack yelled and didn't wait for any response. He knew the two senior detectives would marshal the team as well as he could. The notion that the money was going to end up in the river had been nagging at him, and he wanted to see if he might get a different view, a sense of what the blackmailers' plans were once they got their hands on that bag of money.

He ran, wishing now he hadn't worn such warm clothing. He'd

imagined they might be on some sort of stake-out, but this was all going to unfold in the next minute or so.

Below, Kate cursed her choice of footwear as she slipped in the sliding mud of the towpath. She tried not to think about what it was doing to the suede of her boots and instead focused on the fact that the seventeen minutes had already passed. Were they too late?

Geoff thundered ahead, heroically, no longer concerned with any form of stealth; the sirens would have announced their arrival from far away and Kate could hear people opening French doors and windows to look out and see what the calamity was.

She could hear Geoff like a military general calling out orders and she allowed herself a moment's admiration before she took the risk of increasing her speed.

Luca arrived beneath the bridge as the sirens in the distance cut off. The cavalry was close.

He was breathing hard, but from anticipation and fear, not fatigue. He could have run another half an hour at that pace before he'd have to pause and suck in some air.

'I'm here!' he called out.

A shadow moved in the darkness. 'Fling the bag over here,' a man said. He looked small and wiry, dressed in black, wearing a hoodie and perhaps a beanie. The guy stepped forward. 'Throw it, don't waste time, otherwise . . .' Luca could just make out that he was pointing upwards.

A torch suddenly snapped on above their heads and Luca could see Ally. Another bloke wearing a balaclava and kitted out in all black held a hand across her mouth. Ally was struggling and, in the ghostly light of the torch, looked terrified.

'Ally . . .' Luca whispered, feeling sick with fear, but he snapped his focus back to the man. 'All right, all right.' He threw the bag at the guy's feet.

'Don't do anything stupid,' his foe said, 'or she gets hurt.'

'I won't. But you know the police are almost here.'

'Yep,' the guy said, and Luca watched, helplessly intrigued, as the man got busy winding something around the bag. He couldn't work out at first what it was, but when the fellow stepped back and hurled the bag into the fast-moving waters, he realised it must be some kind of flotation bag. It blinked with what must have been a waterproof light, and then it was gone, carried away on a speeding current.

'Don't follow me,' the guy warned and began to run.

Luca could hear him blundering off into the hedgerow – maybe he knew a way off the towpath. Luca didn't care. He was already looking up again, because Ally was screaming. He saw with horror that the second man had forced her to climb onto the bridge.

'No, don't!' Luca yelled.

Arms grabbed him and he heard Kate's voice and they all watched as Ally was pushed, screaming as she fell. Then silence as she hit the water and disappeared in the darkness.

A motorboat gunned into action in the distance and went roaring off. People – police, he assumed – were running into the water, but Luca was being physically restrained by a man with a beard.

'Look!' His keeper was pointing. Ally had surfaced, gulping and screaming, on the other side of the bridge.

'He's going to do it,' Luca heard Kate murmur and they all watched, still as statues, as Jack Hawksworth, without hesitation, arrived on the bridge, pulled off his jacket, hopped nimbly over the side and jumped.

★

Oof! It's cold! Jack kicked quickly to the surface, looking around wildly. It was Kate he heard first.

'There!'

He looked where she was pointing and he saw Ally being swept away, just like the bag of money presumably, with the fast-moving tide. *Clever*, he thought. They might be amateurs at the business of blackmail, but they weren't without the presence of mind to have thought this part through. At this time of night, the tide would be at its highest and at its fastest as it began to turn.

Jack kicked again, letting the current carry him and using his energy instead to control his direction towards the struggling Ally. She was a fighter, no doubt, but he could see she was panicking, likely thinking about the cold, her babies, her potential drowning.

'Ally!' he yelled. 'Don't fight.'

'Help!' she screamed automatically, now that she could hear him. 'I don't know if my waters broke as I fell.'

Could this get worse? He briefly wondered about infection. 'Don't fight,' he repeated. 'Float! Let the water carry you. I'm coming.' Those were his last words, because he was kicking furiously to swim across the current to reach her.

He looked up and kicked again and suddenly he had connected with her, grabbing her sleeve first and then pulling her as best he could towards him. She began to grab at him, almost climbing on top of him and risking pushing him under the water. 'Stay calm, stay calm, Ally, or we'll both drown,' he pleaded. He could hear her teeth chattering. He hoped someone had called an ambulance.

'Don't let me drown, Detective Sup ... Jack! Don't let us drown. They're coming.' She swallowed water and spluttered, panicked. 'I think I might be in labour,' she said, her voice stretched and thin; her eyes were wide with fear and she was only just able to get her words out.

'I won't let you go. I won't let you drown. I'd let you stand on my shoulders first, I promise,' he said, summoning a smile to calm her. Both of them were breathing hard and shallow. 'Breathe, Ally, do the short breaths you're meant to.' Jack spoke close to her ear. 'Lie back, that's it. I've got you. We're going to let the current take us. My team are at the bank and will work out how to get us, okay?'

'Keep talking,' she pleaded. 'It hurts and I'm frightened I will—'

'Ally, just trust me now. I have you,' he said. He wasn't as confident as he sounded, but he would give his last breath to this woman and her children.

He became aware of people crashing through the undergrowth and the towpath on his right.

'Kate!' He couldn't see her, even though his eyes had adjusted to the darkness.

'We're here,' she yelled. 'Angle towards the bank.'

'Ally's in labour, we think – we need an ambulance,' he yelled through his own chattering teeth.

'I've got a branch, Hawk,' Geoff yelled, also running, and now he just could see his close friend looking ridiculous, holding a long branch as though he was about to pole vault into the water. If the situation wasn't as dire as it was, Jack might have convulsed with laughter. But he knew he had to keep what little energy he had left now to steer them towards safety. He kicked hard, holding Ally tightly and using his other arm as a rudder.

Ally began to moan through a contraction.

And above her sounds of pain, Jack could hear the speedboat disappearing. The blackmailers had stopped momentarily – to pick up their cargo, Jack presumed – and now they were getting the hell away.

I'm coming for you, Gina, he promised silently.

★

Ronnie Barrett was running as fast as he could ever remember. He felt he was running blindly though, and had already fallen twice. He was covered in mud, but he'd done what he'd been asked to do; he had been far too scared not to. The Celik brothers had promised that his life would remain safe if he did this for them.

'But you must do this,' Baris had said. 'You know exactly what to do and when. If you don't, we will kill you, Ronnie.'

Eren had nodded gravely. 'But if you do, you'll be safe always.'

Ronnie nodded. He knew they would follow through on their threats. 'I'll do it. I will. What do I say?'

'Just tell her you know about the plan and you want in on the action or you'll tell the police.'

'How am I supposed to know about it, though?'

Baris had shrugged. 'The other whore is dead. Just tell her she told you about it.'

'But—'

'Work it out, Ronnie,' Eren said in such a threatening way that Ronnie fell silent and simply nodded. 'Now, here's her address. There isn't much time. We only got this tonight. Get to her now, and convince her to include you. When she tells you the plan for picking up the money, tell her what we've just explained to you.'

Ronnie frowned. 'What if she doesn't tell me her plan?'

'Then tell her yours. You can pick holes in hers – it will be rubbish, anyway. Just make sure she goes your way because your life depends on it.'

And he had. He'd performed brilliantly. Sophia's plan was loaded with steps, any one of which could go wrong and might trigger unwanted attention, so he'd found it easy to query some of those steps to make her feel unsure. The Celiks' plan he suggested instead certainly had its dangers, but it required Bruni to simply bring the money and leave. Everything else was on them. Providing they followed their script, then it would work, he assured her. And it had. He couldn't believe they'd pulled it off, even with the cops on their tail.

The bag had gone into the water with its flotation capsules and light, and the police had been diverted by the wife being threatened on the bridge, and the Thames had done the rest. All Ronnie had to do now was get away, melt back into the streets of London, and no one would be any wiser. His life was saved.

He wasn't so sure about Sophia's, though.

Once he'd dumped the woman over the bridge, Franco, wearing training gear and sneakers beneath a black puffer jacket, had legged it across to the Chiswick side where a rental car awaited. He leapt in and roared off into the night. He drove, just as his sister had demanded, for ten minutes, barely knowing the direction he was going in, twisting and turning down streets until he was absolutely sure he hadn't been followed.

Satisfied, he stopped the car, got out and threw his jacket into a nearby bin. In another street, he threw out his hoodie. Back in the car, he pulled on another hoodie in olive green and had an olive puffer coat ready on the passenger seat, so he would look like any other Londoner out for some exercise. Finally ready, he dialled.

She answered immediately. 'You away?'

'Clean away!' He heard her cackle with joy and wanted to press on the car horn for a long time to celebrate alongside her, but he resisted. 'Tell me you got it, Gina.'

'I have it right here beside me. It worked exactly how we planned.'

'How far away are you?'

'Not far at all. I can see the Docklands already.'

'Okay, be safe. I'll see you shortly.'

'You too. Remember, drive slow and steady. Don't draw any attention to yourself. Stop at the lights, and don't break the speed limit. Anything to tell me about Bruni?'

'Nothing to tell. He followed the rules exactly as your friend Barrett said he would.'

'He's no friend of mine, but Barrett has been useful. And Bruni's wife. Did you push her into the water as he said you should?'

'Yes. I wasn't happy to do that to a pregnant woman.'

'I can assure you I wasn't happy about that either, but that little toad said it would be the best diversion. Sounds like he was right.'

'He was. I could see the police arriving.'

'What happened?'

'Oh, some gallant fellow – a police officer, I'm pretty sure – leapt in after her. I knew someone would. We don't have to have her on our conscience.'

'And she has no idea I was involved?'

'None at all. I didn't show my face or give her my name.'

'This is better than I could have dreamed it, little brother. Now, if we're going to make the ferry, we have to be quick.'

'I'm good to go.'

'And I've got the passports. We can be in Europe by the early hours of tomorrow and on our way back to Italy . . . no one any wiser, not even my lowlife, cheating husband.'

Franco laughed. 'Well done, sis. You came through.'

'I'll see you at the meeting spot.'

27

Jack lay on the bank of the Thames, in the mud, sucking air deep into his lungs. Steam was rising from him, he was so cold, but he'd insisted everyone's jackets be tucked around Ally Bruni until the paramedics arrived.

'Jack, you'll die of hypothermia,' Kate said, sounding alarmed.

Geoff peeled off his jumper. 'Put this on, Hawk.' His teeth were chattering.

'I'm all right. Don't need both of us dying of cold, especially now you've lost your special blubber.' Jack found a grin.

'Careful, I'll throw you back in.'

Jack looked over at Ally. Luca was fussing around her much like Kate. 'How's she doing?'

'Shocked and it looks like she's in labour, though what would I know? I'm quite impressed with how composed she is,' Kate said. 'That was no mean fall.'

Jack nodded. 'I wasn't pushed in and it still felt like concrete.'

'Here come the paramedics,' one of Geoff's right-handers noted.

'Make sure they know she's having twins and we think her

waters broke. There's a risk of infection from the river,' Kate
said.

Everyone was drenched. They'd all waded or jumped into
the water to help Jack, whose frozen fingers had been wrapped
around Ally like claws and needed to be gently prised off as they
were hauled up the muddy bank.

Jack felt Kate suddenly tucking an emergency thermal blanket
around him, the kind that made it look like you were being
dressed in tin foil like a roast dinner. 'That was rather heroic of
you, Detective Superintendent,' she said.

He gave a wearied grin. 'I didn't think. I just did.'

'That's what heroes always say.' She smiled and touched his
cheek fleetingly.

Ally was loaded onto a stretcher just as she was beginning a new
contraction, Jack noted from her grimace, and after checking that
Jack didn't need any immediate first aid, the paramedic in charge
addressed him as Geoff helped him stand.

'We're getting Mrs Bruni straight to the A&E at Chelsea and
Westminster Hospital. It's okay, she won't deliver before then,
I promise, but she's begun her labour.'

'Good. Kate, you'd better go with Luca. He must be in a state.'

'Both of them are surprisingly calm,' Kate said, 'but yes, I will.'

'We're leaving now,' the paramedic said, and they strode off,
Ally groaning from the stretcher and Luca soothing her.

Everyone followed to the ambulance and as Ally was loaded in,
Jack took her hand. 'You were very brave, Ally. Everything will
be all right. Now, you go have those twins.'

Her eyes were wide with pain, and she was breathing as she
had been taught. 'Thank you,' she said between breaths. 'Luca
will . . .' She waved a hand, and he nodded that he understood.

Jack turned and Luca hugged him. 'Yes, thanks for what you
did. I felt so helpless . . .'

Jack gave a shrug. 'I reacted as anyone would. I'm sorry about the money, though.'

'Don't be. It was mostly blank paper, with a small amount around it. They may get enough to have a few good dinners and some new clothes before they go to jail,' he said.

Jack, Kate and Geoff stared at him slightly bemused, mostly horrified.

'Ballsy.' Geoff shook his hand.

Jack offered Kate a hand into the ambulance behind Luca. She turned. 'Take Jack home, Geoff, and give him a brandy. He only lives down the road.'

Geoff gave her a salute as if to say 'Yes, ma'am'. After the doors had closed, he murmured to Jack. 'Don't you love bossy women, Hawk?'

'I do.' He grinned. 'I will go home, but not for long.'

'I know,' his friend said. 'Let's wrap up here and we'll start working out the next move.'

Showered and changed, feeling much brighter for the steaming cup of tea warming him, Jack put Sarah on loudspeaker.

'Well, I've checked the current and where the logical points would be to pick up that floating suitcase, and I've checked with the river authorities. They agree that from Kew Bridge, the most obvious place is the Docklands,' she said, having heard how it all played out. 'But that's a needle in the haystack, right?'

'Give it some thought, Sarah. We'll check on the Brunis and then we'll be on the move again. Kate's with Luca if you need her, and if you could let Joan know, that would be good. I think Ari and the others were heading back to the Yard.'

'Right, sir. And then what?'

'Send the youngsters home, but have Ari wait with you. We may need some back-up. Geoff will brief his guys.'

'Glad you're safe, sir. I did hear something about you leaping off a bridge.'

'The tom-tom drums work fast in London.'

'Joan said if she could only get a photo, she'd put it on the wall of the staff canteen.'

Jack grinned at the phone. 'Don't believe her, Sarah. She would rather poke her eyes out than be seen in the staff canteen.'

'Is that Joan being funny?'

'Yes.' Jack chuckled.

'I see. I'm not very good at picking that.'

'But you were smart enough to pick our blackmailer. DCI Benson has already put out an APW for Gina Taylor.'

'And is that all ports warning for her brother as well? We don't know his surname yet. I've already actioned one for Francoise Laurent.'

'Okay, good. Wherever Gina is, Franco likely is too. They'll have to share their spoils . . . except there's a sting in the tail of their success.'

'Oh, what's that, sir?'

'It seems Bruni held his nerve and stayed defiant. He used blank paper, just a token amount of cash.'

'Wow,' Sarah exclaimed. 'Makes me want to watch him play football now.'

Jack smiled. That would be the day. 'Thanks, Sarah. Let me know if anything comes up.'

Geoff had just finished speaking with Kate and he came in to sit opposite Jack, nursing his own cup of tea. 'It's looking good in Emergency. They picked up two strong heartbeats and Ally's being shifted to maternity with a clutter of midwives keen to deliver the celebrity twins,' he said. 'Kate reckons we might be a few hours away, but she's very glad Ally's safely in the hospital. I've put some people around as well, just in case, and especially if the paparazzi get wind.'

'Good. So we've secured the Brunis.' Jack downed the last swallow of the very good tea Geoff had made. It was working. He felt eager, whereas in the shower he had felt drained. Positive news from the hospital had perked him up too. He moved on to their next problem. 'So the bag was grabbed upstream by the speedboat we heard, possibly being driven by Gina, and the bastard on the bridge – potentially the brother, Franco – ran to Chiswick and got in a car.'

Sarah called back and was put on loudspeaker again. 'Sir, they wouldn't want to pass the Met's river police at speed in that boat on their getaway.'

Geoff nodded. 'I agree. So where would they go? You're the boatie.' He looked at Jack.

Jack was frowning. 'Thames Division doesn't have a Met river police unit upstream from memory.'

'Correct, sir,' Sarah replied. 'The nearest unit is downstream at Westminster Pier on the north bank by the Houses of Parliament.'

'Come on, Hawk. We'll have one shot at this, or we'll be relying on border security and Europol, because there's no way those two are hanging around.'

Jack shrugged. 'I reckon they had a pretty clear run to Chelsea Harbour.'

'Okay, just give me two minutes,' Sarah replied. 'I'll put you on hold.'

They waited. 'Do you know it?' Jack asked his friend.

Geoff nodded. 'I haven't seen it but yeah, south end of Chelsea facing Battersea across the water.'

'Exactly. It's a wealthy marina-type development with lots of apartments, offices, shops.' Jack stood and pulled on a dry coat.

'The thing is, you can drive a boat straight in off the Thames there. Or they can moor and jump off. They could be on foot, but there's vehicle access to surrounding streets.'

'No security?'

'Guy in a hut with a barrier perhaps,' Jack murmured, unsure.

Sarah voice returned. 'Yes, sir, the river police agree with that. Chelsea Harbour is their best option.'

'Well, let's focus everyone around there and set up a ring around it. We can't cover the whole Docklands,' Geoff said.

'Okay, call it in, Sarah. We need the SWAT teams there, and thanks.' Jack ended the call. 'I'm just going to see if I can speak with Luca. You fill your guys in.'

Luca answered quickly, speaking over a fair amount of background noise.

'How are you doing?' Jack asked.

'Not bad. We're not there yet though – she's only halfway dilated. Both babies seem fine; they're just printing photos from an ultrasound.' Jack could hear the helpless smile in the footballer's voice. 'Hang on, I'll just step outside.'

Jack also walked but towards his front door. Geoff would follow.

'That's better,' Luca said.

'How is Ally?'

'Spooked and exhausted, but the contractions give her a wake-up.' He laughed. 'She's, you know, relieved. Who was that guy posing as Harry? She says she let him walk right in, that bastard.'

'We believe his name is Franco, but we don't know his surname.'

'Okay. So who's behind this? Those Turkish gangsters you mentioned?'

'Er, not your blackmail, no.' Jack cleared his throat. He didn't want to do this now, but he had no choice. 'Luca . . . I don't want you to say anything to Ally just yet, but where was Gina tonight?'

'She had to go to some family event.'

'But that didn't include Harry, presumably?'

'Er, I don't know, I didn't ask. Harry was at the training ground with the senior coaches at a planning meeting when I called him, and he said he was happy to go wait with Ally. And I let Kate know that Harry would be with her.'

'Franco turned up at the apartment wearing Huxley Arrows' team gear — the type the footballers wear, not the punters. How would he get that?'

'No idea. He must have an in at the club, because normally we leave everything in the changing rooms after training and then that's all taken off for laundering.'

'So you'd need someone on the inside of the club to get that sort of proper kit.'

Luca paused. 'What are you saying?'

'We have a theory. We have no evidence yet, but it does fit all that we know about the people behind your blackmail.'

'Oh yeah? Who is it?'

Jack blew out a breath. 'We believe Gina Taylor might be involved.'

'Fuck off!'

'Mmm,' Jack grunted, knowing that name would shock and hurt the younger man.

'Is that really the best—'

'Listen, Luca, we're on the move, trying to hunt down where your bag ended up, so bear with me. I will explain everything very soon, including why we think she's involved.'

'I don't believe it. Gina's—'

'Like family, I know. Stick close to Ally, all right? Don't leave the hospital. There'll be detectives outside her room. I know

telling you to sleep sounds ridiculous right now, but at least rest
and if you think of anything, especially about the man who—'

'I already have.'

'You already have what?'

'I've thought of something, but it could be my imagination.'

Jack tried to squash down his rising hope. Things were looking
dire. If Luca had something to help them, Jack needed it now.
'Say it.'

'The guy underneath the bridge. He recognised me.'

'You're very well known; him recognising you wouldn't surprise me.'

'No, but there was something else. I could barely see him, but
it was like we weren't strangers.'

'Who did you think it might be?'

'Sounds stupid but I've been racking my brains about why
I feel I know him; I've got a really good memory for faces, but
not names.'

Geoff had finished his calls and arrived at the door. Jack held up a
finger. 'Can you tell me where you think you know him from?'

'I'm sure it was the porter who carried up my stuff to the room
at Lark's Hill.'

Jack's features slackened. 'Ronnie Barrett.'

'I wouldn't know, but he's really small and wiry, short dark
hair.'

Jack felt the Tingler crawl up his body once more. 'Well done,
Luca. Leave it to us now.' Ending the call, he looked at Geoff.
'How does the Celik brothers' stooge, Ronnie Barrett, end up
working for Gina Taylor?'

'Let's talk in the car,' Geoff said. 'It's all happening at Chelsea
Harbour.'

★

As Geoff drove, Jack briefed Kate that he'd spilled the news to Luca about Gina's possible involvement, and filled her in on the Chelsea Harbour theory.

'On my way,' she said. 'Luca and Ally are fully secured and completely distracted – they don't need me. Ally, I gather, is about to introduce her children to the world.'

'No worries. That was just a precaution to have you travel alongside. I don't think they're of any interest any longer to the crims – unless they've opened their package, anyway. Then they might want some revenge, but it's unlikely. Too big a risk. Tell me, did you get Ronnie Barrett's mobile number in any of your dealings?'

'Yes. Why?'

'Luca thinks he was the guy at the drop.'

'Barrett? He's the Celiks' guy though.'

'I know. Trust me. Can you do me a favour and get a trace out on that number? We need to know where he is, because wherever he is, we may find Gina and her brother.'

'And if it's not Gina after all?'

'Then Ronnie can lead us to whoever is behind the Bruni blackmail.'

'Okay, on it. Where do we meet?'

'I'll message you. I have no idea.'

'Letting instinct lead you, eh?' she said. 'Good luck.'

Geoff looked over. 'All okay?'

'She said to tell you how damn handsome you looked tonight in your beanie at the river. And when she saw you running with that branch, well . . .'

Geoff gave him a hurt look. 'I saved your life.'

'That's a lie and you know it.'

'Well, Hawk, it's how tonight will be remembered. Me leaping in to save you.'

'That was one of your blokes.'

'But my branch was the critical factor and, besides, I didn't want wet trousers.'

They shared a chuckle.

'Do you think there's a chance?' Geoff asked as he navigated them expertly through traffic, using only their flashing lights to create a lane for themselves.

Jack glanced over at his friend. 'I do. Take it slow.' They both knew they were referring to Kate.

Geoff nodded and switched back to their problem. 'Okay, so how is Barrett is involved?'

'He knew Francoise, and she's the link between both black-mailers.'

'So you think the Celiks, pissed off at the re-emergence of the scheme they thought they'd put to bed, have somehow embedded their guy into the Bruni scam? That's complicated.'

'Maybe. But I think if Francoise knew Barrett was involved, she would have told us. She only knows him through Lark's Hill, so she likely wouldn't know he was involved with the Celiks . . . I'm sure he was out of the picture when they got involved with her. Rumour has it they threatened him, probably because they suspected he'd become something of a police stooge. He got spooked.'

'Hmm,' Geoff said. 'If Barrett is scared of the Celiks, why is he back in bed with them?'

'Money, fear, greed . . . perhaps they still wield a stick over him – do this or else, or even do this and we'll leave you alone.' Jack ran a hand through his hair. 'He's probably too frightened to defy them. Maybe they knew he was questioned by us, or maybe he was just a convenient mule, but I'm sure they threatened him. He's probably done what he did tonight out of fear for his life.'

Jack's phone rang. 'Hi, Kate. I'm putting you on speaker.'

'We've located Barrett at the former tent site at Chelsea Harbour.'

'Bingo!' Jack exclaimed.

'That's the Imperial Wharf Overground that opened last year, right?' Geoff asked.

'Yes, that's it,' Kate said. 'To the east is Chelsea Harbour Drive and Lots Road, and then Harbour Avenue to the south. He's in there. It's a vacant site – you'll see the old-time Fulham gasholders and heritage buildings associated with the old gas offices all up for planning permission. Good place to hide out.'

'Or disappear,' Geoff offered. 'We know the Celiks have a history of tying up their loose ends. Barrett is one of those.'

'Did you hear that, Kate?'

'Yes. Should I ring him? Warn him?'

Jack wondered. 'Message him. Ask him where he is. That alone might spook him enough to cooperate.'

'Will do. Where are you both?'

'About three minutes out.'

Gina had changed into travelling gear and was loading a small carry bag with a few essentials. Franco was doing the same.

'We take as little as possible,' she told him.

'Have you even checked that bag of money?'

'I glanced in, it's there,' she said. 'I haven't had time to count it, if that's what you mean.'

'What about customs?'

'Franco, we're driving straight onto the ferry in a couple of hours. I'll stash it in the car – they're not going to check beneath the seats. No one even knows we're involved.'

'Won't your husband set off alarms?'

'He wouldn't dare, not after what he did to me. My husband may think everything is coming good between us, but he's forgotten what I told him on our wedding night; it's the same thing I told Ally to tell Luca. Harry knew if he went sniffing around for something on the side I would never, ever forgive him, and I would punish him. This is me doing just that.' *He deserves far more than this*, she thought.

'Gina, the bloke's life was shattered. Can't you forgive him a little?'

'I blame Luca fucking Bruni for the way my life has gone. Suddenly broke, no longer the glamorous wife of one of the top strikers in the country, but the good wife attending to her invalid husband, no use to anyone any more. You saw what happened – you watched him decline into someone I no longer recognised. I had to start a cleaning business and even that's going down the gurgler. Me, Franco. Cleaning!'

'You don't clean,' he scoffed.

'I know that! But I don't even want to be associated with cleaning people's houses. I was a screen goddess! Well, I'm starting again. New identity, new life, new country, new outlook.' She'd never wanted – no, needed – anything so badly.

'Half a million isn't that much.'

'It's enough. Remember, I'm leaving behind a lot of debt. There's no way I could lay my hands on any decent amount to start again. This way, even though it isn't a fortune, we can start something with it. Trust me.'

'I do. I always have.'

She smiled. 'We did it. No one has any idea it's us.'

She heard a commotion as Ronnie Barrett staggered into the old gas station offices, covered in mud. 'Ronnie!' she exclaimed. 'You made it.'

'Were you going to leave without paying me?'

'No, of course not. We were waiting,' she lied, glancing at Franco. 'Five thousand, wasn't it?'

He shook his head. 'Ten.'

She gave a gasp of mock shock. 'Really? Is that what we agreed?'

He nodded.

'Well, you did a good job, Ronnie. I didn't trust you at first, but your clever idea worked perfectly – we couldn't have done it without you.'

He didn't smile. 'Then pay me.'

'Okay, okay.'

'And by the way, *they* want the rest.'

Gina frowned. 'They?'

Ronnie pointed, and Gina turned in the abandoned lobby to see a tall man, built like the very gas tanks that this office was designed to service, standing on the stairs, levelling a gun at her. He had a cigar in mouth, looking just like an old-time gangster. All he needed were the spats.

She squealed and turned for the door, only to see another man, just as tall but very slim. He too carried a handgun, which he lazily waved in her direction, forcing her to step back. She moved towards Franco, who dropped his bag and put his arm around her.

'Who are you?' Gina asked.

'I'm Baris Celik,' the thin man said, 'but a lot of people in England know me as Barry – it's easier for you English. I don't expect you to know me, but you should have done more homework, Gina. You shouldn't play in someone else's backyard without permission.' He smiled. 'Oh, and my brother, up there, is Eren, but for ease, he's known as Eric.' Baris drew level with Ronnie, who was watching with a grin on his face. It died with him as Baris fired his gun into the little man's temple.

Gina screamed and promptly wet herself. 'No!' She shrieked again in disbelieving horror as blood began to pour slowly from the head of the man who had been talking to her only moments earlier. 'Please, what do you want? The money?' She caught on. 'Take it, take it!'

'We intend to,' Baris said, approaching.

For a big man, the brother moved silently; Eren was suddenly nearby, making Gina shrink even further into the safety of her brother's embrace. 'In here?' Eren asked conversationally, kicking the suitcase.

Gina nodded, terrified. Eren picked up the suitcase and rolled it towards Baris, who put his gun away.

'I hate these things,' Baris said. 'As soon as we're done, toss them in the river, and I don't want to see them again.'

Gina thought Baris spoke to his brother with a slightly superior tone similar to the one she adopted with Franco. She could tell straight away who was the elder, and she hoped, somewhere inside him, there might be a connection she could use, because she was feeling like there was no longer any ground beneath her feet. For the first time in her life, Gina had no plan, no fast-moving ideas that could get them out of this; the body of Ronnie Barrett, crumpled like an old pile of clothes, his head and shoulders outlined by his blood, assured her that she had no control over what happened next. In fact, she could almost fall on her knees and pray that somehow the police were about to walk in. Arrest was better than death. Could she talk these two very scary individuals into taking the money and leaving them to run empty-handed? She'd always had a certain power with men – could she use that now?

She'd seen enough television shows though to fear the fact that they hadn't hidden their faces. They were clearly unbothered that she and Franco could identify them.

Gina barely felt the wetness of her jeans, which now clung coldly to her legs. All that mattered was somehow getting away alive.

She was mildly encouraged by the fact that the one called Baris had put away his gun. Maybe that was the end of any further death. She watched him unzip the suitcase, and then he flicked open a knife, took out a torch and slashed at her money. After a few seconds he began to laugh.

28

Police converged on the empty building. They were unarmed; their presence was, at this point, irrelevant to the tactical team, which was now in charge.

Jack never lost his awe at watching these armed units in action; the highly trained operatives moved as stealthily as possible in bullet-proof gear and carrying weapons. A tap on the shoulder here, a finger pointed there, the coded messages were a special language they knew and obeyed like soldiers.

While they silently covered the exits and took up strategic positions, waiting for their leader to give the signal, Jack, Kate and Geoff crouched beneath a broken window, where they could hear the conversation inside.

They'd heard one gunshot only on approach. It was a distant sound and most people around Chelsea Harbour would be none the wiser, too far away from this abandoned area, which had once housed the infamous seventeenth-century performer Nell Gwyn; Jack didn't think Geoff or Kate needed this critical piece of information right now and kept it to himself.

'That'll be the Celiks,' Geoff had warned as they were all moving towards the danger. 'Only they could get access to hand-guns.'

They could hear two male voices and a female, presumably Gina. The men could be Franco and Ronnie, but Jack agreed with Geoff that neither of them would have easy access to guns.

Jack listened. It was only moments now until the command was given to storm the building.

'Bruni royally fucked you, Gina,' one voice said.

Definitely Gina Taylor, then. The three detectives acknowledged their suspicions with a silent glance of triumph.

'What do you mean?' Gina spluttered. 'The money's there. I told you, you can take it. Just leave us alone.'

One of the men inside laughed. 'You've been screwed over. This is mostly paper. What, you didn't check?'

'I don't understand.'

'Come see for yourself.'

Jack heard shuffling, then silence as Gina presumably rifled through the stash.

'What? Luca wouldn't risk—'

'He did though. He's got balls, I'll give him that. And now it's time to go.'

'No, wait! Please!'

The leader of the tactical team gave the go-ahead and the building was stormed, but Jack heard another single gunshot and then a short burst of automatic fire, which ended almost as soon as it began. A man was yelling.

Jack and his colleagues rose from their crouched position and looked through the broken window, where torchlight showed three figures lying on the ground and a huge dark-haired man crouched over them. One man stood, his arms raised high above his head, looking traumatised.

'Franco,' Kate murmured.

The area now secured, Jack, Kate and Geoff were allowed inside. The leader of the tactical unit revealed that Baris Celik was dead, having turned the gun on Gina and then towards them, while his brother Eren had been wounded with a bullet to the shoulder. He would live to serve whatever penalty was handed down to him. Franco was unharmed and Gina had been shot in the chest by Baris, perhaps fatally. Ronnie Barrett was dead, shot by one of the Celiks; they didn't know which, probably Baris.

The tactical leader began reporting back to base while Kate called for ambulance assistance. Geoff had moved to speak with Franco, while Jack crouched by Gina, who was straining to breathe.

'Gina,' Jack said, trying not to look at the gaping wound.

'Franco?'

'He's alive.'

'He always was a lucky bastard.' She began to choke. 'Tell Ally I'm sorry. I never meant for her . . .' Her words faded away as her head fell to the side.

Jack looked over at Geoff and shook his head. Franco began to weep as Geoff gently turned him around and handcuffed him, explaining his rights. He was handed over to Kate's care as Geoff did the same to Eren Celik, whom Jack noted had an angry scratch down the side of one cheek.

'You have nothing on us!' Eren yelled as Jack approached him.

Jack was calm. 'Mr Celik, we have a DNA sample taken from beneath the fingernails of a victim whom we believe you tortured and killed. I'm sure we'll find the match we need to that wound on your face. You're going down for the murder of two women in Southall, a man in Wimbledon and potentially a fourth and fifth right here in Chelsea,' he said, looking over at the bodies of Gina and Ronnie.

Geoff chimed in. 'At the very least, mate, we'll get you and your dodgy cousin on money laundering and tax evasion. You're looking at a long stretch.'

Eren growled and made to headbutt Geoff, but the detective was too quick, ducking quickly out of the way.

'Hope that aggression of yours comes in handy for prison, Mr Celik,' Jack remarked, 'especially when word gets around that you beat up, tortured and killed two helpless women.'

'Fuck you, whoever you are.'

'The name's Jack Hawksworth, and this is Detective Chief Inspector Geoff Benson, who is going to enjoy seeing you in the dock. You'll need a very good lawyer, because we have an exceptionally good case against you. A shame your brother won't get to stand in the dock alongside you.' Jack looked to the police standing by. 'You can take him,' he said to the officers nearby, as carelessly as he could, already looking away as Eren Celik began to foam and froth once more with expletives and threats.

Jack, Kate and Geoff sat in a café, not far from where all the action had gone down. Each of them was silent for a while, going over the night's events in their mind over hot chocolates that Jack had bought.

'I'd like to buy you a stiff drink,' he said, 'but I don't want either of you tested by the breathalyser units.'

It won some tired smiles.

'I checked with Luca,' Kate said. 'All's fine. The babies came safe and sound, a boy and a girl, and they're all tucked away for the night. Ally will be discharged in a couple of days.'

'Did you congratulate him?' Geoff asked.

'I actually told him he was an idiot,' Kate said.

Jack gave a low whistle. 'He plays fearlessly, so I guess we shouldn't be that surprised that he did what he did. It was certainly an edgy move that I wouldn't have recommended.'

'I didn't tell him how it went down. He's shocked enough that Gina was involved, but he admitted he knew the Taylors had some money troubles. Apparently Gina's business was in deep trouble.'

'Did Harry know?' Jack asked.

'Luca doesn't think so. But apparently Harry admitted that Gina always blamed Luca for what happened to him, and his injury was the beginning of the trouble in their marriage – it all went downhill from then. She also blamed Ally for stealing her glory, although I think she genuinely loved her.'

Jack nodded, thinking of Gina's dying words. 'So where is Harry? How did they get him out of the way?'

Kate shrugged. 'I'm not sure, but Luca says he had text messages from Harry citing flat tyres. Maybe the Celiks had Ronnie Barrett slashing tyres? And then other texts growling about traffic. All they had to do was stall him long enough so that they could get to Ally first.'

'Harry's got some bad news coming,' Geoff said.

His companions nodded sadly. 'I reckon Luca will have already told him,' Kate said.

'Hmm, what I want to know though is how the Celiks cottoned on to Gina. They were linked through Francoise, but she never knew Gina's identity.'

'Had to be Ronnie,' Kate mused. 'I wonder if we'll ever find out?'

'The puzzle pieces will fall into place,' Geoff said, some of his marshmallow sticking to his moustache, which made Jack and Kate chuckle. Kate gestured at her own face pointedly. 'Shut up, you two,' he said, licking his lips.

'I gather as Ally's star rose, Gina's went into decline.' Kate shook her head. 'But Gina never let the Brunis know how much she resented their success. Luca says she was the first to raise a glass to them, the first to throw a party for them when the babies were announced, and she'd even made a scrapbook for Ally of the most loved couple in England.'

'Very creepy in hindsight,' Geoff said. 'All the signs were there.'

'Yeah, but you have to be able to read them,' Kate argued. 'And that quartet were just too close.'

Geoff sighed. 'What about Francoise Laurent?'

'Sarah's put out an all ports warning.'

Both of Jack's colleagues looked at him with a suspicious expression. 'Where would she go?' Kate asked.

'France, probably,' he answered. 'But between us, she went back to my friend's place first to get money.'

They both knew him well, because understanding dawned on their faces quickly. 'You're joking, Jack,' Kate said. 'You didn't . . .'

He shrugged. 'She'll hand herself in shortly. She told me she would.'

'You believe her?' Kate said, weary with astonishment.

'I do, actually. I promised Claudia I would go after the big boys, not the pawns, and I know she told Francoise she could trust me.'

'She made a lot of money, mate,' Geoff said, palms in the air. 'Just saying.'

'And she'll do her time, trust me.'

'Rowland will sizzle your balls over a roasted flame and make you watch her eat them in front of you,' Geoff said. At Kate's amusement, he added, 'Just trying to be helpful here, Hawk.'

'Yeah, look, it's on me.' Before they could protest, he put his hands up in surrender. 'I'm just giving her some time to get home to her mother . . . just hours. The red notice is likely already out with Interpol,' he said, and then with a sigh, 'thanks to the expediency of our Sarah. I'm not telling you to make you complicit. Deny you ever knew, both of you. I just don't want to lie to my friends.'

'There'll have to be an extradition hearing,' Kate reasoned.

'I know. She can't dodge answering for her part in it, but with a good barrister in court, we might be able to get her sentence as low as possible. She's small fry. The Celiks were the big haul. Rowland is going to be very happy to have them behind bars. Even if one is dead, she's got the other one off the street. And she's sorted out the Bruni blackmail in no time. She'll be the toast of her superiors, and I'm sure she'll cut me some slack when I say we lost Francoise momentarily.'

'Well, that's not on you,' Geoff said, 'that's on the safe house team being a bit naïve or careless. She took her chance and made it work.'

'Jack, why do you always have to find a maiden in distress and answer her call?' Kate threw up her hands.

Jack's phone pinged and he looked at the message. It was a cute goodnight from Lou Barclay, telling him she was going to dream of him. 'Right, lovely people. I'm exhausted.' He wasn't lying.

'Do you want a lift home?' Geoff asked.

'Not going home.'

'*Ooooh,*' Kate and Geoff said together.

Jack rolled his eyes.

'Why won't you tell us?' Kate said, reaching over to poke his arm.

'Because I like her and don't need snoopy detectives trying to find out more. Night, losers . . . Go and find something to amuse yourselves with if you're not tired, but I'm going to curl up exactly where I need to be.' He deliberately did not catch Kate's eye, just in case. He raised a hand as he turned. 'Good work tonight.'

As he left the café, he messaged Lou: *Can you wait before you fall asleep?*

Coming over?

If I may.

So polite. Yes, please. What about my friend?

He appreciated her being careful. *I'll tell you when I see you.* He sighed into the darkness and wondered what sort of expletives he'd have to face with Rowland in the morning.

That could wait. He let his mind roam to one more task, which was to see to the burial of Claudia Lenkas and safely get her daughter to her grandmother in Poland. He'd already explained to Claudia's mother that regular money would be sent for Hanna's education and wellbeing, and that if she wanted to visit England when she was older, there would always be a safe house for her to stay in for a while. It was the least he could do for Claudia's girl.

It made him think of Samantha, Anne McEvoy's daughter. It was time he visited her too. It seemed he was collecting other people's daughters for supervision and care. He smiled sadly.

Right now, though, all he could think about was wrapping his arms around Lou. He was going to take her to Florence or Venice for a mini break and they were going to get their fill of culture and Italian food. He hoped Kate might be inviting Geoff back to her place for a nightcap, giving him a chance. She was going to freak when she did find out who Jack's mystery woman was, but that drama was for another day too. For the moment, Lou Barclay was his delicious secret, and he would keep it that way for as long as he could.

ACKNOWLEDGEMENTS

There are always many people to thank, because a book might be written by one person, but there are usually a host of others working quietly behind the scenes, lending their expertise, their time and indeed their skills.

I must thank retired Scotland Yard detective Mike Warburton for helping me with the logistics and making sure I got this story right. Once I'd told him the arc, his ideas that sparked for locations were, as usual, bang on. Coming up with the name for our Premier League team was fun, and it helped enormously that Mike is a football fan. His ideas that helped the twists and turns of this story are appreciated, and I love that he is an aspiring author and will, now that he's fully retired, commit himself to writing novels. I can return some of the care.

I must also thank the family of Nick Aretzis, particularly Nick's mum, Suzie, who, more than twelve months ago, sat down with me and walked me through life as a soccer mum in Australia when your son shows sufficient potential that he's earmarked for an international move at the tender age of not quite seventeen.

I couldn't imagine hugging goodbye to one of my sons at that age for a move across to the other side of the world, but Nick had a dream and his family wanted to ensure he had every chance to realise it. Suzie is his greatest cheerleader and I admire her resilience at having to watch him from afar, while raising his younger brother. I used a lot of Nick's story when I was considering the character of Luca Bruni and his early days, so thank you, Nick and Suzie, for your generosity. And go Nick . . . all the way!

I must say watching *Ted Lasso* helped, but so did Mike's drawings of various formations. I look back at those notes now and smile, recalling him explaining the technicality of defence and attack with the pros and cons of a 4-2-4 set up against a 4-3-3, or 2-3-5.

Finding Jack's new home was fun, and it was once we had chosen Kew Riverside, not too far from where the famous Oxford and Cambridge boatrace finishes, that we began to get some plot ideas for the story, including using this location on the Thames for the finale. I walked along that muddy towpath that you read about and feel just like Kate about my boots!

Anyone who has visited or had the pleasure of staying at the very upmarket and salubrious Cliveden House in the UK would recognise it as the setting for my fictional Lark's Hill six-star retreat. The management there were incredibly gracious in allowing me to roam around the hotel and find a perfect room for the main crime to take place. What a splendid spot it is, and I was guided around every corner of it, learning its history (originally Lady Astor's home), its stories and enjoying its fine service. Thank you to the front of house for the team's time and care, especially manager George Kuldo. If you find yourself in London and feel like treating yourself to a quick getaway in the country, don't hesitate (it's pronounced Cliv-den by the way).

Pip Klimentou, thank you for always dropping everything to read my chapters immediately and give swift feedback, and to

Sonya Caddy for doing the opposite and reading the manuscript in one haul at draft time to provide that overview. Your input, since the year 2000 and more than forty books ago, is always appreciated.

Big thanks as always to the whole team at Penguin Random House for loving Jack enough to keep asking for more, and for the generous, good-natured edit that always ensues with Amanda Martin and the constant encouragement from my publisher, Ali Watts.

Booksellers around Australia and NZ, thank you for continuing to recommend the Jack Hawksworth series to your crime readers. He's so much fun to write and with some luck we may just see him on our screens sometime as the producers of TV have discovered his appeal too. Fingers crossed.

For those who worry about Jack, you can rest assured that he might have found his match in this story. I've longed to give him someone special in his life, but he is a bit of a loner and it's taken five books for him to get past all that hurt from the original story. Anyway, his romantic nature has something to look forward to and we'll continue that thought in the next story.

To those I love . . . I can't do any of this without your care and constant humour, which keeps me jollying along. Thank you for being my family. Fx

BOOK CLUB NOTES

1. Blackmailers rely on victims' fear of exposure. What did you think of Luca's refusal to give in to the blackmail demands?

2. Both Luca and his wife, Ally, are famous. Do you think the benefits of being a celebrity outweigh the potential risks and downsides?

3. Can two people be friends if one of them has romantic feelings for the other? Discuss how this dynamic affects Kate and Jack in this book.

4. Did you at any point believe Luca was lying about what happened at the big event? Why or why not?

5. Harry Taylor says he doesn't blame Luca for his career-ending injury. How do you think this situation has affected their friendship and the friendship between Ally and Gina?

6. Is any one of the members of the Stonecrop ops team a stand-out character for you? How do they set themselves apart from the rest of the team?

7. Jack crosses a line when he allows a witness to stay at Lou's house. Discuss whether you think this was justified and why.

8. Many characters in *Foul Play* are involved in criminal activity, and many of them suffer negative consequences. Do you think they deserve what happens to them? Why or why not?

9. If you have read the other Jack Hawksworth books, how do you feel about Geoff being back in the picture?

10. Are there any themes in *Foul Play* that are similar to the other Jack Hawksworth books? Do you think he is learning from his past mistakes? Why or why not?

Start from the beginning

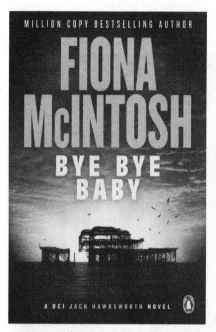

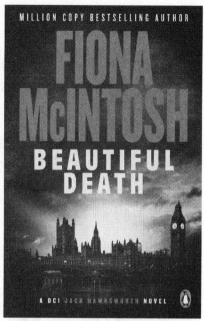

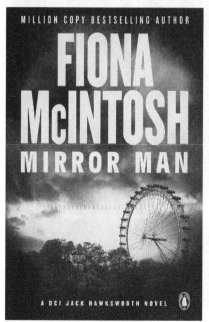

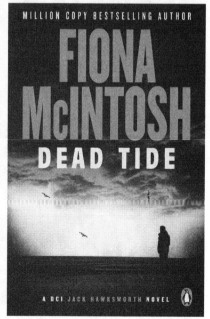

The heart-stopping crime series from a
powerhouse Australian author

MILLION COPY BESTSELLING AUTHOR

FIONA McINTOSH

BYE BYE BABY

A DCI JACK HAWKSWORTH NOVEL

Five cold cases are heating up . . .

Introducing DCI Jack Hawksworth, Scotland Yard's
brightest talent.

A spate of seemingly unconnected murders in southern England
prompt a high-profile taskforce to be formed and led by DCI
Jack Hawksworth, one of the Force's new rising stars who
combines modern methods with old-school instincts.

The victims appear as disparate as their style of death; the only link
that Hawk and his team can pull together is that the murdered are
all men of an identical age. The taskforce has nothing but cold
cases of decades past to comb through in the hope that they
might find a clue to who is behind the savagery.

A heart-stopping tale of brutal revenge with a chilling
twist by a powerhouse Australian author.

MILLION COPY BESTSELLING AUTHOR

FIONA McINTOSH

BEAUTIFUL
DEATH

A DCI JACK HAWKSWORTH NOVEL

A gruesome case just got personal.

DCI Jack Hawksworth is back, working on a high-profile case breaking in London. A calculating serial killer is on the loose, committing the most gruesome of murders as he 'trophies' the faces of his victims. With each new atrocity, the public and police force are getting more desperate for results.

Hawk pulls together a strong and experienced taskforce, who soon find themselves caught up in a murky world of illegal immigrants and human organ trading. As he struggles to find any sort of link between the victims, Jack identifies something unique about the most recent corpse, and things suddenly get very personal.

From the seedy underbelly of London's back streets and New Scotland Yard to the dangerous frontiers of modern medicine, this is a gripping crime thriller from a powerhouse Australian author.

Discover a
new favourite

Visit **penguin.com.au/readmore**